THE STRANGER TOOK GWEN'S HANDS IN A FIRM, WARM GRASP. "GWEN, I AM YOUR FATHER."

She tried to pull free. "Don't be silly—"

"And I am of Faerie."

Gwen went still. A lifetime of stories had laid down fertile soil, and she couldn't quite scoff. Not here. Not now.

Still she had to say it. "You can't be."

"I can. I am." A charming, mischievous smile lit his face. "Though perhaps you should not tell your mother. A charming lady, but conventional."

Gwen had been wondering *how* such a thing might be possible, and now the implication that her mother had no notion . . . She should have been horrified, if she believed it at all, but the image of this rakish gentleman with her placid, extremely conventional mother surprised a giggle out of her.

He joined her in laughter. "You are a delight to me, daughter, and it has given me joy to watch over you." Then he grew serious. "But now it is time for you to meet your faery kin and learn the purpose for which you were created."

—from THE LORD OF ELPHINDALE by Jo Beverley

ROMANCE FROM JO BEVERLY

DANGEROUS JOY   (0-8217-5129-8, $5.99)

FORBIDDEN   (0-8217-4488-7, $4.99)

THE SHATTERED ROSE   (0-8217-5310-X, $5.99)

TEMPTING FORTUNE   (0-8217-4858-0, $4.99)

FAERY MAGIC

Mary Jo Putney
Jo Beverley
Barbara Samuel
Karen Harbaugh

Zebra Books
Kensington Publishing Corp.
http://www.zebrabooks.com

ZEBRA BOOKS are published by

Kensington Publishing Corp.
850 Third Avenue
New York, NY 10022

First Printing: January, 1998
10 9 8 7 6 5 4 3 2 1

Printed in the United States of America

*To Denise Little, who was the first to see the magic,
and Kate Duffy, who made it happen.*

CONTENTS

Introduction   9

THE LORD OF ELPHINDALE   11
by Jo Beverley

THE FAERY BRAID   99
by Karen Harbaugh

THE LOVE TALKER   193
by Barbara Samuel

DANGEROUS GIFTS   261
by Mary Jo Putney

Introduction

Once upon a time a writer dreamed of magic. There are many kinds of magic: babies and kittens, myths and legends, love stories and cyberspace. But this writer dreamed of faery magic. Not Tinkerbell faeries, cute though they are, but the powerful realm of Faerie—the other dimension which, so ancient stories say, sometimes weaves into the human world with volatile results.

Caught by her dream, the writer used the earthly magic of the Internet and found (as often is the case) that the same ideas were dancing in the heads of other writers. Perhaps faery magic was at work, causing the stories to unfold. In fact, one writer had already created a magical court deep in the heart of England, ruled by a beautiful but ruthless queen, peopled by flower-faeries and shape-changers, nymphs and trolls, but needing human help to survive.

Soon the powerlines of cyberspace were humming as four writers spun a unique and powerful dream, four stories set in the same faery world as well as in the enchanting milieu of Georgian and Regency England. Imagine, if you will, fey whisperings of—

"Let's use faery (Faery), not fairy. It's more mysterious."

"What about faeries mating with humans? My group is against it."

"Mine think it's essential for survival."

"My heroine is half faery—and wouldn't her mother be surprised to know!"

"Faeries are creatures of nature and must have greenery to live. How will she survive in London?"

"She could live in Hyde Park."

"Or under a parlor aspidistra!"

"It's reasonable for the humans to be scared. It's not wise to try to fool or foil the Queen of Faerie!"

Faerie is an alluring realm, but it is not gentle. In each story, faeries seek to use mortals in their plans and games, and humans have to decide whether seductive faery gifts are worth the price.

Whenever a writer creates a world and the people to love and weep within it, it is a kind of magic. But the creation of this world was a special magic because it was shared, and the joy and delight shine through.

So come with us now, mortal reader, into the world of Faery Magic. Come share the dream. . . .

The Lord of Elphindale

Jo Beverley

I grew up in England with stories of faeries who live at the bottom of the garden. I've long since stopped believing in Father Christmas and the Tooth Fairy, but I still suspect that those other faeries are there, if I could only see them.

I've been writing stories since I could string sentences together, and always either love stories or weird stuff; quite often a blend of the two. When an editor requested a regency faery story, I leaped at the chance. The bad news came when that whole line folded, taking the collection with it; the good news arrived when I was asked again if I'd like to do a love story with faeries in it.

The Lord of Elphindale grew out of those childhood garden faeries who hide under leaves, or sleep, wings furled, in the heart of a rose, but now my interest is the world to which they belong—the mighty realm of Faerie.

Ancient myths all tell of Faerie, the otherworld of creatures close to immortal who have magical powers and a rather heartless view of "mere mortals." In most cultures, the stories are the same. Despite our mortality, humans are more robust, more aggressive, perhaps because we have such short spans in which to achieve our dreams. Thus we have driven the more ethereal, long-lived creatures into retreat, into other, misty dimensions.

And there they are—lords and ladies, elves and trolls—sometimes—maybe—visible when the light is strange; or audible on quiet, mysterious evenings; or playing tricks on the unwary. Or even, perhaps, shaping human lives to their convenience, as in *The Lord of Elphindale.*

And perhaps, no bigger than damsel flies, they still sometimes hide under leaves, or sleep, wings furled, in the heart of a rose.

—Jo Beverley

In the heart of the woods, in the heart of a dale, somewhere in the heart of England, June 1794 . . .

Call her Mab, call her Titania, call her Kerrigwen.

Ageless and with many names, the Lady sat among her Faerie court considering the emerald globe floating before her eyes. Considering the swirling patterns there.

"The humans betray the bond, Merlon. They do not keep the ways."

"The simple people do," her consort pointed out, lounging on the soft grass beside her. Butterflies danced on his outstretched hand to the sound of elfin pipes.

"But the Lord does not. The Lord of Elphindale sends men to cut our trees while he himself stays out of reach."

"He will die. They always do."

"The next Lord is a child still, and was born out-of-dale. We said no words over his cradle. His mother keeps him away."

The beautiful male stirred, and at a flick of his fingers the insects fluttered away. He raised his hand and the globe floated down close to his eyes. "Ah." He tilted his head to consider the images. "Do the Elphinson family no longer feel the power of the dale? By rights they should be tied here even as we are."

"No. For then they could not serve us in the world." The Lady drew the globe back up to her eyes. "But they must be bound to us, Merlon. *They must be bound.*"

At her tone, the Faery court stilled. Blossom-small or human-size, cobweb-fine or gnarled, the Folk left off play and turned to watch their queen. Trees trembled, and nearby animals quivered in their lairs.

"How long," she asked, "has it been since faery blood was joined with that of the Elphinsons?"

"Perhaps hundreds of their years. You know some think it—"

"That is many generations to humans, is it not?"

"Yes, Great Lady." He faced her now on his knees, as wary as the rest.

She drew a finger down his cheek. "Dear Merlon. How fortunate that you rather like humans. It is time for us to mix blood with the Elphinsons again."

When he made no response, she rapped him with the sharp point of her nail. "Smile. Or I will think you sympathize with those others. Those who do not hold to my rule."

"It is rather a shame that you cursed the Love Talker. He would enjoy—" Her nail pierced his skin.

"You question my wisdom?"

"No, Great Lady." Blood, welled around the nail still in his flesh, began slowly to trickle down his cheek. "But the Lord already has an heir. To kill him would be—"

"Sanctioned if necessary."

Green eyes met green eyes. "The bond says that no one of the lord's family will ever die young, in childbed, or in pain."

"He is cutting the trees. He has broken the bond."

He raised a hand toward her. "Be merciful, Great Lady. He is a child."

"You do like humans, don't you?" Slowly, she took her hand from her consort's face and touched his skin to heal him. Slowly she smiled, teeth small, white, and slightly pointed. "Then save him, Merlon. I will bring this child back to Elphindale. You must create his faery bride."

Elphinson Hall, Derbyshire, September, 1794

Amelia Forsythe read the black-edged letter in a churning mess of emotions. She should have been shocked and grief-stricken by the untimely death of her cousin, Lady Elphinson, but her principal emotion was fear. Selfish fear that she might have to leave the place that had become her home.

She wandered over to one of the long windows and let her eyes relax over the formal gardens. Beyond, the fertile wooded valley called Elphindale was backed by the magnificent craggy Peaks. The Peak District was one of the acknowledged beauty spots of England, but it wasn't just the picturesque view that made it precious to her.

It was security.

Here in Elphindale she never had to fret about scraping together the rent, or secreting enough money to buy food. She never shivered in the winter for lack of a fire, or hobbled in shoes with worn through soles.

For ten years of marriage she had struggled, burdened by a pride that would not tell anyone the predicament created by her husband's gaming. She had even taken in mending to pay for simple necessities. Then, one blessed day, she had encountered her cousin Jane.

They met from time to time, but always when Amelia had warning, and a chance to put on a good appearance. That day, she had not.

"My dear," said Jane, airily kissing her cheek. "How

long it has been." Her sharp eyes skimmed over Amelia. "You look . . . tired."

Amelia knew she looked dreadful, pale with hunger, yet red-nosed with the cold she could not seem to shake. She had no gloves, and her inadequate cloak was frayed at the hem. She tried desperately to think of something to say, but a weary despair silenced her. She and Grayson were virtually penniless, and though he happily scrounged meals from friends, she could not bring herself to do that.

Jane, cozily swathed in furs and with a handsome carriage nearby, linked arms with Amelia and drew her down the street as they talked. "I don't think London agrees with you, Cousin."

Amelia could not dispute it.

Jane chattered on about family and fashion for a while as they strolled up and down, but then she said, "Sir Thomas has a home in Derbyshire, you know. Quite isolated, I'm afraid. We hardly ever go there. In fact," she said in a lowered voice, "he positively hates the place, even though it is his ancestral home. For which I can only be grateful. Mountains!" she declared with a shudder. "Mists!"

"How sad." It was a meaningless phrase, but Amelia had no idea what to say.

"Well, we do feel a little pang of conscience now and then." Jane slid Amelia a considering glance. "We would feel better to have a member of the family there to keep an eye on things."

It took Amelia a moment to absorb this. "But Grayson would never leave London."

"Amelia," Jane drawled with a pitying look. "Marriage is not a ball and chain, you know."

"Yes, but. . . ."

"Can you honestly say he'd object to your living apart?"

Amelia desperately wanted to say yes, but the conventional lies would not come to her lips. Once there had been something in her marriage that might have been love. Now she and Grayson were just two people sharing dingy rooms on the outer fringes of fashionable London. Sometimes she didn't even see him for days on end.

"A rest," said Jane, laughing in a charming but artificial way. "Did you think I was encouraging you to leave your husband forever? Not at all. But you clearly need a rest, my dear. Derbyshire is held to be very healthy. All that fresh air!" Again, she shuddered.

"Will your husband agree?" Amelia asked.

"He'll be delighted. As I told you, he hates to go there, but does feel a proper responsibility. Do say you will."

So, prettily tempted and implored, Amelia had accepted the invitation to move to Elphinson Hall, just for a short rest. In three years she had never experienced the slightest desire to leave it.

But now, with her cousin dead, could she stay? Even though Sir Thomas never came to his house, it could be seen as improper. Was that why Grayson was accompanying the widower and the corpse back to Elphindale? To take her back to London?

Why else? Grayson *detested* the country.

Amelia realized that she was pacing the room and had scrunched up the black-edged letter. Fretfully, she smoothed it out again.

Perhaps Grayson was just penny-pinched at the moment. That certainly would be nothing new. If he was coming to take her back to live with him, she didn't think she could bear it. Oh, she still experienced touches of the delirious love that had plunged her into her disastrous marriage, but she'd long since accepted that there'd be no changing Grayson Forsythe. He'd gamble and drink away any money that came his way, and considered all other aspects of life—including her—mere distractions from the tables.

Amelia spent a week mourning her carelessly generous cousin and dreading the arrival of her husband. She also spent it in a flurry of work. First she thrust three of her best outfits into a black dye-bath, then she supervised a thorough cleaning of the house, top to bottom. Perhaps if she impressed Sir Thomas with her propriety and her care of his home, he might be willing to let her stay.

When the news came that the cortege had arrived in the dale, and that the body was being placed before the altar in the ancient chapel, she assembled the staff in their black-trimmed clothing. When she took her place on the steps, dressed in deepest black, she hoped that her pallor and nervousness would be put down to grief.

Sir Thomas came out of the coach first, a chunky man with a prosperous belly. He stretched and took a deep breath, and despite his black armband, he did not look like a sorrowing widower. He turned and swung down a young travel-weary boy.

Amelia had completely forgotten that Jane had a son. Pity for the poor child hit her first, but hard upon it came calculation. Who was going to look after the child and where was he going to live?

If he lived here, he'd need a governess . . .

She was so wrapped in these thoughts that she hardly realized Grayson had emerged. Loose-limbed and world-weary, he was scanning the beautiful scenery as if it were the worst slum in London. He hadn't changed much. Perhaps his pallor had a yellowish tinge and the bags under his eyes were more pronounced, but he still had a trace of the blond beauty that had stolen her senses thirteen years before.

Ah well, she had only been eighteen. Perhaps wisdom and foresight weren't to be expected at that age.

She welcomed them all, shepherding them in to the waiting refreshments while murmuring the appropriate condolences and statements of shock.

"Yes, yes," said Sir Thomas, flipping up his coattails to sit in the best seat by the fire. "Terrible business. No accounting for it. That horse in the shafts was steady as a rock. Not a trace of vice in him. Then he ups and startles at a dog bark and careens down Pall Mall, pitching poor dear Jane out on her head. Died instantly, which is a blessing I suppose. 'Twas a miracle no one else was hurt!''

"How horrible," Amelia said, passing him tea. She looked a question at her husband and he widened his eyes in disbelief. With a sigh, she sent a maid for brandy. Dear heaven, but she could not bear to live with him again. If she thought there was any chance of saving him, she would try, but she'd put that foolishness behind her years ago.

Little Andrew nibbled a cake but then began to fidget. When he almost knocked a plate of cakes onto the floor, she took him by the hand out of the room, looking for a suitable maid. She saw Nan Ferryman, a good, sensible girl, and instructed her to take the boy out to run around in the sunshine.

When she returned to the drawing room, Sir Thomas said, "Restless little thing. No end of trouble on the journey."

"What happened to his nursemaid?"

"Gave notice. Didn't want to travel here. Can't say I blame her. And damned if I know what to do with such a young child."

Amelia took a deep breath. "Surely he should grow up here. I'd be happy to act as little Andrew's governess." She watched her husband out of the corner of her eye, but saw no objection from that quarter.

Sir Thomas stared at her for a moment, then nodded. "Aye, why not? Good. Fifty pound a year, since you're family. How's that?"

Amelia would have done it for nothing and knew she was flushing. "That will be perfect, Cousin Thomas. Thank you. I'll take the greatest care—"

"Leave it all in your hands, my dear. All in your hands."

* * *

Later that day, Grayson strolled into the dining room as Amelia was checking the dinner table. "Well done, love. I'll be able to touch you up for a loan now and then."

In fact, every penny she earned would be his by right, but he'd never been grasping in that way.

"If I have it, I'll try to help. It'll be a drop in the bucket, though."

He stole an apple from a bowl of fruit. "Once one becomes accustomed to debt, it's quite cozy."

"I never found it so."

"No." He leaned against the sideboard and took a bite. "You're looking in fine twig, my dear. It suits you here."

She faced him across the table. "Yes, it does."

He had his teeth set to take another bite but removed the apple. "Do you think I'm here to drag you away? Why the devil would I do that?"

"I don't know. Why the devil are you here?"

"Damned if I know," he said and took the bite.

Amelia walked around the table and turned an epergne on the sideboard so that its better side showed. "Were you so drunk you got into the coach without realizing where it was going?"

"No. I just took the idea to come here. Damnedest thing. I hate the country, and the Peak District is country at its most extreme. I'm sorry if it'll disappoint you, my pet, but I'm heading back south tomorrow."

She wasn't quite sure how to reply to that and be both polite and honest.

He grinned, looking almost as he had when they were courting. "Don't worry, love. If there's one regret I have in my life, it's involving you in it. You were such a fetching miss, though, I couldn't resist." He kissed her lightly on the lips. "You still are a fine-looking woman. Be happy."

He wandered away, and Amelia stared after him, tempted to try in some way to drag him back from the brink. But the next few hours cured her. His stories were all of gambling and debauchery, and by the time she went upstairs to bed, he was drunk and getting drunker.

She was considerably astonished, therefore, when he came to her bed.

Physical intimacy had ceased quite early in their marriage. Drink seemed to lessen his ability, and after a few embarrassing failures Grayson had rarely attempted to claim his rights at all. Amelia had never found it a potent pleasure and had quickly decided that a child would only make a bad situation appalling.

When she woke to find him sitting on her bed, untying the strings of her nightcap, she was shocked, but strangely stimulated. It had been a long time, and there had been *some* pleasure in it.

"Grayson, what are you doing?"

He didn't even seem drunk, and in the kindly moonlight he looked young and handsome again.

"I want to see your hair." He pushed off the cap and ran his fingers through it. She was suddenly pleased that it was still thick and a rich brown.

"Is that all you want to do? See my hair?"

"No." He smiled in a way she'd never seen him smile before. "I want to see you everywhere."

"Everywhere?" Her voice rose with her embarrassment. They had never looked at one another's bodies.

Rising from the bed, he drew back the curtains so that moonlight streamed into the room. Then he slipped off his long robe and stood in the moonlight, stark naked.

"Grayson!" she gasped, covering her eyes. But she peeked. He looked like one of those Greek marble statues! She was very surprised he hadn't turned flabby in his life of dissipation.

He pulled the covers off her and, despite her feebly protesting hands, stripped off her nightgown, pulling her to stand in the moonlight with him. Her little mantel clock tinkled midnight, and around the house other clocks accompanied it.

"Grayson. What are you doing?"

"This is a special night, my dear, and I think perhaps there will never be another. Let me pleasure you and take my pleasure . . ."

"But . . . clothes . . . why?"

"Perhaps I just want to see you this way once."

"It's indecent." And yet it seemed less so by the moment.

"It's beautiful. You are beautiful." He ran his hands gently down her torso. "Let me show you just how beautiful you are to me."

And he led her back to the bed and lay with her there, astonishing her with the beauty of her body and of his. Frequently she objected, faintly, to his actions, but he always persuaded her, carrying her further and higher until she felt transported to another world entirely.

It's like magic, she thought, dazedly floating, *and I never even suspected this was in us.*

When he settled deep inside her, she stared up at him. A beam of moonlight somehow made his blue eyes seem a shimmering green . . .

But then he raised her so he was even deeper, and moved so her sensitized flesh shot sparks through her dizzy mind, and she knew little more except that she was thrashing and gasping and saying things that were surely going to mortify her when she came to her senses.

And lying later in his arms, that was exactly how she felt, though her body still sizzled with sensations. "Why?"

He kissed her to silence. "Don't, my pretty one."

"But we never—"

"This is a special night. The Autumn Equinox, when magic is alive."

"Don't be superstitious."

"You are charming when you frown."

Amelia was swamped by a too-familiar exasperation.

"And you are charming when you care to be. Have you not thought? What is to become of me if I get with child?"

He soothed a hand through her hair and it calmed her, calmed her almost against her will. "All will be well."

"Oh, Grayson . . ."

"Sir Thomas will not throw you out for bearing a lawful child. It will grow up well here in the beauty and the fresh air."

He sounded so confident. But he was always confident, especially at the gaming table, where he always believed that this time he would win. She slapped his hand away. "I thought you hated the country."

He smiled and touched her nose. "It doesn't agree with me any more than spring water does, but I don't claim it isn't healthy."

He did look just as he had in the early years, and a long-suppressed tenderness swelled like a fertile seed. "Oh, Grayson, I wish . . ."

"Don't." He covered her mouth. "I am what I am, and I will not change. Tomorrow I leave and you will not see me again. If you care for me at all, though, my dear, be happy all your days."

And that was all Amelia remembered before drifting off to sleep. When she woke, he had already left to catch the London coach in Matlock. She felt a twinge of regret in her heart, and in parts of her body still tingling from his pleasuring, but she wasn't sad.

It had been strange, that midnight visit. Very strange. And indecent. Some of the things . . . ! All in all, she'd be happier not to be exposed to that again.

All in all.

When, a few weeks later, she received news that he'd tumbled into the Shoreditch when drunk, and drowned, she wept but was aware of relief as well. Relief for him, for she didn't think he'd been happy, and relief that he would never return to upset her mind and body with midnight madness.

Then she began to suspect that she was, in fact, with child. It was a shock, and rather terrifying, but held some hope of joy. She realized that she had always wanted a child, but had never allowed herself to pine for what she could not have.

When she was certain, she sent up an earnest prayer of thanks, along with a petition that a merciful God let poor Grayson into heaven.

She was a little nervous about writing to Sir Thomas about her condition, and more so when his response was to arrive at the hall in a post chaise. But he was in excellent humor. "Good for old Grayson, eh? And congratulation to you. No, no, don't you fret! You have a home here forever, Amelia, and I'll be grateful to know you have a care to the place. I'll raise your pay to a hundred pounds."

"Oh no. That's too much!"

"Nonsense. And I'm plump in the pockets these days. Regular Midas! Everything I touch turns to gold. I've come to put a stop to the wood cutting. Never liked to see those old oaks going down, but needs must. Anyway, these days, there's no need."

"I'm pleased about that. They are so lovely, and so old. Some of them hundreds of years, they say."

"Aye, well, that's Elphindale for you. Strange place." He went to stare out of the window to where little Andrew played tag with Nan Ferryman.

He frowned, so she asked, "Is something wrong, Cousin?" stabbed by fear that he might find her unsatisfactory. Perhaps she should keep the child at his desk for longer hours.

"No, no. It's just this place. Having been away from it, it gives me the shivers."

"But it's so lovely. And so peaceful."

"Aye, maybe. There's stories, though . . ."

"Oh, the local stories. I'd not have thought you one to pay heed to those."

He turned to face her. "So, you don't mind staying here?"

"I can think of nothing better than to stay here all my days, and raise my child here, too."

"So be it, then. And I know you'll take good care of Andrew. He's blooming already. But don't let him get too stuffed with local nonsense." He frowned out at the child and maid. "They're strange people, here. They hold strange beliefs. I don't want him picking them up. I'll arrange for a good Classics tutor," he suddenly declared. "That's the ticket."

Within days he was off again, and soon a diffident young man called Charles Fenlock came to teach Andrew the sane and sensible stories of Cronos, Apollo, and the fall of Troy instead of the quaint folk tales so loved in the dale.

At first, Amelia had her doubts about Mr. Fenlock, for he was pale, frail, and had an ominous cough. But though the young man put on no weight, he was soon walking the hills and coughing no more.

Yes, the dale was a very salubrious place. As Sir Thomas had noted, Andrew was thriving as well.

Amelia saw no point in keeping the boy locked away, and so—watched over by sensible Nan Ferryman—the Young Master spent his free time with the village children, scrambling over the rocky slopes like a nimble Derbyshire ram.

Soon he was an adopted member of the Ferryman family and Hal, who was just about his age, was his particular friend. Since the Ferrymans owned a prosperous farm and were decent people, Amelia saw no reason to object.

When he took to spending evenings by the Ferryman fireside, listening to the old tales of Elphindale, she did feel a qualm, remembering Sir Thomas's concern about the local superstitions. But the local stories were just harmless fairy tales and Andrew was coming along very well in his Classical studies.

And by then she had her child—her perfect blond-haired, green-eyed daughter.

It was a little strange about Gwennie's green eyes, but she supposed they must be in Grayson's family somewhere.

It was strange about the name, too. She had fully intended to call a daughter Sarah, but somehow the child had been christened Gwendoline, and was known as Gwennie to all.

Such a sweet nature, though, she thought. A mother could never ask for a better child. And though boys were frequently impatient with little girls, Drew adored her, and even let her follow him about without complaint.

Yes, thought Amelia, watching a robust tutor supervise a ball game between his ten-year-old charge and her five-year-old daughter in the lovely summer garden of Elphinson Hall, they were all blessed.

It was almost as if the dale were the magical place the local people claimed it to be.

Elphinson Hall, Derbyshire, September 1807

Twelve-year-old Gwen Forsythe was in the orchard when she heard the crunch of wheels in the driveway. She put down her basket of windfalls and hurried around to the front of the Hall. Visitors were rare, and a pleasant diversion. As she neared the front steps she halted, however, for the carriage door had been swung open by a round, red-faced, almost angry-looking man. He glared at the charming stone house surrounded by the full glory of late summer flowers as if it were an abomination.

It took Gwen a moment or two to recognize Sir Thomas from the portrait in the dining room. When she did, she hurried forward, for she knew her mother would be napping, and this man had the power to throw them out of their home.

"Welcome home, Sir Thomas," she said, dropping her best curtsy.

He stepped down onto the drive and turned the glare

on her. "Who the devil are you? Oh, I suppose you're little Gwennie. Where's my son?"

She cast a quick look around, wondering what he was seeing to make him so angry. "Out angling, sir."

"I thought I sent a demmed tutor here."

"Mr. Fenlock is with them, sir."

"Them?"

"Drew and Hal."

"Hal?"

"Hal Ferryman, sir."

"Blast their eyes!" With that he stalked into his house and Gwen raced up the back stairs to her mother's room.

"Mama! Mama! Wake up. Sir Thomas is here, and he's angry!"

Ever since Gwen had realized that they had no real right to live at Elphinson Hall, she had been haunted by the fear of having to leave.

Her mother sat up, tucking her graying auburn hair back under her lacy cap and blinking. "Sir Thomas? Here?"

"Yes, Mama. And angry."

"Oh dear." Mrs. Forsythe didn't sound particularly agitated. This wasn't reassuring since *nothing* ever agitated her mother. Of course, nothing ever happened in the dale to agitate anyone, and the only newspapers they received here were weeks old. Mrs. Forsythe had been heard to remark that it hardly seemed worth worrying about events already so far in the past.

Gwen tugged her plump mother out of bed and helped her into her gown.

"Does he want to see me?" Mrs. Forsythe asked.

Gwen realized he'd not said as much. "I'm sure he will, Mama. And anyway, we must see to his comfort."

"Oh yes. Comfort," said her mother, like an ancient war horse called to battle. Comfort was something Amelia Forsythe understood and appreciated. "Certainly. Come along!"

Soon Sir Thomas's bed was made up and warming, and

his long-unused rooms checked to see that all was in order. The kitchen had been ordered to produce a full meal rather than the plain one usually taken, and Gwen and her mother even ventured down to the wine cellar in search of manly drinks.

Drew and his tutor returned through the kitchen quarters as Mrs. Forsythe was trying to force the rusty lock to turn.

"What are you two up to?" asked Drew with a laugh. "Finally decided to drown your sorrows?"

Seventeen, nearly six foot tall, and glowing from a day in the fresh air and sunshine, he clearly had no need of alcohol. With the fright of Sir Thomas's sudden appearance made worse by an eerie sense of foreboding, Gwen wanted to throw herself into his arms and hold him tight.

He'd think her demented.

"Your father's here," she said. "And we're sure he'll want some wine or brandy or something. But no one's opened this door since the last time he was here. And that was when I was still in my cradle!"

Mr. Fenlock, a sinewy young man with fine mousy hair but a glow nearly as healthy as his student's, raised his brows. "I wonder what treasures we'll find? But you'd best leave this to me, dear ladies. Though I've no taste for such beverages, I know something of the matter. Old wines need careful handling. In fact, Master Andrew, this will fill in a gap in your education."

"You're going to get me drunk?" teased Drew.

"That will doubtless happen without my intervention, you rascal. I am going to teach you about wines and spirits. And about opening rusty locks."

Gwen and her mother were waved away, but by the time the adults sat to dinner, claret, port, and brandy were available, and presumably handled correctly for Sir Thomas did not complain.

Gwen, of course, ate in the schoolroom, but she heard all about it from Drew when they met as usual in the garden later that night. They sat on their favorite perch, a low wall looking out over the Dale, and Drew angrily tossed bits of rock down the slope beneath their feet.

"Father kept pressing me to drink more. Heaven knows why. Said I had to develop a head for it, but Fen's warned me of the head a man gets from drinking too much and it doesn't appeal."

Gwen plucked a sprig of lavender from the bushes that ran along the base of the wall and breathed in the soothing aroma. "Fashionable men seem to drink a great deal, or so I hear."

"I think that's the plan."

"What?" But she knew and breathed deeper of the plant magic.

"To take me away and turn me into a fashionable man."

"Oh dear." That certainly didn't express the agony in her chest, or the way her lips quivered.

He glanced sideways at her. "That's not much help. Any idea how I get out of it?"

Gwen swallowed. "Can you not just say no?"

"I can try," he said with a grimace, "but something about him . . . It's so strange to have a man appear out of nowhere assuming he has the right to order me about."

"He is your father."

"So I'm told. He last visited here when I was six, and I can hardly remember it." He looked around, and she knew he was drawing in the sights, sounds, and smells of the dale as she so often did. "He hates this place."

"Hates it?"

"Yes. I don't know why." He suddenly took her hand, holding tight. "I don't want to leave, Gwennie."

She squeezed his hand back, knowing he was just seeking friendly comfort, but that she was reacting in a different way. She thought wryly how young she must look to him, with her skirts still at calf length showing her long panta-lettes underneath, and her blond curls tamed into a plait down her back.

A child. That's all Gwennie Forsythe was to him.

But underneath her gown her breasts were budding. She would soon be a woman.

If he were around to see it.

As if he'd caught her thought, he turned suddenly to look straight at her. "I'll miss you most of all, Gwennie."

Her heart somersaulted. "I'll miss you terribly. But it'll only be for a little while, Drew. If he makes you go, you can do what he wants then come back."

"Fen says he probably wants me to go to university. Cambridge. Sir Thomas was lamenting that the war's put an end to young men making a Grand Tour of Europe . . ."

But then his usual spirits shone bright again, and he grinned as he rose and swung her to her feet. "You're right, though. Even if I have to go, it won't be for long. I'll come home for holidays. And we can write. You can tell me everything that goes on here."

She clutched his hands. "Oh, I will. But you'll have to write back!"

"Of course." Then, almost awkwardly, he pulled her to him for a hug.

They'd grown up together, playing and wrestling, and if either of them was hurt, they had hugged. It was not a strange thing. And yet, and yet, thought Gwen, snuggling against his chest, this was different. If she were a little bit older, she thought he might kiss her. But she wasn't so he didn't, though she couldn't help wondering if the idea had been in his mind, too, perhaps a tiny bit.

She'd be older when he came back.

Perhaps by Christmas she could persuade her mother to let her put her skirts down, and her hair up. The trouble was that since she'd never shown interest in such matters before, her mother would either guess, or think her running mad.

After all, penniless Gwennie Forsythe, daughter of the poor relation, was no match for the future Sir Andrew Elphinson.

He pushed her back, but kept his hands warm on her shoulders, frowning as if he would say something important. If the words were there, she never heard them, for Sir Thomas came storming along the path, swinging his cane as if he'd use it on them.

"What the devil do you think you're doing, sir! Unhand her!" He emphasized it with a poke of his cane to Drew's side.

Drew dropped his hands as if she burned him. "I'm not hurting her, sir. We were talking."

"A gentleman talks to a lady without handling her, sir!" *Swish.* The cane broke a line of lavender spikes. "And he doesn't talk to a child at all. What are you doing out here, miss?"

Unused to anger, Gwen felt her knees knocking. "I often come out in the evening, Sir Thomas."

"Well, desist while I and my son are about. Keep to your place, which is out of my sight!"

It was clearly a dismissal, and a very rude one. Gwen hesitated for a moment, thinking Drew would defend her. When he didn't, she turned and left with as much dignity as she could muster, tears streaming down her face. Sir Thomas's words had not just been an instruction to stay out of sight, but a clear reinforcement of her thought that there could be no future for her with Drew.

One day Drew would bring a rich fashionable bride home to the dale, and her heart would break.

She felt as if her heart would break the next day when she woke to find that Sir Thomas had already left, taking Drew and Mr. Fenlock with him. There had been no chance for a proper farewell. The only consolation was that Hal Ferryman had been taken as well, to act as manservant.

Sir Thomas had doubtless shaken the dust of the dale off his shoes. Mr. Fenlock had no real ties here. She hated to think of it, but it was possible that Drew might begin to forget the dale and all its people.

But Gwen knew that Hal Ferryman, son of a family who

had lived in the dale since before the Conquest, never would. Sooner or later, Hal would come back.

Elphinson Hall, Derbyshire. May 1815

Gwen stared at old Matt Ferryman, who'd come up to her in the herb garden. "Go with you into the woods at night, Matt? Certainly not!"

The old man, Hal's grandfather, kept his gray head properly lowered. "I'd keep you safe, miss."

"I'm sure you would." What on earth was wrong with him, seeking her out with such a request? The way he was nervously turning his hat showed he *knew* how peculiar it was. It was years since she'd run wild in the country. Not since Drew and Hal had left, really . . .

"You must see it would be improper, Matt."

Old Matt gave a toothy grin. "Reckon I'm past doing you any harm, miss."

Gwen blushed. "Reckon you're past protecting me, too." She bent to check a chive plant, hoping that would be the end of it.

"The Folk'll take care of you, miss, never fear."

Gwen straightened, gave him a look, and moved on to the dill. She loved the dale stories of the Faery Folk, but she'd hardly trust the imaginary creatures with her safety. "Why on earth do you want me to go with you anyway?"

The old man worked his mouth and glanced around. "Lady wants to see you," he mumbled.

Gwen turned to pay closer attention to his words. "What lady?"

"The *Lady*, miss," he whispered. "The Queen of Faerie."

Gwen managed to hold back a laugh. The local people took these matters so seriously, and none more than Old Matt. Now she thought of it, back when she'd been mingling with the village children, she'd heard him called the faery-man because of his faith in such things.

But really. Clearly the poor man was growing senile. She was sure the five-year absence of his grandson hadn't been easy on him, any more than the absence of his son's master had been on her. She looked at a low wall edged with lavender, and sighed.

But then she put such foolishness aside. "No, Matt. I'm sorry. I could not possibly do such a thing." Trying to turn her refusal into a joke, she added, "If the Faerie Queen wishes to see me, she will just have to come here."

His face crumpled almost as if he'd cry. "Miss Gwennie, please don't be like that about it!"

"Oh, Matt. I'm sorry." She tried to think of something to say that would help and failed. "I don't really believe in all those stories anymore, and I can't pretend I do."

With that, Gwen turned and walked briskly back to the house feeling horribly as if she'd kicked a defenseless creature.

She wished Hal were around, for she could talk to him and see if his grandfather needed any help. The dale folk were remarkably healthy, but if Old Matt was turning foolish, some provision must be made.

If Hal were around, though, Drew would be around. She wasn't even sure anymore that she wanted that, for he clearly had no interest in her, while her obsession with him seemed to grow despite absence. All his rare letters were in her bureau, tied up with ribbon, and when a small portrait had been sent to be hung in the portrait gallery, that had become her favorite place to sit and read.

She sighed. If he turned up, she'd doubtless make an utter fool of herself.

She washed her hands and went into the kitchen to speak to the cook about the evening meal.

"Why, Miss Gwen, has something bothered you?" asked the plump woman, wiping her hands on her apron.

"No, why?"

"It's rare to see you frown."

"Oh." Gwen laughed. "I was just worrying about old Matt Ferryman."

"There's no need to worry about him, miss, that's for sure." With this absolute statement, Mrs. Biggin turned back to tying up a haunch of beef.

"Well, he is getting old."

"Old or not, he's still the faery-man."

"And what does that mean?"

The woman made an elaborate and very secure-looking knot. "Means he keeps the stories, miss. And tells the Folk about our doings here. And brings back words from them."

Or thinks he does, Gwen told herself, but not without a twitch of unease. She'd spent many an evening listening to Matt Ferryman telling stories.

"One thing's for sure, miss. He'll be sound in mind and body till the day he dies. Naught bad'll happen to him."

"Oh, really . . ."

The cook gave Gwen a meaningful look. "Just as naught bad happens to *anyone* in these parts, miss."

Gwen had just thought the same thing, but she was in no mood for nonsense. "It certainly is a very healthy spot, Mrs. Biggin. And before you go on about faery blessings, I'll remind you that one of the legends says that none of the Elphinsons will die young. Yet Drew's mother did just that."

The woman turned back to her beef. "Aye, well, she kept young Master Drew by her side and away from the dale. The Folk have their ways, miss."

Gwen shook her head. Logic made absolutely no impression on the local beliefs. "Did you say you needed new tinning in some pots, Mrs. Biggin?"

The woman accepted the change of subject without complaint, but when Gwen eventually headed off to change her gown and take tea with her mother, she heard the cook say, "Just you don't ignore the Folk, miss. It's not wise to do that."

Goodness, she loved the dale dearly, but there were times when it would be pleasant to mix with more rational people!

Perhaps that was what had seduced Drew away from them all.

After his father had dragged him off to Oxford, Drew had returned only twice, and each time he'd seemed more distant. After that, there had just been letters and excuses that he was busy here, there, and everywhere. Letters from London about balls. Letters from Bath about beauties. Letters from Ireland about horses.

All of them talking of a world Gwen didn't know, a world into which she could never fit.

For the past two years, the letters had been few and far between, for he was now even farther away. He'd joined Wellington's army to fight the French. Gwen tried to bury that deep in her mind, but she could never ignore it entirely, the thought that Drew was involved in war.

That he could die.

She'd wept for joy last year when Napoleon had abdicated and it was—everyone thought—over. But now the man was back, once more trying to conquer Europe. The British army was once more in the field.

She did hope, despite the arguments of logic, that the legend had some basis in truth, and that an Elphinson couldn't die young.

She shook her head and put on a smile as she entered the drawing room. At least her mother could be relied upon not to talk about faery nonsense, or to fret about such distant problems as the war.

Two days later, Gwen became inexplicably lost in the woodlands in the valley of the dale.

She had wandered out to look for wild herbs, not intending to go far. Then, despite the fact that she had been walking and riding these hills and valleys almost from birth, and knew every path and tree like her garden, she had become lost. Suddenly it was as if the woods were not the countryside she knew at all.

Panicked, she pushed on in one direction, hoping to see something familiar. Then, sure she had somehow wandered far from home, she turned back. Only to find that the scenery behind her was now equally strange.

The woodland near Elphinson Hall was not even big enough for her to have walked so far without finding a cultivated field or a sheep-dotted hill. Nor was she walking in circles, for nothing was familiar.

She tried sitting still, thinking to calm her mind, telling herself that sooner or later men would set out to look for her. But it would be hours before she was missed, and it was so silly to be sitting here all day.

So she walked again, sure that at any moment she must come across a landmark, or a person who could help.

Eventually, however, as the light began to fade, exhaustion felled her. Shaking, she collapsed down at the base of an oak, hugging herself against the growing chill of evening and the fear of the peculiar. Her stomach rumbled with hunger, and her mouth was parched, for she'd not even come across a stream of sweet water.

The first hunting owl hooted and she flinched, but she told herself there was nothing to be afraid of, even at night. There were no wild animals here, after all, and no one who would hurt her. She would have been missed by now, and the village people would be out searching. The dalesmen knew every inch of the countryside. They would soon find her.

She'd thought *she* knew every inch of the countryside, though.

She shivered again and glanced around nervously. Where on earth *was* she? Had she somehow managed to leave the dale? She couldn't believe that, for one needed to climb rising ground.

Even though she told herself there was nothing to be

afraid of, fear rose in her, fear all the worse for having no cause or focus. Irrationally, she wanted Drew. He'd find her. He'd save her from whatever it was that lurked in the shadows here.

She sank her head on her knees. One thing was sure. Drew wouldn't suddenly appear. He hadn't even come home last year when his father had died and he'd inherited the estate. Or later when Napoleon Bonaparte had been exiled to Elba and the war had stopped.

Where was he now? They were so out of touch in the dale that he could be in battle and she'd have no hint of it . . .

Suddenly, with scarcely a rustled leaf to announce his coming, a handsome man moved from behind a tree and strolled toward her. His fashionable country wear of jacket, buckskins, top boots, and beaver made him seem quite ordinary, but Gwen leapt to her feet nervously.

He was a stranger. She saw few strangers in the dale.

Inclining his head, he raised his hat with a fine air. "Good evening, miss," he said, as if he were encountering her in the village street.

"Good evening, sir." Good manners made her drop a curtsy. Since there was no way to disguise the fact, she added, "I fear I am lost."

"Poor lady." He extended an arm. "Allow me to guide you to safety."

Gwen hesitated, for she couldn't imagine who this man might be, and his appearance had been so very sudden. Listening most carefully, she could detect no sound of searchers nearby. On the other hand, there *was* something familiar about him. Perhaps he was of the dale after all.

She studied him as best she could in the dimming light. It was hard to pinpoint his age. He seemed about Drew's age, and yet a great deal older. He had blond hair, green eyes, and—

Gwen gasped. "Who *are* you?"

He smiled. "You see the resemblance. Yes, I am a relative, Miss Forsythe. You are completely safe with me."

Reassured by the fact that he knew her name, Gwen allowed him to lead her through the gloomy wood, most of her concentration on the ground before her. She had no wish to crown her foolishness by turning an ankle.

"You must be a relative of my father's then," she said, but doubtfully. She'd never met any of her father's family, but from what she knew, and the portrait her mother kept, there was no resemblance other than fair hair.

"After a fashion, yes." She heard humor in his voice, then he stopped and turned so that she was obliged to look up at him. Strangely, it seemed a little lighter, as if the full moon had broken through the clouds, and yet there was little moon tonight, and the canopy of leaves cut off what light it gave.

"You are going to be surprised, Gwen Forsythe, but you must open your heart and your mind to the truth. Your family needs you."

Gwen frowned at him, puzzled. What surprise? What family? Her only family was her mother. Unless it was Drew who needed her . . .

Her rescuer took Gwen's hands in a firm, warm grasp. "Gwen, I am your father."

She tried to pull free. "Don't be silly—"

"And I am of Faerie."

Gwen went still. A lifetime of stories had laid down fertile soil, and she couldn't quite scoff. Not here. Not now.

Still she had to say it. "You can't be."

"I can. I am." A charming, mischievous smile lit his face. "Though perhaps you should not tell your mother. A charming lady, but conventional."

Gwen had been wondering *how* such a thing might be possible, and now the implication that her mother had no notion . . . She should have been horrified, if she believed it at all, but the image of this rakish gentleman with her placid, extremely conventional mother surprised a giggle out of her.

He joined her in laughter. "You are a delight to me, daughter, and it has given me joy to watch over you." Then he grew serious. "But now it is time for you to meet your faery kin and learn the purpose for which you were created."

When he tried to move on, Gwen pulled back. "I am not a *creation*," she objected. "You speak as if I am a slave."

He turned stern, and even fatherly. "We are all slaves to our heritage. You are needed, Kerrigwen."

"My name is Gwen."

"Kerrigwen," he insisted, "which is a rank, not a name." He released her and stood back, gesturing her to precede him. "Come. Learn."

A glimmering path traced the ground before her, and through the trees ahead, a faint light glowed as if there were moonlight there. But it was moonlight such as Gwen had never seen, holding promise of summer growth and winter ice. Music teased her senses, but so high and soft it could be just imagination.

She was not imagining the impetus, however. Despite a chill down her back, Gwen found herself unable to do anything but go forward on the magical path under the pressure of a man's hand—her father's hand?

"Do not be afraid." Her father's voice? "I will never let anyone or anything hurt you, my daughter."

In the eerily lit glade, a beautiful woman sat on a high grassy mound dotted with flowers, flowers that should not all be in bloom at this time of year. She wore a high-waisted dress in the latest style, but fine enough for Court, surely, having an overdress of spider-fine lace interwoven with gold and flowerbuds.

Her golden hair was fashionably cropped into clustering curls around her face, but at the back it flowed down beyond her waist, seeming to grow into the ground itself. Or out of the ground itself.

Impossible flowers. Impossible hair. Impossible situation. This was Matt Ferryman's Lady, the Queen of Faerie.

She was dreaming, Gwen realized with relief. She'd fallen asleep against that tree, and was now in a vivid dream woven out of fears, desires, and childhood memories.

She'd always loved Matt's tales, and always wanted a father . . .

"Come forward, Kerrigwen," said the Lady, in a soft, melodious voice. "Come sit with me here, so that we can talk."

Gwen went. There didn't seem any point in fighting a dream.

The Lady's soft, smooth hand cradled her face, turning it up for inspection. "You have a pretty daughter, Merlon. And not too much of Faerie about her."

Gwen glanced at the man she had conjured up to be her father and smiled. He appeared hardly ten years older than herself. Impossible again.

But this was the most fascinating dream she had ever experienced, and she intended to enjoy it. She just hoped that something of it would linger in her waking mind.

The Lady released her face and folded her beringed hands neatly in her lap. "Now, my dear, it is time for you to serve your people. You have been brought here to learn what you must know."

Gwen imitated her, folding her hands and paying attention.

"We thought that you would just learn of faery ways by living in our land here, but I fear that you remain unenlightened. You humans are so strange, and grow stranger with each passing century. I must tell you, then, that Elphindale is not just another area of hills and valleys. There is an ancient bond between the humans of this island and Faerie, and the dale is at the heart of it, center of harmony and prosperity for faeries and humans, both."

Gwen found it easy to nod. For her, Elphindale was the heart of everything.

"But we are threatened." The Lady stared into Gwen's eyes as if she would project her words into her heart. "By Dark Earth—the powers that stand opposite Faerie. As people leave the land, lose touch with the land, Dark Earth grows in power.

"Dark Earth?" Gwen had to ask.

"It is always with us, in the earth."

"Like hell?"

The Lady make a click of disapproval. "This has nothing to do with such human beliefs. Dark Earth is not evil, any more than Faerie is evil. It is part of the whole, but the whole must be in balance. Now Dark Earth grows stronger, brought up from the mines and into the lives of humans, changing them, stealing them from us, from the trees and rivers. There must be balance in the dominion over humans."

Dominion. Gwen didn't like that word at all, but something in the Lady's features—a hardening, an aging—made her hold her tongue. In fact, the Lady's small white teeth had grown quite sharp . . .

"Dark Earth grows," the Lady said. Hissed, perhaps. "But as long as Faerie holds here in the dale, we can have balance. If Dark Earth should disrupt the patterns here, however, then the balance would tip, perhaps forever."

"What would happen?"

"Faerie would suffer. Perhaps we would have to leave this . . . this aspect entirely. What must concern you, however, humanchild, is that people would suffer too. Your human kin can never survive under Dark Earth unchecked."

Part of Gwen's mind tried to remember that this was a dream, but it was a small part. She was caught in this story which resonated with beliefs rooted deep in her mind. "How do we stop Dark Earth?"

The Lady smiled, and it was as if the sun shone. "The key to Faerie survival in the dale is our partnership with humans through the link with the Elphinson family. They, like you, are half faery, half human.

"Sir Thomas?" exclaimed Gwen incredulously.

"Indeed, Sir Thomas," said the Lady with a rueful expression. "As you can tell, the blood has thinned. See how he is able to live away from the dale. Think how he once began to cut the trees."

"What of Drew?" Gwen asked urgently, for if the blood was thin, perhaps the ancient faery bond didn't protect him. She realized she was trusting in that faery protection more than she'd thought.

"He was a promising youth, but despite all we did, he, too, has left us. His blood is thin."

Gwen wanted to ask, How thin? Too thin for the bond to hold?

"This is all for you to correct, child."

"Me?" Instinctively, against logic, Gwen turned to the man who claimed to be her father. "What must I do?"

He came forward to take her hand. "You have the blood, daughter. You must give it to the Elphinsons."

Gwen gaped. "A *sacrifice*?"

But he laughed. "Oh, I don't think so. You must marry Sir Andrew Elphinson and bring him back to the dale."

Her heart leaped for joy. Oh, no wonder she was dreaming this dream. It was taking her directly where she wanted to go.

Her father continued. "Here you will birth and raise children in whom the faery blood will once again run strong. You will renew the bond."

Gwen's heart was beating fast and high, but common sense ruled, apparently, even in dreams. She remembered all Drew's letters, letters about dances and house parties, about the beauties of Brighton and the Toasts of London.

He would have no interest in a simple country girl with brown skin, who never tried to do more with her curls than brush them. He'd laugh at the appearance of a person who so hated to leave the dale that her clothes were home-made, and to the simplest design.

She had to swallow before she could say the stark words. "I'm afraid he would not want to marry me."

"Do you not look in a mirror, child?" the Lady asked. "You have beauty such as no man can resist."

Gwen laughed. What foolishness there was in dreams. "Me? I can never be bothered with lotions, or hairstyles, and I design my clothes to need the fewest stitches."

The Lady's laughter joined hers. "What need nave you of beauty aids, child? Or of fashion? You could walk among men in your shift with your hair down to your knees, and they would fall at your feet. How can you be so foolish?"

Then she answered her own question. "Of course. You are bound to the land here, too. Not as much as we, but greatly. You have doubtless seen few men of your station. The lower orders would not dare raise their eyes so far, to a well-born human and a princess of Faerie."

"Is that why . . . ?" Gwen was startled into remembering how the village lads had always treated her in a special way. Even the boldest of them never teased, and if she went to one of their village dances, her partners never seemed to be at ease.

This behavior had strengthened her belief that she lacked what attracted men. It was pleasant of her dream to try to furnish another explanation, but it was foolishness all the same.

"Drew grew up with my attractions," she pointed out, "and showed no sign of falling at my feet."

As if she understood, the Lady touched Gwen's cheek. "You were a child still, my dear. Believe me, when next he sees you, he will not be so indifferent. But if the Lord of Elphindale *is* slow to succumb, there are ways to capture his attention."

"Love potions? That would be wicked!"

Her father answered her. "The love will be real, Kerrigwen, no matter how arrived at. The man will not suffer by all this, I promise you. Do not fail us."

Gwen looked between the two seemingly pleasant, but

clearly ruthless, people. "Don't call me Kerrigwen. My name is Gwen."

"Gwen is your human name," said her father. "Kerrigwen is your title. You were born a princess of Faerie. After your human christening in the church, late that night you were brought here to be named by us, and blessed by us." He drew her to her feet to face him. "I have something to tell you now, daughter. Something important, so pay attention."

"Yes?" Gwen's heart began to speed, for she couldn't imagine what else could be said to shock her.

"You are as much faery as you are human. You can claim that heritage if you wish, and come to live among us."

"Leave the world behind?"

"Yes. You sound horrified, but think. Your lifespan among us would be many, many times longer than among humankind. So long that we are sometimes called immortal. And in all that time, you would never grow older than you wished, never suffer pain or illness, hunger or thirst, or any other of the ills of humanity."

"But I would never marry, or have children?" And it was Drew she thought of. Drew at the altar. Drew's children in her arms.

Oh, foolish dream.

"You could have children by mating with a human, but the child must be raised by humans. That is not easy for a female to do."

Gwen looked between the Lady and her father—perhaps her father—wondering if the Lady had borne babies, wondering about changelings.

It was as if the very trees held their breath.

"But if I stay here with you, what of your plan?"

"We would make another," said the Lady, as if it were of little concern, but a bleakness in her eyes told Gwen it would be a setback.

A setback for the dale and Faerie. Perhaps for all people? It tipped the balance, though it had not been a hard choice. She had no desire for a life of sterile pleasure, and could not endure to leave the world behind, the world that—she prayed daily—still held Drew Elphinson. "I don't belong here," she said.

A gentle breeze stirred, as if the trees sighed in relief.

Her father kissed her cheek, glowing with new hope. "Then you will save us all."

"But I don't know how!" Gwen protested. "What am I supposed to do? We never go anywhere, and Drew's on the Continent. Even when he was in England, he never came here. Mother and I don't have the money to travel, and if we did, we don't know anyone, or know how to go on in Society."

"Everything will be arranged," said the Lady with a confidence Gwen found rather unsettling. "Just be ready to do your part when the time comes."

What part? Gwen felt more worried by the moment. If there was any sense to it at all, her mother had been tricked into bearing her. What other tricks were in hand? Though it took courage, she looked straight into the Lady's emerald eyes. "I won't trick Drew into wanting to marry me. I won't do that."

"You will do what you have to do."

Though she couldn't quite voice defiance, Gwen silently vowed that she would do *nothing* that was wrong. "I don't even know anything about love potions and things like that."

"Betsy Raisley does."

Betsy Raisley was Gwen's maid-companion. She'd come up to the Hall a few years ago asking for a place. Since she had skill with creams and lotions, and seemed able to take care of clothes, she'd been hired as general ladies' maid and rapidly become a friend.

Gwen remembered now that her mother had expressed mild surprise that a Raisley was interested in entering service, for they were an independent family. They made most of their money selling potions at the local fairs.

Gwen shivered at the feel of being entangled in a long-woven web, and at the suspicion that it was not a web easily escaped.

"I won't trick him," she whispered, as much to herself as to the Lady. "How could anyone bear to live with someone they've tricked in such a way?"

"Oh, you humans." The Lady swept out her hand, trailing tiny sparkles of light which became a gossamer curtain. As the curtain faded, Gwen stared at the dark woods behind.

Not woods.

Now she faced a ramshackle building, a row of small white tents, and humps that were doubtless men sleeping in the open. There were no trees nearby at all, and something in the air was wrong as well. This was not the moist air of Derbyshire. This was dry, dusty, and carried country smells different from those she was accustomed to.

She glanced around, but the faery glade, the Lady, the man who claimed to be her father, had all disappeared. She should be frightened, and yet she was not, for she guessed what was before her.

Drew.

Her dream had taken her to Europe, and to Drew, and that was proof positive that it *was* a dream.

Dull noises, distant calls, and the glimmer of banked campfires, told her she was in the middle of a sleeping army. Carefully, she stepped forward over tussocky ground, drawn to one tent, her eyes becoming accustomed to the light.

She had to kneel to look into the tent, and it should have been too dark to see much in there. She saw Drew clearly, though, rolled in a blanket on the ground with only a pack for a pillow. He was alone. Possibly the only concession to his rank.

Major. He'd been promoted to major not long before. He'd not written to tell them. They'd found it in a newspaper.

She worked her way forward until she was kneeling beside him. He was still handsome, with straight nose and square chin, and absurdly long dark lashes resting on his cheeks, but so much older. Perhaps it was just that he looked so deathly weary. She'd never seen him haggard, with a couple of day's growth of dark beard and a nasty bruise on his temple.

He was still Drew, though. Her beloved Drew. Gingerly, she brushed a tendril of hair off his brow.

A primitive instinct surged in Gwen to tend him, to feed and comfort him until he once more glowed with youth, health, and vigor. She doubted her dream would allow her that.

But who knew the rules of dreams? She settled beside him wondering just how far her dream freedom would let her go.

A rough blanket covered him from the chest down, but he seemed to be only wearing his shirt. His open-necked shirt. The years had changed his body, too. Strong muscles rose into a man's neck. Unfastened cuffs exposed brown forearms wound with powerful veins.

How could she picture a man's body so, she who was too well behaved to have noticed such things before? Dreams were strange things indeed, and this dream was summoning a wild desire to touch his skin, to test the warmth and hardness that it promised.

Once or twice, as young children, they'd swum together in the river in their drawers. She'd always known that the boys didn't wear even that much when she wasn't there. She'd seen his body.

A boy's body.

Mr. Fenlock and her mother had taught them dancing, and they'd spun in one another's arms for precious, magical moments.

She'd held a youth's body decently covered in shirt, cravat, and coat.

That night by the lavender-edged wall she'd embraced

a young man's body—the only time there'd been anything remotely lover-close between them, and still they had been armored in the full dress of their station.

Now Gwen wondered what happened in dreams if people touched, if people kissed. Nothing, of course. She leaned forward and gingerly touched her lips to his. She'd half expected him to be insubstantial as mist, but his lips were sleep-soft and warm beneath hers. The bristle around them was rough, though, and prickled at her skin, making this all seem very real indeed.

Telling herself dream kisses didn't count in any scale of right or wrong, Gwen balanced herself farther forward and pressed her lips a little harder, wishing she knew more of the business. It seemed a terrible shame that she was going to waste this unique opportunity because she hadn't much idea of what to do.

His eyes fluttered open. Before she could react, hard hands trapped her, tipping her down onto his chest as he snapped something in a foreign language.

Then he blinked, squinting. "Gwennie?"

Gwen felt horribly embarrassed, as if she had been caught truly kissing a man in his sleep. "You're dreaming, Drew."

"That's certain sure." He let her go and sat up, rubbing his hands over his tired face, then blinking at her again. "What the devil . . . ?"

Free, perhaps for the only time in her life, to do as she wished with him, Gwen captured his hands. Strong hands, rough with calluses. "Don't think about it, Drew. Don't worry. It's a dream." Greatly daring, she raised one hand and kissed his knuckles. "Have you missed me at all, all these years?"

Dark lashes rose from clear blue eyes. "Have I . . . ? Oh, Gwennie." He freed a hand to touched her cheek as if he, too, feared she would melt into mist. "More than you can know." He traced her jaw, her nose, her eyebrows, every touch sending a shiver right through her. "I wonder if you really look like this now? You're twenty, aren't you? Quite grown up.''

"Too long in the tooth for you?" she teased.

He grinned, looking briefly more like the Drew she remembered. "Too pretty in the tooth." He rubbed his knuckle against her lips, against her teeth. "Too pretty by far . . . No." With both hands, he cradled her head, fingers playing restlessly against her scalp. "Too beautiful. God, Gwennie, you've grown into a beauty."

"That's what the Lady said."

"What lady?" But he didn't seem to care. He was looking at her lips. "A dream . . ." he murmured, and drew her head down to his.

She couldn't keep her balance, and so collapsed on top of him to be rolled half under as his lips claimed hers in a rapid education in the art of kissing.

For a moment, Gwen's conventional upbringing stiffened her, urging her to object. But then she realized she didn't have to protest or protect herself. This was a dream.

She could let him do as he wished. Let him push open her mouth, tease her teeth then her tongue, overwhelm her with his hard and rather pungent body. Baths must be rare in an army, but she didn't care about that either.

This was Drew and if he stayed away, if—worse still— he returned with a fashionable wife, she would still have this to remember.

Her hands were in his hair, her mouth was rapidly learning how to savor his, when she startled under a new strange sensation. His hand had found her right breast. Even through the sturdy cloth of her walking dress, his touch was raising sensations she had never imagined.

He drew back from her lips, eyes crinkling with warm appreciation. "Beautiful all over. Gad, Gwennie, you're all grown up."

"Of course I am."

"Are all the boys in the dale mad for you, damn their eyes?" His hand returned to her breast, stroking there.

"Would I were in the dale again, with you in my arms in truth . . ."

Gwen wished she could touch him as boldly as he touched her.

Why not? This was a dream, after all.

No one would ever know.

She threaded her hands into his hair and kissed him back, then let her hands slide down inside his shirt to his muscle-hard shoulders and his satiny back, moving beneath him as his hands and mouth tormented her . . .

He groaned. Pulling their mouths apart, he whispered "Gwennie, sweet Gwennie. How I've missed you. How I've dreamed . . ."

She cradled his face. "Then why not come back, Drew? We're all waiting for you to come back. You're the Lord of Elphindale now."

No. That hadn't been quite what she'd meant to say.

He laughed. "That nonsense." His mind was clearly on other things, such as the curve of her neck, which he was kissing and teasing with tiny, sparkling bites. "That's the trouble with the dale. Stay there too long and a person starts to believe . . ." His fingers traced down the front of her gown. "So many buttons."

"The dale is beautiful." At that moment, Gwen didn't care a fig for the beauty of the dale, and yet the words spilled from her. The Lady . . . The Lady was speaking through her?

"You are beautiful," he whispered, and unfastened the first small button."

She put a hand up to stop him. "Drew . . ."

"Sweet Gwennie. Let me. Let me see you . . ."

"Promise to come back to the dale . . ."

"Anything."

"You promise?"

"I promise."

He'd have said anything, she knew, to still her protests. Hastily, clumsily, he was unfastening the front of her dress, exposing her shift, exposing her skin to his rapt eyes and the night air. Then he was kissing her there, licking her, sucking her . . .

Gwen squeaked with surprise, then hastily covered her mouth. They were alone, but there had been other men nearby. Even in a dream, perhaps they could be interrupted.

She did not want any interruption.

In a state of shocked wonder, she held his head close to her breasts, stroking his hair and skin, relishing the hot weight of his body, and letting him create magic. She could have stayed like that for hours, for eternity, but he pushed back to look at her.

She could see that his weariness had fled, replaced by wondering delight and the flush of desire. She was fiercely glad to be giving him that, even in his dreams.

"You may be twenty but you're still an innocent, aren't you, Gwennie?" Before she could object or apologize, he said, "Hush. I'm glad. I'm glad to see that dazed look in your eyes. I want the honor of awakening you, if only in a dream. How much further can we go in a dream, I wonder?"

"As far as we want, I suppose," she whispered daringly.

He smiled in a devilish way that was so familiar it almost made her cry, and shifted to slide his hand under her skirt, up her leg, until he found her left garter. He tugged until it came undone, then pushed her stocking down, his hand rough against her flesh.

Next, watching her as if he expected her to object, he pushed her skirts up so she felt the night air on her skin all the way up to her naked thigh. His eyes moved then, to look at her legs and she could imagine herself as he saw her—sprawled like a wanton, breasts and legs naked to his eyes, his touch, his mouth . . .

And she didn't care. She loved it because of the way he looked, because of the hunger in him.

"Ah, Gwennie. You are perfect." Slowly, his hand moved

up again, to tug at her other garter. "You are mine. Mine for all time . . ."

But then his eyes began to drift shut.

"Drew?"

His hand stopped, went slack, and then he relaxed back onto the ground, eyes shut once more.

"Drew!" She shook him, thinking he was sick, or dying.

Then he began to turn mistlike in her hands.

"Drew!" she screamed into the shower of light that carried her back to a glade in Elphindale.

She was kneeling on the cool grass weeping when her father's touch on her bodice stung her back to the present.

The real present.

This was no dream.

Or perhaps that had been a dream . . .

She leapt to her feet, twitching her clothing out of faery hands and hastily fastening buttons. "I suppose you watched all that."

"No, child," said her father.

"But can you now give the Lord of Elphindale to another?" asked the Lady, in the manner of one who complacently knows the answer.

Tugging her bodice straight, Gwen faced the Queen of Faerie. "Yes, if he wants another."

"Don't lie to yourself, Kerrigwen." With disdain, the Lady waved her away, and her father began to guide her out of the glade.

Gwen stopped as she realized that her right stocking was down around her ankle. She looked around, but saw no sign of her simple garter. Could she really have left it in a dream?

Her father held something before her, a strip of frivolous pink silk. Lacking choice, she took it and used it to tie up her plain cotton stocking. As she did so, she thought back to the dream that she feared had not been a dream.

She had visited Drew in a camp waiting for battle.

She turned back to the Lady. "Will he be safe?"

The Lady raised her brows in mild astonishment. "Can you doubt it? We are not yet powerless. The Lord of Elphindale could walk through a hail of shot and be untouched. As could you."

"What, then, of his mother? She died before her time."

"An unfortunate necessity. She loved her child too much, and hated the dale."

Which, thought Gwen, showed the other side of the glittering coin. She spoke her fear out loud. "If Drew's death became a necessity, he, too, could die before his time."

"No," said her father. "He is the only Lord of Elphindale, and the bond holds. We must protect him."

There was comfort in that, and Gwen hugged it to her as her father led her through the woods, which gradually became familiar again, until they heard voices calling her name.

Men were indeed out searching.

She turned to him. "I'm finding it hard not to think of this as a dream."

"Perhaps it is, daughter, but dreams are sometimes real. Try not to be seen in the light, but look in your mirror when you get home."

With that he was gone, and Gwen became aware of a soreness on her face. Drew's stubbly whiskers! How could a dream lover abrade her skin?

How could she be transported to an army camp in Europe?

Her agitation was probably just what the searchers expected, though they all expressed surprise that she had managed to get lost. Once home, she claimed an extreme headache made worse by light, and soon found herself tucked into her bed in a dark room.

Once she was alone, however, she lit a candle and looked in the mirror to inspect a distinct reddening of her skin. Her lips were fuller than usual, too. Swollen by Drew's kisses.

It was impossible!

Yet her body had experienced new sensations tonight. She had been visited by sensual dreams in the past, embarrassing dreams, but they had all been vague since she had no knowledge to wrap them around. There had been nothing vague about her dream tonight, about the feel of a hard body, the smell of stale sweat, and the exploration of an urgent mouth.

So, what did that make of the rest of it, of her faery father and the Lady, and her destiny?

She went to her discarded clothes and found one gray garter, neatly embroidered with blue forget-me-nots, and one pink ribbon.

They had said it was her destiny to marry the Lord of Elphindale.

Drew.

She hugged herself, swamped by a blend of horror and longing. There was nothing she wanted more than to marry Drew Elphinson, and their encounter tonight had just enriched that longing.

As it had been designed to do.

On the other hand, she could imagine nothing more appalling than trapping any man into marriage against his will.

In fact, she thought with determination, she wouldn't do it no matter what Faerie wanted.

Gwen soon began to wonder whether Faerie could truly be resisted.

The Duchess of Sommerton, a very grand lady, suddenly remembered her dear school friend, Amelia Carstairs—now Forsythe—and invited the lady and her daughter to visit her in London during the Little Season in autumn.

Gwen argued forcibly that they hadn't the money for it.

"But it would be an opportunity for you, dear," said her mother, fingering the expensive stationery. "The dale is a wonderful place, but you are going to wither into a spinster here."

"Grow into a healthy and happy old maid, you mean," said Gwen briskly.

"You'd miss the chance to have children. My life would have been poorer for not having you, my love." Gwen's mother looked at her with a frown. "You're not . . . you're not waiting for Drew, are you?"

"Drew!" Gwen wished she wasn't turning red, but it was only days since that extraordinary dream. "Of course not. I just think it would be intolerable to be in London, poor as church mice, dependent on the duchess for every little thing."

"I do have some money put aside . . ."

"You can't spend your savings. You know that when Drew marries we might have to leave." With these arguments, Gwen managed to persuade her mother to refuse the invitation.

There, she thought with relief. Faerie's plan—if such it was—had been firmly blocked.

A month later, her mother startled her by rushing up to her in the garden, cap all askew. "Gwen! You'll never guess!"

She was so agitated it was impossible to tell if she were pleased or distraught.

Drew, Gwen thought. Dead?

"Five thousand pounds!" declared her mother, waving a letter.

"What?"

"Isn't it remarkable? Suddenly a few weeks ago, I took it in my head to buy a lottery ticket. I asked the Elphinson man of business in Derby to handle it. And now he writes to say the ticket was drawn, and I have won *five thousand pounds!* I will write back to tell him to have the money deposited in London."

"London?" asked Gwen, dazed and fearing the worst.

"Why, yes! There can be no objection now to our taking

up the duchess's invitation. And you will be able to have the prettiest dresses available! Oh, I do believe your poor, dear father is watching over you."

As Gwen's mother hurried away, more animated than she had been in years, Gwen thought she was probably closer to the truth than she knew.

But it wasn't poor, dear Grayson Forsythe who had a hand in this. Faerie was not so easily blocked.

At least Drew was still abroad, she consoled herself, and with Napoleon on the loose, likely to stay there. She hated the thought of Drew in battle, but if Faerie was to be believed, he was in less danger from canon than he was from her.

Then in June, the Battle of Waterloo put a definitive end to Napoleon Bonaparte, making it more than likely that Major Sir Andrew Elphinson would sell out and return to England in time for the Little Season.

Glaring at the days-old paper containing the glorious news of victory, Gwen wondered exactly how much of the battle had been the work of Wellington, how much of Faerie. Though the rational part of her mind kept struggling to assert that this was all some kind of hallucination, in her heart she believed that she—and the whole world as well—was being ruthlessly forced to serve one particular end.

She put the paper aside and went to look out of the lead-paned window at the fertile valley of Elphindale. To preserve all this, perhaps to preserve England, she was supposed to entrap Drew and live with him here in a marriage entwined with faery glamour.

It was horribly unfair. She might have minded less if she were indifferent, but that dream encounter had shown her that she truly loved him, loved him more deeply than she'd ever imagined possible.

Wasn't it possible, though, that he truly loved her? The way he'd reacted in the dream could indicate that. He hadn't been indifferent, at least.

But she couldn't be sure that the man in that dream had been Drew at all. If she believed anything, she had to believe that a faery creature had impersonated her father once, so another such could impersonate Drew.

On the other hand, she couldn't believe that the man in the tent had been a deceit. Her every instinct, her heart, told her it was Drew, and he had wanted her.

In the coach to London, Gwen held on to that belief. It became almost like an incantation to be murmured day and night as she was welcomed into the duchess's mansion, then dragged around London in a frenzied acquiring of all the latest fashions.

Really, deep in his heart, Drew wanted her.

After all this, she didn't know whether to be glad or sorry that Drew didn't seem in any hurry to return to England. Autumn came, Parliament resumed its sitting, society began to play, and nothing was heard from Major Sir Andrew Elphinson other than a brief note to say that he had come through the battle with hardly a scratch.

It was mid-November when, one day in Hookham's, Gwen's mother exclaimed, "Andrew! How lovely!"

Gwen spun around, heart suddenly spinning like a whirligig, to see her destiny turn from a group of people. He strolled across to them, handsome, elegant, and looking politely pleased to see them, but no more than that. His eyes, still blue, still fringed by those dark lashes, moved over Gwen with only the mildest of smiles, then settled affectionately on her mother.

With the memory of their encounter in his tent so fresh in Gwen's mind, it was like a slap in the face.

And it had been this man she had lain with, kissed, permitted all manner of liberties. Imagination could not have produced so exact a picture of his present looks. She had kissed those lips, that chin, that neck. She knew the shape of h   beneath starched linen and superfine coat.

The memories were drying her mouth and, she was sure, had brought a fiery blush to her cheeks.

And yet he seemed to feel nothing!

After a few exchanges of conversation, the forthright duchess said, "Do you not recognize Miss Forsythe, Elphinson? I understand you haven't been to your Derbyshire estate for some years. Gels blossom fast in their youth."

Drew turned, and Gwen prayed at least for her childhood friend. But this man eyed her casually. "Not recognize Gwennie, Your Grace? Impossible." But then he took her hand and raised it to his lips—not a thing done anymore between acquaintances. "She's certainly blossomed, though."

For a moment, desperation allowed her to hope, but then the tone and the look in his eye crashed on her. It was not the way a gentleman looked at a lady.

She snatched her hand back, fighting a need to be sick.

She had to say something. "How are you, Drew?"

It sounded normal to her ears, but she had no idea what she looked like. Thank heavens the duchess's creams and lotions hadn't made much impression on her brown skin. If she was white as a sheet underneath, it wouldn't show.

"Oh, very well indeed." He was still smiling, and *looking* at her in that way, as if she were a lightskirt. "The luck of the Elphinsons, you know. I wonder, dear lady, whether my luck will hold."

Since the implication was clear, Gwen had to stiffen her spine and her voice. "No one can be fortunate in everything, I fear."

He smiled, but the look in his eyes turned it into an insult. "We shall have to see, won't we, Gwen?" His confidence sent a shiver of alarm down her spine, because he had reason for it. Despite his appalling behavior, she still longed for him, was drawn to him like moth to flame.

Could a man detect such a thing?

He turned back to the duchess. "You must excuse me,

Your Grace. I am with the Baracloughs. If I may, I will call.''

The duchess gave him *carte blanche* to visit whenever he pleased, but as he strolled back across the room, she said, "Soldiers, my dear. We must excuse them much, but a wise young lady does not go apart with them."

So Gwen knew she hadn't imagined his insulting manner.

She watched numbly as he returned to a plump lady and a pretty brunette. The girl, presumably Miss Baraclough, flicked Gwen a suspicious, searching glance. Gwen tried hard not to do the same. Or rather, not to show her sick sense of defeat.

Anyway, Miss Baraclough's attention was soon glued to his face, and Gwen was sure he wasn't paying *her* risqué attentions.

So much for that dream. Clearly it had just been a clever illusion, and clearly her girlhood fears were correct. Sir Andrew Elphinson did not consider Gwen Forsythe worthy for the position of wife, though he'd probably set her up as his mistress for a while if she was amenable.

But that, she assumed, would not serve the cause of Faerie.

"First he as good as cut me," Gwen declared to Betsy Raisley as soon as she was home. "If the duchess hadn't made a point of it, he wouldn't have spoken to me at all!" Gwen was trying hard to show anger instead of tears, but her eyes stung with them.

Even Betsy, a cheerful, easygoing young woman, frowned. "That's not like Master Drew, miss."

"Sir Andrew Elphinson is nothing like Master Drew. He's grown too grand for his family and friends from back home. He as good as pinched my bottom and asked me to meet him behind the bushes!"

"Nay, I'll not believe that!"

"And," said Gwen, ripping her ridiculous bonnet off her beautifully arranged hair and throwing it onto the bed, "he's paying gentlemanly attentions to a little twit called Miss Baraclough!"

"Nay!" And now Gwen really had Betsy's attention. "We can't have that."

Gwen had never forgotten the Lady's words, that Betsy knew all about potions and such. She'd never spoken to her maid about that dream encounter, but she'd noticed that, on this trip to London, Betsy had taken more of a hand in her mistress's affairs than was normal.

During the choice of fabrics and designs for new dresses, Betsy always had advice to offer, insistent advice in favor of this color rather than that, of this trim over another. Gwen told herself that her maid just had good taste, but she feared it was Faerie at work.

Betsy had always made her own scented soaps, and prepared all manner of lotions and creams. Now Gwen regarded them with suspicion. They seemed merely cosmetic, but it was true that the Raisleys were known throughout Derbyshire for potions that were more than cosmetic.

And perhaps the potions were working.

Gwen's success thus far in London had been outstanding, but every time young men gathered around her begging for a smile or a dance, she wondered just what was causing their attraction.

Betsy was frowning now in fierce concentration. "What can have come over the man?"

"A pretty girl with a vast fortune from tin mines . . ." Gwen trailed off, thinking for the first time of Dark Earth and mines. Surely not.

"Tin mines!" scoffed Betsy. "An Elphinson has no need to marry money." Betsy began to unbutton Gwen's dress. "You say he pinched your bottom, miss?"

"No, no. It was just the look in his eyes and the tone of his voice. It made me feel *dirty.*"

Betsy patted her shoulder. "Perhaps you just mistook

him, miss. Men are funny creatures. Now, you lay down awhile, to be ready for tonight. It's Lady Wraybourne's soirée, isn't it? Perhaps you'll see him there."

Suddenly weary, Gwen didn't resist being tucked into bed with the blinds drawn. At home she was full of energy morn till night, but here in London she tired so easily. It must be the late nights followed by rising at noon. She certainly missed the freshness of the morning, but the few times she'd tried to rise with the dawn, she'd been exhausted at midnight with a ball only halfway through.

She longed to be back in the simple life of the dale.

She couldn't sleep now, though. Her mind was too full of Drew and his behavior.

It had been agony to stand by him pretending they were mere acquaintances. And it hadn't been old friendship she'd been feeling, either. It had been desire. She'd wanted a lover's permission to look, to touch, if even only the permitted touch of hand to hand.

She'd needed a hint from him that he felt the same.

She suddenly sat up in bed. Perhaps he *had* shared the dream and now assumed she was no better than she should be!

She collapsed back on the bed, hands over her face. But how on earth was she ever to explain her wanton behavior that night? She'd have to try. When he came to call, she would find an opportunity to speak to him alone and try.

Gwen waited anxiously for Drew to call, determined— despite dread—to have that private discussion. She worried her mother by staying home day after day, terrified of missing him.

He never came.

Nor did she encounter him at social occasions, though three times she caught sight of him at a distance—once at the theater, once in the park, and once at a lecture at the Royal Institution.

Each time he was accompanied by the simpering Miss

Baraclough, and at the Royal Institution they were alone together. An ominous sign.

Gwen was shocked by just how uncharitably she could think about the tin heiress. She prayed to heaven that she didn't have any faery powers, or the young woman would probably wake up as a toad!

When Gwen arrived home from the lecture on the remarkable properties of magnetism, she paced her sumptuous boudoir, deluging her poor maid with a stream of complaints. Then she stopped to ask, "Betsy, what should I do?"

It was an honest question. The thought that she could never have Drew was like torture, but she could bear it. It was the faery plan that tormented her. Was it her duty to do something about all this? And if so, what?

Betsy seemed to have overcome her distress at the situation. She was replacing a flounce on Gwen's cream walking dress, and her nimble fingers never paused. "Dress in your finest and smile, miss."

"Smile? He never comes close enough to notice!"

"Oh," said the maid with a teasing flick of the eyes, "I'll go odds he notices."

Gwen sat opposite Betsy, willing to be convinced. "How can you think that?"

The maid fixed her needle and looked up. "Think about it, Miss Gwen. He'd have no *need* to avoid you if he didn't notice, now would he?"

Gwen slowly absorbed that, hope growing. "I suppose not. But then, why?"

Betsy grimaced. "Who's to tell with men? Sometimes we have to take a hand and straighten them out."

"How?" Gwen thought uneasily of potions and magic.

"We'll have to think about that. Let's see. Tonight is the Duke of Hardcastle's ball, ain't it? Big, important affair."

"Yes," said Gwen without enthusiasm. She found that the young men all flocked around at these occasions, making her very unpopular with the young women.

"From what I hear, it's just the sort of event Miss Baraclough will attend, and she'll want her admirer with her."

"I suppose so."

"You just leave the rest to me, Miss Gwen."

That worried Gwen more and more, for she still revolted at the thought of tricking Drew into anything. But a weak part of her would do anything to draw him back to her, even if just as a friend.

As she prepared for the evening, she tried to be noble. "Perhaps I should let him marry Miss Baraclough if that is his wish."

"Now, you don't want to think like that, Miss Gwen," said Betsy as she lightly tied the stay laces. It was a plain command.

"Why not?"

Betsy turned to pick up the silk gown. "If not for other reasons, because they wouldn't suit. She sounds like a ninny."

And that was true. Gwen might not have encountered Drew in a week, but she'd met Miss Baraclough a couple of times. The girl had no thought in her head other than the latest hair fashions, and no interest in anything outside of London parties. Drew would be bored to tears before the honeymoon was over.

"What other reasons could there be?" Gwen asked Betsy.

The maid dropped the pale green silk gown over Gwen's shoulders, and started to fasten the tiny buttons in the back. "Because it wouldn't be right, miss. You two are meant to be, and be together back in the dale. Can you imagine Miss Baraclough happy to stay in the dale?"

Absolutely not. But *meant to be?* Gwen wished she could ask Betsy straight out about Faerie, but she felt it was a subject better not mentioned.

"There, Miss Gwen," said Betsy, directing Gwen's attention to the mirror.

Gwen looked and saw that indeed she was at her finest yet, and this gown, she remembered, was one that Betsy had virtually designed. She'd chosen the filmy, floating silk sprigged with green ferns and seed pearls. She'd insisted that the bodice be cut noticeably low, and with the stays pushing up Gwen's breasts, the effect was dramatic.

Rather too much so!

Gwen covered herself with her hand. "Betsy, I'm not sure . . ."

Betsy pulled her hand down. "It's decent. But it'll draw the men like nectar draws bees."

"I already draw the men to an embarrassing degree! It's only Drew I want to attract, and if he sees this . . ."

"He'll not be able to take his eyes off you." The maid tugged on the gown to adjust the lie of it. "Perhaps he'll not be able to keep his hands off you, either, miss."

"Betsy!"

"And they do say that if a gentleman forgets himself with a lady, he has to marry her."

"Betsy, I couldn't!"

And Betsy chuckled as she reached for a vial of perfume. "I'll go odds you could, miss. Nature has its ways."

Gwen sniffed at the perfume her maid was dabbing around her, trying desperately to detect faery glamour. It seemed just a light perfume, smelling of greenery and spring flowers. There was a distinct note of lavender, though, that carried her back to that wall in the garden.

The one she and Drew had loved to sit on for their evening chats.

Oh, stop it, she told herself. That young man has gone forever, worn down by education and harshened by war.

"Sit you down, Miss Gwen," said Betsy, pushing her toward the bench in front of the dressing table. "Your mother will be here in moments and we've your headdress to put on."

Gwen's long blond curls had been gathered on the top of her head and now the maid set a silk toque wreathed with delicate ferns and small white flowers to crown it all.

Steadying herself, Gwen knew the Lady had been right. Despite the unfashionable brownness of her skin, she was lovely. Could she really use all this to trap Drew into marriage, though?

Sooner or later, she feared it would come to that. Gwen suspected that Betsy had more powerful weapons in her armory and would use them ruthlessly.

She turned, intending to beg Betsy not to go too far, but Mrs. Forsythe trotted in, happily elegant in crimson silk. The one good thing about all this was that her mother was truly enjoying her London season.

"How pretty you are tonight, dear," she said. "I think that ensemble is perhaps your most becoming. And look what just arrived by messenger." She opened a small box to show a lustrous pendant pearl-drop on a gold chain. It was the size of a robin's egg.

"How lovely! Who sent it?" Gwen's heart quivered, waiting for the answer, "Andrew."

"It came from a lawyer but the note said it was from your father's family." Mrs. Forsythe frowned. "I did think your Uncle Graham was the only close relative, and he's as clutch-fisted as they come. But there, he must be showing a little family feeling. I will write and ask . . ." She clasped the pearl around Gwen's neck. "I must say, it looks remarkably fine. Quite riveting." Her brows rose. "It does tend to draw the eye to your bosom, dear."

Gwen, hopes dashed, looked down at the pearl nestling near the swell of her breasts and knew that was true. She knew, too, that the pearl hadn't come from her Uncle Graham.

"It looks lovely, ma'am," said Betsy firmly, and came forward to drape a long silvery shawl around Gwen's shoulders. Then she picked up the vial and quickly dabbed a bit more perfume around Gwen. For all its spring lightness, Gwen feared it reeked of magic.

She knew with despair that Drew didn't have a chance.

* * *

They arrived at the duke's ball late, having dropped by a rout and a soirée. The glittering ballroom was already crowded, and Gwen had a terror that her faery glamour would stop the room dead. She created only the usual amount of stir, however, as her admirers rushed toward her.

Truly, she disliked it all. She wanted to move through a room without being stared at. She would like to be friends with some of the young ladies rather than an object of jealousy. Searching the room for a friendly face, she was caught for a moment by startling green eyes.

Green eyes very like her own.

Gwen's immediate thought was a gladness to find family here. Then she realized what kind of family it might be.

The lovely young lady with tawny hair seemed as struck by her, but before either of them could make a move, the handsome duke demanded the lady's attention and she turned away. Gwen remembered that there was talk of the Duke of Hardcastle perhaps being smitten at last.

Gwen turned too and caught up with her mother.

There was no cause for joy. If other minions of Faerie were here tonight, it could only be to make sure that Drew had no power to resist.

She saw him then, in elegant black, part of a small circle of men and women including, of course, Cecily Baraclough.

He was the handsomest man in the room, she thought, and then immediately wondered whether she was under some kind of spell herself. He was handsome, yes, but nothing out of the ordinary. As she trailed along with her mother and the duchess, greeting any number of casual acquaintances, she flicked glances at him, trying to compare his looks to others.

There was Lord Randal Ashby, for example, generally considered a very handsome man—blond, blue-eyed, fine featured. Drew's brown hair was less remarkable than gold, but his eyes were as blue. His features went together very well, but . . .

And there was the Earl of Everdon. His Spanish blood meant his skin was as dark as Drew's, and his hair and build were much the same. Perhaps, to an objective eye, he was the handsomer man, but he did not interest Gwen one jot. Drew, on the other hand, was like a magnet to her.

Oh, how could anyone say what made one person special and another not? She would surely go mad if she saw faery fingers in every pie.

Given her way, Gwen would doubtless have skulked in the farthest corners of the room, but her mother headed over to her foster son without any concern at all. "Andrew, my dear boy. How naughty you are not to have called. But there, I suppose you have been busy with your friends."

Introductions were made. Gwen waited for Drew to be smitten by lust—half hoping for it, half fearing it—but as before, his only attention to her was a rather insulting visual assessment of her charms before he smiled at her mother.

"I'm sorry, Aunt Amelia. It's as you say, and I've been caught up in the social whirl. I will try to do better. Are you enjoying Town?"

The first set struck up as they were talking, and Gwen's mother said, "Oh good. You can partner Gwen for this one, Drew."

Gwen wished for a hole to open and swallow her. Drew was too polite to look furious, but a tightening of his jaw showed how he felt. Miss Baraclough was less controlled and flashed an angry glance at both Forsythes. Lord Pasgrove, the Duchess's eldest son, kindly led her out, and Drew had no choice but to ask Gwen.

He might think her worthy of ogling, but as far as proper attentions went, she was apparently not even worthy of a country dance.

Part of her was pleased that all the trickery was failing, but at the same time her heart ached. If he was immune to her at her best, there really was no hope.

As they joined the set, she thought he was going to be distant, but then he turned to her, that disturbing glint in his eye. "I need not ask how your time in London goes, Gwennie, need I? Every male is at your feet."

The dance began, and they bowed and curtsied.

Gwen decided to go on the attack. "Every man but you, Drew."

"Oh," he said, as they danced forward and back, "my aspirations are higher than your feet, my lovely. Somewhere up beyond your garters in fact."

Gwen could only fire him a look of hurt and retreat into silence. He flushed, too, so perhaps he felt a little ashamed of treating her like a doxy.

The dance swirled them from partner to partner and Gwen managed to smile and even chat as she went. She noticed him doing the same. But sometimes their eyes would clash, and she'd look away to smile even more brilliantly at her partner of the moment.

How could he? How *could* he?

And how could she? It had been bad enough to think of inveigling her childhood friend into marriage. How could she bind herself to this stranger, this man who saw her as a mere lightskirt?

There. It was over. Faerie, for all its wiles, had lost.

Then the dance forced them back together for a while, dancing down the middle, hand in hand.

"I'm sorry," he said, staring over her shoulder. "I was ill-mannered."

She couldn't resist this, for it came close to the old Drew. Her friend. "You certainly were. Why?"

They came to the end and stood facing each other, clapping the rhythm. "I don't know. Fear, I think." He was staring at the pearl. "I suddenly felt under attack."

His eyes met hers, superficially charming and rueful. "Can I ask you to forgive a rude soldier?"

"Of course."

But she didn't assure him he wasn't under attack, because he was. Perhaps his trace of faery blood meant that he could detect the glamour all around her, the power of the pearl. After all, beneath his contrite smile she saw a deep wariness. He was afraid of her, and for very good reason.

She wanted nothing more than to protect him, to save him from the snare. And yet she wanted desperately to possess him.

You're mine, Drew Elphinson. Destined from birth. Neither of us can fight it.

The words in her mind were almost like speech, like another person speaking but with her voice, and from her soul. She almost missed a step, and as she collected herself, she gazed at him in despair.

When the set finished, they had to stroll around the room together. Gwen decided she must try. "Drew," she said. "Do you not like me anymore?"

"Like you?" He turned to her in surprise, then seemed caught like a fly in amber. Staring at her, he said, "Of course I like you, Gwennie."

"I'm not a little girl anymore, Drew. I'd rather you called me Gwen now."

His eyes flickered away but came right back. Trapped. "Gwen, then."

"You said you were afraid. Why? Do we embarrass you, your country cousins?"

"Good lord, no. I'm the most popular fellow around. All my friends are seeking introductions." His eyes wandered to the pearl again, and were controlled. "Perhaps it's just that you're not a little girl anymore. I want to kiss you." As soon as the words were out, he flushed. "I'm sorry. I don't know what I'm thinking of tonight." He was staring at her lips now, as he had that night in his camp.

Perhaps had that night.

He looked around frantically. "We need Aunt Amelia. Where is she?"

"In a comfortable corner somewhere." Gwen licked her lips, and he caught the movement. Stared again. She could see each breath he took by the way his chest moved.

She hated this. She hated the feeling that the Lady's beringed fingers were here, moving them both like puppets.

She felt powerless and knew that he was.

How else to explain him standing here with her, dazed and staring between the pearl and her lips?

He was in her power. She suspected that with very little effort she could get him to kiss her here in public. Do more than that, even.

It wasn't right.

"Drew," she said, taking an urgent grip on his arm, squeezing to snap him back into his senses. He started and looked at her, more focused. "Drew, don't scoff at what I'm about to say. I'm covered with faery glamour. The way you feel isn't . . . oh, it isn't the way you feel! It's magic. I'm supposed to get you to marry me, but I won't. Not like this."

He stared at her. "What on earth are you talking about?"

"The way you feel! Andrew Elphinson, you grew up in the dale. You can't have forgotten everything."

He laughed uneasily. "Oh, the dale. You're as bad as Father."

Gwen stared at him, thinking of ghosts and ghoulies. "What has Sir Thomas to do with it? He never came near the place."

"Precisely. He was always going on about the dale being cursed, that it had caused my mother's death. He sent me a deathbed letter begging me to promise to stay away."

"And did you? Promise?"

He shrugged. "Not exactly. I was abroad. It seemed pointless. The whole letter was full of nonsense, especially about you." He laughed almost like the old Drew. "He seemed to think there was something odd about you. That you . . ." He fell silent, staring at her.

"That I'm faery, and I'll try to trap you into marriage?"

He chose to take it as a joke, and laughed.

"Well, he was fading fast," he said. "The dale's a pleasant sort of place, I suppose, but it's a bit bleak. Hardly faeryland."

Gwen sighed. She'd tried to warn him but it was as if he were deaf. Deafened by Faerie, perhaps.

"In fact," he said as he steered her onward in their stroll around the room, "I've been thinking it's time we improved life for the people there."

"They're very happy." Gwen, added pointedly, "Remarkably so, if you think about it."

He wasn't listening. "They need more employment, better housing. I've been talking to someone who thinks he could build a woolen mill there. Use the river for power."

"You can't!" gasped Gwen, stopping so he had to look at her. "It would be horrible!"

"Don't be selfish. Life may be pleasant up at the Hall, but think of the people. Conditions are terrible all over England with so many soldiers coming home from the wars. After all their service, some are starving to death, actually starving to death in the streets. It's our duty to do something."

"Yes, of course it is, Drew. But matters are not so bad everywhere." Then she had an inspiration. She knew that all she needed was to get him back to Derbyshire. "You should visit the dale first and see what's really needed there. Come back . . ."

But the warning bars of the next set sounded and he wasn't listening. His eyes had turned to Miss Baraclough, who sat demurely across the room, fluttering her eyelashes expectantly at him over her fan. "Perhaps," he said.

A young man approached and asked for an introduction. In moments Gwen was off on the arm of a very admiring

Lord Netherfield. She didn't come close to Drew again for the rest of the night.

What pulled him away? Was it pretty Miss Baraclough, or was it Dark Earth? Gwen didn't know which was worse. Perhaps they were the same thing. Had Dark Earth sent a seductress to London, too?

If so, Dark Earth was winning.

As she assisted Gwen to undress, Betsy asked no questions, but disapproval radiated from her. At last, she said, "We'll be staying here till it's settled, Miss Gwen."

Thus the truth was in the open at last.

"You seem to think I'm not trying! He doesn't want me, Betsy."

"Course he does. Perhaps he doesn't want to want you, but why would that be?"

"I don't know. What am I supposed to do?"

Betsy pursed her lips. "We'll just have to try harder. You don't want to stay here. In fact, you probably *can't* stay here for too long without it wearing you down. But you can't go back to the dale without the Lord."

Gwen lay down in bed, knowing Betsy had spoken the truth at last. It wasn't just city life and late nights that were wearying her. It was being away from the dale. Now, she could feel London, feel out-of-dale, weigh on her like a cold, suffocating miasma. It was her faery blood.

What was she to do, though, if the only way home was to trick Drew out of his wits and into marriage?

Though she'd had to give up early rising, Gwen still walked each day in the wilder parts of Hyde Park, needing the pure atmosphere of earth and plants around her. Her mother thought it peculiar but, as long as she took her maid and a footman, made no objection.

Away from the fashionable paths, there were few around

to bother her, though she did sometimes feel presences. Perhaps others of her sort. She'd thought that Faerie was confined to the dale, but she definitely felt something among the bushes and rough trees.

Watched, but not in a frightening way.

She feared it was the forces of Faerie gathered to make sure their plan carried through regardless of the wishes of poor humans. Every day she prayed in the human way for strength to set Drew free, but she knew in her heart that she didn't want that. She wanted him willing, devoted, and desiring, only of her.

The morning after the Hardcastle ball, she was strolling across rough grass toward a favorite spreading oak when Hal Ferryman appeared, heading straight for her. Her footman came forward vigilantly, but Gwen waved him back. "This is a friend from home." She smiled at the stocky young man. "How are you, Hal?" She didn't for a moment think this meeting an accident.

He touched his hat. "Well enough, Miss Forsythe. Saw the world a bit as Sir Andrew's man, but I'm glad enough to be back in England."

"And would be happier still to be back in the dale, I suspect."

"Aye," he said, giving her a shrewd look. "Everything's all messed up out-of-dale, ain't it? So much trouble. So much pain. Beggin' your pardon, miss, but you'll have to make a push."

She didn't pretend to misunderstand. "Why is he so against the dale? He used to love it."

Hal shook his head. "Hard to tell. First it were Cambridge. Had him looking at things too close. Everyone knows there's things you can't see if you look at 'em too close. Now he's fixed that if you can't see 'em close, they aren't there! Then it were going overseas." He considered his words carefully but only said, "Things is different abroad, Miss Gwen. They have their own Folk, but they're different Folk. He knew the difference, but he came to think it proved there were no Folk, if you see what I mean.''

"Yes," said Gwen. "I think I do."

"Aye, well, he's been in a rare stew since he got back. I think he can feel the pull of the dale and it worries him to death. His father warned him of something. He's scared to go back. Has he told you about the mill?''

Gwen nodded.

"Granddad'll have a fit, and the Lady . . ." Hal rolled his eyes. "Well, I tell you, Miss Gwen, I'm right scared. Look what happened to his mother.''

Gwen stared at him. "You think . . . ?''

"The Folk'll do anything to save the dale.''

"But he's the Lord.''

"I *hope* he's needed to keep the line going, but you can't tell with the Folk, and they work on long plans. Perhaps there's another of the blood somewhere.''

Gwen's heart was pounding with fear.

"This Murchison," said Hal slowly. "The one who's after building the mill. He's a very persuasive feller.''

Gwen looked at him quickly. "You think he's"—she whispered it—"Dark Earth?''

"Who knows who that is, or what? But you'll have to make a push, Miss Gwen, and soon.''

Gwen returned home close to panic. Having met the Lady, she had no doubt that she would crush Drew like a cockroach if it suited her purpose. Gwen might not be resolute enough to ensorcel him in her own cause, or even to save England, but she could do it to save him from destruction.

That evening she was to attend Lady Gresham's ball, where she was likely to meet Drew again. She made no cavil as Betsy arranged her appearance.

This gown was of cream satin with an overdress of ecru net woven with gold. Silk flowers nestled in her hair again and a few more formed a posy at the low neckline. Betsy applied the special perfume and hung the pearl around her neck.

Gwen didn't object, but she wasn't sure what she was supposed to do with all this if Drew continued to be wary. To glamour him into ravishing her in the middle of a ball seemed a bit extreme.

As she was preparing to leave, a note was brought to the door. Betsy passed it on. The superscription was a little rough in the lettering. Gwen broke the seal and found it was from Hal.

Dear Miss Gwen,

He's gone and spoken to Colonel Baraclough about his daughter. Nothing's settled, for he's to speak to her tomorrow, but then we'll be in a pickle. Anyway, he's going to the ball with the Baracloughs tonight,

Hal.

Gwen reread the note numbly and made no objection when Betsy took it and read it too. The maid threw it on the fire and tutted.

"There's nothing for it, then," said Betsy and took a small cloth pouch out of her pocket. She tucked it down behind the flowers on Gwen's bodice.

"What's that?" Gwen asked.

"Just some herbs."

Gwen didn't ask. She was swamped with the sudden knowledge that she couldn't let Cecily Baraclough have Drew. There was nothing noble in the greedy feeling. The dale, England, and even Drew's safety could go hang.

Cecily Baraclough just wasn't having him!

She straightened her shoulders and patted the pouch nestled between her breasts. She'd do it tonight, even if it did mean glamouring him into ravishing her in the middle of Lady Gresham's ball.

The event was one of the grandest of the Season, and a tremendous crush. Normally, Gwen would doubt whether she could meet up with Drew and his party among so many people, but tonight she felt certain that faery power would handle it.

She danced the first set with Lord Pasgrove, whom she had come to know quite well. He was rather stuffy, but pleasant enough. She saw Drew in the distance, dancing with Cecily Baraclough. Cecily looked like a contented cat, but Gwen told herself that Drew did not look like a man in love. His eyes met hers, were caught, were dragged away.

No, he did not look like a man dancing with his beloved.

She saw the other green-eyed lady and this time hoped she *was* part of faery reinforcements.

As Gwen promenaded with Lord Pasgrove after the dance, she made no attempt to seek Drew out. She left it to other powers. In the end, he and Cecily came over, and it was apparently Cecily who had been the instigator, claiming to want to speak to Lord Pasgrove, a friend of her brother's.

Drew did not look pleased with the situation, especially when Pasgrove asked for the next dance, a waltz, and Cecily agreed. Certainly the heir to a dukedom was a formidable rival.

Perhaps matters were to be solved without desperate measures, but even so, Gwen must make her push. She looked expectantly at her beloved.

"I don't suppose you have permission to waltz yet, do you, Gwen?"

She didn't, but that hardly mattered. They'd be back in the dale in days. "Yes, as it happens," she lied.

He sighed but made the offer. In moments they were swirling in the daring dance. Gwen found just being in his arms like this enough to bewitch her and she didn't think there was any glamour in it. Even decorously separated, their bodies were joined as if by invisible energy and her senses began to swim with desire.

Drew stared fixedly away from her, jaw tight. She

thought, she hoped, that he was fighting the same shimmering arousal.

"Drew," she said softly.

"Yes?"

"I dare you to look at me."

"I beg your pardon?" he said, still looking away.

"I'm naked from the waist up."

He jerked to look down, then colored. "What a silly tease you are." His words were cross, but his eyes were dark, hot, and hungry.

"You mean you wish I *were* naked?"

"Don't be shameless." He was certainly looking at her now, at her face and sometimes at her bosom and the pearl.

"I have nothing to be ashamed of."

He stared at her for a few turns of the dance, but then his eyes flicked away again, and he assumed the social manner. "I suppose not, living in Elphindale all your life. You must be in alt to be free at last."

"On the contrary, I can't wait to return."

"But will you? Surely you'll marry."

"I hope so."

He looked back, frowning. "And live in the dale? There are no young men of your station there. I suppose you hope to marry nearby, though. Who's the lucky man?"

Gwen summoned her courage. "You, Drew."

He was a picture of blank astonishment, then embarrassment took over. "Gwennie . . . you're like a sister to me."

"No I'm not, Drew. Don't you want to kiss me? You wanted to last night."

He simply stared, but she could tell from his eyes that he did want to kiss her. His arm tightened a little, drawing her too close for propriety.

"There was another time as well," she murmured. "Do you remember kissing me? In a tent?"

He sucked in a breath. "That was a dream . . ."

"Was it? I remember your lips on mine."

"Dear God . . ." He drew her closer still.

"I remember your lips in other places, too."

His head began to lower toward hers.

"Drew," Gwen prompted softly, "we should leave the floor before you kiss me."

He jerked back. "I'm not going to kiss you." But they were at the edge of the dance floor by then, close to a door into a corridor. They stopped dancing and walked through it, arm in arm, gazing into one another's eyes.

Somehow, they found a deserted anteroom and a sofa in an alcove there. Somehow, they were on it, side by side.

He suddenly looked around. "Good Lord, we can't do this. Let me take you back . . ." His tone, however, was vague, as it had been in that tent.

Gwen wanted to cut him free, to shout, "Run, Drew, run!" Instead she rested her hands on his shoulders. "Kiss me," she said. "Kiss me as you did before."

She knew she was shamelessly using the glamour, but perhaps it was using her too. She was breathing high and fast with the need to be kissed, the need to taste him again. She reached up to frame his face. "I love you, Drew. I always have."

"Oh God, I love you too, Gwen!"

His lips were hot and he trembled as he crushed her to him. His hand turned her head and his tongue plunged deep into her mouth. Gwen had no urge to protest this time. She met his kiss and returned it feverishly. When his hand found her bodice, she shifted to allow it, not even complaining when he eased it down to uncover more of her.

Flushed, disheveled, he teased her sensitive skin so her breathing fractured into a moan. She watched him watching her, adoring her with his eyes, and knew this was right.

He loved her and he was hers for all time.

"Gwennie, you are the most perfect creature I have ever

seen." He lowered his head to trail kisses all over the upper swell of her breasts.

Gwen relaxed back against the arm of the sofa, boneless with need. "Drew . . ."

His eyes, hot with passion, burned into hers. "God, but I love to see you like this, melting for me. I've dreamed of it. Thirsted for it. I want you. I've been wanting you so badly it's been hell. You know that, don't you?"

"I know. I want you just as much." And she did. Like the pangs of fierce hunger, she wanted him.

He grinned then, wickedly. "I doubt you know yet just how much, Gwennie. But you will."

"I know I will." She didn't mind him calling her Gwennie now. He wasn't thinking of her as a child. He was slipping back into the closeness they'd known as children when trust was absolute, and secrets unnecessary.

He lowered his lips to her breast again, easing her bodice farther down. Gwen let her head fall back against the arm of the sofa as she savored the exquisite, remembered sensation. Again she held him close, but this was different.

This time he was undoubtedly real, and he was hers.

Hers at last.

Her legs relaxed apart, and his knee came up, parting them farther, pressing on a burning need so she arched back with a cry of delighted desire—

"Good God!"

Gwen and Drew froze. Then, like a shattered machine, they broke apart and looked.

The Duchess of Sommerton—pale with angry red flags in her cheeks—was staring at them through her lorgnette. Behind her hovered a small group of shocked or amused people. Cecily Baraclough, however, looked neither shocked nor amused and burst into tears. Lord Pasgrove led her away.

Muttering a curse, Drew stood, straightening his clothes, and stepped between the observers and Gwen.

Released from the paralysis of shock, Gwen turned away,

fumbling with her bodice. Chills shook her, then her whole body suddenly flushed with shame. What they must have looked like!

She heard the duchess shooing people away, and the click of a shutting door. She peeped around Drew, hoping they were alone again, but the duchess had remained.

"What have you to say to me, Sir Andrew?"

"Of course we'll be married . . ." But Drew sounded dazed and not one bit happy.

When she found the courage to look at his expression, Gwen found he appeared to be every bit as miserable as he'd sounded.

"Indeed you will," snapped the duchess. "I can't imagine what has come over you. Either of you. Gwen, I am horrified!"

So was Gwen, but it had been necessary. And they were to marry. It was all going to be all right.

"You have smirched your name, Gwen, and embarrassed me," the duchess was saying, still looking almost ill in her distress. "You will leave the ball quietly. I will find your mother and tell her the sorry tale. Tomorrow you had best both leave town until the scandal dies down."

The poor lady was seriously upset, and so, no doubt, was Miss Baraclough, though Gwen suspected Lord Pasgrove might be adequate consolation in the end. She went to her hostess, who had been kind to her. "I'm truly sorry to have caused you pain, Your Grace. But you'll receive good fortune out of this. I promise you."

The duchess blinked. "What nonsense you do talk," she said, but more mildly, and her color began to calm. She puffed out a breath. "Get along with you. I suppose some allowance must be made for young love."

Gwen turned back to Drew, but he was standing across the room, looking as if he'd rather never set eyes on her again. Heavens, did the glamour have such a limited scope? Would he long for her when they were side by side and hate her the rest of the time?

She went back to him, touching his sleeve imploringly. He sighed, took her hand, and together they slipped away from the ball.

In the carriage he sat as far away from her as possible and said, "Where shall we go in our exile?"

"Why, to the dale, of course."

"No."

"Why not?"

When he turned to her, his eyes were frighteningly cold. "Because it's where you want to be, Kerrigwen."

So he *did* suspect the truth. Gwen's teeth began to chatter. "I warned you."

"Why?"

"Because I didn't want to do it this way. But you have to return to the dale, Drew."

"Why?" he scoffed. "To be entangled in superstition like you? Trapped into a way of life generations old? It's madness."

"What happened tonight, Drew?"

He caught his breath. "I intended to offer for Cecily Baraclough." With deliberate cruelty, he added, *"She* was my chosen wife."

Gwen's heart ached, but she said, "I know. That's why I had to stop you."

He stared at her. "What the devil are you? A witch?"

"I'm a Kerrigwen. You clearly know what that means. You are the Lord of Elphindale."

"Hell. I should have listened to my father and flattened the place."

"You can't touch the dale, Drew. You know it. Your father knew it. You'd be dead before the second tree fell." Gwen wanted to weep, but she knew what she had to do. She slid over and sat in his lap. "Deny this, Drew," she said and kissed him.

He kissed her back like a starving man first tasting food. It was the footman's polite cough that disturbed them this time. They looked around to see that the door was open and they were at the duchess's house.

Drew pushed her away and cursed. But he recollected himself, handed her down, and escorted her into the house.

"Stay and talk, Drew," Gwen pleaded, making no attempt to go close to him.

He simply headed for the door.

"We have to go to the dale!" she cried after him.

He stopped, back toward her.

Gwen clasped her hands tightly. "Come with me to the dale, Drew. Perhaps there we can find another way. Perhaps you can have your Cecily after all."

He turned and looked at her. Then he nodded and was gone.

Gwen, Mrs. Forsythe, and Betsy traveled back to Derbyshire in a post chaise. Drew and Hal rode. Drew had scarcely come within touching distance of Gwen since the kiss in the carriage the night before.

Gwen's mother was simply bewildered. She could not see why Andrew and Gwen should behave like a clandestine couple when there was no union that would give her greater pleasure. When she wasn't saying this over and over, she dozed through most of the journey.

Betsy and Hal radiated satisfaction. Gwen and Drew exuded misery.

Betsy had little sympathy for Gwen's tears. "How can you think a faery match will turn out wrong?" she demanded as they shared a bed at the first stop. "Now everything's set."

Gwen wasn't convinced. Faerie had apparently once ruled throughout England and was now fighting to maintain its hold on one small dale. Was Faerie immune to making mistakes?

Still, her heart lifted the closer she came to home, and when the road began to wind into the dale, she felt as if she were taking her first deep breath in weeks. She pressed her face to the window, drinking in every slope, stream, and tree. Even the sky above seemed special.

She looked at Drew, wondering if he felt anything, but she could see only his uninformative back.

The servants at the Hall were out to welcome the Squire home. That was only natural, especially after an absence of so many years. Gwen felt a wild excitement underneath it all, however, an excitement which was surely due to another cause.

The Lord of Elphindale was home at last. Soon Hal and Betsy would spread the word that he was going to marry the Kerrigwen and the joy would be complete.

She walked into the hall, stripping off her gloves, certain for the first time of the rightness of it all. After an absence, she knew this earth was necessary to her, and she was sure Drew was needed here, for the good of all.

He, however, was still resisting this match.

How was it all to be woven into whole cloth?

She looked over to where he was talking to the butler. He appeared pleasant and relaxed. If he felt attraction or revulsion toward this place, it was well controlled. She'd learned in the past few days, though, that he had great self-discipline.

That evening at dinner he talked of minor changes he noted in the house and grounds, and minor changes he planned to make. There was no talk of a manufactory, but no talk of Faerie, either.

Days passed. Drew avoided Gwen whenever possible and spent most of his time out in the dale, going over his property as any landlord would after years of absence. He didn't speak of what he saw but he did grow more and more thoughtful. Gwen began to hope that he was seeing the effects of Faerie, and that he would acknowledge the necessity for their marriage.

She still longed for an attraction more personal than dutiful, but if duty was all there was, she must accept it.

His manner toward her did grow a little less cold. One day he told her that he'd written to Murchison to tell him he was no longer interested in bringing industry to the dale. The explanation he gave, however, was a lack of a good source of water power.

That was nonsense when the fast-flowing Youle River tumbled through the dale.

Still he fought the truth.

At times he would speak to Gwen as in the old days, lightly, teasingly. But then he'd draw sharply back and she knew he feared the glamour was affecting him again.

Gwen herself didn't know if their feelings for one another were honest or a product of Faerie. She could not see that Betsy made any attempts these days to incorporate faery glamour into her appearance, but she couldn't be sure it was not there. She never wore the pearl pendant, but was aware of it all the time. Sometimes, empty with longing for Drew, for a smile or a touch, for passion, she would take it out and handle it. But she always found the strength to return it to its box.

After dinner each evening Gwen and her mother sat in the drawing room and Drew took himself elsewhere. Mrs. Forsythe sometimes worked lackadaisically at some needlework but usually went early to bed. Gwen spent lonely evenings with books. She'd spent a great deal of her life like this but had never felt so lonely as now, when she knew Drew to be somewhere in the house.

She was alone one evening, as usual, when he walked into the room. He kept a wary distance.

"It's all right, I think," said Gwen dryly. "I'm not aware of any faery glamour about my person."

He moved a little closer but his manner was stiff. "When you insisted that I return here, you said we could try to find a way out of this tangle."

A way for him to have Cecily. Gwen swallowed tears. She'd hoped he'd forgotten about that. "Yes."

"Well? Have you found one?"

Gwen had thought about it, reluctantly. "We have to have a child, Drew," she said. "The only escape I can see is for us to have a child, and for Cecily to accept it as hers."

He flushed. "Good God! How can you even suggest such a thing? Cecily would be horrified!"

Gwen's temper snapped. "And it would be easy for me, I suppose?" She sprang to her feet. "Drew Elphinson, have you been in the dale for a fortnight without realizing you have a heritage here? A duty? If I am willing to sacrifice myself for it, don't you think you should be willing to do your part?"

"A sacrifice, is it?" he retorted. "*I* wasn't the one playing witch tricks to get us into this entanglement."

"It was no choice of mine, and you didn't fight very hard, did you?"

He stalked over and grabbed her shoulders. "How can I fight your kind of wickedness? When you were a child, you bewitched me, and from the moment I saw you in Hookham's I was like a damned puppet on your string!"

His lips snared hers, hot and angry. Gwen choked a protest, but then desire swamped objection and she kissed him back feverishly. Oh, damn Betsy. She'd sneaked something onto her!

They were sprawled on the carpet, his hand up her skirt, when he rolled away with a curse. "Damn you! Damn you!"

Gwen covered her face. "I thought . . . Drew, I'm sorry, but we have no choice! Could you marry Cecily and bring her here to live with this?"

He pushed to his feet to glare at her. "I'd never let Cecily be under the same roof as you. I'd never bring her here at all, to this benighted place. In fact, I'm leaving tomorrow. I don't have to stay to be driven mad by your games."

She scrambled up and grabbed his arm. "No! You can't leave."

He tore free. "Try and stop me!"

"Drew, think what Faerie might do if you try to leave."

"They can do their damndest." He turned away again.

Gwen took a deep breath. "Very well. Could you resist me if I came to your bed? Could you leave knowing I might be pregnant?"

"Oh, you whore," he whispered, staring at her.

Gwen trembled but faced him. "We have no choice, Drew. You've been a soldier. You know what duty is."

He sneered. "Amazing what someone will do for their country. You'd sneak into my bed, would you?" He stared at her, breathing deep and hard. "Very well, then, we'll do our *duty*. We'll marry, damn you, but once you're with child, you'll never see me again. You and Faerie can care for your beloved dale without me."

Drew rode out the next day to the bishop for a license, and the day after, they were wed in Saint Winifred's Church. Mrs. Forsythe remarked at how little fuss they were making over it, but seemed relieved that nothing was expected of her. The Hall staff produced a handsome dinner, and the villagers had a grand party.

Drew and Gwen ate alone and in silence.

Drew got drunk.

Since he wouldn't stop drinking, Gwen left him well into his second bottle, put on a warm cloak, and headed for the woods. For a while she could hear the merry singing from the village, see the sparks from the roaring bonfire. It was good, she supposed, that someone was happy tonight.

Then she was in the silence of the leafless woods, in the woods that were not the woods. She stood and waited.

Her father came for her. "We're having a party too," he said. "Come and celebrate."

Gwen fell into his arms and wept.

When she recovered, he sat them both down against a tree, she in his arms. "Now, child, what's the matter?"

"He hates me!"

Her father looked at her in puzzlement. "How can he? You are beautiful."

"Beauty isn't everything. He loves a girl called Cecily Baraclough, and he hates me for taking away his chance of happiness with her." She turned to him seriously. "I've thought of a way out. When I've given him a son, can I come and live with you, then Drew will be able to marry Cecily?"

"Ah, child, I doubt he'd want that."

"Oh yes he would. He'd be betrothed to her now if I hadn't turned his wits."

"And how did you do that?" he asked with a smile.

"You know how." She pulled out of his arms and blew her nose. "He'd never have kissed me like that at the ball if it hadn't been for the pearl, and the herbs, and the perfume."

"I don't know what happened at any ball," he said mildly. "We don't have that long a sight. How many men kissed you at the ball?"

Gwen looked at him in bewilderment. "Only Drew."

"Then how can it all have been the pearl, and the herbs, and the perfume?"

"He certainly wouldn't have kissed me without them."

"Can you be sure?"

"It only works when I'm close to him."

"Perhaps."

She glared at him. "What are you saying?"

He laughed. "Oh, you humans. Did you not want to kiss him? You may long for him, but when you are close, do you not long for him more, long to touch him, to join your body with his?"

Gwen shivered. "Yes."

"We've put no glamour on him for you."

"But I *love* him."

"Then perhaps the glamour for him is love, too."

"Love? What of the pearl?" she demanded.

"What pearl?"

"The pearl you sent me in London."

"I sent no pearl." He appeared honest.

"But . . . what are you saying?"

He stood and drew her to her feet. "I am saying that for you humans love is itself a special kind of magic, and one you understand too poorly for safety. We can augment it with our skills, but not overpower it. If Andrew Elphinson had loved Cecily Baraclough, no power of ours would have turned him from her. You were made for one another, yes, and words were said over your cradle, but that was long ago. Now, just call it love, for that is what it is."

Gwen looked down at herself, still in the fern-sprigged silk she'd worn for her wedding. "Do you swear that you've put no glamour on me tonight?"

"None except your beauty, which I gave you at conception."

Gwen bit her lip. "I needn't have asked anyway. He's hardly been trying to ravish me. But what about two nights ago, when we decided to marry?"

"None then, either."

A bud of hope began to unfurl. Had that hungry kiss, that burst of passion, been come by naturally? "He's horribly drunk," she said.

Her father laughed and shook his head. "Even wine cannot drive away magic. He's here."

With a crashing and a curse, Drew staggered into view. He squinted at Gwen. "What the devil are you up to now? Dancing naked around an ancient oak tree?"

Gwen glanced sideways, half expecting to see her father gone, but he was still there, wincing humorously at the sight of the Lord of Elphindale unsteady on his feet, hair on end, cravat askew.

"Who's that?" Drew asked, staggering forward.

"My father."

"Your father's dead. Trying to cuckold me before the wedding night?"

"No," said Gwen with a sigh. For a moment, she'd

believed that lovely idyll of Drew pursuing her with love in his heart, but it was fading fast.

Drew lunged forward and swung a fist at the man of Faerie, but it was easily avoided. Gwen's father spread his hand on Drew's head and he collapsed to the ground like a felled ox.

Gwen fell to her knees beside him. "What have you done to him?"

"Given him rest. And he'll wake without a drunkard's head. Rest here with him, daughter, until the midnight hour. You can wake him then, and we will celebrate your union properly. This will be your wedding bower. It is a fitting place to make a new Lord of Elphindale."

Gwen didn't think so. It was just a space between dark trees. The earth was damp, and Drew was cold. It was November, after all.

In a moment, however, the place turned dry and warm. A faint green light glimmered among the dark branches and fluting music wove through the air. Then the Folk came dancing by, led by the Lady in flowing white silk, all radiating a genuine joy at their salvation. They laughed and sang and each threw blossoms until the ground was thick with them, and fragrant.

When the Faerie Court had passed, only her father remained and Drew was sleeping deeply under a quilt of flowers.

Hope stirred again. "He loves me?" Gwen asked.

"Yes, child. But he never expected it to be so wild a passion, and so he thinks it unseemly magic."

"And you didn't give me the pearl?"

"My word on it."

Gwen decided that was a crucial point. "I need to speak to my mother," she said.

"Very well." He held out a hand and in moments Gwen was back at the quiet house. The servants had all slipped away to the village, to the feast.

Upstairs in her bedroom, Mrs. Forsythe was fast asleep, snoring gently. Gwen woke her.

"What . . . ? Gwennie? What's the matter?"

"That pearl, mama. The one I received in London. Did we ever find out where it came from?"

"Pearl?" Mrs. Forsythe peered around, straightening her nightcap. "What a time to be worrying about your jewelry! Where's Andrew? Oh, you young people . . ."

"The pearl, mama."

"Oh, that. Yes, well, Mr. Reed, who was your father's man of business, cleared it up. It was left you by your grandmother, but with us living so quietly it was forgotten. When you turned up in town, Mr. Reed prompted your Uncle Graham and he, somewhat reluctantly—I told you he was a clutch fist—sent it to you."

"Is that the truth?"

"Of course it is! Good heavens, girl, what's the matter with you? Go to your husband. You were in a fine hurry to be wed. If you've cold feet now, I have no sympathy!"

Gwen kissed her disgruntled mother and hurried out on light feet. Perhaps it hadn't all been faery trickery!

Her father took her back to the flower-strewn glade. "All settled in your mind now?"

"Yes. And I am beginning to hope."

He kissed her forehead. "You are faery-blessed. What you truly wish will be."

With those words, he left her, and Gwen sat beside Drew to study his sleeping features. It was very like that time in the army tent. He'd even managed to bruise his temple again.

Now, however, perhaps she had the right to bring him care and comfort, and perhaps they wouldn't be torn apart before they could complete the act of love.

She smoothed his hair back gently, thinking that it was really not the same. Tonight, far from war and under a faery spell, he looked peaceful and quite young.

She traced his features, discovering what it meant to

have a heart swell with love. She could see why this feeling frightened him. It was not reasoned or calm. It wasn't tame. She lifted a handful of silky petals and drifted them down over his face. He sneezed in his sleep.

Remembering last time, she leaned down and kissed him, playing against his lips.

He didn't wake, though, and so, since there were two more hours to midnight, she lay down beside him. Soon she, too, was asleep.

She awoke to rose petals on her cheeks, to find him looking down at her, clear-eyed and thoughtful. "I'm not sure I want to know how we came to be here. Or even where we are."

"I love you," said Gwen, "and there's no faery magic in that."

"Is there not? But you are part faery. That *was* your father, wasn't it?"

"Yes. But you're part faery too, Drew."

"I'm beginning to think I am. What the hell are we supposed to do?"

"Preserve the dale, and preserve the faery blood in the Elphinsons."

He touched her cheek. "I like that bit. But then maybe I don't . . . You've been driving me mad, you know. I haven't been able to stop thinking of you for weeks. My heart pounds when you come into a room. I want to kiss you, and strip you naked . . ."

Gwen couldn't help but smile. "Did you want to strip Cecily naked?"

A look of anger flashed over his face, but then he laughed. "No, damn you. I wanted her because she was safe. *She* didn't drive me wild. I knew as soon as I saw you again that my father was right, that the faeries had come to trap me." He rolled on top of her. "I was determined not to be trapped. I wanted to drive you away."

His kiss was both snare and surrender, and Gwen accepted both enthusiastically.

She had something to say, though, and struggled free to say it. "The pearl," she assured him earnestly. "It was just an inheritance from my grandmother."

"What pearl?" He was fumbling with the hooks of her dress.

She seized his hands. "The one I wore in London! The one you kept staring at."

He laughed, halting his attempt to disrobe her. "Gad, Gwennie, I was staring at your *bosom*. And having astonishingly lewd thoughts. Which I would put into action now if I could only get your damned dress unhooked."

"But why have you been so horrid since we came home?"

He pulled her into his arms, just a comforting embrace. "I'm sorry, love. But no man likes to feel trapped, by a woman or by magic. I was determined not to give in, but all the time, I just wanted to find you and be with you . . . You've been driving me demented."

"As you have me! What about all the years you stayed away?"

"I wanted to come home. I wanted to come home to you. But I was afraid . . . You see before you a dreadful coward."

She laughed against his chest. "Not you, Drew. You joined the army. I saw you . . ."

He pushed her away a little. "That dream? You really did have it too?"

Gwen nodded. "If it was a dream. That was when I realized I truly loved you, loved the man, not the memory of the friend I'd grown up with."

Slowly, almost reluctantly, he pulled something out of his pocket. A gray garter embroidered with forget-me-nots. "I had this to tell me it wasn't a dream. My old beliefs came back, and I guessed what was in hand. I tried to fight it, though. I thought I could."

"I did, too." She told him about the duchess's invitation and the lottery win.

They both laughed shakily. "No one can thwart Faerie, it would seem," she said.

"I was abominably rude to you at the Hardcastle ball."

"Yes. And it almost worked to drive me away."

"Why didn't it?"

"Because I realized you could be in danger."

He frowned slightly. "Doesn't it worry you that Faerie is so ruthless?"

"Why worry about something we cannot change? Is life in the dale not good? Perhaps the power does spread out from here to make the whole land better. And Faerie is offering us a chance of true happiness." Gwen told him what her father had said about the magic of love.

"So," Drew said in the end, gently stroking her shoulder, "we may have been ensorcelled from birth, but what I feel is normal"—he dropped a gentle kiss on her cheek—"human"—then on her lips—"adoration. . . ."

"And desire," she whispered, her lips soft and ready when he deepened it . . .

Someone cleared a throat.

"Damn it to Hades!" Drew exclaimed as they both looked up.

Gwen's father was there again, lips twitching. "Unwelcome though I suspect it may be, it is my honor to lead you to your wedding, my children."

"We're already wed," said Drew. "Go away."

"By the laws of England, perhaps, but not by the laws of Faerie."

Drew rolled to lean on his elbows. "Are you trying to tell me my father took part in any such rite?"

"No. And there, perhaps, lay an error. The Lord of Elphindale has not made his vows before Faerie for many of your generations. Your father went so far as to marry out of dale, and thus was lost to us."

"He was lost long before that. Did you kill my mother?"

Suddenly frightened, Gwen reached out to grasp his sleeve. "Drew . . ."

"Yes," said her father. "It was as good a death as we could give her."

"Drew . . ."

Drew covered Gwen's hand with his, but his somber eyes did not leave her father. "I should hate you for that."

Merlon inclined his head. "Indeed, by the ways of humans, perhaps you should. But the fault was not in the death, but in the centuries we had let pass which brought such a foreigner into the family. It will not be so again."

"Perhaps we don't want Faerie meddling in our lives, in our children's lives."

"Don't you?"

Gwen bit her lip, wanting to intervene, but knowing this was something Drew must decide for himself.

Silence ran, then Drew turned to look at her. "Faerie has given me Gwen, and the dale. And the faery bond perhaps offers more to all humanity. Very well." He leaped to his feet and held out a hand to her. "Come along, Kerrigwen. Let's plight our troth before Faerie, and then perhaps they'll leave us to finally, finally, consummate our bond."

Hand in hand, they followed a sparkling path to the magic glade Gwen had visited before, and there, in the hearing of all the Folk, and perhaps of all of nature, they made a simple vow, to be true to each other, and to preserve the dale.

The Lady embraced them, like sunlight and starlight all around, then led them—one hand each—back to their rose-strewn bower.

A trailing finger drifted sparkling glamour all around. "Here you will make the next Lord, my children, and make all safe for the next thousand years."

"Willingly," said Drew, drawing Gwen firmly into his arms, "if you will only go away."

And the Lady laughed. "Oh, you humans! I will never understand you." Her green eyes swept over them. "Serve me well. That's all I ask. Serve me well, and I will bless you all your days."

Then she held out her hand to Merlon and, dancing, led the Faerie Folk on their way.

The warmth, the light, and the glamour lingered when they'd gone.

"Well?" Drew asked. "Shall we defy her and go back to our waiting marriage bed?"

Suddenly shy, Gwen shook her head. "I don't want to delay."

"By heaven," he groaned, "neither do I!"

His fingers were swift now, stripping her of her garments, though he paused to laugh when he saw the one gray garter, embroidered with forget-me-nots. She told him why the other stocking was held up by a pink silk ribbon.

"When I woke in the tent," he said, sliding her silk stockings all the way off, "it was all I could do not to rush back to the dale, to see if you were really as I'd seen you. To finish that seduction. To claim you. If I hadn't been an officer, had responsibilities, I might have done it." He raised her foot and kissed the arch. "I want to kiss every inch of you. Every inch, every day. . . ."

Gwen, in nothing but her shift, rose up and hastened his undressing, and did her best to kiss every inch of him, wondering at him, and at herself. Slave to wild desire, she even stroked his erection without self-consciousness. She went further. She kissed it.

That seemed to drive him wild. He pinned her down in their fragrant bed of roses and touched her so that wild desire grew wilder. Wilder and more focused there between her legs where he joined with her slowly, carefully, then thoroughly, making her his wife, his lady, the Lady of Elphindale.

If Gwen had not believed in magic before, she believed it then.

"Oh my!" she gasped when she had breath back.

"Oh my, indeed!" He laughed as he gathered her into his arms, showering her tingling skin with kisses.

"Magic. . . ." she murmured, incapable even of a coherent sentence.

"If you like. But that, beloved, was magic of the most human kind."

Gwen settled into the luxury of his naked embrace. "Mmmmmm. Care to teach me more about human magic then, oh mighty Lord of Elphindale."

"With pleasure, my Lady Kerrigwen, my faery bride."

And so he did. And they taught each other and learned from each other, both human and magic, throughout that long flower-strewn night.

In the heart of the woods, in the heart of a dale, somewhere in the heart of England. . . .

The Faery Braid

Karen Harbaugh

Ever since I was a little girl, I've always wondered about the stuff that the Brothers Grimm never explained in their fairy tales, especially in the story of Rapunzel. Why did Rapunzel's hair grow so long? I couldn't believe it was just for a ladder—the witch could easily have asked for a regular rope. Why did she keep Rapunzel isolated in a tower? And really, could a young woman who knew how to survive in the wilderness have been so clueless as to let the witch in on what she was doing? No, I was convinced there was more to it than the Grimms let on, and besides I figured the prince and Rapunzel did a lot more than just chit-chat when he visited. And when I did just a bit more research, I found to my satisfaction I was quite right.

So when Barbara Samuel e-mailed the rest of us, asking if we wanted to get together and write a faery anthology, I knew this was my chance. At last, I could vindicate Rapunzel! *I* knew the real reason she grew her hair so long, and I also knew there had to be a good reason for the witch to be upset that the prince came a-calling. I've changed some details in my story, but so did the Brothers Grimm in theirs. At least I explain things!

I had an incredible amount of fun writing this story and helping to create our common faery world with Mary Jo, Jo, and Barbara. I hope you have as much fun reading it.

Best wishes,

Karen Harbaugh

Prologue

Somerset, 1760

The faery Aldara could not deny any longer that Faerie had lost something . . . something that made the birth of a faery child so rare that it was both a cause of rejoicing and a cause of sorrow, for the scarcity of children could mean the Fair Folk's power would fade from the mortal world altogether. She had resisted the idea for a long time, and it was why she and those of like mind had split from the court that resided in the Midlands—they who would sow their seed in mortal wombs.

But there was a way around it; it would take time and care, but it would keep their line pure. It was possible to make a human shed mortality and become wholly faery. Some of the knowledge had been lost, but there were many ways to do it. Aldara would use all those ways to ensure it would work.

The unborn babe would be the seventh child born of a seventh child, and this pleased Aldara, for such children, though mortal, had special gifts. Even better was that the child was of the noble Winscombe family, whose roots went back to the days when the Old Ones still laid claim to the hearts and minds of mortals. But what was best of all was that the family's fortunes had failed, and though this child's presence in her mother's womb was greeted with joy, it was also greeted with much sorrow. The child, in a few years, would be for sale.

Aldara laid her trap carefully. She took the guise of a scullery maid and put herbs in the mother's tea to increase the craving for strange foods. And what should be easier than to appear as a farmer's wife on a fine autumn day just when Lady Winscombe was out for her carriage drive, and offer her faery fruit? Of course the mother could not resist, and eagerly ate it, and when Aldara mentioned she was a skilled midwife, it was a simple thing to become Lady Winscombe's.

When the babe was born, under the stars of the Mother Goddess and the influence of the moon, she was beautiful from the first breath she took, and this pleased Aldara even more. The girl-child had hair the color of golden dawn, white skin, and eyes blue like the sky just after a cleansing rain. It was fitting that a child destined to be one of the faery be beautiful, for the Fair Folk preferred beauty in all things. The girl had only one flaw, a tiny red mark on the right side of her chin, but it would disappear once she belonged to the faery woman.

Aldara also became the child's nurse, though she made sure the girl nursed at her own mother's breast, for a mortal child could not live totally on faery milk. But it was in preparation for the time Aldara would take the child away to the place between Faerie and the mortal lands, and train her in the ways of Faery, and slowly over the years transmute the girl from human to one of the Fair Folk. The girl would shed all the baseness of mortal flesh, and acquire all the grace of limb and mind worthy of a faery mate.

And so, as the child—Rowan her name would be, for the name her parents gave her was irrelevant—grew in beauty and grace, Aldara made sure the Winscombe family's fortunes grew worse and worse. Soon, they had no servants except for Aldara, a cook, and the butler, and then the Winscombe children grew pale and listless.

Finally, four years after the child was born, Aldara knew it was time to take the child.

Lord Winscombe came home one winter night, his worn coat frosted with snow. He wore no wig, for he had sold it long ago, and his face was thin and pale, for to get shelter for his horse and himself he had had to go without food.

"Robert . . ." His lady gazed at his bare head then at his tired eyes full of anger and despair. He turned from her to the fireplace, putting out his hands to the feeble fire there. Aldara watched from her place in the shadows and smiled slightly.

"It sank," he whispered. "The bloody damned ship sank. A storm, they said." He put the palms of his hands to his eyes. "God help us. It had gold on it, Mary. *Gold.* We were so close, so damn close." Slowly, he bent and crouched before the fire, his hands now fists pressed hard against his forehead. "God. What are we going to do? There's nothing left. There's nothing *left!*"

His wife bent down next to him, and put a trembling hand on his shoulder, stroking gently. "We had not much to begin with, Robert. And you tried, I know you did, with what we had. But the poor harvest—and the cattle sickened, then the taxes. You can't be blamed for that."

"I should have known. I should have known what my father was doing, wasting my inheritance. But I didn't care."

Lady Winscombe gripped his shoulder. "Don't, Robert, just don't! You *did* care, but he would never tell you, you know that!" Her voice was sharp with mixed anger and sorrow. "We must think of what we can do now, not what is past."

Her husband rose abruptly and turned to her, grasping her shoulders. "And what can we do now, eh? What? The creditors will be at our door soon, I tell you! And we have nothing to give them. Absolutely nothing! The lands are mortgaged to the hilt, and we cannot sell any more of it off.''

"Perhaps we could move to a smaller house, and let this one out to someone—''

He thrust her away, and ran his hand through his hair. "And who would want this ramshackle place? Even if anyone did, the rent from it would not come close to paying what we need to cover our debts! It's debtor's prison for us, don't you see? Oh, God. I can't even sell it . . . though I wouldn't wish such a burden on my worst enemy.''

Lady Winscombe's hand rose, trembling, to her lips. "Oh, no. Oh, no. Debtor's prison . . . our children . . .''

Lord Winscombe paled, and his lips pressed together in a hard line. "Our children.''

Now, thought Aldara. Now. She moved within the shadows of the room, quietly, softly. Quickly she knocked on the door, opened, then shut it, and created the illusion that she had just entered. Lord and Lady Winscombe turned and stared at her as she gave a quick curtsy.

"An it please you, my lady, my lord, Master Robin is calling for my lady—'tis a mite restless he is, my lady, and feverish, I'm thinking.''

"It needs only this,'' Lord Winscombe groaned. "Now our children are becoming ill.''

"It may be nothing, Robert,'' his wife said quickly. She gave Aldara a worried smile. "Thank you, Alyce. I will come up with you.'' She gathered up her skirts and followed Aldara upstairs to the nursery.

Master Robin was indeed feverish. Lady Winscombe groaned aloud, and wept the tears she had kept herself from weeping in front of her husband. It was an illness easily cured, if Aldara so wished. But she did not wish, not yet.

"Go, Alyce, and get me some cold cloths for him,'' Lady Winscombe ordered.

Aldara left and returned swiftly; she did not want her opportunity to pass, though she needed to keep up her pretense. But soon, soon, she would be quit of this place.

She watched Lady Winscombe apply the cloth to her son's head. It did nothing; the boy only shivered and shook the cloths off his head.

" 'Tis a doctor we need, my lady."

It was as if Lady Winscombe did not hear; she only moaned and stroked her son's flushed face and rocked him in her arms. The sound of her voice woke the other children and they sat up in their beds and stared at their mother. One began to whimper with sleepiness. Aldara soothed them, and got them to sleep again. When she turned to Lady Winscombe, my lady was still rocking her son, staring into the shadows with dark and empty eyes.

"What am I to do, Alyce? Debtor's prison . . . my son will become worse in debtor's prison." She kissed her son's hot forehead again and again. "All my children. They may sicken, also. What am I to do? Ah, God." She rocked and moaned again.

Now, now was the time.

"My lady . . . perhaps you may yet save them."

She raised her head and stared at Aldara. "How? How?" Her voice was harsh with hope and grief. Almost, Aldara smiled.

"I . . . know of a barren woman—she and her husband wish for a child, and would gladly raise one of yours."

"No!" Her ladyship clutched Master Robin tighter and shook her head.

"No, of course not your son, not his lordship's heir." Aldara made her voice soft, gentle, soothing. "But you have seven children, and this poor lady—and she is a lady, and her husband a lord—she has none! They ache for a child, your ladyship, any child." She noticed with satisfaction that the baroness's arms loosened around her son.

"Even one girl-child," the faery woman continued, her voice now low and persuasive. "She would be well cared for, given so much, *sooo* much, for they are wealthy, too. They would pay well—"

Lady Winscombe's lips thinned in anger. "I will not sell any of my children."

Aldara almost snapped at her, but she controlled her impatience. "It is not *selling*, your ladyship. They are generous people; they understand what a loss 'twould be to you, and would be grateful. A gift, my lady. You would be giving them a gift, and they would wish to return a gift for a gift. You have known of friends who have got foster parents—patrons—for their children."

"I . . ."

"One less mouth to feed, my lady, and the rest of your children would not go to debtor's prison, nor you or his lordship."

Master Robin moved restlessly and whimpered, and Lady Winscombe pulled him closer to her, whispering soothing words: "Hushabye, love, hushabye."

Aldara pressed her advantage. "And enough to pay a doctor for Master Robin."

Lady Winscombe suddenly rose and put her son down into his cot. She went and gazed at each of her children, touching a soft cheek or pushing aside a lock of hair. Finally, she faced Aldara, her eyes filling with tears.

"I . . . I will need to talk to Lord Winscombe."

"Of course, my lady," Aldara said, and turned away to hide her triumphant smile.

It was done. The child—Rowan—was hers. Aldara almost laughed scornfully a few days later at Lady Winscombe's attempt at impressing some memory of family in the child's mind. The mother had showered hugs and kisses on the little girl and whispered entreaties in her ear. Aldara had overheard one: "Remember, love, your real name is Rachel, Rachel Winscombe. They may change it, add to it, but you are a Winscombe. Remember. Remember. And you will come back to us someday." Her voice had been low and urgent.

Aldara had allowed herself a small smile. How futile an effort! Rowan would remember nothing of her former family. She looked at the grandly dressed man and woman she had brought—Cardain and Elswitha, two of those who had joined her and left the Midland Folk—and subtly signaled them.

"Come, child," said Elswitha, and held out her hands.

The little girl looked at her, then looked at her mother, clearly confused. Lady Winscombe bit her lip and gently pushed her daughter toward the couple. "Go, love. They are your foster parents now."

The girl's bottom lip stuck out and her brows drew together angrily. *"No!"*

Aldara stepped forward. "Come now, child. You will come with me, your Alyce, eh? I shall be with you, when you go with them, and I shall care for you."

This Rowan understood, and smiled, running into her nurse's arms. Had not her Alyce patched her knees when she fell, and had she not given her treats when she was a good girl? Aldara looked into little Rowan's trusting eyes, and felt an odd twisting sensation in her chest. Four years she had watched this child, four years she had cared for her . . . it would not be Cardain and Elswitha who would be her parents, but Aldara, the Lady of the Wildwood. She would be her mother now.

She shook off the feeling and smiled at herself. How sentimental she was being over a creature not far removed from a dog or cat compared to the Fair Folk. She took Rowan's hand and took her to the carriage that would take them only so far as the woods over the hill a few miles away. Glancing down at the child, she saw her waving to Lord and Lady Winscombe. Rowan turned and skipped the rest of the way to the carriage. Aldara smiled, then shook her head. The child would not remember. Somehow the thought comforted her, though why she should feel this way, she did not know. She sighed impatiently. She had spent far too much time among mortals; all would be well once she returned to Faery.

* * *

The carriage rumbled around the bend in the road, and after it did, Lady Winscombe turned in her husband's arms and pressed her head upon his chest and wept. Finally, she looked up at him.

"We did the right thing, did we not, Robert? She will be happy, and she will have a better life than she would with us."

Lord Winscombe did not look at her, but stared at the bend in the road that had taken his youngest daughter out of sight. "Yes, of course," he said. But his lips were white, as if he were suppressing words ready to burst from them. "Come, Mary. Let us go home."

The next day, twenty thousand pounds appeared in their account—it must have come from Rachel's foster parents. But the Winscombes' solicitors did not know how it had got there, for no one could remember anyone bringing it to them. And then a month later, they found the ship they had so hoped for had not sunk, and there was more gold than they had thought they would receive. The next year, the harvest was abundant with fruit and corn, and half their small flock of sheep bore twins.

And yet, though the neighbors congratulated them on their good fortune, they also noticed Lord and Lady Winscombe's smiles did not reach their eyes, for sorrow dwelt there. No, they could not understand it. Oh, their youngest child had gone to live with rich foster parents, but what was wrong with that? It was a common enough thing, and they would see her soon enough.

They did not know that when Lord and Lady Winscombe tried to find the rich lord and lady who had taken their daughter, they could find none by the name they had given them, not in the northern counties in which they said they had their home, not in London, not, apparently, in the whole of England.

Chapter One

A Between Place, 1780

Rowan remembered, at last, her real name. She had a second name also, but it escaped her, submerged in the shimmering warm mist that was her memory of child-long-ago. But at least she knew her real name was Rachel. She had reached that far back, and she held the name close to her, and knew she would weave it into herself today so she would not forget. There was power in knowing one's real name. And she would not tell Mother Aldara.

She closed her eyes, combing out her long hair that was newly washed and anointed with the oil of camellias. The walled garden was bright and warm, and she could feel the sun's heat over her cheeks and neck as she lifted her face to it. The brightness poured over her and Rowan could feel the power of it seep into her flesh and into the waves of hair she held in her hands as she combed, and she drifted, drifted, just at the door of dream time. The shadows and bright sparks of lives and stories long told and not yet told were there at the door of dream-time, and she combed them into her hair as it dried in the sun. The sounds of the shadows and the sparks curled up around her ears with the curls of her hair, and they whispered "Rachel, Rachel" in a woman's sad, soft voice. Now her true name was bound to her, so she would never forget.

She took a deep breath and came out of her trance, and found she had been singing. She did not stop, but listened to her own voice singing of love, a spell of true-love-come-calling. This was a good sign, she thought, for love must have been part of what she had long ago, and even the faeries approached that emotion carefully. It was a song she had learned from Galen, the Love Talker, secretly—another hidden thing. She had not told Mother Aldara of him, but had met him among the trees and the bracken. He had taught her the song on his pipe then told her the words, and she had sung it as he had played his music. She was no fool, however; Aldara had taught her faery ways and Rowan was well aware of his power. So she had put a quick ward upon herself before she had learned various spells from him, and hid her smile at his fleeting frown when she avoided his touch.

Rowan had liked and felt pity for him, however, though a wyrd had been placed upon him. She had managed to see him, though mortals could not, for she was mostly faery; he looked to her as if she gazed at him through a veil of gauze and she could barely discern his features. But he had been a laughing man, a man who loved women, a dark and handsome man of wit and grace. Once, she had touched the skin of his arm, and he had stood still, staring at her, clearly in shock. But then he had reached out to her, and his hand had passed right through her. It was his wyrd that he could not touch a woman, however much he desired her.

"You are faery," he had said, and his mouth had turned down in bitterness and anger. He did not return the next day, and she never saw him after that. But after a while she grew reconciled to his absence. For a short time she understood companionship, and understood what loneliness was after he left. These things made her remember more of child-long-ago, and for that she was grateful. For that, she invoked the Mother Goddess and prayed for his good fortune—faeries never took without giving something in return. Then, too, she had learned the song-spells that Mother Aldara had forbidden her, and it was another thing she stored in her collection of little rebellions.

So now she sang of love and she sang out defiance as well, combing out her hair. Mother Aldara would not return until the sun had risen seven times. Singing love spells was amusing, and it did not matter if she sang them, for it was rare that anyone came to her garden except for Aldara, and whoever came always came with her. So there was little chance Rowan would call anyone to her, much less her true love. She sighed as she sang, then shook her head, and her hair shimmered in a cloud around her.

And then the forest around her garden grew still, and the bees among the froth of alyssum at her feet ceased their buzzing. She stopped her song in mid-phrase, and her body tensed. Listening to the whisper of wind through the branches, she knew it was not Aldara, but someone else entirely. Someone who stumbled through the forest undergrowth, sounding like a boar crashing through the shrubs. She rose hurriedly, gathering her hair together, twisting it then winding it around and around her neck and shoulders like a shawl. She gazed toward the sound in the woods from just beyond the wooden fence, and waited.

At last the crashing stopped, and a heavy thump rattled the gate. For one moment, she stood still, her heart hammering wildly. For one moment she was afraid. It was someone alone, not with Mother Aldara. She would be alone with this person if she opened the gate.

She drew in her breath, ran forward, and lifted the latch. A man fell at her feet, groaning, his face pale beneath the dirt and scratches. He turned his face toward her, and she knew from the way he gazed at her, unseeing, that he was quite blind.

The scent of pine and lavender and honey. Cool smooth cloth under his head. Soft, damp cloth moving gently across his forehead, soothing away the pain.

"Drink this," said a feminine voice that made him think of honey again. He opened his mouth and swallowed sweetness and bitterness, and then opened his eyes.

Light, and a golden haze, so bright that it hurt his eyes. At least the blindness had passed. He sighed with relief and closed his eyes again and then he grew drowsy and slept.

When he woke again, the light was not as bright, and he could still see. Slowly, carefully, he sat up, and noticed the sharp, lancing pain in his head was gone.

He was in a garden, and it was springtime. Wild and damask roses climbed the gray stone walls, bluebells and daffodils nodded their heads beneath them. He smelled a sweet honey-scent, and looked down at a cloud of white and yellow flowers at his feet—he remembered his mother had had them in her garden long ago—alyssum, they were called.

And yet, the woods he had ridden by had been all brown and green and the bite of frost had been in the air, for it had been autumn.

"Ah, you are awake."

He looked toward the voice, and he had to look up, for it came from a tree.

On one long low branch of an alder tree she sat, her body slim, and her face was young and old at once, lovely and remote. Her feet were bare, she wore a dress of green that matched the leaves around her, the sash around her waist was red, and a shawl of golden silk was wound round her neck and shoulders. She looked down at him gravely.

"And you can see now." She looked keenly at him. "What is your name?" she asked.

He bowed carefully, afraid the pounding ache in his head would begin again. But it did not, and he managed a creditable bow. "Sir Jonathan Bradford, mistress, of Somerset." She did not give her name in return, but nodded and leapt down, lithe and agile, from the branch.

And then he drew in a long breath, for the shawl she wore dropped around her and pooled at her feet, and he saw it was not a shawl at all, but hair, incredibly long and lustrous. The sun made it shine like spun spider-silk caught in the colors of dawn, shifting gold and red and white. Some loose strands floated around her like wisps of sun-touched clouds, until, taking it in her hands, she twisted it, then wound it around her again. She looked at him watching her, and gave an irritated frown.

"You came just as I was about to plait my hair, and I thought I should see how badly off you were first. I thought perhaps you might die."

Jonathan grinned. "I'm glad I didn't die and cause an inconvenience."

She gazed at him for a moment then laughed, an oddly rusty, husky sound, as if she did it rarely. "Yes, it would have been an inconvenience." His stomach suddenly rumbled, and she smiled at him. "You are hungry, I see. Come."

She held out her hand and he took it. For one moment she paused, just after clasping his hand, and stared at him as if he had done something shocking.

"Is there anything wrong, mistress?"

For one moment she seemed to hesitate, then she shook her head. "No, nothing," she said and led him to a large cottage at one corner of the garden. Inside, it was bright from the sun streaming through the windows, and he entered a large, neat room. It was spare of decoration but for a few drawings upon the wall and dried flowers and herbs bound with bright ribbons and hanging from the ceiling. A small sofa and chair were the only furniture aside from a table and bench near the hearth. She set out for him some cheese, apples, and a roasted bird—a chicken, he thought, for he could hear the low crooning and clucking from behind the cottage—and she brought a mug of mint-flavored tea. She also ate, delicately and very little, mostly the cheese and apples. She finished quickly, leaving him to continue his meal, and washed her hands in a large bowl nearby. Then she sat down near the fire, and humming a low, sweet melody, she began to comb and braid her hair.

Jonathan stopped in mid-bite and stared at her. Her hair flowed around her like a stream, over her shoulders and breasts, pooling upon her lap and upon the floor. At times it seemed to move about her face, as if roused by some breeze, though there was no breeze in the cottage. He blinked and shook his head—he must be very tired and still ill. He watched her long slender fingers cut through the flow of hair, deftly catching straying strands, weaving it quickly, surely, into a complicated pattern. He wondered what her hair felt like, if it would be soft upon his hands, if it would slip through his fingers like cool water.

He pulled his gaze away and swallowed the bit of apple in his mouth. It was not right that he look at her; he hoped to be betrothed soon. He bit back a bitter sigh. No, truth to tell, he would have been betrothed by now if he were a whole man. But he could not help gazing at the young woman, her eyes half closed as she continued braiding her hair and softly singing an old ballad.

She looked perhaps ten years younger than his own six-and-twenty years, and he would have thought her a child if her willow-slight form had not had such a deep and womanly bosom as well. He watch her sing, and her lips were full like ripe red cherries, and when she turned to glance at him, he saw her eyes were large and greenish-blue, at once full of old knowledge and innocence. Was she young, then, or old? Young, surely, for her face was unlined and fresh. Was she a common farm woman? He remembered her soft and smooth hands—no. Her clothes were of a design that any farm woman might wear without the panniers fashion dictated, but her dress was clearly well made and of fine cloth. Here was a puzzle!

Jonathan looked about him, at the cottage and at the garden outside. He shivered. Perhaps . . . perhaps he was dreaming. Or perhaps even dead. He ran his thumb along a scar upon the side of his face, a wound he had received from the accident some months ago. It had been a race, a bet with his friends. He had driven his carriage—too fast, perhaps—around a bend in the road. He had barely enough time to turn the horses and avoid the children playing in the road. He had missed them but the carriage had overturned into a deep ditch and he had struck his head and become unconscious.

It was a week before he woke from his injury—a farmer had taken him in. But since that time he had suffered from frequent head pains so severe that blindness came over him, and as the months passed, they grew worse. His physicians could give him no hope—and though he was young still, he knew he needed to wed soon to get himself an heir before he died of his affliction. Perhaps it was a judgment upon him for his former dissolute ways. He did not know . . . it did not matter now.

He let out a long breath, pushing back the familiar despair. Well, he could not change the past. At least he had hope, thinking perhaps he could persuade Lady Anne Winscombe to wed him.

He did not know why he still hoped. Perhaps when one had come to care for another, one always hoped, and he believed that Lady Anne would make a suitable wife the moment he had seen her. He had even been encouraged to court her by her father, and so he had hoped even more. It would be a good marriage for both families; though the Earl of Charlton's title was new, the family was very old, as old as his own, and their properties joined as well.

But then he had proposed, and she could barely look at him when she replied with an awkward "perhaps" and ran from the room. He had been riding his horse back from the earl's estate—wandering, really—the memory of her clear aversion to his scar and his admission to his fainting spells still fresh and agonizing, when the pain had struck again like a lance thrust through his skull. Crying out, he had fallen, and his horse had galloped off without him. He did not know how he had come to this garden, only that some sound had pierced through his pain and drawn him here, as if promising surcease of some kind.

It was her singing. He had heard singing in the woods, and had followed it, though why he thought anyone could give him aid he did not know. The doctors in London had bled him and given him draughts that did nothing but make him even more ill than he had felt before, and he would still be wracked with pain so great it robbed him of his sight.

But now his pain was gone, and his sight was clear, and quickly too. It had always taken at least a few days before he recovered from the pain. He looked at the young woman and remembered a sweet and bitter draught and her voice urging him to drink. She had obviously given it to him. Was she an herb woman, then? He smiled. All the herb women he had seen had been old, crabbed, and dry. But he supposed all of them must have started at some time before they had become so. He gazed at the young woman's smooth skin and her golden hair now bound in braids and forming a crown upon her head. He could not imagine her becoming anything like the old herb women he had seen.

"Mistress," he said, and she looked up at him. "Mistress, may I know your name?"

"Ra—Rowan. My name is Rowan." An uncertain look flitted across her face before it became smooth and remote.

He nodded, as if he did not notice her hesitation. It wasn't her real name, perhaps, but it wasn't his business why she might not wish to reveal it. "Mistress Rowan, I must thank you for your help. I would have been quite ill, even badly injured, had you not come to my aid. If there is anything I may do for you—"

She rose hurriedly, grasping her skirts in her hands, looking a little alarmed before her face became placid again. She turned from him and went to a spinning wheel near the fireplace. "No, no of course not. It was nothing," she said. She pulled out fleece from a cloth bag and began to card it, glancing at him from time to time.

He rose, then, and bowed. "Well, I thank you." He reached into his pocket and felt for a calling card. "Here, this is my direction, should you need anything." She hesitated, then took it, but said nothing. "I suppose I should go; my servants will wonder what happened to me, and I would not want to worry them."

She nodded again, and followed him out the door to the garden gate. She opened it and Jonathan went through.

"Wait!" she called when he had gone about ten paces. He turned and looked at her questioningly.

"You are ill, are you not?" she asked. "You have a terrible pain in your head, and it blinds you. It is from your injury."

"How did you know—"

"I can heal it."

"You?"

"I have knowledge of herbs and medicines, and have healed people of their ailments before."

A terrible hope almost choked him. To have no more pain, and not to fear the blackness that came with it, or that his life would be cut short at any time. He swallowed it down and made himself smile. "I have been to many doctors in London, and none of them have been able to do anything for me. How can you do more than they?"

Her brow creased for a moment. "I do not know of doctors. But I do know many things about medicines and remedies. It is worth trying, I believe."

Briefly he closed his eyes. He might be whole again.

Lady Anne might agree to marry him if he were well. He had no reason to believe this young woman might be able to do what London doctors could not do, but what other chance did he have? It could not be worse than what he had been through with them.

Drawing in a deep breath, he said, "Very well. What should I do?"

A certain tension seemed to go from her, though her face was still serene. "Come back in a week. You must come once every week, on this day. Not before. I will have the remedy and the treatments ready for you then." She suddenly thrust her hand into a pocket of her skirt. "Here—you will need this key to find your way back to my garden." She smiled. "I think you must have been pisky-led to have found me the first time."

"Perhaps," he said, and took it, smiling in return. What an odd young woman! She had few social graces, and assumed he would not find his way back again, though he would clearly mark his way back. "And I thank you again, Mistress Rowan." He bowed, and saw a slight blush enter her cheeks before she turned and closed the garden door behind her.

Jonathan saw a small but clear path leading from the garden gate, and it was only a few minutes' walk to the main road again, where he had fallen off his horse. He walked down the road toward his house, and remembered the key she had given him, which he had tucked in a pocket of his coat. It had not felt like a key, not metal. He thrust his hand into his pocket and pulled it out.

It was nothing more than a straight twig with a green ribbon tied in the middle. He shook his head. It was hardly a key! He almost threw it away, but hesitated. No, Mistress Rowan might ask what he had done with it the next time he came to see her, and it would be a discourtesy if he threw it away. As odd as she was, she had made his pain disappear, and he was grateful.

He put it back into his pocket, and began to whistle. It

was only a small chance at being whole again, but his heart already felt light at the thought of seeing Mistress Rowan again.

Rowan did not know why she had made him stop and offered to heal him—it was nothing to her if he was well or ill. But she could not stop glancing at him, and while he ate the food she'd given him, she recalled the images and sensations—a smiling female face that was not Aldara's, soft lips upon her cheek—that had flashed in her mind when she touched his hand. It was only after he had left that she realized they were memories of her childhood. But whatever the reason, she was glad she had told him to return the next week. Perhaps there was something about him that made her remember, and she wished to remember more. If he returned, she would find out.

Then, too, it was a good opportunity to practice her healing arts, and she had little chance to use those on humans and not at all on men. So far, she had worked on animals and women. On a few occasions, she had gone with Mother Aldara to small cottages not far from the woods to attend a birth or cool a fever. Once, she had gone to a great house, where a great lady was ill with the flux; she had never seen anything like the house, for she had grown up in her cottage and had never been far outside of it except when Mother Aldara took her on her travels. It had made her ache to go beyond the perimeter of her garden and discover more of the world she was at present forbidden to see.

But those outings happened seldom now. It was because she was being prepared, and needed to focus on her faery arts. Soon, she would come of age, seven years from the first year of her monthly woman's blood, and she would leave here to wed one of the faery folk. She would wed a stranger, one of the tall, shining, beautiful men she had seen from time to time from the upper window of her cottage. He would put a child in her, and she would give birth to a faery babe, and the faery race would continue. She had never been allowed to be near any of the men and, aside from Galen, had only seen them strolling past the fenced garden, laughing with the faery women who were equally beautiful. Mother Aldara had said once that Rowan was not wholly faery yet; for her to mate before her time would not produce a child that was purely faery.

Rowan stared at the gate through which Sir Jonathan Bradford had gone, and slowly ran her fingers across the hand he had clasped earlier. Touching him had stirred a memory, had called to something that lay deep inside of her, something not faery. It had startled her and was something akin to child-long-ago, and the memory of her true name.

Bradford . . . neighbor. The words pressed upon her from within, and she let out a slow breath. At one time, she had had a neighbor named Bradford.

She smiled and closed the hand he had touched tightly against her chest. Another memory of who she really was! It could be, when he returned the next week, when she touched him again, she would remember more. It could not hurt to do so. She would wed as Mother Aldara bid her, of course, and no memories would stop that, she was sure.

Rowan thought of touching Sir Jonathan and thought of how different he looked from herself or Mother Aldara. His face was all spare, hard planes, and he was taller than herself, and broad of shoulder. And yet, his eyes had been large and tired, and his lips looked as if they were used to laughing and saying soft words. She had never been so close to a mortal man before, at least, not that she remembered.

She shivered. Perhaps he should not come here . . . it was not precisely forbidden, for Aldara had brought patients here before. But her foster mother had never brought a man here. Rowan pressed her lips together and shrugged. If Aldara did not specifically forbid her, how was she to know?

Rowan frowned. How had he come here? He was not of faery, as Galen had been, and so should not have been able to find her cottage door. The Love Talker . . . she shivered. She thought of the spell-song that faery had taught her, a song to call one's true love. She had sung it for amusement and out of, admittedly, resentment that she would not be free to choose a mate as any of the faery did. Never had she thought it would work; she was not all faery, after all, and so her spells were weaker than theirs. She doubted she had much influence beyond the walls of this garden. Indeed, she could not go very many paces beyond the door without getting turned around and arriving at the door again; something about the garden or walls must be ensorcelled.

Again her hand touched the other hand Sir Jonathan had held and a yearning came over her. Was Sir Jonathan her true love? Rowan smiled wryly and shook her head. No, she doubted it. She was destined to wed one of the faery folk, and but for a small taint of human still left in her, she was as good as faery herself. So Mother Aldara had said, and had worked to accomplish it.

And yet . . . it could not hurt to have Sir Jonathan visit her from time to time. He was only a mortal, after all, and was no threat to her. Aldara might object . . . Another flare of rebellion sparked in Rowan's heart. Her foster mother need not know, and he would be gone soon enough. He would come when Aldara was not here. Rowan would heal him and touch him as she pleased and perhaps that deep-down memory would surface again and she would know her whole, true name at last.

Chapter Two

Sir Jonathan looked out of his chamber window at the gray mist rising over the fields and between the smoky branches of the autumn trees beyond. He thought of his promise to go back to the garden in the woods. Had it been a dream? He felt better in the past week than he had for a long time, and he had been very busy talking with his bailiff about the harvest on his lands and making improvements here and there—a thing he enjoyed. His family had been on this land from before the Normans had conquered England; it was a part of him. Though it was a foolish thing to admit, he often felt as if his feet could take root into the earth and imagined he could feed off the richness of the soil when he pushed his fingers into it.

His London physicians had warned him against doing strenuous work of any kind. A flare of anger and resentment burned in him at the thought. They had also said he would die during one of his spells of pain and blindness, and that could be soon. So what did it matter if he dug in the earth like a peasant? He could walk and he could work when not in pain, and he would not lay in bed like a puking, mewling babe, but work like a man instead, as long as he could.

He grinned suddenly. Sometimes he could not help himself—he sometimes found himself digging a trench beside his tenants, which made him laugh when he saw the scandalized looks he received from both them and his neighbors.

An image came to him of a cottage—it was in his dream, a vivid dream, for he could see it in detail. An abandoned gardener's cottage not far from his house was very like the one in his dream—old, but made of sturdy gray stone. Perhaps that was what he dreamed of, yet another task he could put his hand to, to keep him occupied until—

He looked about his room, and suddenly his house seemed too large, too empty. Perhaps, just to occupy himself, he would renovate the cottage, make it like the one he had dreamed of. It would keep him busy.

Until he died.

His hands turned to fists and he pushed down the rage that flooded his gut. Slowly the heat receded from his mind, and despair replaced it. He shrugged. He would work and make himself useful until he literally dropped. Quickly he pulled on some old clothes, and smiled slightly, thinking of the appalled looks he would receive from his valet if he were seen. He strode out of his room, out of his house . . . he would survey the gardener's cottage and begin work on it immediately.

But near the end of the week, Sir Jonathan experienced the painful blindness again—not as bad as he had had it in the past. It was enough for him to take to his bed, and while he lay sweating in pain, he remembered a cool touch upon his brow that had seemed to soothe it away, and the sweet and bitter draught he had taken. Rowan—Mistress Rowan was her name. He had slept at last, and dreams of the lady were the only thing that had disturbed him that night. His dreams were full of her touch, cascades of dawn-colored hair, and her lips and body soft against him. He had awakened in the middle of the night, breathing quickly, his body hard with desire, and he banished the errant images to a far corner of his mind. He wished to pledge himself to Lady Anne before it was too late, but his dreams were all of another lady, perhaps all concocted from his pain-filled mind. How could such a place be real? And yet, the dreams laughed softly at him, and pressed hope into the furrows that despair had scored into him, deep in his heart.

The next day he felt better, enough to arise from his bed, though his head still pounded and his sight dimmed at times. It was near noon when he finally decided to ride his horse to the woods he had left a week ago, if only to see if the path had been born of his imagination. If it was not, he had promised Mistress Rowan that he would return, and he kept his promises if he could.

He came at last to the stretch of road that passed through the wood, and he reined in his horse. He frowned. He had thought there was a path through it to the cottage. But he could not see any such thing, though the leaves had fallen from the trees and the undergrowth and would have shown even the smallest trail through the woods. He turned his horse around and went back the way he had come for a space, but there was no path in that direction, either. Once more he searched . . . nothing.

Was it a dream, then? He remembered the warmth of the garden after the chill of the surrounding autumn woods. It had been like late spring, and flowers had bloomed that were long faded and gone in his own gardens at home. It could not be real.

What a fool he was! He had chased a will-o'-the-wisp called hope, and the hope had been so strong, it had conjured up a vision of spring and healing and the gentle touch of a woman. No doubt it was a phantasm created while he was ill with pain and blindness the last time.

A sudden freezing wind blew in his face and he pulled

up his shoulders against it. His fingers grew chill and he thrust his gloved fists in the pockets of his coat to warm them. Something hard poked the fingers of one hand, and as he retrieved it from his pocket, he drew in a long breath.

It was the twig with the green ribbon around it. Mistress Rowan had given it to him, telling him . . . He frowned, trying to remember, and an ache began to move behind his eyes.

A key. She had said it was a key. He had thought it was nonsense, and had just concluded the whole incident was a fantasy, but here was the twig she had given him. Some part of it, then, must have been real. There was no reason why he would tie a ribbon around a twig and place it in his own pocket.

In that case, he must find the path. He looked up again searching the trees to the right and left of him . . . and there it was right in front of him. He shook his head. Perhaps his injury was worse than he thought—he should have seen it immediately, for it was broad enough for a horse to walk upon.

It took only a few minutes to ride down the path to the gate of the cottage. Jonathan was surprised it was not easily seen from the road. But the brush and trees were thicker here than at the edge of the road, and perhaps that was why it was obscured from sight. He tied the reins of his horse to a wooden post next to the door and knocked.

He thought he heard soft footsteps, and then silence. Almost he turned to leave, for he heard nothing more, and thought perhaps he had mistaken the day. But then the door opened, and Mistress Rowan was there smiling widely up at him.

For one moment he stared at her, for he did not remember her smiling thus before, only a few small brief ones. But this time her smile reached her eyes and she took his hand and brought him into the garden. He could not help smiling back, and when her own smile grew wider, he caught his breath.

She was beautiful. Very. Why had he not remembered this before? For some reason he had not recalled it. The sun streamed through breaks in the clouds, and a beam of light struck her head, making her hair shine like gold. The brightness seemed to course through the strands of hair braided round her head in a crown and the long locks flowing down behind to her waist, making her hair seem a living thing. When she walked, she seemed almost to float over the ground and he would have thought he was dreaming again except for the warmth of her hand in his. And when she smiled, her lips looked soft and he wished, suddenly, that he had not decided to try to ask Lady Anne Winscombe to be his wife again. Lady Anne. He firmly reined in his thoughts. It was for her that he was here, after all.

"I am glad you have come," she said. "I almost thought you would not." Her voice was low and sweet, just as he had remembered. She led him to the cottage and made him sit in a chair by the fire.

He sat, slowly, and gazed at her. "I almost didn't." He stopped—it was a boorish thing to say. "That is, I thought all this was a dream, for I could not find the path at first."

Rowan nodded. "But you brought the key. That is the only way you will find this place, you know." She shook her head. "I wonder how you came here last week, for no one does, unless it is Mother Aldara or someone who accompanies her. I almost think someone led you here." She busied herself opening different cupboards, bringing out bags of herbs and bottles of liquid. She glanced at him. "Are you hungry? Do you wish for food?"

"No, I thank you." He smiled at the brief flicker of disappointment upon her face. "I had my luncheon before I came." She nodded and continued rummaging about in the cupboards.

The wool collar of his heavy coat itched against his jaw, and he realized suddenly that he was too warm, and that sweat prickled his hands inside his thick gloves. Slowly, he took them off, looking about him carefully now. Outside the cottage, it was unchanged from what he remembered—there were the spring flowers and the roses, flowers long gone from his own land. The alder in which she had sat before still had green leaves where the woods outside the garden had shed half their yellow ones. And when he had stepped from the wood into the garden, he remembered feeling the warmth of the sun on his face, where the sun in the wood seemed distant and cool. He shivered slightly, not from cold, and stared at the young woman before him.

"What is this place?" he said abruptly.

Her hand paused for a moment over a bottle before she picked it up, then she turned to look at him.

"It is where I live," she said.

"Oh, really?" he said, and could not help the sarcastic tone in his voice.

She laughed softly, and this time it was musical sound, not halting like the last time when he'd been here. "Yes." She paused and gazed at him, as if trying to decide something. "I will not insult your intelligence by telling you it is part of the world you know," she said. "You clearly have noted the difference between what is outside the walls and what is within. What is outside is the mortal world, the world in which all may come and go. Here . . ." She stopped and her brow creased as if trying to search for the right words. "Here is a *between* place."

"Between what?"

She cocked her head, looking at him. "Between the mortal world and Faerie."

He said nothing, but stared at her, trying to make sense of the words she had just spoken.

"You do not believe me, I see," she said. She turned to the door of the cottage and waved at the garden beyond. "In your world it is autumn, is it not? The leaves are gold and brown, and some have fallen. But here it is spring, and the air is warm, not cold. Time marches differently here—and no, you need not be alarmed." She smiled slightly. "It is not like the stories. This is a between place. You will not leave here to find everyone you cared for dead or aging. The time you spend here is the same as you would spend in your mortal world." She turned to her herbs and bottles again, and he could see her lips move as she went over them. "There," she said. "I have all I need."

"You are joking," he said. Faerie . . . such things were not real. They were only stories told by mothers to their children.

"Joking? No. You have seen the difference of seasons yourself. What else could it be?"

"Then I am dreaming."

Mistress Rowan stepped toward him and pinched him. "Ouch!"

She raised her eyebrows. "Dreams do not pinch."

"No, I suppose not," he said, and could not help laughing at the mischievous look on her face.

She turned and poured some water into a kettle and set it on a hook above the hearth, then came to the table at which he sat and set down the herbs she had gathered. "I will give you tea to start. When you are done, I will work the pain away from here . . ." She reached out and touched his temple near the scar. "And here." Her fingers ran down the back of his neck to his shoulders.

His breath caught at her touch and he stared at her; he should have been indifferent to the sensation, for her voice was impersonal, instructive. But her fingers had lingered as they flowed from temple to shoulders; he had not been touched like that for a long time. For one moment there was silence as she stared in return, and a slow blush rose in her cheeks. Then she shook her head slightly as if dismissing some thought.

"Did—did that hurt you?" she asked, her eyes growing worried.

Jonathan smiled and brought her hand to his lips. "No. It was pleasant, Mistress Rowan."

Again the silence as she gazed at him, and her blush rose higher. She pulled her hand away, and hastily took up a cloth to take the kettle from the fire. "I . . . I am glad it did not hurt," she said. She did not look at him when she poured the hot water into the teapot into which she had put some herbs and dried flowers. But then she seemed to shake herself and she smiled at him. "If it is pleasant, then the healing will be that much faster for you." She brought a mug from one of her cupboards then poured out the tea, straining it through a fine cloth sieve. She pushed the mug toward him. "There, you must drink all of it, and then I will rub away the pain."

It was a sweet and bitter drink, much like the drink he had tasted when he'd first arrived in Mistress Rowan's garden. Better tasting, certainly, than the draughts that had been forced down his throat in London. As he drank it, he became conscious of her hand upon his arm and that she stared at him, as if trying to discern something from his face.

"Is there anything amiss, ma'am?"

She opened her mouth, then closed it. "I—I sometimes remember things when I touch you." The words rushed from her, and for a moment she looked surprised before her expression became distant.

"I hope they are pleasant memories," he said.

A little smile curled up one corner of her mouth, oddly defiant. "They are," she replied. She let out a breath, then rose and stood behind him and he almost rose as well, but she pressed her hand down on his shoulder. "No, sit. You must relax yourself." Her hand came up and settled on his jaw, then slipped upward to his temple. It was a simple touch, but he caught his breath again, and the dreams he had of her last night flashed in his mind. He had not lain with a woman for a long time. The mistress he had kept before his accident had shuddered when she looked at him, and he could hardly blame her; the scar on his face was still red and would repulse anyone.

But it did not seem to repulse Mistress Rowan. He felt a hot damp cloth pressed against his face, and then caught a glimpse of her fingers laden with a thick ointment that smelled slightly of camphor. Then her fingers moved in a smooth, slick motion against his wound and upon his temples, and he closed his eyes.

There was only the soft sound of the sighing breeze among the trees outside, the brooding of the hens behind the cottage, and the quiet sound of her breath behind him as she rubbed his temples. A long sigh left him, and his shoulders loosened.

"Tell me of yourself," came her soft voice behind him, almost a whisper, and her breath was warm against his ear.

"There . . . there is not much to tell." He felt her fingers at his throat, and his cravat suddenly came loose and his shirt came open. Again he caught his breath, opened his eyes, and seized her hand. "What are you doing?"

"I cannot stroke away the pain and apply the ointment if your neck is covered."

Jonathan relaxed again, and again the thought of his abstinence from women flickered in his mind, and his eyes went to the large fleecy sheepskin rug near the hearth. He felt her hands upon his collarbone and imagined them slipping downward upon his chest, and a heat rose up from his loins. Abruptly he stood up.

"I think perhaps this will be enough for now," he said.

Her hand pressed hard upon his shoulder. "I pray you let me decide this, Sir Jonathan. No, it is not enough for now. You *will* sit and you *will* let me apply the ointment," she said, and her voice grew angry. The cottage dimmed, and an odd threatening pressure surrounded them. Reluctantly he sat.

The pressure lightened and the sun streamed into the windows again.

"Who are you? Are you—are you a faery?" He blurted

the words, then felt foolish. Such things were only children's tales, and Mistress Rowan was solidly real, as her touch and his resulting imaginings clearly showed. Yet, the garden, and sudden shift in atmosphere . . . a "between place" she had said. . . .

A pause, then: "Almost. I am almost faery." This, a whisper, so that he would have not heard it had not the cottage and garden been so silent.

"There is still a part of me that is mortal," she said, and her words came from her haltingly. "I have been here since I was a child, being made ready for the time I am twenty-one years. Then, I will be all faery, and a worthy bride of a faery lord."

Jonathan could hear uncertainty in her voice. "But that is a few years from now," he said, wanting to comfort her, though he had an uneasy feeling at the thought of her being wed. "You are young yet to be thinking of marriage. And no doubt your faery lord is handsome and pleasing to you."

"I do not know what he will be like," Rowan said, and her voice was flat. Then she laughed and her breath stirred the hair on the back of his head. "And I have only a year until I am one-and-twenty—what, did you think me a child?"

He did, and did not. He had thought of her face and how it looked at once child-like and full of old knowledge. He felt her body against his back as she worked upon his neck, holding him up when he had relaxed, and the occasional brush of her skirts against him. He stiffened his back and drew away from her. "I thought perhaps you were younger—sixteen or so. It's hard to tell."

"The faery are ageless, unless they choose to look otherwise."

Her touch lingered upon his skin for a moment before she left him to pour more hot water into the teapot. The pouring of tea, the cottage, the room—these were mundane things, and here she was talking of Faerie as if it were just as mundane. And yet, it was not autumn in this garden . . .

Suddenly remembering the stories he had heard as a child, he said, "Why are you doing this for me?"

He almost missed the hesitation before she said, "For the practice, of course. I am a healer; I heal."

"And?"

She gazed at him, her brows raised haughtily, but said nothing.

"I remember the stories my nurse told me when I was a child," he said. "Faeries don't offer gifts without a reason. What do you gain by healing me? Tell me, or I shall leave."

Her smile was touched with scorn. "I doubt you will leave. You wish to be healed of your injury, after all."

He rose from the chair and strode to the door.

"Stop!"

He turned and faced her. She gazed at him, at once angry and anxious, one hand curled into a tense fist at her chest. "Sit, and I will tell you."

He returned to the chair and sat.

Rowan glanced away, then gazed at him steadily, though she bit her lower lip briefly before she spoke. "I . . . I told you I remembered things when I touched you. I don't remember what it was like before I came here, what my mortal life was like, only a few things. But I remember when I touch you—perhaps it is because you are mortal, and that calls to the mortal part still in me. But I wish to remember more, and so . . . and so I wish to touch you again, to see if I can." Her hand closed under her breast, as if she were holding something precious to her heart.

Jonathan rose and took her hand in his, and her fist gently uncurled. He smiled and brought it to his lips as he bowed. "If that is all, then I will stay, and count myself fortunate that I have found a physician whose fee is so easy to pay."

For one moment she stared at him, and her eyes were wide and vulnerable. And then she let out a long sigh and pulled her hand from his to pick up the teapot. "Thank you," she said, and gave him his tea.

"Mother Aldara . . . if the Fair Folk are superior to mortals, why is it that you chose a mortal child to become faery?" Rowan asked the next time the faery woman came to see her.

The question made Aldara look at her sharply, and Rowan wondered if she would say speaking of it was forbidden. But then the woman put down her pestle with which she was grinding some herbs and smiled and touched Rowan's cheek affectionately.

"I suppose you are wondering why you were chosen, child?"

It was not precisely what Rowan wished to know, but her foster mother's sharp look made her wary, though she kept her face serene. She had learned faery ways well. "Yes," she replied.

"I should not be surprised you asked it; it's true faeries are superior to mortals, and that you were brought here to become one of us. It probably seems a contrary thing for one of us to do." Aldara set aside the mortar and sat down at the cottage table. She looked as young as Rowan herself, and more beautiful, with her brilliant red hair and skin as pale as a lily flower delicately touched with pink. Suddenly it struck Rowan odd that she called "mother" someone who looked so young. She had learned that mothers in the mortal world looked older than their daughters, but Aldara had never changed from the day she had brought Rowan to this cottage. Or rather, Aldara had never changed unless she so chose. A quick disorientation seized Rowan, and for a moment she wondered if the shape Aldara took whenever she visited Rowan was her true one. But of course it was. Rowan was mostly faery now, after all, and she was good at discerning a changed shape. Then, too, Aldara would have little reason to hide her true shape from her foster daughter. Rowan relaxed and took up the mortar and pestle Aldara had set aside and continued grinding the herbs in the way she had been taught.

"You know there are many ways for a mortal to turn faery; I have taught them to you by applying as many of them as I know upon you," Aldara said, looking beyond the window of the cottage to the garden outside. "But one must choose carefully. Those that conceived and birthed you were of old stock, and strong of body and quick of mind. They had forgotten the old ways, but their blood still held a touch of the Old Ones. I could tell—like calls to like, after all."

Like calls to like. The image of Jonathan—he had become Jonathan to her now, at least in her thoughts—came to Rowan. He had come every week for six months now, and it was spring in the mortal world, unlike the unchanging face of the garden; so he told her and so she could see from her upstairs cottage window, beyond the garden walls. She liked to listen to his voice, telling her of the changing earth as she applied her herbs and healing unguents. She would watch him as he talked, watch how his expression changed with the recounting of seasons, as if he were part of the land he worked.

A slight triumphant laugh pulled her attention around to Aldara again.

"It made your change to faery very quick. Except for the last taint of mortal you have within you, the change was almost complete by the time you were fourteen. It has slowed considerably since then." Aldara smiled at her. "But I am sure the taint will disappear by your twenty-first birthday. And then you will wed one of us, and bear children who are faery from their birth."

"Can . . . can you not bear your own?"

Aldara's brow creased in a frown and for a moment her green eyes became cold. "You are full of questions today!"

Rowan gazed at her steadily. "But of course. Am I not

to become faery soon? Shouldn't I know the reason for
my purpose as one of the Fair Folk?''

Her chin was suddenly seized between Aldara's thumb
and finger, and she stared into her foster mother's suspicious eyes. "Almost . . . almost I would think you have been
seeing someone, someone who has caused you to ask these
questions.''

Rowan twisted her lips in a skeptical smile. "And who
would know to come here, Mother Aldara, unless you bring
them? Did you not just say you chose me because you felt
sure I would be quick of mind? And if I am, and if I ask
questions, who is to blame for that?" It was bold of Rowan
to speak so, but after a last searching look, Aldara laughed
and released her chin.

"You show yourself to be one of us, by your answer! I
will tell you, then." She sighed, stood, and stepped toward
the hearth in a restless movement, her skirts swirling about
her like rivulets of water. "Faery children are rare, and
grow rarer as the years pass. It had not occurred to us that
it was important, for we are long-lived; immortal, compared
to mayfly humans. But the mortal race was created from
earth, and as the earth gives birth easily to all manner of
life, so do mortals give birth easily, and with great regular-
ity. We, the Fair Folk, were created from all the elements,
and we choose what element we prefer, so . . .''

As she had always been taught, Rowan listened and
remembered. But this time she listened to the meaning
underneath her foster mother's words, as she was taught
to listen to mortals. She had never done this before, always
taking what Aldara said as truth. Now, she brought her
lessons to bear even upon Aldara's words, and saw that it
was not as it had always presented to her: The Fair Folk
lacked or had neglected something that mortals had, and
thus faeries were, perhaps, not as superior as they claimed
to be. This was something to think further upon, and she
would do so as soon as Aldara left her today.

"And that, my dear, is why you were chosen, and why

we wish you to wed one of us when you are wholly faery, with not one taint of human in you." Aldara smiled and touched Rowan's cheek gently. "How we shall celebrate when we welcome yet another one of our kind into our group, and even more when you are wedded and bedded and with child! I shall be your midwife, and shall care for you as I have cared for you all your life, for you are like my own daughter, as if I had birthed you from my own body." She bent and kissed Rowan upon her forehead. "Indeed, I have loved you as my own child, even though you are not all faery—an odd whim for one of the Fair Folk, I know, but an old woman should be allowed a few fancies, yes?"

Rowan laughed, though guilt and rebellion mixed with the love she felt for her foster mother. "Old! As if the Fair Folk could ever look old, for they can look as they please."

Aldara laughed as well. "True. Now, shall we turn to your lessons? You were very strong last time you cast a defensive ward against me. Put away your herbs and I will sing the magic into your hair, then we'll try new spells."

Rowan smiled and nodded, and poured the herbs they had ground into tightly woven bags. She liked to practice her spells and was very good at them. But she remembered what her foster mother had told her about the nature of humans and of faery, and tucked the words in a corner of her mind to ponder over later. She would think over them tomorrow, the day Jonathan would come to see her again, and when she would touch him and remember more of her mortal self. Her breath quickened at the thought of his return, and she remembered, not the flashes of child-memories, but the feel of his skin beneath her hands, and how it felt different from her own. She saw Aldara give her a questioning look, and Rowan smiled at her. "I was thinking of becoming all faery," she said. "I wonder how different it will feel from the way I am now."

Aldara shrugged and smiled in return. "What you feel now is not important. To be faery is more than anyone

could wish." She began to hum as she took up the comb
and pulled it gently through Rowan's hair, and Rowan
could feel the magic set itself in each strand as the music
flowed around her, high and sweet and comfortingly
familiar.

Even so, an odd tendril of fear pushed its way up through
Rowan's feelings of anticipation at joining the Fair Folk,
and she almost shook her head at herself. What had she
to fear, after all? To be faery was to be much more than
a mortal, and something she should be happy about. But
though she pushed the fear away and turned to her lessons
with eagerness, it settled down in a corner of her heart
and joined with the rebellion that had grown faster since
the day Jonathan Bradford first stumbled into her garden.

Jonathan gazed at the old gardener's cottage before him.
He nodded, satisfied. The renovation was going very well,
although he was going mostly from memory. He grimaced
at the sketches he had made of Rowan's cottage—he was
a poor draftsman, unfortunately. But the image of her
house was clear in his mind, for he dreamed of it every
night he was away.

For one moment he frowned, then shook his head. He
did not know why he spent so much of his time here,
overseeing the refurbishment of the old cottage. It did not
matter—it kept his mind away from his illness.

Illness . . . he had not felt as ill as he had been for about
six months now. The progress was slow, but at least the
pain and the blindness were not so severe and not as
painful. That was something, at least. Perhaps Mistress
Rowan did have it in her to heal him completely.

He could not help feeling uneasy . . . truth to tell, he
dreamed not only of her cottage but also of her, the way
she looked and moved, full of lithe grace. She said she
was faery . . . he was not sure of that, for she showed no
real evidence of it, except in her healing skill. That could

easily be explained by the knowledge she had of herbs and remedies, something his London physicians lacked, certainly. But he could not ignore the fact that the garden never varied in season, but was always warm and full of flowers and fruit, spring and summer at the same time— an impossible thing. But it did not mean she herself was faery; it could mean she was under an enchantment, per- haps. His heart lightened at the thought, and he grimaced at himself. He'd much prefer to think that she had not ensorcelled him into thinking and dreaming of her—or perhaps he did. His wish was to make Lady Anne his wife, for she was of good birth and her family's land marched with his. If Mistress Rowan had put a spell upon him, then he would not have to think he was to blame for his wayward thoughts.

Jonathan crumpled the sketch he had drawn and thrust it into one of his pockets. He smiled bitterly. It mattered not what he thought—he would be lucky if any woman wished to wed him. A woman might wish to wed his money, perhaps, or his land, but not, willingly, him.

He gazed at the gray stones the workmen were unloading from their wagons and noted the angle of the sun. He sighed. At the very least he could try to ask Lady Anne to marry him today, and see what came of it. If she said no, at least he had his work, and he could take a little comfort in Mistress Rowan's company, faery or not.

When Rowan woke the next morning, she drew in a long breath to still the anticipatory hammering of her heart. But she could not prevent the smile that grew on her lips at the thought of Sir Jonathan Bradford. He would come today, and she would listen to the deep tones of his voice, and touch his skin, and remember. An intriguing man, she thought suddenly. She was not sure why it had not occurred to her before. It was true, however; the thought settled down inside of her comfortably, a familiar thing.

It was something she had felt, if not known, for quite a few months now. He was only a mortal, but he was interesting, for she had not seen his like before. Galen had been charming and all smiles and seductive looks—she had seen such actions and heard such words among the faery men and women when she listened from her upstairs window overlooking the walls of the garden.

But Sir Jonathan did not cajole or charm . . . or indeed smile often. Rowan wondered why this was, for his lips looked as if they should turn up happily more than they did. Perhaps it was because of his pain. His mouth lifted on one side more than another when he did smile, an awkward expression, devoid of the grace and beauty in the smiles of the Fair Folk. Yet, it made her wish suddenly that she could somehow make him do it more. Perhaps once she healed him completely he would smile more at her. Rowan ruefully shook her head at herself. Why should she care whether he smiled at her or not? Regardless, his healing was very slow; she would look deeper into his ailment today to see if she could speed his recovery. He was a distraction; the sooner gone, the better, she was sure.

She rose and dressed, then hummed as she went down the short flight of stairs from her bedroom to prepare her breakfast. Once she was done eating, she hummed through the preparation of herbs she would use when Jonathan— she felt a secret guilty pleasure in thinking of him as "Jonathan" and not in the formal distant way of the faery when addressing mortals—came to her cottage today.

Sunlight shone bright and warm through the windows, and a gentle breeze blew in the scents of the garden to her, beckoning her outdoors to tend her herbs and flowers. Though she heeded it, and fed and watered her chickens as well, a restlessness made her impatient with her work and she finished it quickly instead of lingering over it. Later, she regretted it, for after she had swept the cottage from top to bottom and spun a skein of yarn from fleece, she had little else to do until Sir Jonathan came for his treatment.

At last, however, she heard a knock at her garden door and she ran to open it. Her heart beat quickly even after she stopped and put her hand to the door latch, and when she opened it, she understood why. At first a shadow of sadness seemed to sit within his eyes. Then he smiled and his eyes were warm when he looked at her, and Rowan realized that no one else had ever looked at her like this, as if she, herself, was someone—even with a taint of mortal left in her—who was all he could wish her to be.

"Welcome," she said as he took her hand and raised it to his lips, a courtly gesture.

"I thank you, Mistress Rowan," he said, and that was all. And yet, though it was only polite, and kissing her hand was only courteous, a rush of more than childhood memories came to her—a rush of warmth, a shimmering tension like the promise of summer rain upon dry earth.

Rowan gazed at him, and it seemed that both their breaths halted for one moment before he dropped her hand and she turned, leading the way to the cottage.

"Come," she said as she stepped into the kitchen. "I have the tea for you . . . and do you wish for luncheon?"

This time he smiled, and put his hand upon his stomach. "Yes, if you please. I didn't have luncheon, so I would be glad of some, thank you."

She was absurdly happy he had not eaten, for he smiled at her in that ungraceful lopsided way when she asked. Quickly she seized a bowl from her cupboard and filled it with dried fruit and cheeses that a merchant's wife had given her and Aldara not long ago. The woman had been in labor for two days, and her physician had given up. But Aldara gave her a draught of pennyroyal and turned her baby slightly in the womb. It had eased her labor and the babe was born easily after that. The new parents had been grateful and had offered money, but Aldara never took coins, only goods. One's healing power lessened if one took coin; why it was, Rowan was not certain, but so Aldara had said.

Rowan watched Sir Jonathan as they ate their luncheon, and noticed the sad cast of his expression again, but said nothing. Something troubled him, something other than his illness, she was certain. He had not looked like this the last time he had come. Not that she truly cared, of course; she was almost all faery, and whatever mortal concerns he had were certainly not hers.

She put away the food and the dishes when he shook his head and thanked her for her offer of more, then she went to the cupboards and took out the salve she had used the last time. She saw him watching her as she took out her remedies, and wondered if he liked to watch her; his eyes seemed to follow her as she worked, and she thought perhaps he was only curious. Well, who would not be, who had never encountered Faerie before? She certainly was curious about him, she admitted that, though she had restrained herself from asking all the questions she had wished to ask of him. He was a novelty to her, even though he was only a mortal.

Jonathan *was* curious—he was still not used to the idea that she might be faery even after all these months. He watched her drag a huge wheeled wooden tub in front of the fire, then she went outside. Soon she returned with two buckets of water. As she bent over the tub, her pink tongue curled over her upper lip as she lifted one bucket and poured it into the tub, and then the other bucket into a large pot over the fire. The flames threw red lights into her hair pulled up high upon her head and left to cascade over her shoulders, breasts, and hips in a golden stream. One long strand of her hair slipped forward over her breast and would have gone into the fire if he had not quickly risen and pulled it back.

She jumped back and stared at him. "Why did you do that?" she asked.

"I am sorry if I startled you, mistress, but your hair would have caught fire if I had not, or would have been badly singed." He smiled at her. "It would have been a pity to have damaged something so beautiful."

She gazed at him, her eyes wide. "Beautiful?"

"Yes," he said. "Has no one told you?"

"No." A pink tinge colored her cheeks, and she glanced away and pulled her hair from him, and he realized he had not let go of it. It slid over his hand like water and silk.

Hastily she turned to leave again with the buckets, but he stopped her. "If you are going for more water, please let me get it."

A startled look crossed her face, and she slowly let down the buckets. "If . . . if you wish. The stream is behind the cottage . . . it flows through the garden from beyond the walls." She looked away from him, clearly discomposed, and he cursed himself for an inept fool.

They worked together in silence, and soon the tub was filled with steaming water and fragrant with the herbs Rowan had put in it. Finally, she turned to him. "Take off your clothes, please."

"I beg your pardon?" He could feel his face become warm—surely he did not hear correctly.

She frowned at him. "I said, take off your clothes, please. You must bathe. It is part of the treatment." She took a large towel from the cupboards and laid it on the back of a chair next to the tub.

"I think not." Why he hadn't thought the tub would be for him, he didn't know; it should have been obvious— well, he'd been too busy watching her, that was why. But he'd be damned if he would strip as bare as a babe in front of her. The thought of it made the rest of him become warm as well and his imagination run wild.

"Then you may leave, and I am well rid of you." She stared at him, and the hair about her face moved as if a breeze had suddenly sprung up in the cottage. "You may go back to your doctors and to whatever foolish quackery they care to force upon you."

The sunlight streaming in from outside dimmed, and the air became suddenly chill. She continued to stare at him and then suddenly she grinned. "Ah! You don't wish me to see you without clothes. Believe me, I am used to it—I have seen babies born and put plasters on weak chests. One more unclothed body would make no difference to me."

"It would make a difference to *me.*"

Rowan cocked her head to one side and frowned. "I don't see why it should. Think of me as one of your physicians—surely they saw you without clothes."

"They were not, however, young and beautiful women."

Her frown deepened. "You are speaking nonsense. What I look like should make no difference. I require that you bathe in the herbs, so you must do it, and not act like a recalcitrant child."

Jonathan gazed at her and the look in her eyes was both exasperated and bewildered. She truly believed that it made no difference. Well, if he were to disrobe, she'd see some definite differences, and despite her air of competence, she must be an innocent if she could not understand his reluctance.

He sighed. On the other hand, he did wish to be cured. He cleared his throat. "Let us compromise: you turn your back and I shall disrobe and get into the tub."

With a shrug, she turned away from him. Quickly, he took off his clothes and sank into the water. "You may turn around."

She turned and her eyes widened then became curious. Jonathan grimaced. It was obvious—she no doubt had rarely, perhaps never, seen an undressed man before. He wondered if she could really effect a cure . . . perhaps. He sighed. It was his last hope. However, if it did not help, he'd be in the same state he was before. He'd almost decided not to come after his disappointment today regarding Lady Anne. But he had oddly not been as disappointed as he thought he would be, and the thought of visiting Mistress Rowan for his treatment had made him feel more cheerful than a man should have felt whose proposal of marriage had just been turned down. A reluctant smile formed on his lips. At least he could enjoy the bath.

Water suddenly poured over his head, and he sputtered. "What the devil!"

"The herbs must be all over you to work," Rowan said primly. "Now, please sit back. Here is some tea to drink."

He gave her a grudging look, but that only made her grin, and reluctantly he sipped the tea. At first he thought he'd simply sit in the tub, soaking in the herbal remedy. But the scent of the ointment she had used before came to him, and then her hands touched his shoulders. He took in a long breath at the silken pressure of her fingers spreading the medicine across his skin. It had been so long since he had lain with a woman, but he had no taste for suffering rejections, especially after Lady Anne—no. He did not want to think about that now. It was better to think of becoming well, and it could not hurt to look at Mistress Rowan while he did.

He discovered that while it did not hurt, it was very distracting to watch her as she went to the hearth to get more hot water to pour into the tub. He closed his eyes instead, then felt the softness of her hand making circles upon his temples and down his jaw. Her fingers slipped down, and caressed the muscles of his neck and then his shoulders. She did not go farther down, but it did not prevent his imagination from having her do so. He tensed. She was a beautiful young woman and touching him when he was covered up to his waist only with warm water made the images in his mind turn erotic and his flesh turn hot. She touched him again, and he caught her hand.

"Don't."

"You are tense, Sir Jonathan. You will suffer more if I don't work out the tension."

She is an innocent, he reminded himself, and smiled wryly. He'd been in worse situations and had kept himself in rein. There was no reason he could not now. Perhaps he could distract himself in conversation with her. He released her hand.

"That's better," she said, and began to hum a quiet melody. One of her hands rested upon the top of his head, and then he felt her fingers run through his hair and upon his scalp. His shoulders ached suddenly, and he realized it was from the sudden release of tension. He had not known his muscles had been so stiff. He sighed and closed his eyes.

Rowan watched him relax and hummed her spell of healing. It had been difficult to focus upon at first, because a sudden onslaught of childhood memories had flashed in her mind as soon as she touched him. But she took them in and consigned them to a corner of her mind for later sorting. Healing was more important now.

She smoothed her hands over his flesh, massaging gently, then more firmly. He relaxed under her ministrations even more, and sighed deeply. This was when people she healed were at their most vulnerable, when they relaxed . . . and she could not help taking a little advantage of it.

"Tell me," she said softly, "tell me what has been troubling you." She was curious about the dark sorrow that had been in his eyes when she had first opened the gate to him. She had rarely been very curious about the people she and Aldara had tended in all the years she had gone about with her. Her foster mother did not encourage it.

"I . . . it is nothing," he said, and tensed slightly. She waited until he relaxed again under her hands.

"I saw your sadness at the gate this morning . . . I thought perhaps you were not pleased to see me."

"No . . ." he sighed and relaxed further as she pressed her fingers against a hard knot on his shoulders. "No . . .

of course not. Lady Anne . . . I thought to make her my wife someday.''

A tight knot formed briefly in Rowan's stomach, and her hands stilled for a moment before she resumed massaging his neck. "And . . . and she has said she will have you," she said.

A dry laugh burst from him. "That would not have caused me to be sad," he said.

"Then she has refused you?" Rowan kept her voice serene, though elation jumped in her heart thinking that he would not be married. The thought that Jonathan would cease visiting her because of it was . . . unpleasant. She wished he could visit her for much longer than the time it took to heal him, and she realized she wanted to see him more than once a week.

He let out a long, shuddering breath. "I should have guessed it," he said, and his voice turned rueful. "I'm not pleasant to look at, and she has suitors better than I."

"Did you love her?" Her stomach tightened again.

"I . . . I became fond . . . I respect and admire her, of course . . ." His voice slowed, sounding drowsy.

So, he was not sure. Perhaps he was in love with her. Rowan found she had stopped rubbing his shoulders, and that her fingers had tightened on his flesh. She dipped her fingers in the pot of ointment and began rubbing again. She thought of how he must have been disappointed and hurt, and her lips thinned in a frown.

"She is a fool." The words slipped out from her with a vehement edge. Rowan caught her breath, and calmed the sudden anger that surprised her. "That is—I do not know her, of course. But there are more important things than one's appearance to consider. Appearances can change." She thought of how the Fair Folk could change theirs at a whim, and knew this was true. "And I would think your character would speak more to her than your appearance. Besides, I tolerate your looks quite well. Other people should be able to, also."

"Thank you." Jonathan's voice quivered, not drowsy any longer, and then he chuckled.

"Don't laugh at me. What I say is true."

"I am sure it is," he replied, and though his voice was quite serious, she thought perhaps he was smiling. She could not help smiling herself, thinking of it, and then turned her attention to the healing.

She could see he had been badly injured. Closing her eyes, she passed her fingers over the scar on his face . . . she could see in her mind a thin bright line upon his skull there, where he had broken it and where it was healing. She ran her fingers along the scar—ah, there! There was darkness deep beneath the break—a clot of blood—which caused the blindness. She would need to clear it and make the coursing of blood through the veins smooth and even. She sang a different song, a cleansing song, and behind her closed eyes *saw* the clot slowly dissolving. It would take time, but at least he would not have as much pain as he had had before, and the spells of blindness would not be so frequent.

She heard him gasp, and she said before he could take her hand again, "Do not move, and do not disturb me at what I'm doing. I am clearing away that which has caused your blindness."

His muscles tensed under her hands. "Can you?" he asked.

"Haven't I said so?" she replied irritably. "You are so full of questions and doubts. I will do what I said I will do. I even give my pledge that I will. There! You must know that the Fair Folk always carry out what they pledge."

"I know nothing of the sort," he said, but his voice sounded amused.

"Well, it is true." Her irritation grew.

"They have been known to use trickery, I believe—and I can tell by the dimming of the sunlight and the wind coming through the door that you are irritated at me."

"Why shouldn't I be? You accuse me of incompetence

and trickery, and then you laugh at me.'' But even as she spoke, her irritation grew smaller. She could hear the lightness in his voice, and she was sure he was smiling, though she could not see his face. Even now, she was pleased that she had made him smile, though at her own expense.

''I? When have I laughed at you?''

She moved around the tub to face him, and took his chin between her thumb and finger, staring into his eyes, as Aldara had often done to her. ''You laughed at me earlier for saying I liked the way you look, and you are laughing at me now—I can hear it in your voice.'' But he was not intimidated at all and grinned at her instead.

''No, I didn't laugh at you for saying you liked the way I look.'' His blue eyes danced now, clearly amused.

''How can you say that? I heard you!''

''I laughed because you said you could *tolerate* the way I look.''

Rowan released his chin and looked away, feeling a heat rise in her cheeks. ''Yes, that was what I meant.'' She moved away from him, but he caught her arm, his hand dripping water on the floor.

''Is that true, Mistress Rowan?''

''Is what true?''

She could have made him release her, could have blasted him where he sat for demanding an answer from her. But though his voice was still light, there was a hesitant wistfulness underneath, and the sound of it made her swallow a lump in her throat.

''Is it true that you like the way I look?''

She closed her eyes for a moment, feeling the heat rush to her cheeks. Then she took a deep breath and said, ''I won't answer that. It will do nothing but feed your vanity.''

''But I am not vain at all,'' he said. ''Haven't I been mourning my lack of looks for the past few minutes?'' He put on a sad, wistful look, but his eyes were still laughing.

''Mourning the loss of your looks *is* vain,'' she said

severely, and turned to the hearth to warm the tub with more hot water.

"Most certainly, Mistress Rowan!" he exclaimed, eyeing the steaming kettle warily as she came toward him.

She stared at him a moment, then caught the gleam in his eyes, and burst out laughing.

"You are a horrible man for teasing me! I don't know why I bother with you."

"For my fair face, of course," he said, and gazed innocently at her.

She laughed again and shook her head, turning to go back behind him to resume her massage, but he caught her hand again before she could.

"No," he said, "I am unjust. It's because of the kindness of your heart, and I am grateful." He drew her hand to his lips and kissed it.

For one moment, her heart beat fast as she gazed at him, for the gentle touch of his hand and the kiss he pressed upon her skin was not merely courteous this time, but warm and caressing. No, he was not handsome, certainly not like the Fair Folk, she thought, and she should not wish that he would kiss her hand again. But she gazed at how his dark hair, released from the queue he normally kept it in, dried in the heat of the hearth and waved and curled about his shoulders and face. It was unruly and unlike the sleek straight locks or the bright riotous curls that danced about the faces of the faeries. His face was not well put together with its straight harsh planes of cheekbone and jaw and hawklike nose but with lips that looked soft and inclined to laugh. He should have had black eyes to go with the black hair, but they were blue eyes—warm blue with flecks of green, like summer skies and the budding leaves of trees. He had the scar, of course, from temple to mouth on one side of his face, but it was already becoming pale and not red anymore, and it was no more than a slight annoyance upon something that was . . . not handsome, not beautiful. Or perhaps beautiful in its own way, in the way tall cragged mountains and stark rocky earth were beautiful, instead of the air and dew and moonlight beauty of the Fair Folk. It made her wish he would kiss her.

One of his hands still held hers, but with the other he took the towel from the back of the chair near the tub and shook it out. With a last kiss upon the back of her hand, he released her.

"Do you think perhaps I have soaked up enough of the herbs?"

She continued to stare at him, then took in a deep breath and glanced away. "Yes . . . yes, of course. I—I will turn my back, and you may dry yourself and put on your clothes."

Turning away, she let out her breath again, and listened to the splash and drip of water as he rose from the tub, the light shush-shush of the towel rubbing the wet from his body. She wanted, suddenly, to turn around and look at him, to see how different he was from her, if the rest of him was as harsh-planed as his face. But she had said she would not, and he would be displeased if she looked upon him . . . and she cared whether he would be displeased or not.

"You may turn around now."

He was dressed, though his shirt was undone still, and she could still see dark hair upon his chest, curling hair, now that it was dry. She gazed up at him, and he smiled and stepped toward her.

"I feel much better now. Is this all, or am I to come back again?" he asked.

A sudden fear clutched her heart. "Oh, no! You must come back—that is, the treatment is not done yet. Perhaps a few more weeks."

"I am glad," he said, and instead of bowing over her hand as he usually did when he left, he raised her hand to his lips, causing her to step closer. Again she stared at him, and the warmth in his eyes made her tentatively touch his cheek with her fingers.

"I am glad, also," she said. "Because then—because then you will become better."

"But when that happens, will I have a reason to return?" His eyes held a question, and he still held her hand, tighter now.

A twisting of her stomach, a hard lump in her throat, and a prickling in her eyes made her incapable of doing anything but saying "Please" and clutching the cloth of his shirt. She felt something strange—a wetness coursing down one cheek—something she had not experienced in all her life that she could remember.

His hand came up to her face, and his thumb wiped her cheek. "Don't cry, Rowan," he said, and kissed her gently.

She moved her arms up around his neck so she could be closer to him and in return he pulled her to him, against his chest so that her breasts pressed hard against him. She remembered then that she had wept before, long ago when she was a child, when she had first left . . . her mother and her father. Overwhelming loss and grief swept over her, and she drew in a long, shuddering breath. She tightened her hold upon him, wanting the comfort of his solid presence against the ghosts of old memories.

His lips feathered over her lips, then his mouth came down firmly over her mouth so that she opened it and his kiss deepened. Tiny shivers flowed over her as if she were in a fever, and a heat rose up from her belly. She moaned and ran her fingers over his cheek and jaw and up through his hair that flowed over the backs of her hands.

"You taste sweet, like honey," he whispered against her lips, and kissed her again, more fiercely, and she felt the touch of his hand upon her breast, then upon her hip, pressing her hard against him. The heat within her grew into a flame, a growing ache deep in her womb, making her move upon him and moan.

"God, Rowan. Have you ensorcelled me? Your songs,

your touch . . ." He kissed her cheek, her jaw, and the soft spot under her chin. "I have even dreamed of you. . . ."

"No," she gasped as his lips went lower, between her breasts. "No, I sang only healing songs."

He parted from her, taking her face between his hands, and looked deeply into her eyes. "Tell me. The song you sang that I followed when I first came here. Was that an ensorcellment?"

It was he who ensorcelled, thought Rowan, for she could not look away from him and felt compelled to tell him whatever he wished. "No. It was a calling," she whispered. "A stupid thing. I thought it would be amusing to try a song to call true love to me—I did not think it would work."

"Did it make me love you?"

"No!" she cried, pulling away from him. "We cannot compel love, only create lust at most, and even that is difficult."

He gave a short, halting laugh, and she saw that the sadness in his eyes was gone now, replaced by something tender, warm, and so deeply intense that it made her catch her breath. "It is much more than that I feel for you, Rowan," he said gently and kissed her again.

She felt like a flower opening to the sun, and she almost wept again feeling it, for though she had known and taken pleasure in each season when she ventured as far as she could past the garden walls, it seemed she had lived in winter all her life. She kissed him in return, as fiercely as he had before, and pushed her hand beneath his shirt, wanting badly to feel him, to see what was like and unlike between them. He groaned and moved against her, and they bumped against the tub, splashing water. They laughed breathlessly, and gazed at each other.

"I want to love you, Rowan," Jonathan said, kissing her again.

"Yes," she said. "Yes." She closed her eyes at the almost painful opening of her heart, and knew she loved him.

She did not want to wed a faery lord, did not want to bed anyone but Jonathan. He was mortal, and the thought of losing him was like the thought of losing that last mortal part of her—frightening, like the darkness of winter, like death. She had never said so to Aldara, but it was the root of her rebellion, that fear that she would lose everything that she truly was. No, she could not let herself lose it. Just as she had bound her name to herself, she would bind that mortal part of herself to her spirit and never lose it.

Taking his hand in hers, she pulled him upstairs to her room, and they tumbled upon the featherbed, kissing, hands searching and tugging at each other's clothes. Rowan rose from the pillows, kneeling over him, and Jonathan pulled down one shoulder of her dress and unlaced her bodice, kissing the skin he exposed from shoulder to breast, then tugged her skirts down over her hips. She dragged away his shirt with trembling hands, then touched his chest, soft with light curling hair, and hard with muscles underneath the smooth skin. She followed the line of hair from chest to belly and he gasped and seized her hand.

"Not yet," he said, and rolled her down to the bed. She heard the rustle of cloth upon the floor and knew her dress had fallen from the bed, but had no time to think of anything else, for his hands were upon her now, touching and caressing her breasts and belly and thighs.

He moved upon her and the hardness she had felt earlier against her pressed against the apex of her thighs, back and forth until the fire in her grew hot and she moaned, seizing his face and bringing his mouth down to hers.

"God, Rowan," he groaned and kissed her, his tongue slipping into her mouth. She tentatively touched her tongue to his and he rocked his hips against her more quickly, making her open her thighs and curl her legs around his. "Rowan . . ." he groaned.

"Rachel," she whispered in his ear. "My real name is Rachel." She wanted him to know her real name, for she suddenly felt it was important for him to know. Rachel was who she really was—she wanted him to know it now that flesh touched flesh, now that she had the chance to know all of him.

He gave a choked laugh. "Now you tell me," he said and kissed her again.

"Say it," she said. "Say my real name."

"Rachel," he said, and kissed her lips. "Rachel." He kissed her chin. "Rachel." He kissed her throat and the place between her breasts. "Rachel," he said, and put his mouth upon the tip of her breast. He suckled upon it and caressed her hip and slipped his hand between her legs, moving his fingers in small, slow circles there.

She gasped and her hips rose against him. The fire in her womb burst suddenly, making her shudder and cry out with the heat and the light that struck her there and through her belly and breasts. But he did not stop, only shifted on top of her, and the hardness he had pressed earlier upon her moved between her legs. She closed her eyes, moaning, and pushed against him and the heat struck her again, making her shudder and forcefully clutch his hips with her legs, skin now pressed tightly to skin, binding all that was mortal to her. Instantly, pain and surprise made her open her eyes and grip his arms tightly with her hands, interrupting the pleasure. "It hurts," she whispered.

He kissed her mouth gently, and kissed the tears that trickled from the corner of her eyes. "Ah, love, I'm sorry. I wasn't sure . . . you seemed so eager." He closed his eyes tight for a moment and breathed deeply. "It will be better, I swear it."

Slowly he pushed in, and Rowan drew in her breath, anticipating more pain. But there was only a slight stretching ache and she relaxed again and shifted her body more comfortably in the featherbed, fitting herself a little closer to him. Jonathan groaned, pressing deeper, but did not move any faster. His hands pushed under her body, and suddenly he rolled over, pulling her around so that she was above him.

"Move, like this," he said, gasping, and lifting her hips and pressing down again.

Rowan looked at him, at his hair tousled around his flushed face, and her gaze traveled down his chest and the line of dark hair that led to where they joined. She wet her lips and tentatively moved as he had shown her. It did not hurt now, not at all, and his groan and tightened grasp on her hips gave her a triumphant joy that she could give him pleasure as he had given her. She closed her eyes and shifted upward, then down. His hands trembled upon her skin as they slid from her hips and upward to her breasts, lingering there until the bright tension she felt earlier began again. She felt his hands rise behind her neck and then fingers plucked at the pins in her hair and her hair fell down.

Her hair fell like a river down the peaks of her breasts and swirled over her hips rising and settling upon him. Jonathan had dreamed of this, of her hair cascading down over her and over his body. But he had banned it from his mind during the time he had hoped for Lady Anne. Night had brought the dream upon him again and again, and perhaps it was that which made Lady Anne's refusal of his proposal much less painful than he thought it would be. He'd dreamed of the golden strands of Rowan's— Rachel's—hair twined around his fingers and arms, sliding against his skin like silken water, binding him to her, soul to soul.

Now, now it was real and not a dream, for her hair flowed around him and between them like molten gold. A fire burned in his body and mind as he watched Rachel moving as she pleased upon him, her eyes closed, her mouth half open and panting. Her hair shimmered in the sun that poured through the window of the room, and shifted around him, caressing like feathers upon his flesh. The scent of honey came to him; he had tasted honey when he kissed her, as if she had been made of it. She trembled and her movements became uncontrolled; he pulled her down to him and kissed her lips and rolled her beneath him. He tasted the honey again, and pushed his hands through strands of sun-gold hair, pushing himself deep inside her until the sweetness and heat burst through him, and he groaned, deep, sinking deep, kissing the low singing moans from her mouth, breathing her breath like his own breath.

Jonathan could feel her still trembling beneath him, her quick breath slowing, matching the tremor in his own body and his long deep sigh. He began to move from her, but she made a protesting sound, so he only pulled her to him, shifting them both on their sides. He gazed at her then kissed her eyes and lips again gently, touching her face hesitantly. He had thought to wed a suitable wife— one who could bear his looks. He had never thought he would love as he loved now, that someone like Rachel would wish to lie with him, she who knew little of him. It was not something he understood, but he was grateful for her trust in him. He kissed her again, and gathered her to him in his arms.

Rowan sighed and pressed herself close to him. She was Rachel now, for in the bursting heat of their joining she had bound the mortal part of herself firmly to her spirit. She sighed again and shifted next to him, wanting to feel her skin move upon his for the sheer sensation of it. This was mortal flesh, this was part of who she was. She did not think she would ever tire of it. Jonathan kissed her again, gently now, upon her eyes and cheek and lips.

"You are beautiful, love, so beautiful," he murmured, and gazed at her and touched her face with his fingers as if he could not quite believe she was real.

She smiled. "You are, also."

He laughed, and she could feel the laughter rumble through his chest. "You cannot have seen many men if you think that."

Rachel watched her fingers run across his brow, down his nose, and along the scar upon his face. "Yes, I have—

faery men—and they are all more beautiful than you. And yet," she said wonderingly. "And yet, I would not have any of them, only you. Do you think . . ." She hesitated and gnawed her lip. "Do you think it is because I love you? The Fair Folk don't talk of love much, so I don't know if it is because I love you that you look beautiful."

He laughed and kissed her. "Only you can know that, sweet one. And when you decide, then you can tell me whether you will marry me or not, because I do wish to marry you and have you with me forever. But I—I would love you and want to marry you whatever you looked like."

A speculative look came into her eyes. "Really?" she asked. "What if I looked like this?" She made herself have black hair and a longer nose and made her shape more voluptuous than it normally was.

He gasped and grasped her shoulders, staring at her. "What the devil?"

She laughed. "Or this?" Red hair now, and thin as a stick. "I told you I am almost all faery. We can shape-change, you know."

"How do I know which one is really you?" he asked, his voice distrustful.

"Kiss me. Then you will know."

Jonathan closed his eyes and brought his lips to the red-haired woman's thin lips and after a moment felt, not what he had seen, but Rachel's full lips. He put his hand to her face and touched not bony nose or hard chin but Rachel's soft skin instead. He opened his eyes, rolled over onto his back, and began to laugh.

"What is so funny?"

"I was thinking some days ago that no woman would want me. But now I've just been in bed with a black-haired witch, a gawky red-haired girl, and a golden goddess." He turned to her again, grinning. "I definitely think you should marry me," he said. "I would be the envy of all the men in England."

Rachel looked at him suspiciously. "I think I should not

be entirely flattered by your proposal. Why do you say that?"

His grin widened. "Because then I shall be the only man in England who has got himself a harem all in one woman."

She sat up indignantly. "If that is what you think, then I shall change myself into an old hag," she said and did just that.

Jonathan laughed and pulled her down. "And I shall love you anyway," he said, and kissed her again. Her lips felt dry and leathery at first, an old peasant woman's lips, but he touched her breast and kissed her more firmly. Her breast suddenly filled his hand and her lips became soft and smooth as they opened beneath his, and she was Rachel once again.

Again they loved and for a while they slept until the lowering of the sun in the sky struck Jonathan's eyelids and woke him. He kissed her awake, and her response almost made him plunge himself into her again, but he pulled away.

He pushed aside the hair that had fallen over her face, incredulous that someone like Rachel should care for him. She was beautiful, and had not looked upon him with revulsion even the first day she had seen him, had said she had liked the way he looked, and had even brought him into her bed with eagerness.

"Do you love me, Rachel?" he asked. He could not help asking it; it seemed impossible, even now.

She rose up and kissed him. "Yes," she said. "Yes." She smiled at him. "You are my true love; I did not want to think it at first, because you are a mortal. But when I sang my true love to me, you came here. What's mortal in you called to that part in me, and you intrigued me from the first." She laughed, a little sadly. "I thought I might find out all of my name, not just Rachel, when I touched you, but I haven't. But I am glad you are not just a way find it, but so much more."

He kissed her hand. "You can have my name, sweet one, until you find your own."

She nodded and looked at the setting sun, and rose from the bed. Jonathan felt a certain dissatisfaction as he rose also and put on his clothes. She said she loved him, but she had given him no outright answer to his marriage proposal. But she did love him—she had said so, and it was in her eyes when she looked at him, and in her kiss.

It could be he had gone about asking her in the wrong way—he didn't know the ways of the faery except in the stories his nurse had told him when he was a boy. He cleared his throat.

"Is there someone I should ask for your hand in marriage, Rachel?"

She stopped in the middle of her dressing and turned to him, her eyes frightened. "No—don't!"

"Do you not wish to marry me?" he asked, then wished he hadn't said it, for he anticipated pain in her answer. She might even regret that she had lain with him. A flicker of anger began to burn in him. Perhaps she intended to wed the faery lord she had spoken of, after all.

A smile lighted her face, so full of love that she glowed with it—literally, for it seemed the room was filled with sunlight though the sun was clearly setting—and his anger faded with the warmth of it. "Of course I wish to marry you," she said. "It is just that I cannot leave here. At least, I haven't found out how to leave . . . I had no real reason to do so until now."

"I don't understand. I can come here easily with the key you gave me. Can you not do the same for yourself?"

Rachel pulled on the rest of her clothes, frowning in thought. "I have left when Mother Aldara goes with me, but I have not seen her cast a spell or do anything when we did. I have tried to go outside, and I can step twenty paces and back from the walls of this garden. But beyond that . . ." She sighed. "Beyond that, I find myself back at the garden door, no matter how many paces I have gone."

She gave a last tug to the laces of her bodice and tied them. "The place is ensorcelled—or I am."

"Perhaps you only need someone to lead you out," Jonathan said. He hoped it was so; he wished her to come home with him, now, and they would wed immediately. His hope was clearly reflected in her face, but there was doubt and fear also.

"I . . . I don't know," she said.

He grasped her hand. "Come," he said. "Let's try."

She gazed at him, then laughed, and there was eagerness in her eyes and voice. "Yes," she said. "Yes!"

They ran like children to the door of the garden, and Rachel fumbled with the latch then pushed the door forcefully open. She stopped. "There is no path," she said, "but perhaps we can make our way out in spite of it."

Jonathan stared at her. The path was clearly before them. "But there is a path, right in front of us," he said. "Perhaps you don't see it because you haven't a key like I do." He took it out of his pocket and pressed it into her hand. The path faded from his sight when she took it, but she shook her head.

"No, I still don't see it." She gave the ribbon-bound twig into his hand, and the path appeared before him again. "You will have to lead me."

He took her hand in his, lacing his fingers with hers, and she smiled at him. They went forward.

The path seemed to go on longer than it had when he came there earlier, but he walked on, pulling Rachel behind him. From time to time, she raised her hand in front of her face, as if warding off branches and tall bushes—she was under an illusion, he realized, as he would have been without the key in his hand.

A sharp twist in the path made him pause. He didn't remember this turn before; though the path had curved this way and that a little, it been fairly straight.

"Is there something wrong?" Rachel asked. She looked

about her, unseeing, as if she were blind to what he encountered.

"The path isn't going as I remembered," he replied. "Let us go back a little and see if we have somehow gone down another path." Rachel bit her lip, then nodded.

They retraced their steps, but Jonathan saw no other path than the one they were on. There was no choice but to keep going.

The path twisted and turned wildly, and then Jonathan saw a clearing ahead. But his sigh of relief halted in mid-breath as he approached it, and turned into a groan.

"It's the door to your garden again," he said.

Rachel shook her head. "It's my fault—that is, I'm the one who cannot leave here. There must be a way, though." They went into the garden again, and she took his hands in hers. "You must go—it is late, and your servants will wonder where you are. We can do nothing about my leaving here for now." She laughed wryly. "Besides, I was so eager, I forgot to pack my belongings."

"You need not pack anything, love," he said, kissing her. "You may come to me in your shift and it would not matter to me."

She laughed. "How impractical you are! I would become very cold if I did that. Besides, I would like to take some of my belongings with me." She gazed at him, at his cragged face and his eyes that looked at her with such love that it made her catch her breath. Suddenly she felt a week would be too long to wait for his return. "You may come here tomorrow, too, if you wish. Mother Aldara will not be here then, either."

Taking her hand to his lips, he smiled. "I will . . . and I think even when she is here. Can't she be persuaded to let you leave here and marry me?"

"No! No, you do not know what you will be facing." She clutched his hand tightly, as tightly as fear clutched her heart. "She is ancient and powerful, Jonathan, and knows more than I. This is not what she wishes for me—

she wished me to wed a faery lord, not a mortal. If she should hear of this, I would never leave here, and the Goddess help us, I do not know what she will do to you—turn you mad, perhaps, or curse you. That is wholly within her power.''

"Is there nothing you can do, then?''

"I . . . I can, perhaps, put a protective ward upon you.'' She sighed. "At least I can do that. Wait here, please.''

She went into the cottage and returned with a small clay pot. Dipping her finger into it, she touched his forehead with a slick ointment that smelled of honey. Closing her eyes, she began to hum, and then sang a song in a strange language. For a moment the air about him shimmered and shifted, growing warm as the light in the garden brightened to the brightness of noon, though the sun had nearly set.

And then as the light dimmed, he felt the cool afternoon breeze of spring, and heard Rachel's long sigh.

"There,'' she said. "You are protected as much as I can protect you. I hope it will be enough.''

"I hope so,'' he said, and kissed her again, lingeringly. After a moment, he sighed and moved away. Rachel opened the door of the garden, and with one last quick kiss, he left and she closed the door behind him.

Chapter Three

Jonathan returned the next day, and again Rachel applied her healing arts; again they kissed and loved and ate of bread and cheese and loved again. Whispered stories spoken into each other's ears nested into their hearts as they lay in bed; they told of their lives and each heard the loneliness and longing underneath the other's words. Jonathan had friends, true; but he had no family, and had come into his inheritance very young, for his parents had died when he was a boy. In a way, Rachel thought, he was like herself, having parents taken away when she was but a child. She, in turn, told him all that she remembered of hers, and her upbringing under Aldara's care.

Then, all too soon, he had to leave. Five days would pass before he returned. Rachel, meanwhile, could not help thinking of him all the while he was gone, how he looked and how she loved him so that her heart ached with an emptiness more profound for the new knowledge that it had been empty for much of her life until now.

Rachel searched desperately through her mind for a way to leave the garden and be with him soon, before she turned one-and-twenty, before a faery lord would be chosen for her. But spring turned to summer, and then to autumn, and still she found nothing. The only remaining way was to search beyond herself, beyond her own knowledge; though Mother Aldara would come in the next two days, Rachel dared not ask her. Even so, there was only a slight chance she'd find an answer at the door of dream-time; she'd tried once, before she met Jonathan, to find a way out of the garden, and had found only whispers of light and shadow. Sighing, she took a chair and went out into the garden and the sunlight, unloosing her hair from her braids with one hand as she walked.

She closed her eyes, feeling the sun upon her face, combing its power into her hair, feeling it seep into her flesh. The power came quickly, so quickly that she almost gasped and lost the trance she was beginning to enter. She never remembered it flowing so quickly, and it almost took her unawares—a dangerous thing. But she drew in a long, slow breath and let it out again, and the power slowed to a manageable flow, steady and strong, stronger than it ever had before. It disturbed her, however . . . the texture of the power was different. It made her think of the budding and branching of trees and the scent of newly turned earth, of ancient mountains worn with wind and rain, instead of the air and mist and light she was used to.

The luxury of studying it was not hers, however. She turned her mind toward the door of dream-time, the source of all things now real and would be real someday. She flew to it instead of drifting, and the shadows and bright sparks of lives and stories long told and not yet told were there at the door of dream time, as it was before. But this time they reached out to her and called her name— "Rachel, Rachel," now in Jonathan's voice, now in her birth mother's voice.

"The answer!" she cried to them. "Tell me the answer, what keeps me in my garden!"

The shadows and the sparks that swirled in the misty

door before her stilled for a moment, and the whispering that came from it stopped. She almost turned from it, thinking she would get no answer this time either. But then a warm chuckle floated toward her, and a womanly voice said, "Come here, child."

Rachel hesitated. She had never gone past the door of dream-time. Aldara, who had shown her how to come here and summon spells and answers from it, had never stepped into it; Rachel had once asked her about it, and the faery woman had only shaken her head and looked grave, refusing to speak.

"Do you have the answer?" she asked.

"Come here, and I will tell you," the voice said again. "You cannot learn while you are out there."

Rachel frowned. "How do I know you will not trap me there?"

"You do not, of course. But your power is different now . . . nothing will keep you here against your will."

"Will I find the answer in there?"

"Yes, of course." The voice laughed warmly again.

What did she have to lose? If she did nothing, she would stay in her garden, and Aldara would find out what she had done, and she was sure her punishment would be severe. Aldara had so much more power than she, for Aldara was all faery, after all, with no taint of mortal in her. Rachel breathed in and out slowly, then stepped through the door of dream-time.

The sparks and shadows danced around her, and for a moment she could not see anything else. She felt a great power here, and it joined with the power that flowed through her already, deep, earth-deep. She felt almost as if she had grown roots that sank themselves into the core of the world. Taking another breath, Rachel moved forward.

And fell into sightless dark.

For one moment fear seized her and she froze. But the dark was warm and she felt a soothing presence around her. The sound of rustling leaves and the scent of spring breezes made her turn, but she could still see nothing.

"There, now, child. Was that so difficult?"

Rachel shook her head slowly. There was something familiar about the voice and the presence, but not familiar. Power emanated from all around her, but it was different from that of the Fair Folk, for it seemed to draw from the very earth itself.

"So many questions you have!" The womanly voice chuckled. "I will tell you who I am, at least, and then you may ask me the question that you wish to know now—the others can wait for another time." There was a pause as Rachel felt a comfortable *settling* around her, like a hen covering her nested chicks with her wings.

"I am she under whose sign you were born," the voice said, "And whose blessing you have requested from time to time."

Rachel trembled, fear and awe clutching her heart. Aldara had never told her that the Old Ones spoke to anyone anymore. Who was she, Rachel, to be spoken to by the Great Mother?

"Come, now, you need not be frightened," the voice said comfortingly. "You have chosen to balance the elements within you, and very little can harm you unless you believe otherwise. Now, ask your question."

It was true, Rachel did have a million questions rising behind her lips, and the voice's words only brought more questions to her mind. But she closed her eyes and felt the power coming from all around her, and knew that it would be here should she ever wish to return. She drew in a breath then released it.

"My Lady, how may I leave the garden I have lived in for so long? I have tried, and have failed again and again."

The Lady's voice chuckled. "I will give you an answer that will infuriate you, you know. Such is the nature of oracles, yes?" She laughed and it flowed over Rachel like warm water. "The answer is all about you, of course; it surrounds you and it has flowed through your fingers, the fingers of the mother who birthed you, your foster mother, and those of your lover. All have twined their hopes and dreams into it . . . and now you cannot leave because of it. You must decide if you would rid yourself of it or not." The voice seemed to come a little closer, and sounded a little lower, almost as if confiding something. "It isn't as necessary to you as you think," it said. "There now. You may go . . . and I think I will also tell you one more thing, though you have not asked it."

Rachel had halted in midstep away from the voice, but turned back. "Yes?" she asked.

"You are with child, my dear . . . but I think you already know this."

Rachel's hand moved over her belly, a protective gesture. She swallowed the dread that rose in her throat. She had taken no precautions; she had not thought to do it, for children came so seldom to the Fair Folk that they did not bother with remedies to prevent a babe from forming in a mother's womb. Closing her eyes, she *looked* within, beneath her hand upon her belly. "Two, I believe," Rachel said wryly as she opened her eyes again. "Mother Aldara will not be pleased, should she find out."

"Yes," the Lady said, then the voice became grave. "They will be quite safe, however, so you need not worry about them."

Rachel nodded wordlessly. "I need to leave," she said at last. "Quickly."

The presence grew warmer, washing over her like a benediction. "Go then, child. What comes will not be easy, and you will need your wits and your strength about you—you are stronger than you know."

Rachel curtsied deeply. "I thank you, My Lady," she said, and turned away. She did not know where the door of dream-time was, but suddenly the darkness faded, and she was again in her garden, singing a lullabye. She smiled then shook her head, thinking of the Mother's words. The answer was around her, and all who cared for her had twined their hopes and dreams into it—but it made no sense. Rachel pressed her lips together. She would find the sense in it, and find the way out of the garden so she and Jonathan could wed.

"There is something different about you," Aldara said, the day before Jonathan was to return, and during Rachel's magic lessons. She frowned at Rachel and looked her up and down.

Rachel shrugged, pressing down the fear that crept into her. "How different? Perhaps stronger, a little, than I have been before. But you have taught me well, and it is coming close to the time I will be fully faery, isn't it?"

Aldara's eyes narrowed into slits as she stared at her foster daughter. "Yes, stronger. Much stronger. And yet, you have not lost that mortal taint. If anything, it is lodged even more firmly within you."

Rachel made herself frown as if puzzled. "I don't know why that should be so. Isn't it enough that my power has become stronger? That is all due to you, I am sure. Where else could it have come?" Rachel's fear grew. She *had* grown stronger, so much so that she had deliberately tamped down the force of her magic when practicing with Aldara. But it was obviously not enough; her foster mother had noticed, and was now suspicious. And it was true— Rachel had bound that last bit of humanity to her, and all her subtle wards had not kept Aldara from noticing it.

There was a brief silence, then Aldara gave her a sidewise glance before cupping her hands before her. A glow formed above her hands. It grew brighter, then crackled with force. It was a thing that could kill. Without warning, she threw it at Rachel.

Instinctively Rachel raised her hand in defense, splaying her fingers as if to catch the white-hot ball. Warm darkness and thunder rolled through her body, then lightning seared the air. Mist touched her face . . . and then it was gone.

There was no sound. No breeze ran through the leaves of the trees in the garden, no birds sang, no bees buzzed among the flowers. Rachel looked at Aldara's face, pale and full of grief and anger. The attack had been a test. The faery woman's shape shifted, becoming sharp and angled, and the air around her became heavy.

"Who is it?" she hissed. "What man came here?"

Rachel raised her chin, though she shook inside. "I don't know what you mean." She stepped backward from Aldara, but the faery woman seized her chin and her hand.

"This!" she cried, and pulled up Rachel's chin. "This blemish you had as a child—it has returned!" She released it with a jerk. "And this!"

She held Rachel's hand at the wrist—the hand that Rachel had placed unthinkingly, protectively, upon her belly when Aldara had attacked her. Aldara stared hard into her eyes.

"Whose child is it?"

Rachel merely stared wordlessly at Aldara. She could not tell her—she could not put Jonathan in danger.

"Is it Galen's?" Aldara's eyes narrowed speculatively. "I have heard he has been sniffing around here. It might not be a loss, if it were. His child and yours would only have perhaps a trace of mortal. Then I could start anew with it, and the change to faery would be quicker than it has been with you."

Claiming she had taken the Love Talker's seed would delay things a little, thought Rachel, perhaps until she found a way to leave the garden or at least warn Jonathan. But Aldara would not believe it if she outright said she knew Galen. She deliberately shifted her eyes away from Aldara's then said, "Galen? Who is Galen?"

Again, Aldara took her chin in her hands and stared hard into her eyes. "Do not lie to me! I can see you know very well who he is," she snapped.

"He—he has not been here this age," Rachel said, letting the trembling she felt come out into her voice. Great Mother, protect him, she prayed, and do not let him come to harm despite what I do now, for he had been a friend, though only briefly.

"So, he *has* been here." Aldara let out a sharp laugh. "And has been after you like the rutting boar he is." She gazed at Rachel suspiciously. "And yet, he is under a curse—how is it that you were able to touch him?"

Rachel stared back at her foster mother. "I am almost faery, and you yourself said I am stronger than ever. Perhaps I ended the curse."

Aldara released her and stepped back, her form returning to her usual shapeliness. She smiled cynically. "I suppose if you had to defy me, it was just as well you did it with a man of the Fair Folk." She laughed again, this time with more humor. "And he is a persuasive one, is he not? I can hardly blame you. I myself have desired him more than once, though he had the bad taste to desire mortal women more than faery ones. No doubt that was what brought him to you, that taint, and coupling with you must have ended the curse upon him in some way." She shrugged. "We could make him wed you, perhaps. Or if not him, then another. At least I know for certain now that you are a good breeder."

Rachel clenched her teeth and closed her eyes in humiliation, anger, and grief. She had thought her foster mother had cared for her, even loved her . . . but now she spoke as if Rachel were no more than a beast of the field, to be futtered and bred like a cow. Rachel had defied her, true, and she had expected some punishment. But she had thought Aldara would care for her still, like the mother she had replaced. Had she not healed the skinned knees and tenderly twined the magic into her hair as she braided it? The thought of being tied to some stranger, even Galen, when she loved Jonathan made her feel ill. But she swallowed down these feelings and stared into Aldara's eyes.

"Whatever you will, foster mother. I do not care." She shrugged. "Shall we continue my lessons?"

Aldara gazed at her assessingly. "No . . . no, I think that is enough for now." She turned toward the garden door, then paused and stared at her narrowly before she opened it. "I think I will find you a mate sooner than I had planned. Perhaps that will keep you from straying from Faerie." She left, closing the door firmly.

The trembling that Rachel had held at bay took hold of her at last, and shook her so that she fell to her knees. "Ah, Goddess. What am I to do?" She covered her face with shaking hands. "You said I had the answer—but I can't see it! I can't see it!" She knew from Aldara's last considering look that the faery woman would stay near the garden, to watch and see who came.

A whisper of enfolding warmth came to her mind: *You are stronger than you know. Rest now, then think.*

Rachel rose slowly. Tomorrow Jonathan would come; it was dangerous, for Aldara would come to the garden before a week was through, perhaps even tomorrow, and there was no way to warn him. She hoped she would be able to turn him away before Aldara saw him—and hoped with all her heart that she would find out the secret to leaving this place.

Jonathan had dreamed of Rachel every night he was away from her, and his nights were full of her smile, her face, her body. But she seemed to change slightly as the days went by; a look of worry came into the face he saw at night, a tension to the atmosphere of his dreams. He wondered if she was in trouble, and almost dismissed the thought for it arose only from his dreams. Only dreams— only Faerie! No, he couldn't dismiss such things any longer. He was more in health than he ever had been after his accident, and he remembered clearly the magic Rachel worked. He rose from his bed, rang for his valet, and quickly dressed.

There was, perhaps, nothing he could do, for he knew nothing of magic. But at the very least, he could talk to her, and perhaps they could find some solution together. Even if they did not find an answer right away, he could try to comfort her. And if that didn't work, he'd face the faery woman who kept her imprisoned. He could tell from Rachel's expression that she thought it dangerous, but in truth, he'd prefer to face Aldara and honestly claim Rachel for his own.

He rode swiftly to where the road and cottage path met, and hesitated before going upon it. He'd ridden up to it before, but this time felt perhaps he should not. He dismounted, and led his horse to the gate and tied it to the post next to it.

This time he didn't knock, but pushed upon the door. It opened easily—did Rachel ever latch it? He couldn't remember. Slowly he opened the door and looked about him. Rachel was not in the garden, but she would not be, not if she didn't hear him knock. He turned toward the cottage.

"Boo!"

He jumped and turned around, then laughed. "Little witch! I'm going to exact payment for that." He pulled her from behind the door and into his arms. He looked down at her smiling mischievously, bent down his head, and kissed her.

"Jonathan!"

He stiffened. It was Rachel's voice, but it did not come from the woman in his arms but behind him toward the cottage. The woman's shape shifted and changed, and quickly he pushed her away. This was not Rachel, but a red-haired woman who stared at him with glittering green eyes in a pale, cold face. He turned toward the cottage and there was Rachel, her face white with fear.

"*Ssssooo,*" hissed the red-haired woman. "This is your

lover, Rowan." Her shape shifted again, and she seemed to become all angles and sharp teeth, beautiful and terrifying. The air rumbled with subtle thunder, the sun dimmed to twilight.

"Jonathan, get away, quickly! Go, leave now!"

He glanced at Rachel, her face clearly frightened. She had said Aldara was powerful, more powerful than Rachel . . . and it was clear Rachel could be hurt. He did not know if he could prevent it, but he could not leave her, either. He ran to her, taking her into his arms.

"Ah, Goddess, you are a fool, Jonathan!" she cried, clinging to him for one moment before thrusting him away. "Why did you not go? You are in danger here!"

"So are you, love—and I could not leave you to face it alone."

Her face was full of despair and love for him, but she shook her head. "It is too late now."

"Jonathan," the woman said. "Sir Jonathan Bradford, I assume?" The air about her grumbled, and a sickly light glowed around her.

He nodded once, curtly.

"A mortal." She turned to Rachel. "You could not even choose a man of the Fair Folk—you had to couple with a mortal, and breed brats from him."

Jonathan stared at Rachel. A child—no, children—she bore his children. Hope for the future died as fear for Rachel seized him. He must do something, think of something to save her.

Aldara's face grew hard and she lifted her hand, clawlike, in the air.

Quickly, Rachel stretched out her arms and the air shimmered with silver light and lightning flashed against it, blinding bright. Again and again it flashed, and Rachel gasped and closed her fists against the onslaught and the silver shimmering grew thick and close around them. For one moment she seemed to wilt, but Jonathan grasped her around her waist and held her firm.

"Thank you," she gasped. She opened her hands and the shimmering shield pulsed outward, still thick, and the woman took a step backward and dropped her hands. Rachel took a deep breath, and he felt her lean against him.

"There must be something I can do," he said urgently. "Can you or I not strike against her, as she has done to you?" he asked.

Rachel's lips trembled. "No. No, she is my foster mother, the mother I have known most of my life."

"She is trying to hurt you, Rachel."

She shook her head. "She is trying to keep me from leaving. Think of how I may leave here, and perhaps we might have a chance—ah!"

He held her up as she fell back from another onslaught. Jonathan cursed himself for a fool—she might be in less danger had he not come. His arrival in the garden had caused her more trouble than she deserved, she who loved him and had brought all her healing powers to bear upon his injuries. And now, now all he had done was bring this terror upon her. He looked at the furious blaze of the faery woman in front of them, and saw how her anger was mixed with a certain grief—and there was nothing that hurt more than grief. Perhaps Rachel would be punished, but it was clear the faery woman still cared for her foster daughter, both from what Rachel had told him of her life and what he saw in front of him. The Fair Folk were an alien race . . . but they could know anger and, it seemed, a measure of caring.

It would be better if he left. It made him ill to think of it, but there was nothing else he could think of. The cure was not done, and he did not know what Aldara would do to him—he might die, perhaps, and all that he had worked for on his land would be lost to some stranger. Bitterness seized him. He would lose everything—he would not see Rachel again, or even his children she bore. But it would also mean she would be safe and not be troubled. He gazed

4 BESTSELLING HISTORICAL ROMANCES BY YOUR FAVORITE AUTHORS CAN BE YOURS, FREE!

Kensington Choice brings you historical romances by your favorite bestselling authors including Janelle Taylor, Shannon Drake, Rosanne Bittner, Jo Beverley, and Georgina Gentry, just to name a few! Each book is filled with passion, adventure and the excitement of bygone times!

To introduce you to this great club which is part of Zebra Home Subscription Service, we'd like to send you your first 4 bestselling historical romances, absolutely free! And once you get these 4 free books to savor at home, we'll rush you the next 4 brand-new books at the lowest prices available, as soon as they are published.

The way the club works is that after your initial FREE shipment, you will get our 4 newest bestselling historical romances delivered to your doorstep each month at the

preferred subscriber's rate of only $4.20 per book, a savings of up to $8.16 per month (since these titles sell in bookstores for $4.99-$6.99)! All books are sent on a 10-day free examination basis and there is no minimum number of books to buy. (And no charge for shipping.) Plus as a regular

subscriber, you'll receive our FREE monthly newsletter, *Zebra/Pinnacle Romance News*, which features author profiles, subscriber benefits, book previews and more!

So start today by returning the FREE BOOK CERTIFICATE provided. We'll send you 4 FREE BOOKS with no further obligation: A FREE gift offering you hours of reading pleasure with no obligation...how can you lose?

*We have 4 FREE BOOKS for you
as your introduction to
KENSINGTON CHOICE!
To get your FREE BOOKS, worth
up to $24.96, mail the card below.*

FREE BOOK CERTIFICATE

Yes! Please send me 4 Kensington Choice (the best of Zebra and Pinnacle Books) Historical Romances without cost or obligation (worth up to $24.96). As a Kensington Choice subscriber, I will then receive 4 brand-new romances to preview each month for 10 days FREE. I can return any books I decide not to keep and owe nothing. The publisher's prices for Kensington Choice romances range from $4.99-$6.99, but as a preferred subscriber I will get these books for only $4.20 per book or $16.80 for all four titles. There is no minimum number of books to buy and I may cancel my subscription at any time, plus there is no additional charge for postage and handling. No matter what I decide to do, my first 4 books are mine to keep, absolutely FREE!

KF0198

Name _____

Address _____ Apt. _____

City _____ State _____ Zip _____

Telephone ( ) _____

Signature _____

(If under 18, parent or guardian must sign)

Subscription subject to acceptance. Terms and prices subject to change.

AFFIX
STAMP
HERE

KENSINGTON CHOICE
Zebra Home Subscription Service, Inc.
120 Brighton Road
P.O.Box 5214
Clifton, NJ 07015-5214

at Rachel, at the stubborn tilt of her chin. She was strong—
even he could feel the power now emanating from her.

He was powerless against Aldara, and he hated it, as he
had hated how his illness had made him weak. But for
Rachel and his children, he would talk with this faery
woman, and perhaps convince her that he held Rachel's
well-being above all else. He looked at Rachel and an odd
certainty seemed to rise up from the ground he stood on
to settle in his heart. It made him certain that whatever
he promised the faery woman, he would see Rachel again.
He could bear anything if he could have that.

"Stop!" he called out. He saw Aldara pause and took
heart. He swallowed. "If . . . if I promise to leave here, will
you leave Rachel alone?"

"No, Jonathan!" Rachel seized his arm. "No, I wish to
go with you," she cried desperately.

The faery woman cocked her head to one side and
looked at him skeptically. "Would you leave, and never
come back here?"

"Only if you promise that she will not be harmed or
that she will not be punished for any of our actions."

Aldara smiled, showing teeth grown sharp. "Not
enough. You have fouled my plans and have set them back
many years. I demand a price."

"Then punish me, and leave her alone. I swear I will
not come looking for her."

"No, Jonathan, you don't know what you're saying,"
Rachel cried.

He turned to her, and touched her cheek gently. "It
doesn't matter, love. You've given me something wonderful
. . . and I think you are stronger than you know." The odd
certainty that had come upon him grew stronger, and he
smiled and whispered in her ear, "And I may know more
than your foster mother thinks. Promise me that you will
seek a way out, and bring our children to my home. I will
make sure all will know they are my heirs." Rachel nodded,
though she looked confused. "Now, put a ward upon me

like you did before, or as much of one as you can. And heed my words carefully.''

Rachel stared at him, hearing his words and the words she had heard from the Mother Goddess repeated in his voice. Did the Old One speak through him, somehow? She closed her eyes and held his hand tightly, calling upon the faery magic and then the earth magic she had felt when in the Goddess's presence. It did not seem to do anything—there was no protective shimmer around him as there had been with any other warding she had ever cast. She shook her head at him, but he merely smiled at her. "It's enough."

He turned to Aldara. "I swear that I will not come looking for Rachel. And you may punish me any way you see fit—me only, for the people and the land who depend upon me are innocent.''

Aldara frowned for a moment, then nodded, and a sly smile grew on her face. "Very well."

"No, Jonathan," Rachel pleaded desperately. She clung to him, but he pushed her away, hard enough for her to stumble and fall.

In that moment of parting Aldara struck. Rachel quickly put up her hand, trying to shield Jonathan, but it was too late.

He closed his eyes and groaned, then fell to his knees.

"No! Ah, Goddess, no!" Rachel ran to him and tried to hold him up, but he slumped to the ground. He groaned and gasped as if in deep pain, twisting and rocking his body. The fading scar upon his face reddened, and when he opened his eyes again, they looked upon her, unseeing.

"Stop!" she cried, and turned to Aldara. "You will stop this, now!"

Aldara stared at her coldly. "It is too late. He has taken the punishment upon him. All you have done for him is gone. I have reversed the healing; it is as if he had never met you. Worse, for I have made his injuries twice as bad as they were before." She looked coolly at Jonathan. "He may die of it. It depends on whether he goes back to his mortal physicians again.''

She turned to Rachel. "See, Rowan, how weak and inferior they are. We do not have to suffer such things." Her voice turned persuasive. "Really, you would be better off with a faery lord. He could pleasure you ten times better than this—thing." She gestured at Jonathan contemptuously. He lay still now, still breathing fitfully, as if it hurt to take in air. "Become wholly faery, as we are, and know what it is to be truly strong." She waved her hand again at Jonathan, and the air about him wavered and shimmered. Thunder roared, and then he was gone.

Rachel closed her eyes and stood up. Hot, dark rage rose in her, making her hands clench tight into fists.

"No," she said. "No." Wind suddenly swirled around her, lifting her hair away from her face, and a low tremor built beneath her feet.

She opened her eyes and stared at her foster mother. "You are wrong." She pressed her fist against her chest. *"I* am mortal, too, and it will never leave me, because I have bound it more tightly to myself than the magic you have woven into me. *That* is stronger than any magic of air and fire, something you have not, and so in the end cannot bring forth children of your own. Have you never thought it?''

Aldara's lips twisted in disbelieving scorn. "You have been talking with someone of the High Court."

"How can I?" Rachel said. "I who have been penned here like a cow raised to breed to your liking. You say I am to be faery—but when have I been given the choice to wed whom I like, as you have?" She shook her head. "No. I think no matter if I become faery, I will be nothing but a thing to breed from, and no joy will I have of it, for I shall never willingly do it."

Aldara jerked as if struck. "Ungrateful wretch! Have I not brought you up as my own daughter? Have I not given you knowledge far beyond any mortals, plaited the magic into your hair so that you would become one of us?''

"For your own amusement," Rachel shot back. "To turn me into something *worthy* of Faerie. No more than a pet, at best." The rage grew in her, making her spit out the words. "You didn't even let me know who I really am."

"Your mortal life was irrelevant."

Rachel stared at her foster mother. Aldara would never understand—how could she? The Old One, the Mother Goddess, had hinted that Rachel had something the Fair Folk did not—and what else could it be than that part of her that was mortal?

Aldara shrugged. "Why do you bother to discuss this with me at all? You know you can never leave here, unless I wish it. And why should you? Even if you found the way to do it, you would lose your power, depend upon it."

Hopelessness almost threatened to overcome her—what was she, if she did not have her healing powers and her magic? Mortal, certainly, but how would she make her way in the world?

It is not as important as you think, whispered the Goddess's words in her mind. *The answer is all about you; it surrounds you and it has flowed through your fingers, the fingers of the mother who birthed you, your foster mother, and those of your lover. All have twined their hopes and dreams into it. You must decide if you would rid yourself of it or not.*

She was Rachel. She could love, and she could laugh and think and do as she pleased if she left here. She had that, at least, and she would find out the rest of what she could do if it took the rest of her life. That was more important than magic, more important than any power.

"I don't want the magic," she said. "And if I must, I will rid myself of it to leave here."

And then she laughed with sudden realization. Where did the magic reside but in her hair? Did not Aldara herself say that she had woven the magic into it? Rachel thought of how she herself had plaited it, how she had twined whatever magic she had found in it, and how Jonathan had twined it in his hands as he had loved her and kissed her mouth. She recalled an image of a soft hand stroking her hair, and a woman's fair face so like her own singing a lullabye.

She could be wrong, but perhaps, just perhaps she was not. Quickly she ran into the cottage.

"Where are you going?" Aldara called after her, but Rachel ignored her.

A razor hung from beside her spinning wheel—she had used it in the past to cut fleece and flax. She took the long, thick length of hair that hung down her back and wound it around and around her hand. Taking a deep breath, she raised the razor, then brought it down upon her hair.

"No!" screamed Aldara from outside the cottage.

Rachel raised the razor again and cut more hair. It fell to the floor, and she could not stop the tears that fell from her eyes as well. She could feel the magic fading from her—she had lived with it for so long.

"No!" Aldara was at the door now, but it was too late. Rachel looked at her, and dropped the last handful of hair onto the floor.

"You fool!" The grief that had been hidden underneath Aldara's anger came to the surface now. "Do you know what you have done?"

"Yes. I have got my freedom now."

"You have been like my own child ..." whispered Aldara.

"But I am not a child," Rachel said gently. "*I* must choose where I go, and how I must live." She went about the cottage and picked up a shawl and a warm cloak—it would be midwinter beyond the garden—and put on a pair of thick woolen stockings and stout boots. She packed a small bag with herbs and various simple and sovereign remedies, as Aldara watched silently.

She stepped out of the cottage and walked toward the

garden door. She could feel Aldara watching her still, could hear her following behind her.

"I will not let you leave," Aldara said flatly.

Rachel turned around in time to see her foster mother raise her hand in a spell-casting. Instinctively she raised her own hand against it, and low thunder rolled up from the earth into her body.

Bright light flashed between them . . . and then nothing. Aldara's eyes widened, and she stepped back. "You . . . there is magic in you still."

Rachel's breath halted for one moment. Magic . . . if so, it was not something she had been taught.

She could not stay. Jonathan could not seek her out, for he had promised it; but she had listened to him carefully. Nothing was said that prevented her from seeking *him*. She looked at Aldara's face, confused and bereft, and quickly ran to her and kissed her cheek.

"I know you cared for me in your own way . . . even if we see it differently. I will always remember you, and love you, too," she said, and ran out the garden door.

The path was clear now, and as Rachel ran farther and farther from the garden, the cold increased, the trees lost their leaves, and a chill wind bit into her flesh. She pulled on the cloak and the shawl, and slowed as she saw where the road and the path met ahead.

Where would she go? She searched her pocket for the pasteboard card Jonathan had given her when they first met . . . she would have to find someone to tell her where he might be. She needed to hurry; if she had magic even with her hair cut, and if the ward she had placed upon Jonathan protected him, he may not be as ill as Aldara said. But she could not be sure of that. She left the path and put her foot upon the road at last.

A cry almost burst from her—but the thousands of images and sensations choked it off. Flashes of memories, touches, scents, textures, words roared within her until she was almost blind and deaf with it. She sank down upon the road and covered her ears—

Then it stopped. She looked up at the trees and the blue skies above and drew in a slow breath.

Rachel. She was Rachel Winscombe. She had a mother and a father, and they lived in Somerset. She even had brothers and sisters.

And they had a neighbor named Bradford.

Hope rose in her heart. If she could not find Jonathan right away, perhaps she could find her family, and they could tell her. She had more choices now.

The Countess of Charlton ruffled her grandson's blond hair and tickled his neck until his giggles turned to squeals and he pushed against her. A knock sounded on the drawing room door then, and made her look up.

The butler came in, looking troubled. "My lady, there is a young woman here to see you."

"Who is she, Norton?" Lady Charlton rose, signaling her grandson's nurse to take him away after she kissed the boy soundly.

He hesitated, and his thick gray eyebrows drew together. "She . . . she says her name is Rachel . . . Winscombe, my lady."

The countess closed her eyes and placed her hand upon the back of a chair to steady herself. No. The young woman could be an impostor. There had been a few who had come to the Winscombe estate, claiming to be their long-lost daughter, but none of them had the look of Rachel, and no identifying marks. But she and Robert had always hoped, and always agreed at least to talk to them.

"Bring her in, Norton."

A few minutes passed, and the door opened again. A cloaked figure stepped lightly into the room, and Lady Charlton hid her clenched hands in her skirts. She wished her husband were here also, but he had left briefly on business.

"Lady Winscombe?" The voice was low and sweet, a young woman's voice, not a child. But of course Rachel would be a woman grown now. "Or no—I am sorry. I understand you are Lady Charlton now."

"What do you wish of me?" she asked.

A slim, delicate hand pushed away the cloak's hood, and Lady Charlton drew in a long, shuddering breath.

It was as if she were looking into a mirror and saw herself as she had been more than twenty years ago. But this young woman was far more beautiful. Her hair curled raggedly around her face as if hacked off with a knife, but it was the same color as Lady Charlton's, only more richly golden. Her face was delicately slender, her mouth curled at the corners as her own had curled before care and sorrow had made them droop. And her eyes—they were Robert's eyes.

"I . . ." The young woman gave a halting, uncertain laugh. "I don't know what to say, now that I am here. So many things . . ." She squared her shoulders and lifted her chin, a proud, arrogant gesture—Lady Charlton swallowed hard, for it was something Robert did, and many of her children did also. "I believe I am your daughter," the woman said stiffly. "I remember you, but you look different now. And . . . and I remember that Aldara—you called her Alyce—took me away in a coach with a fine lord and lady. But they weren't who they said they were. They were only Elswitha and Cardain. Aldara—Alyce—took care of me all these years. She was your midwife, and then my nurse."

"How . . . how do I know you are telling the truth? Anyone might have found this out." Lady Charlton's knees felt weak. None had known their nurse's name—it was a test that they gave to all who claimed to be their daughter.

The young woman's shoulders slumped. "I suppose you cannot know . . . and I do not have the time to confirm every aspect of my childhood with you. I can make my own way in the world." She walked toward the window and looked out. The sun glimmered upon her face and hair, and Lady Charlton drew in her breath; the girl's profile was just like Anne's, her next-to-youngest daughter. "Could you tell me one thing, my lady? I remember my family—I am sorry—you have a neighbor by the name of Bradford. Is this true?"

"Yes, Sir Jonathan Bradford. That is his estate over there you see, beyond the trees." Lady Charlton could not help herself; she would have liked to have acknowledged this girl as her daughter, and she was curious. "May I ask what your business is with him? He is ill right now, and has been this past week."

Rachel—Lady Charlton could not help thinking of her by that name—turned to her, an anxious look upon her face. "Is he very ill? Not . . . not dying?"

"No, not dying. The doctor believes him to be in remarkably good condition for the injuries he has suffered."

Rachel gave a relieved sigh. "I must go to him. You see," she blushed and hesitated. "You see, after Anne—that is, Lady Anne—refused his suit, he asked me to be his wife."

Lady Charlton raised her brows. Sir Jonathan's proposal had been quite private—the young woman could not have got that news from anyone but him.

"I . . . I hope you are not offended. We fell in love, you see," Rachel said simply.

"No. No, of course not."

Rachel curtsied. "I thank you, my lady. I must go to him quickly." She grinned suddenly. "Does Anne—Lady Anne—still get a rash from eating strawberries? I remember she vomited on me once when she ate them."

Lady Charlton gasped and abruptly sat down on a chair. No one could know that except herself, Anne, and . . . and Rachel. They had been alone in the garden, picking strawberries, and Anne had eaten too many of them. Such things could stain, and she had taken off Rachel's frock immediately to rinse under the pump. Anne had been too embarrassed to speak of it, so no one knew.

"Rachel . . . Oh, Rachel!" She covered her face with her hands and burst into tears. "We have been looking and looking for you—years and years—we could not find you—I'm so sorry!"

A soft rustling sound and a shaking hand smoothing her shoulders made her look up. Rachel's face was pale. "You know now? It's true, I am your daughter?"

Lady Charlton took Rachel's face between her hands. "Oh, how can you not be? You have your father's eyes, my mouth and face, and I would think you Anne's twin in profile. And . . . and here, the mark on your chin—oh, dear heaven. I used to call it the mark of a faery's kiss."

Rachel's hand went self-consciously to her chin. "Aldara—Alyce—called it a blemish."

Lady Charlton smiled through her tears. "Never a blemish, love, my own Rachel."

They talked and talked until the sun set, and Lady Charlton would not have believed half of it, had not Rachel shown her how she could conjure a fire in the fireplace instead of using a tinderbox, and how butterflies fluttered suddenly into being when Rachel blew embers into the air. But she noticed a restlessness in her newfound daughter, and saw her look out the window toward Sir Jonathan's estate more than a few times.

"We will call upon him tomorrow, Rachel," Lady Charlton said. "He has been ill, and has not been receiving any callers."

But Rachel did not see him the next day, or the day after that. For it seemed he had left Somerset, and had gone to London, for how long, no one knew.

A month passed, and then another, and Somerset saw an uncommonly warm winter, with heavy wet snow. There had been a great deal of activity, the neighbors heard, at Sir Jonathan Bradford's estate, but he had not yet returned. No doubt the difficult travel conditions were what delayed him so. Rachel went each day to the edge of the Winscombe estate, hoping to be the first to see him return, but had seen nothing.

She had written to him—of course he could not write back, for he had promised not to seek her out. But surely that could not extend to her parents' letters? It was not that she was unhappy now that she had found her family. She was very happy, for they had completely taken her to their hearts and she could scarcely believe the abundance of joy and love surrounding her. She met her brothers and sisters—she did not know how to behave around them at first, but had finally succumbed to their laughter and teasing. Neighbors and friends came to parties hosted by the Winscombes—she had to remember they were the Earl and Countess of Charlton now—and greeted her kindly, and she was never without a partner at a dance. She was surprised to find a mix of faery in a few of them, too, and though those such as Sir Thomas Elphinson frowned in displeasure at a chance mention of Faerie, there was a strong strain of it in him, too.

But though it did not show quite yet, the babies-to-be—she could sense it was a boy and girl—were growing inside her womb, and though she had not told anyone of her condition, it would be known soon. She knew well by now that one could not bear children outside of wedlock without bringing scandal to one's family—and she would not want to bring that on hers. And Jonathan . . . her heart ached when she thought of him.

At last her maid spoke of Sir Jonathan's carriage rumbling up to his house, and Rachel could bear it no longer.

It was not proper, she had learned, for a lady to call upon a gentleman by herself, but she did not care. She would find Jonathan, and ask him why he had left for London and stayed for so long.

His butler did not seem surprised when she told him her name; indeed, it seemed as if he expected her. "Sir Jonathan is in the garden behind the house, my lady."

She followed the directions he gave her, going down a path around the house. There was a huge walled garden there, newly made, the butler had said, and when she saw it, she stopped.

The walls were made of the same gray stone that made the walls of the garden she had grown up in. Slowly she approached the door—it was made of the same wood as her garden door. There was a latch on it. She lifted it, and entered.

A cottage sat at one corner of the garden, almost exactly like the one she had lived in for so long. Around her were alders and a young apple tree, bare now, for it was late winter. But early snowdrops thrust themselves through the thawed ground, and the way the flower beds were arranged was exactly like that of the garden in the between-place she had lived. The sound of shifting feet made her turn to the cottage.

"Jonathan?" she said.

He came out of the cottage, tall, stronger than she had hoped, his beloved craggy face pale. "Rachel?" he called out. "Rachel?" He turned toward her.

He was blind.

She could see it in the way he turned his head this way and that, trying to hear some sound she might make. With a sob she ran to him, and flung her arms around his neck.

"Oh, Jonathan! Was this why you did not come home sooner? Because you could not see?" He did not answer, for she drew him down to her and kissed him.

"God, Rachel . . ." He kissed her over and over again, his lips moving over her mouth, cheek, and throat. He laughed huskily, and moved away from her slightly. "A little, perhaps," he said, moving his fingers across her chin and cheek, and then her hair. "You are not hurt? You are well? Your hair—"

"I am well, love. It was the only way out—I had to cut it."

He smiled slightly. "It will grow out, I'm sure. I somehow

felt you would find a way." He drew her toward the cottage. "Come—I had it built, hoping you would come someday, in case it might be difficult to become used to a larger house at first." He hesitated. "I could only describe what I remembered, and I can't see now if they've built it correctly."

Rachel closed her eyes against the tears building in them, but they fell down her cheeks and she could not stop them. "Why? You left me there—I could have wed a faery lord."

His face became bleak. "Yes. But I was afraid you would be punished—and the way Aldara struck at you, I thought it could be deadly—and I could not bear the thought that you or the children should be hurt for my blundering. But you said that the Fair Folk keep their promises—so I made her promise. And you see, your warding protected me quite well. I do not get the headaches like I used to and . . . well, I suppose what I am left with is a good trade for your safety."

"No," Rachel whispered. "Oh, no."

He touched her face again, and shook his head when he wet his hand upon her tears. "Don't cry, Rachel." He gave a dry chuckle and wiped her cheeks with his fingers. "I suppose, since you came here and kissed me in that wanton way, that you would not mind becoming my wife, even with the way I am?"

She seized his face between her hands and kissed him fiercely. "You stupid man! How can you even suggest I would mind, when I have been waiting and waiting for you to return from London? Why did you leave, when I might have come to you?"

"I had to go—I wished to be sure our children would be my heirs, whatever happened to either of us. And then the snow prevented me." His laugh had a note of frustration in it. "I was beginning to think that Aldara was planning to keep me from you forever—the carriage broke down, and two horses threw a shoe. And all the time I could think of nothing but you.'' He grasped her hand tightly in his. *"Will* you marry me, Rachel?''

She gazed at his sightless eyes, and rage and grief and love twisted and twined about her heart until she almost cried out with the pain of it. "Yes,'' was all she could say. "Yes.'' And pulled him down to her, kissing him hard.

They tumbled to the ground, and it was not hard dirt but grass, and the sun suddenly shone hot upon them as if it were midsummer and not the end of winter. Jonathan kissed her mouth and her eyes, and kissed her breasts as he uncovered them, unlacing her bodice as she pulled at his shirt. The scent of honey came to him, as it had when he had first made love to her, but it had an overlay of flowers. We should go into the cottage, he thought, but Rachel pulled him on top of her, moving sinuously against him, and all thoughts fled.

They loved wildly, and when he came into her, he rolled onto his back. She seized his face and kissed him and wept until his face was wet, and his closed eyes pooled with her tears as if they were his own. She held him tight, and poured all her strength, all her grief and love into him. What magic she had left was weak, but she willed him to be whole, so that he might see what he had created, so that he might see the children they would have soon. At last he arched hard into her and she shook and shook with the power of it, then sank down onto his chest.

There was only the sound of their breathing for long heartbeats of time, and then the slight sound of the breeze rustling the leaves of the trees. Leaves. The quick buzz of a bee flickered past Rachel's ear, and the scent of alyssum wafted past her nose. She opened her eyes and looked up.

It was not winter in the garden, but spring. New buds of flowers covered the apple tree, and new leaves sprinkled the limbs of alder and oak. Her hand touched thick grass, warm with the sun upon it, and snowdrops and daffodils in full bloom lined the flower beds.

Somehow they must have been taken back to the between place, back to the garden in which she had grown up. Rachel shuddered and hid her face on Jonathan's chest. Aldara would come, and all would be lost to her again.

A low rumble shook her, and her head jerked up at the burst of laughter from Jonathan.

"Good God! I have heard of the earth moving, but I never thought a good loving would cause this."

She looked up at him, and saw him grinning and looking at her—*looking* at her!

He turned toward the cottage, and cocked his head to one side, gazing at it critically. "It's not exactly what I had remembered, but I suppose it's close enough."

Rachel stared at him. "You . . . you can see."

"Yes," he said, and touched her face tenderly. "And I thank you."

"But I have only a little magic left . . . and I didn't think I could heal anyone again."

He kissed her. "You are stronger than you know."

He took her hand and raised her up from the grass, and as her feet touched the ground, she felt a warm power rise up from the earth through the soles of her feet, and a motherly chuckle murmured in her mind. *He is quite right,* said the voice of the Goddess, wafting softly like a soft warm wind through her thoughts. *But then, he would know, for he is a son of my heart, like his father and his father before him. Be happy with him, child.*

Joy rose in Rachel's heart, and once more she brought her love's lips down to her own. They would live in the mansion, but here was their own place, and they would bring their children to play among the flowers and the trees. She had never imagined such abundance before, but as she looked into Jonathan's eyes so full of love for her, she knew she would have it forever.

* * *

Occasionally visitors would come and marvel at the walled garden Lady Bradford tended, for it was always warm there, and winter always short, unlike anywhere else in Somerset. Lord and Lady Charlton, her parents and neighbors, often said that it was because it was full of the laughter of their grandchildren—what else could keep it so warm? And Sir Jonathan would smile and nod.

But sometimes during the dead of winter, Lady Bradford and Sir Jonathan would disappear for a space, and if anyone came near the garden, the scent of alyssum would flow over the walls, and the buzzing of bees could be heard among laughter and soft sighs.

Magic, some said. But magic, of course, lives only in fairy tales.

The Love Talker

Barbara Samuel

The Love Talker is a fixture of Irish faery lore, a seductive and dangerous being indeed, a conscienceless faery who ravishes the senses of unsuspecting women and leaves them to pine away to their deaths. In all the poems and stories, he is the King of Rakes, a libertine of unholy power.

When Jo, Mary Jo, Karen, and I started batting around actual legends and story ideas for this collection, I knew which faery I'd most want to spend an evening with, and wondered if it would be possible to redeem him. What greater challenge, after all, than the most unrepentant rake?

It meant moving him from his traditional ground to a location in keeping with our English setting, but we all agreed the doors to the world of faerie are many, and their land is not bound in the same manner as our own.

So move him I did, and plunged into his story. He proved as seductive and entertaining as I'd hoped—we do so love to see rakes fall to love. I hope you enjoy his journey as much as I did.

—*Barbara Samuel*

Prologue

Rosewood Manor, 1502

The maid lay beneath a gauze shroud on a bier strewn with violets and roses. The tenderness of the petals served only to underscore the fragile beauty of her face and the slim, youthful form dressed in the red velvet gown she'd been wearing when Galen had first spied her.

Mourners wept as the lady was carried into the crypt, her beauty there to wither away unseen, unused, unforgotten. As if the earth itself mourned, a thin gray mist fell from a leaden sky; every stalk of grass, every leaf, every flower, wore a silver cloak of sorrow.

Even Galen felt an ache, just below his breastbone, a thudding emptiness he did not know how to ease. Watching from his hidden place in the thick trees of the Rosewood estate, regret needled him with pointed fingers.

By the Lady, 'twas never meant to go so far. Who could have known she was so delicate that she'd pine unto *death*? That was the wretchedness of the mortal coil—the poor creatures were so ephemeral, so easily wounded or pierced.

And even those who weathered the wanton finger of fate were destined to grow old. Beauty faded or died. 'Twas always one or the other. It seemed a great cruelty to him.

And yet, it was that same evanescent quality that made them seem so much more alive than Faerie; 'twas the quickness of their hours that gave them a passion and heart unknown to his own kind.

Next to him stood the Queen. He felt her judgment, cold and grim, as she watched the burial. "I am most displeased, Galen."

"Aye, My Lady. I did not intend—"

Her fierce gaze silenced him. "I am weary of your roguish ways, Galen. You cannot be sated with women of your own kind, women who would not face this end, no matter how you mistreated them. You run forever to the mortal realm to seek your amusements, with no care for the delicacy of these creatures."

"My Lady, I do take care, but—"

"Not enough, Gancomer. Not enough." Her eyes glittered, green as a misted field. "On this sorrowful day, I curse you."

His throat went dry. "A curse?"

One elegantly shaped brow rose the slightest bit as she passed her gaze over him. Galen knew she desired him, and he allowed himself to hope the curse might only be a ban against his presence in the mortal realm. 'Twould not be so terrible. Perhaps he might serve as her consort for a time, appease her unhidden wish to lie with him by his own choosing.

Then, when she was well and thoroughly sated, she'd lift her curse and he'd be free again to spend his time with mortal women.

He glanced toward the mourning party, and caught sight of a ripe beauty with the golden locks of a faery, but all the warm earthiness of a mortal. A wisp of desire brushed his loins, and he smiled. Not even the Queen of Faerie could equal the lure of that rich, scented flesh, the poignancy of their fleeting time—

"Ah, Galen," the Queen said. "It grieves me, I admit, but even as one is buried, you plot the seduction of the next."

Guiltily, he looked back. A poor misstep, that. He gave her his best, most crooked smile. "I am only as I was made."

"And I do what I must, to keep the balance between our worlds." Her voice was cold as a winter moon. "I curse you."

A gray disturbance began to blow around them, lifting his hair, stinging his eyes.

"I curse you, Galen, to wander between the mortal and Faerie realms, never to cross to either. None but the beasts of field and sky will be your companions. All will hear you, but none will see you, though I will not be so kind as to give you blindness, for that would defeat my lesson."

"Good Lady! I beg you—"

"My curse on you, Galen, is loneliness so vast 'twould make stones cry. You'll wander alone till I see true remorse in your heart for your crimes." Her gaze was sober. "And when you have repented, true love will set you free, Galen. True love."

The world seemed to shimmer all around him, fading on both faery and mortal sides till he was the single figure of substance in a world made only of gray.

"My Lady!" he cried in panic. "Might I have my pipe at least?"

Even she shimmered now, near invisible. "Very well." He found the instrument in his hands. "Farewell, Galen."

He was alone.

Chapter One

Rosewood Manor, 1787

Waiting till very late of a September night, Moira Ryan slipped through the halls of the very grand Rosewood manor to her cousin's bedchamber. Deep in the bowels of the old part of the house, where stones were said to date back to medieval days, the chamber was tall and drafty, and not at all what Moira thought Blanche required.

But who listened to a poor Irish cousin? Worried as they all were over the mysterious illness that had fallen upon the celebrated Blanche Rosewood, they only laughed off Moira's demands and complaints.

Moira intended to take matters into her own hands. With charms she'd learned at her grandmother's knee and the good common sense bred into a country girl, she slipped into the room.

A blast of heavy, hot air nearly choked her, and Moira saw a servant asleep by the roaring fire, her plain face dotted with beads of sweat. Moira coughed at the smoke of the pungent herbs burned to chase away the illness, and she choked it back with her hand, lifting her apron over her face.

She tiptoed to a window and flung open the casements, waving her hand toward the smoky dead air to get it moving, then hurried over to her cousin's side.

Blanche Rosewood, pretty as her name, lay against the cloud of her long golden hair, still as death. A feverish color burned pink against her white skin, and her eyelids showed thin and blueish. Her pretty figure had melted these past three weeks to a gauntness that gave her an even more ethereal beauty. Moira sighed. Only Blanche could still manage to be beautiful in such circumstances.

The manor was in a tizzy. Lady Blanche lay dying of some mysterious malady only three weeks from her wedding. There was no reason the doctors could find. She'd been bled and rubbed; sweet potions were burned to purify the air. And still she lay abed, restless with a fever of no source, babbling of some sweet music only she could hear.

Moira knew the source, and the cure, though none would listen to her. As cool, light air wafted through the open windows, Moira glanced over her shoulder at the servant. Still snoring.

She took the heavy counterpane and pulled it from her cousin's sweat-soaked body, and climbed up beside her. "Blanche," she whispered, touching the delicate cheek. "Blanche, you must rouse yourself."

Her eyelids fluttered. Prettily. Eyes the color of pansies showed the drugging influence of laudanum. Seeing Moira, Blanche smiled faintly. "Can you hear it? The music? Isn't it lovely?"

She nearly drifted away again. Moira lightly slapped her. "Blanche! I cannot hear it! I need your help."

"There," she said dreamily. "That sweet, sweet pipe. 'Tis unlike any I have heard."

"Where did you hear it first? So I may hear it with you, my sweet."

Blanche smiled. "In the meadow, by the pond. You know

it. Where the old oak grows. The one we climbed as children.''

"What're you doin', girl?" The servant, jolted awake, hurried over to the windows. "You trying to kill her now?"

"She does not need all this heat," Moira said, stubbornly, sitting on the counterpane so the servant could not pull it over her mistress. A minute or two of the cooling air would be better than none at all. She crossed her arms and tried to imagine herself as heavy as a boulder, but she proved no match for the burly servant who simply plucked Moira up as if she were as light as one of the pillows. "Get now," the servant said, "or I'll tell her ladyship you've been causing trouble again."

"Very well." She had accomplished her purpose. "Sleep well, Blanche," she whispered, pressing a kiss to her cousin's hand. "Sleep true." She slipped out the way she'd come, and hurried to her own chamber.

It was a much less grand room than her cousin's, though that was Moira's choice. She liked plainer things. Her uncle George had taken her in when her parents were killed three years before, in spite of his lingering fury at his sister, who'd dared run off with an Irish youth without a farthing to his name. Love was for fools, George blustered often, when Moira reminded him that her parents had been happy to their very last moment on earth.

Love, indeed.

For love of his sister, Sir George of Rosewood had sought his orphaned niece and brought her back to his estate, where she was treated as daughter, not a poor relation at all. There was even talk that she would be married next year to some suitable younger son, a fate Moira accepted with her usual good humor. Happiness, her mother always told her, was Moira's gift. She'd be as happy with a younger son as in a cottage by the sea or even simply here in Rosewood.

Her dog waved his tail as she came in. "You're right to look alert, Desi, my dear. We're off tonight on a mission."

The trouble with the English, Moira thought, putting on her good boots, was their sensibility. No appreciation at all of the world beyond this one, not the world of heaven to which they gave mannerly lip service at dignified services, nor the world of Faerie about which they sang in a hundred little ballads.

No, the English world was one of reason and science, as her uncle so often reminded her. But neither reason nor science would cure Blanche.

Moira tossed her cape over her shoulders and drew up the hood, then crept into the kitchen, Desi's nails clicking on the parquet floor behind her. From the stillery she took a jug of cold milk, carefully stoppered, and burrowed about in the pantry until she found an unopened jar of honey. For good measure, she also took a loaf of newly baked bread, fragrant and faintly warm from sitting atop the mantle. In the hall, the clock chimed once to mark the half hour. Nearly midnight.

"Come," she said to Desi, and they slipped out together into the crisp night.

It was very dark and quiet. The moon was a far, high silver amid a black, black sky that showed every star in twinkling splendor. Beautiful, Moira thought, but wondered if she ought to take a lantern. For a moment, she hesitated.

Fear at what she was about to do rushed up to her throat. To crush it before it halted her entirely, she hurried down the steps and into the garden. Desi could see well enough in the dark; he would lead her.

Still, her heart skittered as she made her way through the shadowy forest, tripping sometimes on roots or rocks. The path was often used, so even in the dark, she did not stumble too much, and there was Desi, big and comforting, to lead the way.

It was a fearsome thing she was about to do. Against her breasts hung a protective amulet, agelessly ancient, that her grandmother had given her, and her pockets were filled with charms she'd made against Faerie. Even so, when she reached the edge of the meadow, she froze in sudden breathless terror.

The tree grew by itself in the middle of a field that had likely once been used for crops, but now lay fallow and grassy in the faint light. Perhaps those who'd cleared the land had left the oak for its age, or for shade during their work.

But perhaps in those days the country folk had known what Moira did: that an oak so sturdy and tall, so revered, was like as not the mark of a doorway to the land of Faerie, and was best left alone. She'd shivered with terrified glee when she and Blanche climbed this tree when they were much younger girls, fancying she could see the Gilded Land from the uppermost branches. For endless hours had she entertained her cousin with tales of the forbidden fruit in those unholy orchards, and the care one took with the *sidhe.*

But Blanche was English and did not really believe. Not until a faery had seduced her. Now she pined away for love of him, and would die unless Moira acted.

Next to her, Desi whined softly. Gooseflesh rose on Moira's arms and prickled up the nape of her neck. Swallowing her terror, she lifted her chin and marched into the clearing with her offerings, which she put below the branches of the tree, and stepped back.

Desi trotted along beside her, still making that soft noise. "Will you stop, Desi," she whispered fiercely, and put a trembling hand on him for courage. "I'm already frightened half to death."

The meadow was still. Moira took a deep breath. "Come out to me, Gancomer," she cried, hoping his name was the same in this land as it was at home. "Come and drink the milk I've brought, and eat this sweet honey, and allow me to lay my petition at your feet."

Desi barked. The sound was loud and sudden in the silence, and Moira started so violently she thought her heart would stop entirely. She peered into the darkness, but saw nothing.

Then it came, the soft, high notes of a flute played with such exquisite perfection it could only belong to the other world. The sound plucked her very soul with its wistful beauty, and tears stung her eyes. "Oh," she breathed. "That *is* lovely. But can you not come out, Gancomer, and let me see you? We must speak. 'Tis most urgent."

Again Desi barked, and suddenly bolted forward, heading for a place in the deepest shadows of the tree. Moira clutched her talisman with one hand and held the herbs in her other, and for good measure, began whispering the Lord's Prayer.

The music halted. "Must you?" The voice was uncommonly rich, braided with the sound of cello and rushing water and the wind's melancholy sigh.

Moira started again, making a little sound of terror as a figure emerged from the shadows. It was too dark to make out details, only a tall, deft grace that might have been part of the shadow, a branch walking free. "I will not," she said, bobbing in a curtsy for good measure, "if it displeases you, sir."

"I have not had an offering of milk and honey for . . ." he paused as if he could not count so high. "Centuries, I think."

"Then I'm glad to have brought it." She forced herself to let go of the charms, forced herself to breathe as normally as possible. "Perhaps you will not mind listening to my petition, then."

Desi had rushed over to the tall shadowy figure, and nosed around his knees, as dogs always seemed to do. "Desi," she admonished firmly. "Leave him."

"He's a fine creature," the shadow said, and Moira saw him bend to put his hands on Desi, who groaned happily at the way the faery scratched him.

Moira frowned in puzzlement. " 'Tis not usual for your

folk to befriend canines, is it? I thought they rather disliked you.''

"Is that why you brought him?"

"No," she said. "He goes where I go." She smiled as the faery—in an oddly comforting gesture—coaxed Desi onto his back so he could scratch his belly. "He'll be your slave forevermore if you rub his belly like that. I'll never get him to come home with me."

The faery stood, and even in the darkness, she saw the poised alertness of his posture. "Madam, can you *see* me?"

"Not terribly well, in this darkness."

He moved urgently toward her. In terror, Moira stepped backward, holding up a hand to ward him away. "Stay back!"

Instantly, he halted. "Forgive me. I did not intend to frighten you."

Gripping the charm in her hand again, Moira looked at him. He'd halted a few steps distant. His face was still indistinct, but there was a wealth of long black hair trailing down his back. And in this, too, she found she was wrong. "Are not faeries all golden and light?"

His chin lifted. "They are not. I am a rare one, 'tis true, but I've heard me no complaints."

That reminded her of why she had come. "I have a complaint, sir. Not of your hair, but of your pipe."

"My pipe?"

"It is wooing my cousin to death."

A short, harsh curse came from him. "To death? But how?"

"That I do not know. She hears you play, and now pines and pines, until she wastes to nothing. I have come to ask you to cease playing, so she might mend and make a pretty bride three weeks from now."

"My music woos her? Unto death?"

He seemed so bewildered, Moira stepped closer. "You didn't know? She is not the first to have pined away for the sound of your playing, though I admit she is the first in a long while.''

He turned away.' 'I did not know.''

In his resonant voice, the words were a mournful sound that near brought tears to Moira's eye. In defense, she slipped her hand in her pocket and found the bundle of herbs.

"I am doomed," he said.

"Doomed?"

"Aye." He raised his head. Moira saw the shadowy outline of his face before he turned away again. "I have repented, but now there is another for which I will be blamed."

Moira did not quite follow this, but she sensed his remorse for the unwitting seduction of Blanche. "She is not dead yet. If you will only leave off playing, she might mend."

He looked at the pipe in his hand. "I have no other amusement. Nothing. It's all I have."

"You need not stop forever, I don't think."

"If I agree to your petition, will you come again? Here, to speak with me?"

Some sense of sorrow or sadness plucked at Moira. "I will."

Teeth flashed, so quickly it was gone before she fully realized. "Are you not afraid of seduction yourself?"

Moira inclined her head. "I am wiser than these modern folk, sir. I have my protections against your wiles."

He laughed, and even with both hands filled with that protection, Moira felt the power of it. A sound like a sunrise, or a great feast with free-running red wine, or a wind dancing through an orchard of blossoms. "Very well, then. As long as you come to talk, I will not play. You have my promise."

The bells in the village rang suddenly, and Moira turned. "I must go! Good night."

Chapter Two

Galen waited by the tree the next night. The bread and honey and milk the woman had left the night before were gone, taken by some less hapless faery than he. But he sat close by where she'd left it, the knowledge of the offering a warmth in his belly. His belly did not need food.

Only craved it. Craved the taste of things on his tongue again. Craved the feeling of a cold cup of milk in his hand. Other things he craved, too—the breath of wind in his hair, heat on his neck, the scent of grass in his nose.

Once he had believed the most wondrous things to be a woman's flesh, her breath on his mouth, her breasts heavy and hot in his palms, her thighs twined around his own. He'd lived for it.

After so long a time between worlds, his longings were far simpler. Simple words, simple gestures, simple pleasures.

How many years had he been cursed? He looked at the moon, little more than a thread as it waned, but it held no answer. Long enough to see multitudes of children in this tree, children who sometimes heard him, sometimes

did not. How he'd treasured the ones who could hear him!
Like jewels they were, precious and rare.

A great depth of despair near swallowed him as he
thought of the pretty maids who had also come to hear
his songs, to sit in the sweet-smelling grass beneath the
spreading boughs of this tree and cock their pretty heads
as his notes danced around them. Danced as he could not.

How many? he wondered with anguish. How many like
the one who pined away in a sickbed, haunted by the pipe
she could not see? Had they all pined away at the sound
of his pipe? The girl said there had been others besides
her cousin.

It made him feel an anguished frustration. Why had the
Lady not halted his damaging music, or at least given
warning? Did she mean to let him languish forever between
worlds?

He'd never escape this purgatory.

But, too, he was puzzled. The Queen said he had to find
"true love." Surely a woman who pined so deeply that she
neared death, simply from hearing his music, had shown
love true enough.

Or perhaps the Queen meant a woman had to see him,
know him, not simply love some idea of him. If that was
true, perhaps this new woman was his chance. Perhaps
she'd be the one who would love him truly enough to set
him free. By some old magic, she'd dented the curse
already, speaking his true name so he had to come to her.

A swish of sound reached him, and eagerly, Galen stood.
Through the grass of the meadow came the hound, an
enormous friendly creature with a thick, lustrous coat that
was very fine to touch. That had been more a kindness
than the Queen had known, he thought as the animal
barreled eagerly into Galen's waiting embrace. The feel
of dogs and wolves, and squirrels he managed to tame
from the trees, had kept him from starving unto death for
lack of companionship and warmth. This one was solid

and his soft fur a pleasure against Galen's touch-starved fingers.

Only when the dog had been properly greeted did Galen lift his head to the woman, somehow a little afraid of her or the test she might represent. What if he fell into his old habits—as he nearly had last night—and ruined his last chance? Ever had his impulse to seduction and charm been his flaw.

He could see little of her in the darkness. Her hair was sensibly bound into a long braid, the style of a country maid, and the color was hard to discern. Dark, but whether black or brown, he could not tell. Her body was cloaked against the cool night air, and in the shadows all he knew of her face was a smooth pale oval with luminous eyes.

Tonight, she had brought again an offering. More milk and bread and honey. She held them out to him, but Galen deferred, gesturing that she should put them on the ground. His hands held no weight in her world. The jar would shatter.

"How fares your cousin?" he asked.

"No better, but this is only the first day."

A fist struck his gut. "Is there some blessing we might say to help?"

"Give it a day or two," she said with a smile. "I'll not give up till she's a pretty bride, which she'll certainly be."

"I did love mortal weddings," he said, half to himself. He'd loved the dancing and the pretty gowns. He'd liked, too, the ease of conquests at such times, but that seemed a petty thing to him now. Distasteful. "I do long for the sight of another."

She laughed, a light sweet sound in the night. "Now there is one I was not wrong about. Your folk like a party."

"We do." It was easy to smile. "Music and feasts and the liveliest of your days. I liked fairs, too, and that sweet cherry cider made hereabouts."

"Then next I'll bring you cider."

He said nothing about that. It would not hurt to leave

it for the others. They would like it, too. And it was true the people had forgotten to leave offerings for the Folk over the years, save the stray romantic child.

"Will you tell me your name, madam?"

"That I will not."

He smiled in the darkness. "Then give me a name that I might use."

She tipped her head sideways in thought. A wash of light spilled over one round cheek. "Tara."

Galen laughed, for it was the name for the ancient seat of Irish kings. "All right," he said amiably. "Tara. I was there, you know, when the kings sat upon their thrones, and the land of Erui was a mighty place. Would you like to hear of it?"

"Oh, yes!"

So simple a thing, so rich, to give her a tale of a time long ago. "Sit then, and listen awhile."

"Only a little while," she said. "I will be missed, and must check my cousin again before I sleep. They'll half strangle her with their cures if I do not air that chamber."

Every minute was a gift, every minute he could sit with another—human or faery mattered little to him now—and he nodded. "I'll choose a short tale for this night's telling, then."

He did not notice the wind that blew in his hair as he spun his tale, in his best voice, simply for her pleasure. Did not notice it at all.

Moira hurried back through the wood, sure she had sat too long with the faery and would have been missed by now. But when she arrived, breathless, at the back door, she peeked into the kitchen window and saw the girls still at work with the dishes. Relieved, Moira ran around to the side door and ducked inside.

She followed the twisting halls through the rambling house to her cousin's door. The doctor in his black coat was coming out, and his voice was grave as he murmured to Moira's uncle.

"What news?" Moira burst out. "Is she no better?"

Her Uncle George looked grim. "She is not, my sweet. Go and sing to her, will you? She keeps crying out for music."

Moira rushed into the room, flying across the room to Blanche's side. The room was hot and foul with burning herbs, and in frustration, Moira cried, "Let her breathe! How could anyone recover in such a room?"

"I have my orders from the doctor," the servant said stubbornly.

"Leave us," Moira commanded.

The woman blinked. They were not used to her orders.

"Go on," Moira said. "I want to be alone and sing and pray over her." She turned toward Blanche and, after a moment, heard the servant leave.

In one day, Blanche seemed to have withered far more than was possible. All flesh was gone from her once rosy cheeks, and blue smudges ringed her eyes. Moira could see veins through the thin flesh at her temples.

"Blanche," she whispered, kissing her cheek, stroking her brow. "Blanche, my sweet, wake up. You must not sleep and drift away from me. You are my sister, my friend. What will I do if you go?"

"Moira." The voice was soft and breathless, as if Blanche had some wasting disease. Her lips were pale. "I cannot hear the music anymore. Where did it go?" Her thin fingers gripped Moira's urgently. "Did you find him? Did he play?"

Moira hesitated. "It's only faery music, Blanche. You must not listen. You must not let it take you away. You must get up! You're to be married in three weeks!"

"No," Blanche said. "I think I will not rise again. Do not be angry."

"Stop! You must not fade away like some tragic heroine.

Shall I sing? I cannot sing so sweet as he plays his pipe, but perhaps it will ease you."

"You've heard it!" Blanche opened her dark violet eyes. "You have, I can tell."

"I did," Moira admitted, and a queer little shiver walked down her spine as she thought of his shadowy form in the darkness, that arrogant tilt of his head, the lilt in his braided-music voice. "I asked him to cease to play till you are well. If you want the music, you must not fade away."

"You asked him to stop? Oh, no. You must tell him to play again."

"No. You can't see what's happening, Blanche, but I can. It's stealing away your soul, a tiny bit at a time."

"I don't care." Blanche turned her face away. "The music I will have."

Moira stood. "No. If you want the music, you will fight the spell and get to your feet," she said. "Like it or not, I'll see you live."

Blanche did not answer, her face turned stubbornly away as if she did not hear. Moira narrowed her eyes. Blanche was spoiled by beauty and position. She was accustomed to getting everything she wished, even if that wish was to die.

But Moira loved her as a sister. She could be sweet and generous, and her laughter was like butterflies swirling in a garden. She could not help being spoiled.

"I'll not let you die, Blanche Rosewood," Moira said quietly and fiercely. "I won't."

Moira could do nothing till morning, and then she walked to the village. It was a quaint spot, nestled close to the old forest. Pretty thatched cottages lined the cobblestone streets. As a byway with a fine inn on the highway, Rosewood village flourished. Healthy matrons shopped the stalls for fresh onions and apples and cider, gossiping and comparing, and boasting of the accomplishments of their children. It was sunny and cheerful, and Moira resisted the temptation to linger.

The house she sought lay far to the end of the village, tucked away at the very edge of the forest. A woman in a plain dress sat on a bench in her garden, drinking a cup of tea in the warm sun. A yellow cat sat on her lap.

"Good morning, Mrs. Hadrian," Moira called.

"It's a pretty one. What brings you out so far to see an old woman?"

Moira settled next to her on the bench, and busied herself for a moment with petting the cat, trying to come up with some way to ask her a question without sounding daft.

Or Irish. That's what they all said about her: *"What amusing Irish ways you have, girl."* Moira hated it.

"You know my cousin Blanche is ill," she said finally.

The woman's brown merry eyes clouded. "So I've heard. A wasting disease, they're saying."

"That's what they say." Moira frowned. There was no way to say it but spill it out. "Mrs. Hadrian, I think she's faery-cursed. She's heard the Love Talker and his music has bewitched her."

Mrs. Hadrian stroked the cat, and pursed her lips. "Well."

"I know it sounds mad, but there's no harm in trying to break a spell, is there?" Earnestly, Moira rushed on. "If it's a wasting disease, 'twill not hurt her to be blessed, or to have herbs in her clothes or whatever it is I am meant to do."

"True enough. A good prayer can cure all manner of ills." She peered into the distance, deep in thought. "I know some herbs that are said to be a cure, but they're harsh and we'll wait to try them later. I remember a ritual or two said to break the thrall of a faery. We'll try those first."

"Thank you," Moira breathed.

"Have you heard him?"

"Him?" A movement in the forest beyond the cottage caught Moira's eye, and she turned. Nothing.

"The Love Talker."

"No," she lied, somehow reluctant to admit it to anyone. Those moments spent in the dark field felt . . . private. "Blanche says his pipe is more heavenly than all the angels of the heavens."

"So it is said."

Again Moira felt a sense of presence or a feeling of being watched. She looked around, behind her and in the forest. Nothing. She shook it off and leaned toward Mrs. Hadrian. "So, what shall I do to save my cousin?"

Time and distance in Galen's cursed plane were vague. There was the Faerie world on one side, and sometimes he heard music coming from there, high and sweet. Sometimes he heard lovers murmuring endearments, or caught the edge of a thunderstorm in the mortal realm.

But mostly, it was as if he existed in a silent forest, where only animals ventured, and birds. He could see a house here and there, and sometimes inadvertently wandered into some enchanted realm. Once, he'd thought the spell broken when he found a young woman in a garden. He'd taught her some notes on his pipe, and been charmed by her beauty, then learned she, too, was faery, and under enchantment.

So when he found himself nearby a cottage that tugged at his memory, he feared it was another such place, where a witch or faery worked some magic that did not shut him out. He did not know how he'd come here, or how he'd return to his oak.

It was the lure of sunlight that drew him first. Sunlight falling in butter yellow bars across a garden near the end of its season. It had been . . . he didn't know, a long, long time, since he'd seen clear, unfiltered sunlight. He moved toward the puddle of light with a mingling of anticipation and fear. If he saw it, would he also be able to feel it?

He put his hand into the light. For a moment, he felt nothing, only the same faint chill of the air in his own world, and disappointment ripped through him.

And then, then, he did feel it. Not the heavy warmth of summer, but the less fierce sunlight of autumn, warm on his knuckles and the back of his hand. Damp, cool air from the forest floor rose to touch his palm. Galen laughed, turning his hand over, back to front and front to back, taking a child's delight in sensation. Any sensation.

After a moment, he stepped into the pillar of light to feel it on his whole body, and tipped up his face to it as if it were a rain shower or a waterfall. The light turned red below his eyelids, and poured over his cheekbones and danced upon his mouth, and Galen only stood there, drinking it in. He moved in a slow circle and stretched out his arms and let it spill all over him, then tugged his tunic over his head and stood naked in the forest, absorbing the pure, life-giving warmth of the sun.

He might have stood there all day, drunk on the feeling of sunlight against his flesh, but the sound of voices reached him. Curious what else this spot might hold, he put his tunic back on and brushed his hair from his face and crept toward the sound.

The cottage sat at the very edge of the forest. It looked familiar, but he could not place it, and at any rate, did not linger on the thought for long.

For one of the voices was known to him. It was the voice of the woman who'd brought him milk and honey, the one who had begged for her cousin's life. Galen halted, blinking.

She was no beauty. A smooth white face with a faintly snub nose, the sort of round, near-plump body born of peasant stock. Her eyes were big and brown and earnest, and in daylight, were as luminescent as they appeared in the darkness.

But her hair—her hair made him sigh. It glittered in the morning, red and gold, almost afire with the colors of coins and autumn maples and the sunlight spilling over her. She'd pulled it, as always, into a neat braid, but that braid was thick as his thigh, and long, past her hips. It was worthy of the faeries themselves.

For the first time in hundreds of years, Galen felt his loins leap, felt the old heat rise in his blood, and his mind filled with visions of how she would look, naked, with that red-gold hair loose and—

He found himself no longer in the sunlit forest, but back in the dull, pale world of his exile. Beneath the tree were untouched empty cups of cider and the crumbs of a sweet cake.

He stared at the remains uncomprehendingly for a long moment. Not only had he been torn from that sunlit world, but he'd lost time as well. She had come, bringing cider as she'd promised, and Galen had not been here to receive it. Or to hear her voice, or listen to her laugh, or tell her another story.

It seemed brutally unfair. He cried out, a wordless roar of despair and frustration. It did not even echo, but was simply absorbed into the thick walls keeping him from the world. He fell to his knees and buried his face in his hands. "Please," he said to the void, knowing She heard him no matter where he spoke. "Please tell me how to free myself."

Silence, unbroken by laughter or tears or the voice of the wind, was all he heard. And Galen, broken at last, wept.

Chapter Three

Moira dozed in a chair at her cousin's bedside. It was late, and very dark when she started awake, thinking at first that Blanche had called to her. A quick glance at the bed showed Blanche to be sleeping. Not peacefully, for she tossed a little and made quiet protesting cries. Moira rose and put her hand on the girl's forehead. Cool now.

As she straightened, a low sound moved in the room. She froze, listening. It was not a human sound, nor that of a screeching banshee—the ghost who warned of coming death. This was lower, more musical, a melancholy symphony of lonely grief, and hearing it, Moira could not move. The sound pierced her, called to some well of sorrow in her soul, and she found tears in her throat.

It ceased and began again, quieter now, fading.

But then, as if the animals heard it, there came the sound of cows singing in their mournful, sad voices, and a dog howled. And most poignant of all, the blackbirds in the evergreens beyond the windows added their bittersweet notes, until the whole world seemed to be weeping.

Moira could not bear it. She bolted from the room and

ran into the cold night, and here, here it was louder still, the voices of the beasts adding harmonious notes to the beautiful and woeful sound of that low cry. Her dog, Desi, waited for her in the yard, as if he knew, and he gave a sharp, hard bark when he saw her. He ran forward and nipped at her hand, and ran toward the forest. Moira, feeling ensorcelled, followed.

Desi ran at top speed through the forest, into the meadow, and Moira did her best to keep up. Her breath came in ragged gasps by the time she reached the clearing.

And then she knew. It was the faery who mourned. There could be no other, no one else who could make a sound of that sorrowful depth or unholy beauty. She hesitated on the edge of the meadow, for she had only her grandmother's talisman around her neck, no herbs or other protections against his spell of seduction if he chose to draw her in.

She might not be strong enough to resist him, and then there would be two daughters of Rosewood pining away in their beds. It would kill her uncle.

Beneath the tree, she saw a soft white glow, as if the moon had fallen to earth. In the pale ghostly light, a figure bent in deepest sorrow, head in hands. Moira stepped forward against her will, drawn to comfort. She thought she saw something—or someone else—at the edges of the light, and her fear dispersed.

She ran, and called out his name. "Gancomer!" And again, running closer.

The pale cold light washed over him and Moira was struck with the beauty of his form against it, his lean grace so expressive of sorrow, his hair raven black and shimmering, his hands long and lean and beautiful.

But as she approached and he lifted his head, when she might have seen his face at last, the light faded till he was left only in blackness.

There was no moon. Moira stopped, afraid she would

stumble if she continued. It was only then that she realized how cold it was, and put her arms around herself, shivering.

He stepped from the shadows. "You came." His voice ran in dark silver spirals down her back, and Moira closed her eyes in a soft prayer of protection—not against his faery charm, but against the passionate need he roused in her to comfort him, to give him peace.

"I did," she whispered.

"Why?"

She raised her head. "I heard your sorrow."

He stiffened. Even in the darkness she felt it.

"The world felt it. I feared you would call my cousin into your realm forever."

"No." At his feet, Desi whined, and Moira saw Galen simply sink down into the grass and put his body close to the dog. He lay his head against the broad back and she heard him sigh, as if in great weariness. "I have no such designs on anyone. Not any longer."

She rubbed her arms, fought against her teeth chattering. "What grieves you so, sir?" she asked quietly. "Is there no cure?"

"You are cold," he said, lifting his head. "I have no cloak to give you. Go. Go back to where it is warm."

"I don't want to leave you in such pain," she said.

This time his voice was softer. "For that I thank you, Tara. But you must go so you can come another day."

She didn't argue. "Come, Desi."

The dog shifted from foot to foot, and licked his lips, but did not move.

"Come," she said again, and slapped her leg.

Desi whined, as if he wanted to obey but could not.

Moira understood. "Stay and comfort him then, for I will freeze if I do."

His tail wagged happily. Moira lifted her head. "Care well for him, sir. Good night."

*   *   *

The Faerie Queen, in her court of pearl and gold, watched carefully. Her present consort stood beside her, looking into her green globe that showed a red-haired girl gently washing the face of an invalid. "Is that the one who is pining away?" he asked.

"It is."

"How can you let him do this, over and over? Was not his punishment fashioned to keep girls from dying?"

The Queen inclined her head. "He does not cause it. I have no power over the foolish fantasies of mortal maids. Those who would pine for the sound of faery pipe would find some other thing if the pipes were never heard again."

"What of Galen, then?"

Her eyes softened, and her consort knew a flash of purest jealousy. "I have faith he is nearing the end of his exile."

"Will he return to us then?" he asked, thinking darkly he'd be cast out on that day.

"Only he knows that answer," the Queen said, and her consort thought he heard a wistful note in the words.

Moira waited till everyone was about their chores before she crept into Blanche's chamber the next morning. Only a single young servant girl sat with her, and Moira smiled. "Run away and get a cup of tea. I'll sit with her."

The girl bobbed happily. "Oh, that does sound fine. Thank you."

When she was gone, Moira removed everything from the night table beside Blanche's bed. From her pocket, she took a handkerchief filled with salt, and fashioning a spout from a corner of the cloth, spilled out three lines. Putting the napkin aside, she made sure the rows were exactly even, height and width and length, then knelt to put her arm in a circle around them. She bent her head over them and repeated the Lord's Prayer. Over and over,

till she had done it thrice times three, one set for each
row of salt.

Blanche still slept. Moira took her limp hand. In her
most commanding voice, a voice kept quiet so none outside
would hear, she said, "By the power of the Father and Son
and Holy ghost, I command this spell to be broken. Let
this woman be free!"

And though it was not part of the spell, Moira bent her
head over the fine white hand, cold with so long an illness,
and pressed a kiss to her fingers. "Please, Blanche. Be
well."

Blanche slept.

The wedding preparations had halted completely, and
Moira felt depressed as she walked through the house.
There was a pall over every room, a worried frown on every
face. The ballroom, half festooned with colorful ribbons,
sat abandoned, and the kitchen, which should have been
cheerfully alight with cooking for hundreds, was somber
as maids stirred daily offerings of bland porridge and milk
toast instead. Moira's aunt had taken to her own bed out
of worry.

Moira waited as late as she could, but it was only evening
when she slipped from the house this time. No one would
notice, and she most urgently needed to speak to the faery.
Perhaps he could appeal to someone in his world.

She carried a pot of soft cheese and a bottle of wine, all
she could steal without notice at this hour. The cheese
had been sitting on the table, and the wine came from the
cellar, and she stowed them away under her cloak, hoping
he would not be angry that she couldn't bring traditional
things. She had forgotten to ask how he'd enjoyed the
cider she left last time.

In the gloaming, the meadow with its huge ancient tree
was a very different place. Birds, who favored the stream
that ran close by, whistled and chirped in the trees, lending

a sweet music to the hour. The sky had gone a pale purple from the clouds on the horizon, giving the landscape a gray and silver wash. Moira remembered the moon-like shimmer of light she'd seen the other night, and wondered where it had come from. Had Galen cast it, or had some other being been present that night?

Standing there with her hands filled with cheese and wine, she wondered suddenly if she had simply gone mad, babbling about pixies and faeries and otherworldly music and light. Would she have believed the tale from another?

But as if to reassure her that her mind was sound, Desi came bounding toward her from some hidden place, a grin on his chops, his tongue lolling, and he jumped on her with such glee that Moira nearly dropped everything. "I missed you, too," she said, letting him nuzzle her neck. "Where is our companion?"

"I am here, at your bidding, my lady."

The words carried a strangely pleasing, old world courtliness, and Moira looked up with a smile.

And lost her breath.

She closed her eyes to block the sight of him, but once seen, he could not be unseen, and she opened them again. In the twilight, he stood straight and tall, possessed of the otherworldly grace of bearing she would have expected. His figure was lean of hip, broad of shoulder, which was also not surprising.

She had already known his coloring differed from the usual, but had not been able to see just how. In her imagination, in all the stories, the seductive faeries were gilded beings, with silvery gold hair and light eyes and skin of unholy beauty.

If those creatures were diamonds, Galen was a ruby. There was that richness about him, in his long black hair lying against his back, and the warmth of his flesh, and the jeweled brightness of green eyes framed with lashes black as raven wings. He looked like some prince from a

Renaissance painting, with that sensual red mouth, and the clean angles of his face.

"Oh, God," she breathed, and covered her face with one hand, and turned away. Her breath stuttered in her chest as if her lungs had forgotten their purpose, and her heart thudded. But worse—worst of all—was a well of something hot moving through her arms and hands and breasts, something heavy and thick and completely unfamiliar.

"Do I displease you?" he asked, slightly mocking.

Moira shivered at the sound of his voice. "I cannot look on you," she said in a tight voice. Turning back to him, she kept her eyes lowered, and put the wine and cheese at his feet, then backed away. "I could not get milk and honey tonight. I hope this pleases you as well."

"All of your offerings please me, madam." He made a short, quick noise. "Oh, must you act so humble and keep your eyes lowered? I have so few companions, I was glad to see you in the light."

"I am afraid."

"Afraid?" he sounded bewildered.

"Afraid of seduction."

He gave a short, humorless laugh. "Raise your eyes, Tara. I'll not seduce you. I *cannot.*"

"Cannot?" Moira looked up, and again his beauty was like a blow, but she saw a little beyond it now, to the sorrow in his vivid green eyes.

"I'll show you." He reached out a hand and it passed through her, or by her. "I am cursed by my Queen," he said. "Until you came and called me, I had not spoken to another in many, many years."

"Cursed? Why?"

Weariness crossed his face, weariness of such depth Moira could not fathom what caused such a thing. "I was . . . unfeeling. I caused the death of one who loved me, and felt no remorse. To teach me a lesson, the Queen cursed me to be alone till . . . till I have learned compassion.''

Against her will, Moira was moved. Inclining her head, she asked, ''Cursed to be alone with nothing but your pipe? How long has it been?''

He took a breath, confusion on his brow. ''I do not know. Elizabeth was queen. How long since then?''

''Nearly three hundred years,'' she said quietly. No wonder he mourned so deeply. ''And in all that time, you've not been with other people at all?''

''Only when I played my pipe, or when I came on another enchantment.'' His mouth was grave. ''That was why I played for your cousin—'twas the only way I could make myself heard. She was pretty the day she came in the meadow, and I tried to speak, but she did not hear me until I played. Then she sat''—he gestured toward a place beneath the spreading boughs of the oak—''and listened all day. But she did not come back. They never come back.'' He raised his eyes. ''Only you.''

''And I used your true name, Gancomer. That was why you were compelled to come to me.''

He lifted his shoulders. ''I suppose. I truly have no answer for that.'' He frowned. ''How fares your cousin?''

Moira shook her head. ''Nothing helps. I came tonight to ask if there is some appeal you might make to the Faerie world to break the spell on her. Your Queen cursed you. Would she have the answer to this quandary?''

''I had not thought to ask.''

''Will you?''

His gaze was fixed upon her with a peculiar intensity. ''Will you come back, even if your cousin heals?''

Moira gave the only answer she could. ''Yes,'' she whispered.

''And if she dies? Will you hate me?''

''I don't know.''

He nodded, and in the angle of his neck, she again saw

the weight of weariness he carried. "I don't know if the Queen will listen, but I will ask her help."

"Thank you." Relieved to escape his beauty, she turned away. "I must go now."

"Can you not linger even a little while, sweet Tara? If my face disturbs you, I wouldn't mind if you sat with your back to me. Just stay a little longer."

Moira resisted the urge to cross herself as she met the appeal in his eyes. The greenest, most beautiful eyes she'd ever seen. But it was not the beauty that snared her now, it was the loneliness in them. She smiled bravely. "I think I can bear to look on you, Gancomer. I'll stay for a little if it pleases you."

"Call me Galen," he said.

"All right." She settled on the grass. "Sit with my dog and me, then, Galen, and tell me another tale of great Tara of old."

His smile was almost heartbreakingly grateful. Gracefully, he sat down. "Would you tell me of your life instead?"

"It's very boring, sir."

"Not to me."

She peered at him to see if he teased her, but he seemed quite serious. "If you wish."

Chapter Four

Galen stared at the girl hungrily as she told him of her life in Ireland, and now at Rosewood. There was a curious energy about her, an appreciation of daily things that moved him as much as the prettiness of her red lips and the dancing light in her eyes. She made him laugh more than once with tales of mischief and impersonations of servants or lords, or grand ladies. He wondered what she'd make of the Faerie Queen, and the thought amused him enormously.

But as darkness gathered in deeper and deeper pools, she finally stood. "I must go."

Galen gave her a bow. "Thank you, my lady. You've been a wondrously fine companion."

She smiled, then sobered. "You will not forget to ask for cures from your Queen?"

"I will not forget."

"Till tomorrow, then."

He watched her go, the long red braid swaying, bright even in the darkening evening. He liked the sturdiness of her bearing, the sensible swing of her arms, and the air of purpose she carried with her always. Her cloak billowed behind her in waves, and Galen found himself smiling softly. An unusual woman. He'd not met one of her ilk before.

Watching her go, a strange yearning under his ribs, it occurred to Galen that before he was cursed he would not have spared a glance for her. He would have bewitched her cousin, the fair beauty who had sat under this tree, and not even noticed this robust country girl.

But tonight, it was for Tara he acted. When the moon had risen, nearly to the first quarter, he called the Queen by her private name, knowing she had to come, as he'd been compelled to come to Tara. He was not disappointed.

She came from the west on a great white steed, her gilt hair streaming down her arms and over her legs, clad only in the lightest gossamer. "At last, you've called," she said in a slightly mocking tone.

He blinked, dazzled a little by her beauty after so long a time. "I've not called for myself, but to ask your help with a matter I know not how to solve."

"Speak, then."

He outlined the tale to her, and she waved it away. "I know of the pining girl. 'Twas not your doing, else I'd have punished you more. She's a vain and foolish girl who does not wish to wed, but be admired all the day." She lifted a pointed silver brow. "Once, Galen, she would have suited you well."

He bowed his head, knowing the truth of it. "Her cousin is most distraught, My Lady," he said, and took a breath. "She loves the girl, and I feel responsible. Is there no tune I can play to release her? Some words for Tara to say?"

For a long, long moment, the Faerie Queen was utterly still, her eyes sober. "Her true name is Moira," she said in a hushed voice. "Thank her for her offerings. I had the cider myself. Mortal food is rare in these times, and I do enjoy it."

Galen smiled, remembering her fondness for mead. "There is wine and cheese there tonight."

She only shook her head. "I'm on my way to a gala, and must go."

"Wait," he cried. "Is there nothing, My Lady?"

"Let me think on it," she said quietly. "It is a most serious matter."

And as quickly as she'd come, she was gone, leaving Galen to his dull silence and darkness. With a sigh, he turned—and halted in confusion, for he was not where he had been, under a canopy of trees and an unnatural sky, but in a darkened room. He could not see for the gloom, and dared not move till he knew what place he was in.

After a moment, his vision cleared and he saw the nearly quarter moon shining through a mullioned window, uncurtained to allow the night in. In the faint light, he saw a shadowy figure in the bed. He could not think why he was here. Was this the fair cousin, who mourned some vision of him that had no reality? Was he meant to be part of her dream? He stepped closer.

And halted again, his heart hammering. It was not the cousin. It was Moira, who started awake even as he peered at her. She sat straight up, and he glimpsed the soft white plumpness of an unbound breast at the neck of her nightrail. "What are you doing here?" she whispered.

Galen had no answer for her. No answer for anything. He looked around him and out to the silver of moon, and back to her in confusion. "I don't know," he said simply.

"Oh, you are so weary," she said, and held out her hand. "Come, Galen, lie down."

He moved without knowing he would, moved toward the place she made for him, and with a long sigh, lay next to her. He could smell her skin, a scent of morning and dew, but even that could not match the pleasure of falling prone upon a down-stuffed mattress, or putting his head into the cloud-like softness of a pillow she plumped for him. "Sleep," she said. "Sleep, Galen. I will keep watch for you, and you will have to go before morning."

And Galen, a faery who should not have needed the rest, fell into a deep healing sleep. Before he drifted away, he thought he felt her fingers on his brow, but it was too faint a touch to be sure, and he was too weary to drag himself back again.

Moira kept her promise. She kept watch through the night, as if goblins might spring from the walls and take him off to hell. Once, sleepy herself from nursing her cousin and making so many late-night trips to the fields, she drifted off.

When she awakened, she found herself nestled close against his back, her brow pressed against his shoulder. Her hand rested upon his waist, as if she had instinctively gravitated toward him as she slept.

It bewildered her at first. She remembered his illustration of his inability to touch her, but he was no wraith now, but solid and real and warm as any man.

Any man. Darkness still covered the windows. She knew she ought to push away in alarm, ought to put him away from her, but his sleeping form, so warm against hers, roused a curious mixture of protectiveness and desire in her.

She had never touched a man. Unable to resist her curiosity, she spread her fingers a little, gauging the sensation of supple flesh over lean muscle. He smelled of some elusive note that made her think of primrose blooming in the shadows of the forest. Very gently, so as not to disturb him, she pressed her face closer to his back, till her nose touched his spine, and breathed it in deep. A soft wash of awareness moved through her body as she inhaled the essence of him, an awakening notice of her own back, and her limbs, and her hands and breasts. She wanted to straighten her legs and uncurve her body and press the whole of herself against him.

It was hard to say when he wakened, what little thing gave him away first. There was a tiny movement in his hands, a shift in his breathing, a soft sound of surprise. Then, as if startled, he turned suddenly to face her.

"I can feel you," he whispered, and touched her cheek with his fingers in amazement. In wonder, he stroked her face, her brow, her neck, very gently. "Your skin . . ." As if overcome, he closed his mouth.

Looking up at him, Moira was flooded with tenderness. "Did you sleep well?"

"Yes." He stared at her mouth, and she saw him swallow. He closed his eyes, and Moira recognized the wish to unsee what had already been seen, to avoid temptation. He opened his eyes. "I have thought of kissing you many times. You were protected then, because I could not." His thumb grazed her lower lip restlessly. "May I kiss you, Tara?"

She lifted her hand and drew him down.

It was exquisitely gentle, just a soft, sweet brush of lips and mingling breath. He touched her nose with his and looked at her, so close. His hand, when he lay it against her cheek, trembled slightly, and Moira felt a swift agony of yearning bolt through her. She shifted toward him, and felt his chest against her breasts, and sighed, her eyes closing.

His hand closed in a fist next to her ear, and his brow pressed close to hers. "I must go," he whispered. Another soft kiss feathered over her lips, and then he moved away.

"Oh, please don't," she protested in a fierce whisper. "Stay a little more."

He stood rigidly by her bed, looking down at her. "I cannot," he said, and she heard the strain in his voice.

Moira did not know what thing inside her made her shift suddenly and capture his hand. But she did it, took that slim, long-fingered hand in hers and drew it to her lips, and pressed her mouth to his palm and his wrist. She felt his other hand fall to her hair, his fingers tangling in a tight grip close to her scalp. A low groan came from his throat.

Then he was on his knees in front of her, tugging her head up with that fierce grip in her hair, and he kissed her. Hard and deep, with the unfettered loneliness of three hundred years behind it. Moira's breath left her, and she returned his passion without thought, with no sense of past or future, only now, and his mouth, and his low moan of yearning.

He broke free, breathing hard. "I must go."

He stood and walked away stiffly, and then he was simply gone. Moira fell back on her pillows with a soft cry of disappointment. She felt in her a roaring madness, a depth of yearning entirely at odds with her sensible ways. She touched her still tingling lips, and smelled him on her fingers, and she closed her eyes, and restlessly rubbed her neck and breasts, as if to ease the ache in them.

The wantonness of her gesture at last shocked her from the enchanted state of need, as if she'd been doused with water. Blinking, she sat up in her bed and clutched the coverlet to her.

Madness. What had she done?

Invited him to her bed, she who had never even kissed a man. Let him sleep beside her, then let him kiss her. And then, she, who had never been moved by a man one way or the other, had tried to seduce him. A faery.

She was too honest with herself to call it anything else. When he'd stood beside her bed, so beautiful and straight and struggling to restrain himself, the only thing in her mind had been to have him lie beside her, and take off his clothes so she could touch all of him, and feel his flesh against her own.

Even now, the idea made her feel dizzy. Even now, she wanted him. She pulled the covers over her head, shivering in reaction. What had possessed her?

The answer was clear, and all the more humiliating for

the plainness of it. Her own cousin pined away for the very same man—he obviously possessed a magic that worked on women's senses. By his own admission, he'd been a rake; it had led to his curse.

And Moira Ryan, known to all for her sensibility, had fallen like an autumn leaf to the wind of that charm.

No, she thought in some relief. Not fallen completely. She remained a virgin with an unsullied reputation. Her uncle would still be able to find her a respectable husband. She had not entirely fallen.

But only because Galen had resisted her. Resisted because he found her unappealing, or because he was noble? She thought of his first tender kiss, thought of his fist balled beside her cheek and knew it was not lack of desire.

So he had honor. The knowledge pained her in some way she couldn't name. She wanted him to be a brutal rake, for then she would not have to think of him anymore. Would not feel this need to ease that weariness on his face, or the need to sing him a sweet song, or the wish to make him laugh.

Burrowed there under the sheets that still smelled of him, Moira closed her eyes and prayed fiercely that she would not fall in love. Not with a faery. What a terrible fate that would be!

He could barely breathe as he stalked through his grove in the unholy light where it never was cold or hot, or rainy or bright. He did not notice. His blood was afire with the taste of Moira on his lips, the feel of her satin skin below his fingers, the lushness of her breasts pressing into his chest. And more—the passion that burned in her, lurking below the surface like a wild sea battering at the walls of her upbringing. Most maids had to be softly coaxed, sweetly wooed, and even then, their passion often frightened them.

Moira would not be frightened.

He halted, breathing hard, and leaned his back against a tree. Unthinking, he raised his palm to his mouth and remembered the way she had pressed kisses to the place with such ardent petition, her hair falling in copper rivers over her shoulders, down to the floor beside the bed. He had struggled with himself, fearing the penalty, but the white-draped curve of her back had proved his undoing. Before he'd even known he would act, he was kissing her.

He dropped his hand and lifted his face to the bland sky and thought of the way she had simply gestured for him to come to her bed last night. Innocently, she had invited him, for she witnessed his weariness. Innocently, too, he had gone. And innocently slept in her bed after three hundred years of aching for a woman.

Even this morning, when it would have been so easy to take what she offered, he could think only that he could not bear to be yanked from her again. In her bed, and even when he knelt, kissing her like a wild lost man, he had dared not think of any carnal thing.

"Well done," said a dulcet voice at his side.

Galen looked at the Queen in misery. "Why did you send me there?"

"That answer is plain, Galen, my sweet. To see if you had the will to resist her."

He narrowed his eyes. "It was a test?"

"Yes," she said with amusement, then sobered. "Do you love her?"

"How can I know? She is the first woman I've spoken to, touched, in centuries. I'd love my shadow after so long a drought."

She smiled her pointed little smile. "Ah. Perhaps. You will know it soon enough, I suppose."

"How?"

Coyly, she drifted a little way from him. "I have decided to let you try to save the cousin. There is an old cure for the faery-struck: you'll take mortal form for seven days and seven nights."

"And then?" Galen suspected another trick. "If she recovers, will you lift this wretched curse?"

She waved a hand airily. "We shall see. There will be much temptation, dear Galen. I wonder how you will manage that?"

His mind strayed to Moira, but just as quickly, he turned his thoughts away. "How am I to go among them?"

"It has been arranged." She lifted her hands. "Are you ready?"

He picked up his pipe and lifted his chin. "I am."

She clapped her hands.

Chapter Five

Two nights in a row Moira went to the oak tree and called to Galen. Twice she was disappointed. As she returned from the meadow the second night, Desi gloomily walking beside her, one of the maids called to her urgently, "My lady, come quick! The lady is asking for you. Hurry!"

Lifting her skirts, Moira bolted for her cousin's chamber, fearing the worst. At the threshold, she stopped, stunned. "Blanche?"

Her cousin was sitting up in bed, her cheeks rosy as dawn, her eyes clear and heartbreakingly beautiful. The blond curls that had lain so dispiritedly on the pillows now fell around her face in an airy cloud. "Moira!"

Gladness burst in Moira's chest, and she rushed across the room to fling her arms about her cousin's shoulders. "Oh, I am so happy to see you back to yourself!" she cried. "When did you awaken?" She looked over her shoulder to the maid. "What healed her at last?"

The servant shrugged. "She just woke up and said she was hungry. Just like that." She made the sign of the evil eye, and Moira scowled.

"Now they believe me," she muttered under her breath.

"Have they not brought my tray yet?" Blanche said. "I vow I could eat every bit of food in England."

When the servant had gone to check, Moira turned back and peered hard into her cousin's face. "Tell me what happened. Did the music cease?"

"Music?" Blanche echoed.

"Never mind." She stroked her hair. "What do you remember?"

Blanche cocked her head. "Nothing. Did I hit my head?"

"No. It was a sudden fever. We don't know what it was."

"My wedding!" she cried. "How long till the wedding?"

"It has been postponed."

"No, it must go on." She moved, tossing back the coverlet. Moira had a glimpse of her pretty white shins before the nightrail fell down to cover them. "How long? What is the day today?"

"It's impossible, Blanche!" She captured her arm. "You must stay in bed a little longer. At least one day, to regain your strength."

Imperiously, Blanche shook her off. "Tell me what day it is."

Moira had her own core of stubbornness. "Get back in bed and I will. Get back in bed and stay there till I say you may get out, and I will personally carry all your messages out to the world beyond."

A glitter shone in the pale blue eyes. "Very well," she said with mock meekness. When she pulled the cover up, she said, "Tell me."

"One week from today," she said.

"A week!"

"I told you. But if you are so eager, and you do not have a relapse, I don't see why we can't manage to make it all work."

Blanche took her hand and kissed it. "You're too good, cousin."

"I am," she agreed, but smiled to take the sting from the words.

It was only later, alone in her room, that she remembered Galen's absence from the grove. Had he made some bargain to free Blanche from his spell?

He must have. She stared at herself in the mirror. Would she never see him again? Was that the price of saving Blanche? Her face paled visibly at the thought, and a sharp pain arrowed through her chest.

She sank down to the little chair before her writing desk. "I've fallen in love with him, Desi," she said to her dog. "What am I to do?"

He only groaned.

For an entire day, Galen could only drift from one sensory pleasure to the next. He ate and drank, reveling in every morsel and sip, taking an hour to eat a hunk of bread and butter and drink a glass of wine. He bathed in water up to his neck and gloried in the soft currents around his body, in his hair, on his face, sitting so long the water grew ice cold, and even that was a pleasure.

He'd found himself in a sprawling country house, manned with servants who seemed to think him a long-term resident. His valet laid out unfamiliar clothes for him, and told him he preferred reds and blues to the washed-out pastels that were so insipidly in fashion. Galen allowed himself to be trussed in the strange, tight-fitting clothes when he saw how they suited his form. He also allowed his hair to be tied back in a neat queue down his back, but drew the line at powder or wig.

He learned he was a lord, neighbor to Rosewood, and was expected at a pre-wedding supper the following evening. He did not wonder at the power of the Queen to bewitch the entire county, but he wondered if Moira would be included in the bewitchment. Would she know him as himself, or would she, too, think of him as Lord Woodman?

Woodman. He chuckled a little over that.

As his carriage pulled up before the sprawling old manor of Rosewood, Galen blinked at the visual splendor. A spill of brightly gowned ladies and dark-coated gentlemen poured into the drive, and at the edges of the lawn, trees boasted dressings of yellow and scarlet and pumpkin-colored leaves, dazzling against the dark blue-green of fir and purpling evening sky. After so long an exile, Galen felt nearly breathless with wonder at the brightness of the mortal world.

From the protective cocoon of his coach, he watched the mortals in their finery ascend the old stone steps he remembered. There were newer wings that had been added to the house during his exile, but this part he remembered of old. Many a generation had he climbed those steps. The daughters of Rosewood had ever been exceedingly fine.

As if called by his thought, one of those daughters emerged from the house now, and Galen had to admit she was one of the finest of all. Her deep blue gown displayed shoulders as unblemished as new fallen snow and a demure plumpness of breasts that promised to be as soft and white as rose petals. A shimmering golden curl lay across her collarbone.

That was surely Blanche, the cousin about whom Moira had been so worried, the girl who was to be married. He eyed her with a sort of delicious absorption, remembering all at once how mortal women had felt, how they smelled, what sort of cries they made when in the throes of pleasure.

But even when he probed for it, he could find no desire in him for the woman. He took pleasure in her beauty in much the same way as he drank of the look of late roses climbing the walls, or the trees against the sky. Pleasing to gaze upon, no more.

In some relief, he tapped on the roof and climbed down. The force of his delight in sensory pleasures this day had worried him. His starved senses were like beasts unchained, and he'd been sorely afraid he would not be able to resist the lure of mortal flesh. But Blanche was surely the most tempting and beautiful of woman there that night, and he'd felt not even a stir for her. He let go of his breath with a smile. It was only women he was bid to forgo. The rest of it—the food and wine and conversation—were his for the indulgence.

And he intended to indulge most heartily.

He gave instruction to the driver and took up his walking stick, turning with a jaunty little whistle to ascend the stairs with the rest. He nodded to a paunchy squire in an ill-fitting coat, finding the man's name miraculously upon his tongue. "Sir Edward."

But as he reached the top of the entryway, Moira came out of the doors on some errand, whispering something into her uncle's ear. Galen's carefree cheer evaporated. He had never seen her dressed for a party.

She wore a jeweled shade of silk. Green, the color of the Faerie. Like her cousin's, the gown displayed her shoulders. But Blanche was thin and willowy, where Moira was voluptuous. What seemed modest on the blonde was sinfully wanton on the other. His gaze swept the exposed flesh and his mouth dried with longing.

Her skin near glowed against the green, and her breasts were high and full, her waist slim, and the silk clung in a way that made Galen clench his fists. Her hair, thick and lively, could scarcely be contained in the arrangement upon her head, and wisps of it framed her face, fell down her neck, brushed her shoulders. As Galen stared, transfixed, something her uncle said made her laugh, and Moira gave that surprised hoot of earthy laughter he enjoyed so much. Her lips parted and her head went back and Galen stared at her white throat.

He burned, looking at her. Burned. His blood all leapt to life at once in his veins and roared through his body till he could hear nothing but his own chemistry responding to her. Deep in his loins there rose an almost unbearable yearning, and it seemed his mouth and the heart of his palm tingled with the ghostly imprint of fervent kisses.

The force of his lust made the glory of sunlight and chocolate and beauty seem very small and far away. Every moment of every one of his years of exile coalesced into now, into this moment, and from the depths of him, from that place mortals called a soul, came a silent, piercing cry.

Moira.

As if he had roared the name aloud, she turned abruptly, the smile fading from her mouth. Her luminescent eyes widened in recognition when she saw him. Staring, he moved toward her.

"Woodman," George said heartily. "Heard you'd got back in time. Good, good. You remember my niece, Moira, don't you?"

Galen managed a polite smile, and bent over her hand. His fingers trembled faintly as her flesh and his met, and he looked at her, unable—and unwilling—to hide his roaring desire.

"I do remember," he said in a voice that was raspier than it should have been. "I wonder if she remembers me?"

She swallowed. There was fear in her eyes, but the tiniest shudder shook her, and a flush stained the upper curve of her breasts. "Of course," she said, and her voice, like fingers, stroked his body, all over, all at once. He forced himself to straighten, let go of her hand. He was dizzy with the look of her eyes, the impression of her soft mouth, and looked away.

When he'd reined himself, he clasped his hands behind his back. "Do you have a moment to spare, my lady?" he asked smoothly.

Pure terror blazed in her eyes. "My uncle needs me just now," she said. "Perhaps later."

"Oh, don't be silly, girl!" George cried. "Run along. Show our guest to the punch. I'm fine here."

Moira smiled stiffly. "Very well. Come, Lord Woodman. Shall I show you the gallery?"

"Delightful," he said, and offered his arm.

She led him through the foyer, and into a long hall where few guests lingered. Neither of them spoke. Galen could not. He was formed of pure desire, his only thoughts, his only need to put his hands on her, his mouth to her lips, his body against hers.

Her hand trembled on his arm, and he saw that she was as moved as he; her skin glowed with the rush of blood in her, and the tips of her breasts showed as alert and hungry points beneath the glazing of green silk.

But she was not starved, as he had been, and managed to wave a hand toward one painting and another, naming ancestors who stretched back to the Crusades.

At last the gallery was empty, and Galen halted, turning toward her with an urgent hunger, intending to steal a kiss here in the dim brown quiet, with only the last of the day's light coming through a long narrow window to the south.

She halted him. "No!" she cried sharply and quietly. "Stand back."

He stopped. "Tara," he said softly, using the protective name she'd given him out of respect. He held out his hand. "I only want to kiss you."

"What are you doing here?"

"It was the only way to break the spell." The small light from the window illuminated her cheek, the side of her neck, one lush slope of each breast. He could not tear his eyes away. "Are you so displeased?"

"I—you look . . ." she shook her head. "I am surprised."

Galen took a step toward her. "You are beautiful." As if the sound of his voice wounded her, she closed her eyes. "Like a flame," he said. "Like all the colors of autumn."

She opened her eyes. "Galen, please, I beg you to leave me. To leave here."

"I cannot."

"If you seduce me," she whispered fiercely, "I will be ruined."

Ruined. "And I would be doomed."

She softened suddenly, and took a step toward him. "Then why do you look at me that way?"

Drawn by her movement, Galen, too, stepped forward, until they stood only a hand's breadth apart, not touching but for their locked gazes. "I will not lie, Moira. I ache to touch you." He looked at her mouth, red and ripe as the cider he loved, "Kiss you." He tried to resist temptation, but failed, and let his gaze fall lower, over the soft shoulders, and lower still, to her plump breasts, "I want to stroke your breasts, and kiss them till you cry out."

"Stop," she whispered, but did not move. Her breath came in shallow, hurried bits, and her hands were balled into tight fists.

Galen made a low noise and looked at her eyes again. "It might be worth my doom," he murmured. "But it is not worth yours."

She stared at him, and he saw everything, saw the world in her eyes, before she lifted her chin and, with an act of purest will, took a step back. "We must not be alone."

"No." Taking a breath, he managed a small humorless smile." 'Tis only six days and nights, not an endless, unthinkable sojourn."

"Oh." Impossible to tell whether the sound expressed disappointment or relief. Perhaps both.

"Shall we return to your guests?"

She nodded, puppetlike, and smoothed her gown as if they'd been embracing, then she, too, took a deep breath. Only to steady herself, he was sure, as he had done, but the movement made her breasts swell, ripe and soft and white, against the emerald silk and he groaned, turning away so he would not slam her against the wall and ravish her there. Now.

"Give me a moment," he managed.

He stared at the painting before him unseeing, calling

up visions of the dead world he'd inhabited these long, long centuries. Bit by bit, the turmoil in him slowed, and he forced himself to focus on the painting itself. The colors, red and white and bits of shiny gold. A Renaissance gown. He smiled bitterly as he realized what he focused upon: the bosom of a woman, displayed proudly by red velvet.

It calmed him somehow. This could be done. Seven days and seven nights. Only six now. And perhaps, at the end, he would at last be free.

With a dry smile, he raised his eyes to the face of the portrait.

The air left him, the smile bled from his face, and he must have made some sound of protest or sorrow, for Moira asked, "Did you know her?"

"She died young," he said, thinking of the day even the leaves had seemed to weep for the loss of a beautiful daughter of Rosewood. The day she had lain under a shroud of gauze, with rose and violet petals scattered over her tenderly. "By her own hand. I had seduced her."

"When Elizabeth was Queen." Her voice was stronger now. "I see."

Galen turned away, a thickness in his chest. "Tongues will wag if we linger here anymore, my lady."

She nodded, and moved forward as if to take his arm. He drew away. "You must not touch me," he said in a choked voice.

For a moment, she only looked at him, her wide brown eyes filled with compassion and worry. Then she bowed her head and moved away. Galen followed a step or two behind.

Chapter Six

Supper was an endless misery. Moira felt only the thinnest, brittlest hold over herself, as if her face with its tight smile was a fine glass mask that would shatter at the faintest touch. She chatted with her neighbors at table, laughing lightly in the right places, and picked at her meal. But all through it, Galen was there at the edge of her vision, drawing her attention to him, as he drew the attention of everyone in the room.

In the smoky twilight of the glade the first time she'd really seen him, then again in her dark bedroom, she had not had the full benefit of his beauty. Tonight, she was forced to take it in all at once, and it very nearly overwhelmed her.

It was not so much his tall grace, or the seductive gleam of his bright green eyes, or even the promise of sensuality that hung in the air like a musky scent, capturing the attention of every female from six to ninety. It was not his lyrical voice, or the laughter that made them all want to laugh with him, or his beautiful hands or the hair that lay in glossy rippling invitation on his neck.

It was all of that, and more, and less. It was the enchantment of Faerie.

She was most desperately torn. Her flesh ached for him, for the feel of his hands and lips. Need pulsed in the crook of her elbow and the joints of her toes and the edge of her earlobe, making her restless and irritable. But her soul wanted to protect him, protect him from the despair she'd glimpsed on his face when he looked at the painting, protect him from having to return to the lost world of his exile, protect him from himself. And from her.

Six days, he'd said. Surely he would not be among them much—though she suspected she would have to endure at least one more day with him. The day of the wedding.

Blanche found her as the quartet tuned its instruments. "Lord Woodman has not stopped staring at you since he came in this evening," she whispered. "He fair burns, by the look of him."

Moira blushed. "Don't be silly. He's a rake and a gambler. He stares at all women."

Blanche inclined her pretty head. "He's not looking at me that way." A tiny smile curled her pink mouth. "If he had, I might have been determined to marry him instead of Robert."

"Marry?" Moira tamped down her jealousy. "What possible good could such a man be to an honest woman?"

"You are too innocent, cousin," Blanche said, her eyes on the Galen. "Turn around and look at him."

Moira ladled punch into her cup. "No."

Blanche laughed, and grasped her by the shoulders. "Just look, Moira."

"I've seen him."

"Look." Blanche put her arms around her cousin and rested her chin on her shoulder. "He's looking at you."

Moira lifted her eyes reluctantly, and it was true. Galen stood near the door to the hallway, all lazy grace and charm. His coat and waistcoat were cut of scarlet brocade and she remembered thinking he was like a ruby, burning with color. He stared at her with a sober, intent expression on his face.

In her ear, Blanche said, "Think of pressing your mouth to those lips. Think of those beautiful hands on your body, sliding all over you."

Oh, she had! Once snared, she could not seem to turn away, and her imagination poured forth pictures to illustrate the words Blanche purred in her ear. "Think of him lying in your bed next to you. Can you imagine what might make such a marriage worthwhile?"

Moira turned away abruptly, her skin hot. "He would take a thousand mistresses."

Blanche laughed. "Perhaps. But you know what they say, a reformed rake is the best husband."

"But those who truly reform are counted in smaller numbers than the hairs on Lord Unwin's head." Blindly, she helped herself to a sweet and put it in her mouth. The taste appeased her hunger a little, and she eagerly took another.

"Ah, well," Blanche said with a shrug. "You've missed your chance now. Lady Greythorpe is bearing down upon him as we speak."

Moira could bear not another moment. "Excuse me," she blurted out, and bolted for the garden. And silence. And some semblance of sanity.

She found a bench in the darkness, and gulped in the clean night air. Her flesh was so overheated she did not even feel the cold.

Six days. Six days and he would be free. If she had to lock herself in her chamber for that time, she would not venture near him again until that time was done.

In her green globe, the Queen watched avidly as the days passed. Six left, then three, then two. He had not broken. But he had not seen the girl. She suspected he did not know he was walking her world as mortal only, with no faery charm to help him.

"Will he break the curse laid upon him?" The question came from her lover, who lay in long-limbed golden splendor beside her.

She did not take her eyes from the globe, which showed Galen staring out a window of his estate toward Rosewood. "He's not been fully tested to now. He's not seen the girl. Tomorrow," she said. "Tomorrow we shall see."

With a twist of her wrist, she sent the world within the globe swirling, and waited with her tiny tongue between her teeth for the magic waters to settle. It showed a girl sitting before a mirror in a simple, armless chemise. Candlelight shimmered in the glass, and sparked red and gold fire from her hair.

The Queen's consort rose on one elbow. "He could bring her to the land of Faerie, could he not?"

"Not this one," she said slowly. "She's a child of the earth. She would be unhappy here."

"She would adjust."

The Queen narrowed her eyes. "Fancy her, do you?"

His smile was triumphant, and she smiled in acknowledgment of her own jealousy. Tit for tat.

The girl's aura shone with the braided colors of passion and loneliness, and to the Queen's surprise, there was love there, too. "Well," she said in surprise, and smiled. Tomorrow would be amusing indeed. She was fond of the child; too many had forgotten Faerie in this modern world, but Moira had not.

A pity it was for Galen she'd conceived her passion. The Queen did not think he'd changed much, even after all these years.

But she'd been wrong before. Tomorrow would tell. So much emotion these mortals had, and Galen had grown to be much like them. She wondered if he had the will to resist the subject of his passion, and if the girl would prove stronger. The Queen had done what she could for them. By nightfall, the end of this story would be told. Both would be doomed or both would rejoice.

The days passed in a kind of sensual haze. Galen dared not drink spirits, fearing his control would snap entirely, but he ate until he thought he would burst. He swam in the river, naked, and did not care that his flesh ached with cold when he emerged. He walked ceaselessly, marching the lanes and byways and paths till he knew the entire county and his bones were heavy with weariness. At night, he slept like a mortal, and did not dream.

Six days, then three, then only one more to survive. He had not seen Moira for even a moment in all that time, but this last day, he could not avoid her. He was to attend the wedding of her cousin, and Moira would be there.

And this was his test. He felt it in his bones.

There was to be a grand ceremony at the local church, then a wedding supper at Rosewood. Tonight, the full moon marked the seventh night of his walk in the mortal realm. By tomorrow, he would be free if he could prove himself.

If.

But as he entered the church, the first person he saw was Moira, standing in the vestibule with flowers in her coppery hair. The gown was a terrible shade of pink for her, a muddied shade that clashed with her hair and made her skin look sallow.

But it did not matter. His skin, every inch, rippled with awareness at the sight of her. He drank in the look of her thick hair, so richly colored, and the glory of her pale, smooth skin, and the bow of her mouth. As if she cast some glamour over him, he found himself drawn to where she stood, her dark eyes full of misery.

"You're lovely, Tara. Fit to sit at the court of your Irish kings." He dared not touch her, and laced his fingers tightly behind his back.

She lowered her eyes, and a pain went through him at the dip of her head, the shape of her nose, and the curve of her ear. "I look a sight," she whispered. "It's an awful color for me." As if to wash it to a better shade, she smoothed the skirts over her legs with a restless movement.

Pierced by her embarrassment, Galen gave in to his wish and took her hand in his, lifting it to his mouth for a kiss. The dry, light curl of her fingers over the edge of his hand made a prickle of sensation rush down his neck, and he stepped closer, willing her to lift her eyes. "You are beautiful," he repeated.

She stared up at him. "Don't flirt with me, Galen. I cannot bear it."

But wrapped as he was in his desire for her, he could not halt. He pressed her palm to his lips, slowly, and kissed the tender center.

She did not move away, and he saw a faint shudder pass through her. With a soft cry, she turned her head.

Only the hearty laughter of a man behind him brought Galen to his senses. He dropped her hand and stepped back, his heart pounding with fear and desire. With a soft curse, he left her, willing himself to keep his distance for the rest of the day. Only hours now till he won his freedom.

Somehow, Moira managed to get through the ceremony and supper, clinging to the knowledge that the dress made her look like a dowdy country cousin—which in fact she was. Not even Galen could desire her at the moment. It was a shield of pink silk.

But it was not so much that she needed protection against him as much as protection from herself. Every night this week, she had dreamed of him, and wakened to memories of him lying next to her. As he moved among the guests, laughing and talking, she stared at him hungrily, wistfully, wishing he were anyone but himself, a magic being from the Otherworld.

She had never been so miserable in all her life, and there was a part of her that resented Galen for stealing away her gift for happiness. She was even tempered. Everyone said so. She was cheerful and calm and sensible by nature. Nothing rattled her for long.

Except Galen.

The long windows around the ballroom began to darken with sunset, which served only to illuminate the gaiety within. Moira stood near one corner, watching the dancers in their finery spin like flowers on the wide floor.

Galen appeared at her side, so suddenly she started. He took her arm with a firm grip. "Come with me," he said in his silvery voice. "There is a sight you must not miss."

"But—"

His eyes shone as he covered her lips with one finger. "Please. I am only a man, like all others—I cannot bewitch you with some glamour."

The long black hair glowed with candlelight, inviting a woman's fingers to muss it, and his eyes were green as emeralds. Against her elbow, his hand was strong and dry and unbearably arousing. Mortal or faery, he was the most alluring creature she had ever known, and she had no wish to resist him. Still, she frowned. "We are not to be alone."

His mouth sobered, but there was still a dazzling light in his eyes. "Only for a moment." He tugged her hand urgently. "Please come with me to the garden. I must share this with you."

Moira, a little bewildered by his excitement, nodded.

With musical laughter, he rushed toward the French doors closest to them, pulling her along behind him. In spite of her wariness, Moira was swept into his mood as they dashed into the cold night and ran down the stone terrace along the house to the east, where a wall of hedges cast long shadows. Just before they moved into the open promenade, Galen halted. "Close your eyes."

She'd gone along with him thus far and saw no reason to quarrel now. She did as he requested.

He tugged her hand, leading her beyond the hedges and into the open, then put his hands on her shoulders to turn her around. "All right," he said, his voice a nectar in her ear, "now open them."

She did. And gasped. For to the east, the moon had risen, an enormous ball of pale orange, as big as the entire mansion of Rosewood. Moira covered her mouth with her hands. "Oh!"

"The harvest moon," he said. "There is no night in all the year on which it is more beautiful than this."

She laughed happily at the sight, letting it fill her, forgetting all but the wonder of such a thing. "It's beyond lovely."

He stepped toward it, as if he would walk on the path of the light into the glowing sphere itself. His face shone, and with a purely pagan gesture, raised his arms to either side, as if to encompass it, clasp it to him. "I have not seen it in three centuries," he said, and tipped back his head to the light.

Moira stared at him, at the light on his throat. It haloed his lean form, glossed his hair with hints of yellow, and it seemed to her he was all that was beautiful and good and holy in all the world.

She stepped close, slipping behind him so she wouldn't block the path of light falling on him, and put her hand on his back, then sighed and put her head against him, too, breathing of the smell of him, and his warmth. "Galen, I will miss you so," she whispered.

His arms came down and his body grew utterly still beneath her cheek. Shamelessly, Moira did not move. Her heart pounded heavily in her chest as she waited, but some voice told her this was the right thing to do now. After tonight, he would be gone from her.

Slowly, he turned. "Moira," he whispered, and the sound was choked. She had a blurred impression of his bright eyes, and a circle of light around the edges of his hair, and then he crushed her to him, his whole body against hers, his mouth desperately hungry as he kissed her. A sound rose between them, low and soft, half moan, half cry of joy.

And here was true magic—the taste of his tongue, which was moonlight and honey; the low sound of his need, spiraling with silver warmth down her spine, through her breasts and belly, into her heart. Hunger, sweet and dark, rose in her, filled her, made her nearly weep with wonder. His lips moved over her face, on her neck; he bent and kissed the swell of her breasts.

Moira kissed him back, his mouth and his neck; she poured her fingers through his hair, reveling in the cool heavy texture of it.

He gasped and raised his head, and put her away a little. Both of them breathed unsteadily. "For this, Moira, I would willingly trade all the days and all the nights that lie ahead of me." He closed his eyes, put his brow against hers. "But I will not ruin you."

Moira wanted to protest, wanted to beg him to bring his lips back to her throat, but his honor stopped her. She stepped back. "And I do not care for my own ruin, but will not condemn you to your endless loneliness again."

Quickly, fighting tears that washed down her cheeks, she stepped forward and kissed his mouth. "But I do love you, Galen. With all my heart. If you are able, show yourself to me one day. I will wait."

He cried out and captured her in a close embrace, burying his face against her neck. "I cannot bear to leave you," he whispered, and she thought she felt dampness on her jaw. "I love you," he whispered, and breathed deeply, as if to inhale her, make her part of him. "I love you," he said again, brokenly, then let her go. "Be well," he said.

And strode away under the great harvest moon, toward the forest, and the Faerie Land that lay somewhere within.

In her bower, the Faerie Queen sat alone, her green globe in her hands. Tears ran brilliant as quicksilver on her moonwhite cheeks as she watched the lovers part. They were tears of victory—for at last Gancomer had learned his lesson, and he would now be free. But they were tears of sorrow, as well, for she knew what his choice would be.

He cried out the Queen's name, the sound echoing with unholy power through the court of Faerie. The Queen smiled. Adorned in a gown of moon beams, she rode into the night to meet him.

Chapter Seven

Galen strode to the ancient oak in the middle of the field and roared the Queen's name. As he waited, silence ringing around him, he turned and paced, then unable to bear it, cried her name again.

Her laughter, like the ringing of crystal, wove through the trees, and he stormed toward the sound. "Free me," he said when she appeared. "You must free me."

She inclined her head. "Tell me first what you have learned, Galen, my sweet."

"Nothing," he said. "Only that I love her. And I cannot have her as long as I am faery."

"You wish to become mortal."

A tightness marked her voice, and Galen felt the smallest flush of shame. Among his own race, such a request would be met with gales of laughter at best. Horror, at worst.

But there was no hesitation in him as he knelt at his Queen's feet. "I do, My Lady. It has ever been my wish. I did not know it till now."

"But you will die, as they die."

He raised his head. "And come back, as they do. To love again."

"I can make it seem you are mortal for as long as she lives." She touched his head. "It would grieve me to see you age, but even that could be managed."

He gazed into her ancient and unmarked face. "No. I wish to be truly mortal," he said quietly, surely. "To live beside her, forever."

The Queen bowed her head, and for a moment, he thought he saw a tear on her white cheek. "You are already mortal, Galen," she said softly. "I saw it happen. I thought, once you'd tasted of it, once you'd regained your freedom, you would be glad to be faery again." She paused. "I was wrong."

Joy crept into him. "I am mortal *now?* And she loves me as I am?"

"Yes. Your love transformed you."

"Then what . . ."

She sighed. "I had hoped to bring you to the land of Faerie, where you would not grow old, or die, Galen. I am fond of you. I had hoped you would come and ask me to change her heart to come to us." Now he was sure there was grief on her mouth, in her eyes. "But I will grant your wish, for you have earned the right to ask for your reward."

He stood, and lifted her hand to his lips. "You are the finest of all women, mortal or faery, My Queen."

The Queen swayed forward and pressed a magic kiss to his lips. He felt it through him, a blessing and a benediction. "It will give her, too, the gift of long life. For both of you."

Then she was gone, and Galen, Lord of Woodman, stood in the middle of a plain grove, a mortal man with his whole life before him. Moonlight washed down upon him, and filled him. Wind blew on his face, cold and sharp. Above him the branches soughed and creaked, and leaves blew free to dance in the air.

He threw back his head and laughed.

*   *   *

Moira paced the ballroom, restless as a cat. At last, realizing no one would miss her, she gathered her cloak and tossed it around her shoulders, escaping into the moon-drenched night.

Here it was quieter, and the wind cooled her heated cheeks. She leaned on the balustrade and gazed up at the risen moon. From the doors behind her came the sound of the hired string quartet playing something sad and sweet. She hummed along, trying to regain her lost sense of happiness. Happiness, she knew, did not come from big things, but from little ones. From stopping to gaze at a moon or a flower, to smell bread baking, to listen to the sweet strains of a pipe.

A shiver went through her. There had been no piper in the quartet. But there it was again, a light sweet sound, as delicate as the wing of a butterfly. It danced through the air from some invisible source, and Moira felt she could almost *see* the sound—an incandescent swirl there against the trees, where blackbirds began to sing with voices sweet and beautiful as morning.

A ripple of anticipation rose on her flesh, and she straightened almost without realizing she did so. The music swelled, richer now, not so delicate, fuller and stronger and more compelling, and as it grew, so did the voices of the birds. Not only blackbirds now, who were known to sing at night, but sparrows and wrens and robins joined in as well. A gull cried counterpoint, and a jay with his unpleasing caw even gave a kind of leaping life to the swelling of the symphony in the air.

Louder and fuller and wider the music grew, and behind her in the ballroom, the quartet seemed to be moved by it, for their viols and cellos turned to a lilting, resonant piece in perfect harmony with the pipe and birds, and now even the sweetness of laughter ringing in the ballroom.

And from the garden came a lone figure, playing his

pipe. A tall, lean figure, so familiar to her from those days—only weeks before—when she had not been able to see his face in the dark grove. With a catch in her throat, she watched him come ever closer.

Her heart swelled with the joy in the music, with the life of it leaping through the air, with the wild celebration and wholeness it expressed. She covered her mouth, afraid to hope.

But then he stopped at the foot of the steps and threw out his arms and laughed. "I am mortal, my love. Forever." His face shone with a joy of such depth it moved Moira nearly to tears. "Come!"

Something bright and wild burst in her, and with a cry, she hurtled down the steps and into his arms with such force that he spun around with her, lifting her feet off the ground.

And then he kissed her. And around them broke a new burst of birdsong, and the viols and cellos danced. Pure light filled Moira as he kissed her, pure love, purest, most perfect joy.

In a moment, he lifted his head, and his face was ablaze. "You will be my wife."

"Yes. Will we be poor? I do not mind it, but—"

"No! I am yet Woodman, with my estates and my servants who will never question why I am there. Or you." He put his hand on her face. "Or our children. Oh, children, Moira! Our own."

His wonder was almost childlike, and it touched her. "You do not mind dying one day?"

"No immortal can ever know the truth of the love we have found, Moira. Not of this depth, not of this perfection." Soberly, he said, "It is worth whatever I trade for it."

Moira could not halt the soft, grateful tears on her face. "Oh, my love," she whispered, and kissed him.

"And now," he said, his eyes glittering. "I think we

should go tell your uncle that his niece is to be wed. Quickly."

Moira laughed. "Oh, yes."

He bent his head to lightly kiss her once more. "I burn for you, Moira, but will you mind waiting for our wedding night? I want it to be blessed and holy and pure."

It pierced her. "Not as long as we marry soon."

He halted. "There is one more thing, my love."

"Tell me."

"Though I am mortal now, our children will be half faery. If one wishes to go to that land, we must not stand in her way."

Moira imagined her children with his green, green eyes and gilded flesh. "I will not mind."

He slid his hand around her neck and, as he had before, pressed his brow to hers. "You are the finest gift I have ever known, my love."

And as they stood there, washed by the bright light of the harvest moon, Moira thought she heard a chorus of voices, unearthly and joyous, singing in celebration of the love she had found with Galen, a love for all time.

Dangerous Gifts

Mary Jo Putney

Most of the time, being a writer is a great life. You get to set your own hours, wear clothes that most people would turn into car wash rags, and when you're caught staring out the window, you can justly claim to be working.

However, writing is also the hardest work I've ever done, which is why when I was invited to join three friends in a faery anthology, I gave a sigh of pure delight. It was clear from the get-go that this project was going to be *fun*.

And so it has been. As a child I loved reading fairy tales, myths, and legends, and later I graduated to science fiction and fantasy. However, my own writing has tended to maintain at least a nodding acquaintance with reality, which is why it was so stimulating to debate the fine points of faery/mortal relationships with three marvelous, diverse authors.

Every life can use a little magic. I hope that you enjoy reading this tale of Faerie as much as I've enjoyed writing it.

Mary Jo Putney

Prologue

Liquid harp notes floated down the wind, gentle as a dream. The faery lord listened with closed eyes as the melody twined warmly around him. The harpist was a young mortal female, and she had played her haunting tunes in his wood many times. At first he had merely enjoyed the music. Then, when the winter chill kept her from the wood, he had realized how much more satisfying it would be to make the harpist his own. Then he would always have music.

When she returned to the wood in the spring, he had studied her and woven his plans. Today he would put them into motion. Impatient to begin, Ranulph of the Wood opened his eyes and set off toward the glade where the girl played her instrument with a power and passion that made the leaves and sunbeams dance.

At the edge of the glade, he paused in the shadows to study his quarry, Leah Marlowe. She sat on the trunk of a fallen tree, caressing the small Celtic harp like a lover as her fingers rippled out a tune that pierced the heart.

Slight of build with pale skin and straight brown hair,

the girl was not a beauty even by mortal standards. Compared to a lady of Faerie, she was positively plain. Yet there was a sweetness about her, and she had a magical gift for music. He would have that sweetness and magic for himself. Beguiling her would be an easy task, for she was shy and lonely. Perhaps, if he was lucky, he would have her in his gilded lair this very night.

He smiled at the thought, and prepared to step into the glade.

"Why don't you leave the child alone?"

Jolted out of his reverie by the husky feminine voice, Ranulph whirled, his hand falling to the hilt of his sword. A scant two yards away, a female of unearthly beauty lounged gracefully against an oak.

She was of Faerie, of course, for few mortals could see him until he revealed himself. But her complexion was dusky, not the snow-pale hue of the Folk, and silken hair of raven-wing black floated around her shapely form and cascaded to her heels. Her garb was as exotic as her person, a length of shimmering fabric that wrapped around her in a most revealing way, exposing one flawless shoulder and slim bare arms circled with dozens of gilded bangles.

Ranulph's gaze went over her appreciatively. Even by the standards of Faerie, she was stunning. "What is your name? I've never seen a faery like you."

"My name is Kamana." She smiled with feline amusement. "Most assuredly you have seen no one like me, for none of my Folk have ever journeyed so far. I come from the other side of the world, from the land of Hind."

"India," Ranulph said, intrigued. "So Faerie extends even there?"

"Faerie is everywhere, for we are of nature, not man." Kamana bent to pluck a sprig of woodruff, her bangles tinkling musically. "There are differences from land to land, of course. The mortals of Hind reflect us, just as your Anglish humans reflect you."

"English," he corrected.

"As you wish, my lord." She crushed the woodruff stem, releasing a scent like new-mown hay. "And what is your name?"

"I am Ranulph of the Wood. How did you manage to come so far? Did you travel through Faerie?"

She shook her head. "No, for that is a dangerous shifting way, more perilous even than the lands of men."

"Surely the mortal world was even worse!" he exclaimed, appalled. "Such great spans of desert and sea would be lethal to one of the Folk."

"I traveled with a shipment of shrubs and flowers brought back by an Anglishman who had lived many years in Hind. Townley filled half a ship's hold with his specimens, letting in the sunlight when the weather was fair. It was near enough to a garden for me to survive." Kamana's eyes, a shade of dark gold as unique as the rest of her, darkened to pure night. "For eight long months, I dwelt in that hold as the ship ran before the winds and rolled between the seas. I know now what human hell must be!"

Ranulph nodded, understanding how wretched such confinement would be for one of the Fair Folk. "Why did you undertake such a perilous passage?"

She shrugged, her garment shimmering with the iridescence of a butterfly wing. "From curiosity. For amusement." Light sparked again in her slanted eyes. "For destiny, perhaps, Lord Ranulph."

"Destiny," he snorted. "In this land, we forge our own fates."

"Or think you do," she said cryptically. "In Hind, we know that all beings dance to the measure of the weaver of the web, whether they recognize that or not." Her gaze went to the clearing, where the girl still played her harp, oblivious to the fact that she was observed. "The child plays exquisitely."

"It's hard to believe she is mortal," he agreed.

Kamana's eyes narrowed. "I suspect she has some faery

blood in her. See the shimmer of magic when her fingers touch the strings?"

The cursed female was right. Irritated that she had seen what he had not, Ranulph said shortly, "Whatever her blood, soon she will be playing her music only for me."

"You mean to ensorcel her?" Kamana arched her dark brows. "In Hind, we cannot bind a mortal unless he or she consents to be placed in our power."

"The law is the same here." His possessive gaze went to the girl again. "I shall offer her the dearest wish of her heart. She will accept, and soon she will be mine."

Kamana frowned. "You shame yourself to enslave an opponent so unequal to you. She is but a child."

"She will be my consort, not my slave," he said brusquely.

A faint expression of distaste showed on Kamana's exquisite face. "Among my Folk, it is considered . . . vulgar to take mortals for mates. Oh, lying with them is all very well—indeed, it's a great pleasure. But for consorts, we keep to our own kind. Surely there are ladies of Faerie who would suit you better."

"In this land the Folk are of two types, those who live in courts and celebrate together, and the solitaries, like me." He thought of the Love Talker, another solitary who'd been a friend of sorts until the lecherous fool had gotten himself exiled from both Faerie and the mortal realm as well. Voice clipped, Ranulph went on, "Oh, there are court ladies willing to come and share my bed for a night or two, but none would ever consider becoming consort to a solitary." He knew that for truth, because more than once he had invited one of the gilded court ladies to share his life, and been laughed at for his trouble.

There was flicker of brighter gold deep in her eyes. Then she nodded gravely. "It is the same in my own land. But the price for a mortal to leave her own kind and dwell in Faerie is high."

"So are the rewards." He moved his hand impatiently. "Begone, lady of Hind. I've work to do." He turned his back and moved into the glade. But behind him he heard laughter, and perhaps a trace of mockery.

Chapter One

Eyes closed and small body rocking gently, Leah flowed with her music, losing herself in the pulsing rhythms of the harp. In music, there was no loneliness or sorrow, only sweet abandon.

She came to the end of a long ballad and bent her head with a sigh. It was almost time to return home, and to drab reality.

Very near, someone cleared his throat. Her eyes flew open. To her surprise, a man of terrifying elegance stood right beside her. He was incredibly handsome, his immaculate London garb not concealing the strength of his tall frame.

Instantly tongue-tied, she clutched her harp and stammered, "A . . . are you lost, sir?"

He bowed, sweeping his hat so low that it brushed the verdant turf. "Not in the least. I came to find you, Leah, and in that I have succeeded." His hair was golden, and when he straightened, she saw that his eyes were a startling true, clear green.

She held the harp even more closely. "Why would you want to find me, sir?"

"I have often heard you playing your harp in my wood, Leah. Because of the pleasure I've had from your music, I've come to give you a gift."

"They are not your woods," she said politely. "This land is part of Marlowe Manor, so it belongs to my father, Sir Edwin Marlowe."

The stranger smiled, a chancy light dancing in his eyes. "There are many kinds of ownership, Leah. The wood is mine in a way that it will never belong to Sir Edwin."

"I have not given you leave to be free with my name." She stood, her harp in her arms, and began to edge away warily.

"I shall not harm you, Leah," he said as if reading her mind. "I desire only to grant your dearest wish."

Her mouth twisted. The late child of elderly parents, she had known she was an unwanted nuisance before she learned to walk. If she had been pretty and charming, she might have won her parents' hearts, but she had been as nondescript as the faded wallpaper in the hall. She had caused no trouble, and in return was treated with absent-minded courtesy. And this man spoke of granting her dearest wish! She wanted to be lovely and lovable, but even a London gentleman could not give her that.

"Ah, but I can," he said softly. "I am Ranulph of the Wood, a lord of Faerie. I can give you beauty so great that it will bring all mortal men to their knees. Wealth, fame, the love of heroes—you can have whatever, or whomever, you most desire."

She gaped at him. He was mad; there could be no explanation. Or perhaps she was merely dreaming.

"This is no dream." Ranulph took her right hand and raised it to his lips, pressing a cool kiss on her tense fingers. "It is a sign of your own magical gift of music that you can see me. Usually only sorcerers or simple country people can see the Folk, but sometimes artists and poets and musicians can also."

She pulled her hand away, beginning to wonder if by some wild chance this encounter could be real. The woods around her had always had an uncanny reputation, and the villagers avoided the area. Leah came to this glade to play because the music inside her was always most powerful here. "If you're a faery, prove it."

He shook his head sadly. "So skeptical, you modern mortals." He reached inside his coat and drew out a small looking glass. Then he extended it to her, his fingers trailing sparkling light. "See what you might be."

Leah looked into the glass, and almost passed out with shock. The image revealed was stunningly beautiful. Her mousy brown hair had become a marvelously thick, glossy mane streaked with sun-kissed blondness, while her nondescript, gray-green eyes were a striking shade of green. Her fair skin seemed almost to glow and her features had been refined to exquisite perfection. Yet eerily, the face was still hers.

The image shimmered, and suddenly it showed plain Leah Marlowe again. She gave a small whimper of protest at the loss of that vision of loveliness.

Ranulph lowered the mirror. "You can look like that, Leah. Say the word, and you will be able to go to London as an acclaimed beauty and take your choice of the finest gentlemen in Britain. You shall be declared a diamond of the first water. Become a duchess, perhaps, if that is what you wish."

"Such beauty would be wasted, for my parents would never take me to town." She tried to sound as if that deprivation did not bother her.

"There is more than one way to get to London."

Nervously she brushed back her hair, torn between disbelief and the palpable reality of her surroundings. The scents and sounds were of the familiar glade, and this Ranulph seemed as genuine as anyone she'd ever seen.

He smiled at her. "I am as real as you, though of a different nature."

He could also read her mind, which certainly supported his claim of being a faery. Warily she said, "You will give me so much simply because you've enjoyed my music?"

He gave a world-weary shrug. "You would also have to make some small future payment when I come to claim it."

She looked into his eyes, and suddenly believed that he was what he said, for there was something deeply alien in those green depths. Something ancient beyond words, even though his face was that of a man in the prime of his life.

"You want my soul," she said flatly. "There are stories of faeries stealing human souls because they have none of their own."

He laughed, as charming as the London gentleman he resembled. "You mustn't believe all those old tales. I have no interest in stealing your soul."

"Do you have a soul of your own?"

"I really don't know," he said thoughtfully. "The Folk live so long that the issue is not one I have considered. But I assure you that even if I lack a soul myself, I wouldn't know how to take yours, much less what to do with it."

Oddly, she believed him, even though this conversation was increasingly bizarre. "If not my soul, what would you want of me?"

He shrugged again. "I haven't decided."

Relieved to have a good reason to deny his gift, she said, "I can't possibly agree to something when I don't know the price to be paid."

She started to move away, but he caught her gaze with his. "When the time comes, I will give you three choices. I shall not ask for your soul or your life—my oath upon it," he said with cool deliberation. "Surely one of the choices offered will be something you shall not mind paying."

She hesitated, knowing she should leave, but unable to deny the mesmerizing lure of his green eyes. Trying to sound firm, she said, "No."

"You will be beautiful beyond words, Leah," he said softly. "Men will offer you their love, their wealth, their devotion. Heroes will lay their glory at your feet. You will be the most envied woman in the land."

To be loved, not alone. To be beautiful. She thought of that entrancing image in the mirror, and wanted to weep with longing.

Seeing that she was weakening, he said in a voice like honey, "I am not asking you to do evil, my dear girl. You have blessed me and my wood with your music. I simply want to give you a token of my gratitude. But according to the laws of my world, a faery cannot give a gift without some kind of exchange. I say again, you will not have to forfeit your soul, or your life. You'll have three choices, Leah. Surely one will be the merest trifle for you to pay."

Treacherously, he raised the mirror again. The beautiful Leah was there, garbed in silk and lace instead of the drab, worn gown that the real Leah wore.

She looked into the eyes of her false image, trying to find evil or corruption. But she saw only herself, happy and beautiful. She ran her tongue over dry lips. To be lovely and loved . . .

With sudden reckless passion, she knew that she wanted love at any price. Even if she possessed it for only a handful of days, it would be better than the emptiness of her present existence. She drew a ragged breath. "Very well, Lord Ranulph. I will accept your offer of beauty and love. In return you will give me three choices of repayment, and will not ask for my mortal life or immortal soul."

His smile was dazzling, though his teeth were rather . . . pointed. She reminded herself firmly that cats had pointed teeth, and she was very fond of them. She still missed her old tabby, gone since the last winter.

With a glitter of light, a silver dagger materialized in his hand. As she stiffened, he coolly sliced the center of his left palm. A crimson line appeared. Before she could retreat, he caught her hand and made a matching cut in her palm. Strangely, even though blood formed along the wound, it did not hurt. Rather, it stung like ice against bare flesh.

He pressed his palm to hers. "Flesh to flesh, blood to blood, a faery bond is formed." His voice was soft, but in his piercing eyes was a wild, alien light.

She gasped and snatched her hand away. "What wicked magic have you done?"

Lord Ranulph smiled, a sophisticated London gentleman again. "It was the merest formality, my dear girl." He took her hand again, but this time he only bowed elegantly over it. "You will not regret this, Leah. Go home now, and enjoy the blessings of faery magic." He straightened and gestured across the glade at a bird perched on a branch. "Very soon you shall take flight like that turtle dove."

Her gaze followed the fluttering wings as the dove rose into the air. She watched until it soared out of sight among the trees, then turned back to Ranulph of the Wood.

He was gone, leaving not so much as a single footprint or broken blade of grass.

She drew a dazed breath and sank onto the fallen tree trunk. The cool wind slid over her heated face. Had the faery vanished, or never existed?

She looked at her left hand, but there was no trace of a cut. Pressing her cheek against the silky wood of her harp, she bent her head and closed her eyes. The encounter must have been some sort of dream. She had dozed, and dreamed of a magical offer that would bring her happiness. She'd had many such fanciful daydreams as a child, though never one so realistic.

Face taut, she stood and slung her harp over her shoulder. Now she was grown and knew that happiness did not come with the swish of a magic wand—or the slash of a magical dagger. The reality was that eventually she would inherit a comfortable independence and would never want for anything. She was a fortunate woman, for she did not need a husband or children or passionate, romantic love.

It had only been a dream.

Leah entered the manor house quietly and headed for the stairs. Her dream of Faerie had delayed her, and she barely had time to change before dinner.

Then her mother called, "Leah, dear, come in here, please."

"Yes, Mother." Leah smoothed a hand over her wind-whipped hair, then slung the harp as far behind her as possible. Her parents approved of her skill on the piano-forte, but they had never understood her strange passion for a common, old-fashioned harp.

The instrument had been the gift of the old Irishman who had been her father's forester until his death the previous winter. McLennan had taught her to play. He'd also filled her ears with tales of the Fair Folk, of how they loved music and how he himself had once spent a midsummer's night listening to the wild melodies of faery harpers. Then he'd nod and say that Leah had the same gift.

The memory relaxed her. It was McLennan's tales that had produced that strange—dream? Hallucination? A faery in the woods! She must have been mad.

Leah entered the morning room, where her mother reclined on a brocade sofa. "Do you need something, Mother? Your shawl, perhaps?"

Lady Marlowe, gray-haired and chronically vague, but still retaining some of the frail prettiness of her youth, looked up from the letter in her hands. " 'Tis the most extraordinary thing. This has just come from your father's cousin, Lady Wheaton. She's one of your godparents, you know."

Leah nodded. Her ladyship had sent her goddaughter an elaborate silver christening cup twenty-one years before. That was the extent of their relationship.

"Andrea wishes for you to join her in London for the Little Season. She's a widow, you know, and she's decided that it would be amusing to present a girl to society."

Leah gasped. "London—me? I . . . I would have no idea how to get on."

"Nonsense," her mother said reprovingly. "You're well bred and a very handsome girl. You shall be a great success. Your father and I have often discussed taking you to London, but . . ." Her shrug delicately explained that such a project had been beyond her strength.

Leah scarcely noticed, for she was stunned by the remark that she was a very handsome girl. Apart from an occasional sigh after studying her daughter's unprepossessing countenance, or perhaps a remark that it was a pity Leah resembled her father's side of the family, Lady Marlowe had always been silent on the subject of her daughter's looks.

Weakly Leah said, "I have no clothing suitable for fashionable society."

"You'll need a new wardrobe, of course. Andrea shall select it for you." Lady Marlowe refolded the letter neatly. "Since you will be taking few of your own clothes, it won't take long for you to pack. You can leave tomorrow morning. Andrea is most anxious to welcome you."

"As you wish, Mother." Still dazed, Leah left the morning room and headed upstairs to her room. In her—dream—Ranulph had said that there was more than one way to get to London. Could he have arranged this visit? Absurd!

Then she passed the gilt-framed pier glass that hung in the upper hall, and came to a dead stop, as stunned as if she had been hit with a hammer. The image in the mirror was that of the beautiful, faery-touched Leah that Ranulph had shown her. But now she could see all of herself. Her hair was a sensual, tawny mane and her figure was alluringly petite instead of merely thin.

She touched the reflection with shaking fingers, half expecting it to vanish like an image in a pond, but there was no change. As her mother had said, she was a remarkably handsome girl. No, more than that. She was beautiful. Achingly, heart-stoppingly beautiful. Even in her worn gown, she looked like a princess. No man would be able to resist her.

Yet as she had noticed earlier, she was still herself. Each of her features was much as before, but now refined to perfection. Her fair complexion, always good, was now flawless. Her formerly average gray-green eyes had become a riveting shade of green—exactly like those of Ranulph of the Wood.

Involuntarily she glanced down at her left palm. The sunlight revealed a faint, silvery line across the center, exactly where Ranulph had drawn his dagger.

Her hand dropped. With eerie calm, she accepted that Ranulph had been real, and she had pledged herself to an unholy bargain. What would she have to pay when the time came? For now, it didn't matter. As her eyes drank in the sight of her new self, she knew that what she had received was worth an uncertain price.

She tore herself away from the pier glass and hurried to her bedroom in the east wing. As soon as she closed the door, she looked into her own mirror, half afraid it would reflect the drab image of her old self. But it was the beautiful Leah who looked back, and who reflected Leah's joyous laughter.

Exuberant, she set down her harp, then whirled across the room in a mad dance. She was beautiful and going to London and she would have admirers by the score. She would enjoy the attention, then love and marry the best of her suitors. Everything she had silently yearned for would be hers.

Still laughing, she threw open her casement windows and leaned out. "Look out, London, here I come!"

Leah did not expect a response, but a ladylike "Meow" sounded from very close at hand. She glanced to her left in surprise.

Perched daintily on the branch of a tree that grew near Leah's window was a magnificent cat with long black hair and golden eyes. It was quite unlike any other cat Leah had ever seen, but quite in keeping with the events of the day. "Good day," Leah said courteously. "Are you a magical faery feline?"

The cat compressed itself like a coiled spring, then made an amazing leap that took it all the way to Leah's window. After landing lightly on the sill, it rubbed its cheek against Leah's arm, purring powerfully.

Leah stroked the cat's back. The splendid black fur was silky soft. "What a beautiful lady you are. You couldn't be anything but a lady."

The cat raised her aristocratic head and regarded Leah with huge golden eyes that seemed as intelligent as those of any human. Leah blinked. Perhaps this really was a faery being. Feeling absurd, she asked, "Did Ranulph send you to watch me?"

Making a disdainful feline sound, the cat jumped from the sill into Leah's room, glided across the carpet, then leaped onto the bed. There she circled thrice around before settling down to sleep in a furry ball.

"You certainly believe in making yourself at home," Leah said with amusement. She sat on the bed by the cat and began petting again. "I'd love to keep you, but I'm sure that you already have a home." Though she could not imagine who in the neighborhood might own such a rare and obviously valuable cat. Leah knew every pet for miles around, and none of them were remotely like this lovely creature.

The cat purred ecstatically as Leah's fingers found the

sensitive spot under her throat. Leah asked, "What shall I call you?"

The cat opened her eyes for a moment. As her gaze met Leah's, a word formed in Leah's mind. Half convinced she was ready for Bedlam, Leah asked, "Is your name Shadow?"

Radiating satisfaction, the cat closed her eyes again and tucked her nose under the magnificent plumy tail.

Leah was definitely ready for Bedlam. Nonetheless, she hummed with pleasure as she changed her clothing for dinner.

All was chaos at Marlowe Manor the next morning. Ranulph drifted across the grounds and took refuge in the shade of a topiary hedge as he watched the preparations for sending Miss Leah to London. First the massive travel coach lumbered out of the carriage house. Then a footman brought out a small trunk of the young lady's clothing. Ranulph was glad to see that she was not taking much; he'd never been impressed by her wardrobe. Luckily that would be improved in London. And of course when she was his, he'd garb her in moonbeams and faery silks.

Leah herself appeared, looking harassed and a little frightened to be leaving home for the first time in her life. In her arms was the case that held her harp. Behind her trailed the elderly maid who would accompany her to London, then return with the coach. Last of all came her parents, dutifully bidding their daughter goodbye.

Ranulph studied Leah hungrily. Mortals had such enticing vitality. The addition of faery glamour had made her lovely indeed. But his magic was limited by the fact that she was not yet bound to him; all he could do was maximize the features she had.

When she was fully his, he'd be able to alter her appearance at will. Make her tall, perhaps, or voluptuous, or give her the silvery blond hair of a faery queen. It would be like having his own private harem. Perhaps he'd give her black hair that swirled and danced about her heels. Though he'd never fancied black hair, it might be a pleasant change since most ladies of Faerie were blond.

Leah was on the verge of climbing into the coach when a fluffy black cat streaked by her and leaped into the vehicle. Leah removed the cat. It was back inside before she'd straightened up.

Ranulph laughed as he watched the ensuing battle. Cats were uncanny beasts who wandered freely between Faerie and the mortal world. This one had obviously been drawn by the scent of magic.

A footman caught the cat, only to have it wiggle loose in the blink of an eye. After the beast was removed from the coach again, Leah and the maid were hastily shut inside before the cat could rejoin them. It countered with a magnificent leap onto the coach, landing on the seat next to the driver.

Since the cat was clearly set on going to London, Leah wisely surrendered and opened the carriage door. The creature lightly sprang into the coach beside her and curled up daintily on the seat. Lady Marlowe suggested that if her daughter must take that *feline,* at least put it in a basket. Leah smiled and said that wouldn't be necessary. Ranulph was pleased by her insight and flexibility; she'd do well when he brought her into Faerie.

With a mighty lurch, the coach set off. The Marlowes and the servants who had come to send the little miss off returned to their normal activities. Only Ranulph was left to watch the coach disappear around the bend in the drive.

He felt a surge of sadness, coupled with flashing impatience. Goddess, but he wanted her! But he must wait, give her time to become addicted to the power of her beauty, and to become infatuated with some mortal man. Then she'd be ripe for the plucking. To move too quickly would be to risk losing her. He'd realized the day before that she could not be rushed.

Briefly he considered Lady Kamana. An odd creature, but amusing and quite attractive in her foreign way. Perhaps he could use her as a distraction for the next long weeks. But she'd left the wood; he'd felt the moment when she slipped away, as he sensed everything that happened in his territory. In her desire to explore her new land, Lady Kamana could be anywhere by now.

He wondered what the other Folk would think of her. Sometimes the Folk could be cruel to those who were different, as he knew from hard experience.

The idea struck when he was returning to the wood. Why not go to London himself? The place was a great sink of dead stone and teeming humankind, but there were parks with enough greenery for him to endure a visit. He would be able to see not only Leah, but other sights as well. It had been long since he'd traveled to London.

He tried to remember just how long. That fellow Henry, the one with the six wives, had been king then. The city would be much changed. Probably not for the better, but still, a visit would be interesting, and would fill the empty hours.

He'd wait a bit before going. Give Leah time to adjust. With luck, she might be ready for him sooner than he expected.

Steps light, he glided into the welcoming depths of the wood.

Chapter Two

Shadow in her arms, Leah descended wearily from the coach in front of Lady Wheaton's immense London townhouse. It was late afternoon, and two days of rattling around inside a badly sprung vehicle had left her exhausted and depressed. She was so far from home. Why had she willingly gone among strangers? She and her party had spent the previous night in a coaching inn, and the stares of the men there had been positively rude. Even with her maid and coachman near, she had felt nervous.

Dispiritedly she followed her maid up the steps, then waited for admission to the house. When an elderly butler opened the door, she said, "I am Miss Marlowe. Lady Wheaton is expecting me."

The butler gaped at her before giving a little shake, like a dog after a bath. "This way, miss," he said, in control again. "Her ladyship wishes to see you immediately."

Cat still in her arms, Leah followed the servant upstairs to a small, richly decorated boudoir. A tall woman of middle years reclined on a brocade-covered chaise longue, a letter in her hands and a small dog curled up at her feet.

Solemnly the butler announced, "My lady, Miss Marlowe has arrived."

Lady Wheaton lowered the letter and looked up. Dressed in the height of fashion, she had strong, handsome features and an air of command.

Leah curtsied as well as she could with a substantial cat draped over one shoulder. "Good day, Lady Wheaton. It is so kind of you to invite me here to London."

For a moment Lady Wheaton stared with the stunned expression Leah was becoming used to now that her appearance had changed. Then her ladyship rose and came forward, the small dog at her heels. "How lovely you are! Your mother was too modest in singing your praises." She studied Leah with interest. "You shall be a great success. I guarantee it. But my dear child . . . a cat?"

Leah, who had begun to revive under the admiration, blushed. "I'm sorry, my lady. Shadow would not be left behind."

Her godmother frowned. "Neither Rex nor I are at all fond of cats."

A sharp canine yip identified Rex. The dog bounded toward Leah, looking ready to chase or eat the feline invader.

Shadow jumped from Leah's arms and stared at Rex. The dog skidded to a stop. Then he whined and flattened his belly to the floor, all the fight gone out of him.

The cat stalked forward, gaze locked with the dog's, until their noses touched. After a moment of whimpering panic, Rex gave a kind of sigh and relaxed.

Shadow turned to Lady Wheaton and began to strop her ankles, purring vociferously. Her ladyship's first expression of distaste vanished almost immediately. "It's quite a friendly creature, isn't it?" She bent and patted the cat's head, as if Shadow were a dog. "And rather pretty, for a cat."

Leah almost laughed as she watched Shadow charming her hostess.

Lady Wheaton straightened. "Since Rex doesn't seem to object, I suppose there's no harm in having the creature here, but don't allow it to scratch my furniture."

Clearly her ladyship knew nothing of cats, or she would not have the foolish idea that they could be trained to obedience. Still, Shadow hadn't scratched anything yet, and she seemed to have a clear sense of which side her bread was buttered on. Meekly Leah said, "Yes, Lady Wheaton. She is a very good cat."

"Call me Aunt Andrea," Lady Wheaton said warmly. "You must be tired. You'll want to take supper in your room. I shall have a tray sent up. Then you must get a good night's sleep, for tomorrow we'll be off to the modiste to order your wardrobe. I am giving my autumn ball next week. It will be the perfect occasion to present you."

She slowly circled Leah. "Wait until Lady Hill sees you," she said with satisfaction. "The whole spring season she went on insufferably about how beautiful her daughter Mary is, but you quite put the girl in the shade. Presenting you will be a great triumph for me. You'll be the belle of the season."

A little dismayed, Leah collected Shadow and withdrew. She hadn't known that she would be used to score points for her godmother in what looked like a long-term rivalry. Still, she supposed it was harmless enough.

As she settled into an airy, attractive bedchamber, she turned her thoughts to the far more pleasant prospect of a new wardrobe.

The footman handed Leah into the carriage. She collapsed on the seat opposite her godmother with a sigh. "I had no idea how fatiguing it is to be fashionable. It's been three days now of shopping and fittings, being pinched and pinned." She glanced out the window as the carriage began to move. "May I remove the veil? It is not comfortable on such a warm day."

"Wait until we are away from Bond Street," Lady Wheaton ordered. "I don't want to risk anyone seeing you in public before the grand presentation at my ball." She pursed her lips. "Instead of introducing you in the usual receiving line, I shall wait until most of the guests have arrived. Then we will make a grand entrance down the front staircase."

Leah suppressed a sigh, not sure she would like being so much the center of attention, but knowing it was her duty to cooperate with Lady Wheaton's plans. Luckily, she was becoming quite fond of her tart-tongued but generous-hearted godmother. "Very well, Aunt Andrea."

Still full of energy despite so much shopping, her god-mother said, "It's time to start discussing potential husbands. There are several available royal dukes, of course, but they are an unreliable lot. I want better for you."

Thank heaven for that. Even Leah knew that the unmarried royal dukes were fat, middle-aged, and chronically in debt. And from what she inferred from news stories, they were not very bright. She wanted to marry a man she could talk to. "I wouldn't want to be a duchess. Indeed, I would make a sad muddle of such a high rank."

"You simply must put a higher value on yourself, my dear," Lady Wheaton said briskly. "I've never known a beautiful woman who had so little confidence as you. In relations between the sexes, a woman's beauty is power. You must use yours to acquire the wealth and security that ensure a woman a comfortable life. Granted, the royal dukes are poor choices, but there is the Duke of Hardcastle. Much more handsome than any of the Hanovers, and in the market for a second wife."

Lady Wheaton's brows drew together as she continued, "Hardcastle is the greatest prize in the Marriage Mart, but there is young Lord Wye—you could win him with a snap of your fingers." Grandly she demonstrated a snap. "If you like the military sort, there is Duncan Townley, who is a Peninsular hero and heir to his uncle's viscountcy. Not the best title or the richest man, but very dashing. Or if you prefer poets, there is Lord Jeffers. Not so handsome as Byron, nor so good a poet, but far wealthier and better behaved."

Before her godmother could continue, Leah said with alarm, "But which are *agreeable* men? Sure that is paramount when choosing a husband."

"When enough wealth is involved, one scarcely needs to see one's husband after the heirs have been produced. A wife who has done her duty to her husband's family has enormous freedom," Lady Wheaton said with an airy wave of her hand. "To continue, it is as important to know who is *not* eligible as to know who is. Under no circumstances can you accept dances from the following . . ."

For the rest of the ride, her ladyship rattled off more names and pungent descriptions of each gentleman's virtues or failings as a potential matrimonial partner. By the time they reached Wheaton House, Leah's head was aching in earnest. She went directly to her room and flopped onto the bed.

Shadow, who had been watching the passing scene from the window seat, jumped to the floor and came to join Leah on the bed. Leah cuddled the cat, grateful for the undemanding company. In a strange and disorienting city, she sometimes had the odd feeling that Shadow was her guardian angel.

Even more than her cat, she needed music. Her gaze went to her harp, which sat silent in its case beside her wardrobe. She hadn't played since arriving in London; she had simply been too tired. Perhaps after dinner . . . No, drat it. A dancing master was coming to make sure that Leah was proficient in all the latest dances.

She sighed and her eyes drifted shut. In a few more days, she would be presented. Then she would be a belle, and it would all be worth it.

* * *

Monique, Lady Wheaton's French maid, was putting the last touches on Leah's coiffure when her ladyship herself appeared in Leah's bedroom. "The ballroom is full, and almost every man on my eligible list has arrived. It's time for your grand entrance, Leah." Lady Wheaton smiled, eyes dancing. "For the last week I've been dropping hints to friends about how beautiful my goddaughter is, so everyone is madly curious. Now stand up and let me look at you."

Leah stood obediently while her godmother examined her appearance, her shrewd gaze missing nothing. "You'll do, girl. You'll do."

"What I might do is faint," Leah said weakly.

"Nonsense. Look at yourself." Lady Wheaton drew Leah toward the mirror. "You're a warrior girded for war, armored in beauty to fight the great battle of the sexes."

"I thought I was in London for love, not war." Then Leah saw her image in the mirror and gasped, all other thoughts forgotten. Her tawny hair had been swept into an irresistible confection of shining curls, secured here and there with golden combs. In a fashionably low-cut gown with a gauzy overskirt studded with brilliants, she looked like an exquisite faery princess.

The thought made her flinch. In a sense, she *was* a faery princess, or perhaps a faery doll, decorated as a plaything to amuse a faery lord. Her gaze lingered on her reflection. She must give Lord Ranulph credit—when he came to collect his price, she would be unable to say that he had stinted on his part of the bargain. Shining hair, perfect complexion, alluring sylphlike figure—she had received beauty in full measure.

She glanced at Shadow, who was sitting on her haunches watching. The cat's golden eyes seemed to gleam with warmth and approval. Absurdly comforted by the cat's expression, Leah said, "I'm ready, Aunt Andrea."

Arm in arm, the two women left Leah's bedroom and descended the sweeping staircase into the vestibule that opened into the flower-filled ballroom. Leah felt as if she were wading into a river of sound as the roar of conversation clashed with the energetic playing of the musicians.

Halfway down the stairs, heads began turning toward Leah and her godmother. Silence fell, rippling from the vestibule into the ballroom. One man said reverently, "By Jove!" while another exclaimed, "She's a goddess!"

Guests in the ballroom began crowding into the vestibule. Before Leah's startled eyes, the area at the bottom of the stairs filled with people, their eyes fixed on her. Most of the expressions were stunned admiration, but here and there tight-lipped women resentfully analyzed the new competition.

Leah froze, wanting to run back upstairs, but the pressure of Lady Wheaton's grip kept her moving down. "I told you," her godmother whispered triumphantly. "Look at them! You'll be betrothed before the month is out, my girl."

They reached the bottom of the stairs and were instantly surrounded by men with avid eyes and lusting hearts. A tall, heavyset fellow demanded, "An introduction please, Lady Wheaton!"

Beside him, a soulful gentleman said with a French accent, "A dance, mademoiselle, you must save me a dance."

A wide-eyed young man called out, "Your hand in marriage, my dear goddess. I shall make you Countess of Wye."

Other demands, other needs, chewed at her. Leah could feel the lust coming from the men like animal heat. They were tall, strong, closing in like wolves. . . .

You wanted to be admired. The words formed in her mind, light and ironical. Lord Ranulph, perhaps, watching her in some strange faery way?

The faint mockery of the thought steadied her. Well, she *had* wanted admiration. She simply needed time to become accustomed to so much attention. Already that first rush of panic was retreating.

Lady Wheaton began making introductions and allotting her protégée's dances. Leah was more than willing to let her godmother handle such things. Her own energy was engaged simply in keeping her wits about her. A pity she had never attended a ball as her normal, mousy self. If she had, she would have been better prepared. But of course, her normal mousy self had never been invited anywhere.

After the flurry of introductions, she was handed into the keeping of her first dance partner, Lord Wye, the young man who had virtually proposed before he'd even learned her name. He was one of the eligibles Lady Wheaton had described, which meant that he was possessor of a vast fortune and an impressive title.

Unfortunately, he possessed neither a chin nor conversation. Throughout their dance, he simply stared at Leah adoringly. She guessed that he was no older than she. She felt torn between sympathy for his shyness, and amusement at the way he blushed whenever she ventured a comment. The smile she offered him at the end of their quadrille reduced him to babbling incoherence.

Her next partner, the Duke of Hardcastle, was more articulate. He was in his middle thirties, a widower and man of the world who was at the top of Lady Wheaton's list of eligibles. He was quite a handsome man, and he made witty comments whenever the patterns of the dance brought them together. Altogether a good husband prospect, except that his hot, hungry gaze seemed to strip her naked.

Yet even though Hardcastle made her nervous, she felt a glow of triumph at the knowledge that he wanted her. No one had ever wanted her old, plain self.

She curtsied prettily at the end of the dance. 'Thank you, Your Grace. You are very kind.''

"Kindness has nothing to do with it." His heavy lidded gaze studied her with searing intensity. "Until next time, Miss Marlowe."

He returned her to Lady Wheaton, who took advantage of an interval between dances to introduce Leah to some of the powerful women who ruled London society. Leah had recovered enough from her earlier nervousness to smile, curtsy, and acknowledge the introductions without stammering.

Her progress was followed by approving comments such as "What pretty manners the girl has," and "She does you credit, Andrea."

Leah was tempted to laugh. She was merely practicing the courtesy learned by any child in the schoolroom, yet some of the women acted as if her behavior was unusual. That meant either that great beauties were often rude, or that Leah was getting more credit for good manners than a less beautiful girl would.

By the end of the long evening, she was enjoying every shred of admiration that came her way. Lady Wheaton was right—this was power. The warm gazes were balm after a lifetime of being ignored. Leah's simplest remarks were greeted with laughter, as if she were a great wit. Her every smile was received like a precious gift. Her dances were sought after as if they were the holy grail.

She had become a belle—and she loved it.

Chapter Three

By the end of a fortnight's social activity, Leah was universally acknowledged as the Beauty of the season. So many flowers had been delivered that every room of Wheaton House was perfumed with blossoms. She had started a collection of the poetry that had been sent to her. Half of the pieces came from the adoring Lord Jeffers, society poet and eligible bachelor. As Lady Wheaton had said, he wasn't the poet that Byron was, but the man did know how to turn a pretty phrase.

Resting in her room before preparing for a ball at the Duke of Hardcastle's famous mansion, Leah smiled over Lord Jeffers's latest effort, then tucked it away. The poet was quite charming, but in love with the idea of love rather than with her.

She relaxed into her wing chair, welcoming the interval of peace and quiet. There had been few such times in the last fortnight. "It's very exciting being a belle, Shadow, but I haven't fallen in love yet," she said with a sigh. "I haven't even met someone I *want* to fall in love with. Is there something wrong with me?"

The cat turned her head to Leah, for all the world as if she were listening. A thought appeared in Leah's mind. *You haven't met the right man.*

Leah was no longer surprised at such incidents. Admittedly all cats were rather fey, but she was half convinced that Shadow had been sent by Lord Ranulph as some sort of guardian. If witches had familiars, why not faeries?

A wordless note of disgust touched Leah's mind. She grinned at the cat, who was twitching her plumy tail with irritation. "Do you find that thought insulting? I'm sorry." She went to get her harp from its case, then sat again and ran experimental fingers over the strings. The familiar singing notes made her smile with pleasure. She settled down to play seriously. Her fingers were a little stiff, but they loosened rapidly.

It seemed no time at all before Monique entered. The maid said, scandalized, "M'zelle, you should be dressing for the ball!"

Leah almost protested that she wanted to spend the evening playing, but stopped herself. She had come to London to find love. There would be time for music later.

The dance ended and the Duke of Hardcastle bent to kiss Leah's hand. "You waltz beautifully, Miss Marlowe. But of course, you are beautiful in all ways."

Flushed from the swirling dance, Leah inclined her head graciously. "A good waltz requires a good partner."

The duke's mouth curved in a predator's smile. "As witty as you are lovely."

It hadn't been that witty, but by this time Leah had become used to such exaggerated reactions. The duke tucked her gloved hand into the crook of his arm and continued, "The ballroom is very warm. Come into my garden for some fresh air."

Leah hesitated. He had called at Wheaton House several times, always claimed two dances at each event, and had taken her driving once. Aunt Andrea said that bets were being laid in the clubs that Leah would be the next duchess. Leah was not sure how she felt about that. Hardcastle cut an impressive figure and he was certainly a great catch, but he still made her nervous. She needed to become better acquainted with him. "I should like some fresh air, Your Grace."

As he guided her across the crowded ballroom, Leah studied the other guests. She had assumed that in London she would make friends with other young women, as she had at home, but that hadn't happened. The really pretty girls were jealous, and the average ones avoided her. Remembering her own plain days, she guessed that they thought she was interested only in finding foils for her own beauty. The knowledge saddened her. She had not thought beauty would come at the price of friendship.

Her gaze touched a strikingly lovely young woman with golden hair. She was about the same age as Leah, and instead of scowling, she offered a tentative smile. Leah started to smile back—until she realized that the blonde had vividly green eyes. Exactly like those of Lord Ranulph, or Leah.

Hardcastle made some remark, and Leah hastily turned away from the green-eyed woman. Was she a faery, or another mortal who had made a devil's bargain? Leah realized that she didn't want to know the answer.

As the orchestra struck up a new dance, the duke led Leah through the French doors. Several other couples were on the stone patio in plain view of the ballroom, so this must be proper. But when he steered her toward the steps that led into the dark garden, Leah balked. "My godmother said I should not be alone with a man."

His brows rose impatiently. "I am not *a man*. I am the Duke of Hardcastle. Lady Wheaton would approve entirely."

Before Leah could protest again, they were on a gravel path that led into the heart of the immense garden. It was pleasant to be surrounded by dark, shadowy trees and the scents of growing things rather than chattering ball guests and sweaty bodies. Leah relaxed, enjoying the cool air and the knowledge that she was being escorted by one of England's greatest lords. This scene would have been unimaginable a month ago. "Your garden seems very lovely, Your Grace. I would like to see it in daylight some-time."

"Whenever you wish, my dear." There was an odd, rough quality to his voice.

The tree-lined path led into an open space. Though the night was moonless, there was just enough starlight to see the outlines of a marble statue set in the middle of a gently splashing fountain. Leah squinted at the statue, then blushed, glad for the darkness. The sculpture appeared to be a naked woman entwined most improperly with a swan.

Deciding that she had bent the rules of propriety far enough, she said, "Please take me back, Your Grace. I'm beginning to feel cold."

"I'll keep you warm." The rough note she had heard before was stronger, and suddenly his arms were around her and his mouth grinding into hers. When she tried to utter a protest, his thick tongue slid between her lips.

She gagged, feeling as if she would be physically ill. She pushed against his chest, but managed only to pull her face away from his revolting kiss. "Your Grace, please!" she pleaded. "You forget yourself."

"It's because of you, my sweet," he said hoarsely. His hand slid down and he squeezed her buttock, pressing her hard against his hot, obscenely swollen body. "You're the most exquisite creature I've ever seen. You make me mad with desire."

Shocked by the unwanted intimacy, she snapped, "That's not my fault!" She tried to twist away, but he maintained his grip. One of his groping hands caught her breast. Near hysteria, she gasped, "Let me go or I'll scream!"

"For God's sake, don't make such a fuss," he said impatiently. "I wouldn't seduce you in my own garden if my intentions weren't honorable."

Before she could say that this was not seduction but rape, his mouth crushed down on hers again. She realized with horror that he was tugging at her skirt. Dear God, she would never be able to break free. He was too strong, too intent on having his way. And if he did, she would have no choice but to marry him.

In her mind, she heard the cool words *You wanted a beauty that would drive men mad.* Lord Ranulph again? But she hadn't wanted *this!*

Suddenly a hard voice snapped, "Let her go!"

The newcomer enforced his command by physically breaking the duke's hold on Leah. Panting for breath, she retreated several steps and tried to see her rescuer. In the darkness he was only a faceless shadow. Of middle height, perhaps, with broad shoulders—and wonderful timing.

"Damn you, sir, do you know who I am?" the duke snarled at the interloper.

"I believe so," was the icy reply. "You do yourself no credit, Your Grace."

"You criticize *me?*" Hardcastle said, incredulous. "How dare you interfere between a man and his affianced wife!"

"She looked like an unwilling woman to me," the other man retorted. "Was I wrong about that, miss?"

"Tell this lunatic that we're betrothed," Hardcastle ordered.

Leah wanted to say that she wouldn't marry the duke if he were the last man in Christendom, but barely in time remembered that it would not be wise to humiliate a man so powerful. And in fairness, he'd had no reason to think she would not accept an offer.

"Though I do not question your honorable intentions, Your Grace, you neglected to go through the formality of making an offer," she said carefully. "You do me great honor, but . . . but I do not think we would suit."

"Wouldn't suit!" Hardcastle said with disbelief. "A nobody like you is turning down the chance to become a duchess?"

"Yes," she said in a small voice.

His jaw dropped. Then his expression changed to disdain. "I thought you worthy to be my wife, but you're only a foolish, impertinent little girl. You're quite right—we would not suit at all. I shall tell your godmother to summon her carriage because you are not feeling well. And I suggest that in the future, you avoid your sly tricks that lead a man to misread your affections." He spun on his heel and stalked off.

Leah stood there, shaking, until her rescuer said gently, "Sit down."

He guided her to a bench. She folded onto the cold stone. "Thank you," she said unevenly. "When we came out for air, I . . . I had no idea what he intended."

"It's a fair guess that a man who takes a girl into a dark garden is up to no good," her rescuer said dryly as he peeled off his coat and draped it over her shoulders. "I suggest that you accept no more such invitations unless you are in favor of accepting the gentleman's advances as well."

He had a really wonderful deep voice. As she gratefully wrapped the body-warmed fabric around her, she tried again to see his face, but couldn't. He was simply a silhouette against darker shadows. Wanting his good opinion, she said earnestly, "Truly, I did not encourage the duke's advances, despite what he said."

"Then I presume you are very beautiful," he said cynically. "Wealthy men tend to believe they are entitled to beautiful women, and beautiful women tend to assume that they deserve wealth. It's a bargain that has existed since time immemorial, so perhaps the duke can be forgiven for misunderstanding."

"What nonsense," she retorted. "Marriage should be more about love than wealth and beauty."

"You are very young," he said, but his voice had softened.

Her mouth curved ruefully. "I suppose so. But I don't appreciate having that pointed out to me."

"Neither would I," he agreed. "If you're feeling well enough, allow me to escort you around the house. Your godmother should be waiting for you there."

Silently Leah rose and took his arm. It was firm and well muscled beneath the linen of his shirt. Strength that had been used for protection, not assault. As they moved through the garden, she said, "I hope the duke does not choose to ruin me socially."

"He won't," her rescuer said confidently. "The situation reflects badly on him."

When they reached the side of the mansion, the flaring torches lining the driveway revealed Lady Wheaton waiting beside her carriage, her expression concerned. Though Leah would like to see her rescuer's face, she did not want it to be at the price of him seeing hers, not after what had happened.

She stopped and slipped off his coat. As she handed it to him, she said, "You have my deepest thanks, sir. And—please don't watch me go."

Understanding, he said with amusement, "Leaving us strangers in the night, with all embarrassment safely covered by the dark. But what if we meet again?"

"We'll pretend this never happened," she said firmly.

"As you wish." He executed a courtly bow, his shirt pale in the darkness.

She gave him a sweeping curtsy, hoping they would meet again under more normal circumstances. Then, head high, she crossed the soft lawn to her godmother.

Her rescuer watched her for a moment, unconsciously raising the coat to his face, as if seeking for a trace of her scent. Then he turned back to the dark garden, before she was so well lit that he could not fail to identify her in the future.

* * *

Hidden in the deepest shadows of the garden, Ranulph watched Leah join her godmother, his faery sight giving him a cat's vision at night. He'd been in London for several days, exploring the great parks but always coming back to the dense patch of bushes and trees in the center of the square where Wheaton House stood. Hungrily his gaze followed as Leah climbed into the carriage. Goddess, but he tired of waiting!

His hand tightened on the hilt of his sword. If he had been closer tonight, he might have slain the duke when the drunken sot had attacked her. Luckily that other mortal had happened along in time to save Leah from harm. It would have enraged the powers of Faerie if Ranulph had killed the duke because of a mortal woman. Debts must always be paid, and those between Faerie and the mortal world weighed heavy indeed.

Intent on his thoughts, Ranulph spun about with dangerous alarm when a warm hand touched his wrist. His grip on his sword relaxed when he saw that he had been accosted by Lady Kamana, the Indian faery.

"You again," he said, voice cool though in truth he was pleased to see her. "I thought you would have joined one of the faery courts by now."

"Nay, my lord." She tossed her head. Her long black hair was pulled into a luxuriant silken rope, banded every six inches by a circlet of gold until the tip brushed the earth. "I will not choose a permanent home until I've seen more of your land."

He'd forgotten how richly purring her voice was. Instead of her Indian silks, she was garbed in the provocative evening gown of a grand London lady. Perversely, the English garments made her seem even more exotic.

"You've made your little country girl very beautiful," she observed.

"You recognized her?" he said, surprised.

"Of course. You could not have made her outward appearance so beautiful if it did not reflect her soul. She is young as only mortals can be young, but her heart is good, and music runs through her like pure fire. Otherwise the faery glamour you laid on her would be a pale thing, fit only to convince mortals."

"Mortals are easily deceived," he said dryly. "I've made her the toast of London, but the foolish girl has not yet fallen in love, and I cannot ask my price until she does."

"Patience, Lord Ranulph. She will find the love of her life soon." A smile touched her voice. *"Very* soon."

Ranulph frowned. "Do your Folk see the future clearly? I can sense it sometimes, but not with any detail."

"When I concentrate, I can see patterns of destiny like silver threads that run through time and space," Kamana said slowly. "They touch each other and create shining webs of love and hate and friendship."

"You can see Leah bonded to me?" Ranulph asked urgently. He'd sensed that he would soon be sharing his domain with another, but desire might be distorting his intuition. "She will be my consort?"

"Never fear, my lord. I see your thread intersecting that of your consort, forming a knot that will bind you together for eternity, or near enough." Kamana drew the heavy rope of her hair through her fingers, absently toying with the gold bangles that circled it. "Like all gifts, mine is a mixed blessing. I followed my own thread of destiny here, not knowing how close it would come to destroying me."

"You said the passage was difficult," he said as he imagined the months of confinement on shipboard.

She was silent for a long moment, her habitual shimmering vivacity stilled. "Even more difficult than I told you when we first met. At the start of the voyage, there was not enough of nature living on that ship. The mortal who was bringing the specimens back to England found me dying among his shrubs. He understood my malady, though I could say little, and demanded that the ship stop at a small tropical island. Days we stayed there, and I recovered my strength among the flowers and palms. When the ship continued, the mortal brought more greenery into the hold to sustain me for the rest of the journey.''

''But he extracted a price from you,'' Ranulph said flatly. ''It is ever the way of mortals to extract treasure from the Fair Folk when they have us in their power.''

She flashed a smile in the darkness, shimmering again. ''Aye, he asked a price, but not for himself. Merely to preserve his beloved nephew from death in battle, then find the boy a good mate. 'Twas not a price I mind paying.''

''You were fortunate.''

''I merely followed destiny's thread.'' She swept a perfect English curtsy. ''Good night, my lord. I intend to stay in London for a time, so we shall meet again.''

He bowed, then vanished into the shadows of the duke's garden.

Kamana stood and watched him leave, her inner vision studying the silver thread of his destiny.

Chapter Four

Lady Wheaton at her side, Leah entered the Duke of Candover's ballroom with the graceful confidence that came to her naturally now. She had recovered from her encounter with the Duke of Hardcastle, and never let herself be caught alone by any of her other admirers. She had also improved her flirting, which made it easier to control the men who flocked around her. Flirting was a game, enjoyable in itself and also good at keeping people at precisely the distance one wanted them.

Lady Wheaton murmured, "Brace yourself, my dear, you've been seen."

Already men were flocking toward them. Most Leah knew, though a few were strangers drawn like moths to the flame. Several of them immediately demanded introductions from Lady Wheaton. Lord Wye planted himself in front of Leah and bowed. "You are in exceptionally fine looks tonight, Miss Marlowe."

"Thank you," she said with a friendly smile. She had already turned down three proposals from Lord Wye, but he had not given up yet.

Lord Jeffers intoned, "She walks in beauty, like a swallow's flight." He hesitated. "That's the first line of my new poem, but I'm not sure I've got the right phrase yet."

Leah touched his hand. "I'm sure you will," she said warmly. Then she turned so Lady Wheaton could make introductions. In the last weeks Leah had mastered easy social intercourse. In fact, she'd learned that beauty made almost all things easy.

Yet she was no closer to finding someone to love. The most attractive men she had met were those who were happily married, like her newly wed host, the Duke of Candover. Wanting nothing from her, such men were relaxed and charming companions.

At every social function she attended, she looked for the man who had rescued her from the Duke of Hardcastle, but without success. Instead of a guest, might he have been a servant, perhaps a gardener? She wanted to kick herself for running away in embarrassment that night instead of making his acquaintance. Ah, well, he was probably married and unavailable.

Leah had just returned from waltzing with a portly baronet when Lady Wheaton murmured behind the cover of an opened fan, "Captain Duncan Townley has just arrived. He doesn't go out socially very much, so he's the only one of my eligibles that you haven't met." She tapped her lips with the fan reflectively. "Since no one else has taken your fancy, perhaps he will. Half the women in London dote on him. A hero of Waterloo, you know, and heir to a viscount."

Leah glanced toward the door, then caught her breath involuntarily. The man who had just entered was stunning, the epitome of the bold, dashing hero who would make any woman's knees melt. Though not exceptionally tall, his lithe, broad-shouldered form radiated intense virility. A lock of dark wavy hair fell over his forehead as he surveyed the ballroom with hooded eyes. Leah tried to estimate his age. Not old, though, certainly under thirty. Awed, she whispered, "He's magnificent."

For an instant, she thought that he had noticed her. Then her view was blocked by women crowding forward to see him. She understood perfectly. In fact, she had to suppress a mad desire to walk up to Duncan Townley, link her arms around his neck, and announce that she was his destiny.

Such foolishness! Or was it? There was magic in her life now. Could Ranulph have sent her to London to meet Duncan Townley? The faery lord had said that she could command the love of heroes if she wished.

Smiling at her protégée's reaction, Lady Wheaton said, "Shall I introduce you?"

"Not yet. I must go to the ladies' retiring room and fix my hair." More nervous than she had been since the night of her presentation, Leah made her excuses to her circle of admirers and left. But instead of returning to the ballroom after checking her appearance, she detoured to the music room, which was blessedly empty.

She dropped onto the bench in front of the pianoforte and forced herself to breathe slowly. She must be calm when her godmother introduced her to Duncan Townley. With a man like that, who could have any woman, she would need every iota of her beauty, and charm as well. Nor could she appear too eager. She'd learned enough of men in the last weeks to know that many were captivated by a woman who seemed unattainable.

Her gaze went to the keyboard of the pianoforte. Unable to resist it, she stripped off her gloves and began to play, keeping the sound soft so that it would be inaudible in the ballroom. Mozart soothed her, reminding her of who she really was. Some days she feared that she was in danger of losing herself.

By the end of her first piece, she was so caught up in the music that she went immediately into Beethoven's "Moonlight Sonata." The knot of tension that had been part of her since coming to London dissolved. Eyes closed, she played by touch, gently rocking back and forth as her hands coaxed the divine melodies from the instrument.

At the end she sighed with happiness, head bowed as her hands stilled on the keyboard. Then the sound of clapping hands startled her from her reverie.

Her lids snapped open. To her shock, Duncan Townley was standing in the doorway applauding. Their gazes met for a charged moment. In his eyes she saw the same kind of intense interest that she felt for him.

He entered the music room with a pantherlike smoothness that riveted her attention. "So this is where you've been hiding, fair lady," he said in a voice like deep, rich chocolate. "I saw you across the ballroom earlier, but you vanished before I could find you. I've been looking ever since." He halted beside the pianoforte. "You play extraordinarily well."

Leah's heart began to beat in triple time. The voice, the height and build—this was the man who had rescued her from the Duke of Hardcastle. "Thank you," she said, amazed at how steady her voice sounded. "You're Duncan Townley, and I am Leah Marlowe. Since my godmother intended to introduce us, we can now say that the formalities have been duly performed."

As soon as she spoke, his brows drew together in puzzlement. He must find her voice familiar also. How foolish of her to think that it would be possible to pretend their first meeting had never happened. She continued, "Besides, we have already met, in the garden of Hardcastle House. I am very much in your debt, Captain Townley."

"So it was you," he exclaimed. "With your voice like singing bells." His gaze was almost fierce in its intensity. "Hardcastle's behavior was despicable—but I understand better now why he forgot himself as he did."

Leah blushed, and wished that she hadn't. With this man, she cared about the impression she made. Cared desperately. He was glorious, the most attractive male creature she'd ever seen, except for Lord Ranulph, who was too alien to affect her heart.

Dear God, Duncan Townley couldn't be faery, could he? Her gaze shot up as she looked to see if his eyes were the same emerald green that showed in her own mirror. She exhaled with relief when she saw that they were a rare and striking transparent gold. Not green, thank heaven.

She must say something before he decided that she was an idiot. Casting about for a topic of conversation, she said, "My godmother says you are a hero of Waterloo."

Wrong topic. His golden eyes darkened. "I simply did my duty. There were many heroes that day, and too many of them are now dead."

The tan skin tightened over his face, revealing the fine line of a newly healed scar over his sculptured cheekbone. She guessed that it had been made by the slice of a saber. He might have been killed or blinded, but instead, the scar enhanced the rugged masculinity of his appearance.

The thought of him being wounded brought the reality of war to her as newspaper stories never had. On impulse, she stood and lightly touched the scar. Since her gloves were still off, there was an intimate contact of skin to skin. "I'm sorry," she said softly. "It must be bitter to lose so many of your friends, and then be acclaimed when they have been forgotten."

The warmth returned to his eyes. With utter simplicity, he turned his head and kissed the palm of her hand. "Thank you for understanding."

The touch of his lips sent fire shivering through her, warming deep places that she had not known existed. This was what she had longed for, she realized dazedly. The first tentative recognition between two souls that, God willing, would lead to love.

Without haste she lowered her hand. "I should return to the ballroom. My godmother would not be happy to learn that I was alone with a man." She made a face. "You know what happened the last time."

His brows arched. "Do you think I am like the Duke of Hardcastle?"

She considered flirting to keep him at a distance, but decided that it was already too late for that. "No. You are unlike anyone I have ever met."

For a moment, there was an expression that seemed almost like pain in his golden eyes. Then he smiled. "You're right that it is time to return to the ballroom. The next dance is a waltz, and you will dance it with me."

The thought of being held in his arms sent a delicious shiver through her, but she shook her head regretfully. "I'm sorry, this waltz is spoken for." She lifted her fan from the pianoforte and studied the sticks, where she had written the names of her partners. "Sir Amos Rowley, I believe."

"What a pity that you lost your fan." Duncan plucked the fragile object from her hand, then folded it neatly and tucked it inside his coat. "I shall gallantly volunteer to see that you are not forced to sit out this dance."

Her mouth curved. "I shall miss that fan," she said as she drew on her gloves again. "It was a gift from my godmother."

"I foresee that I will miraculously find it later." He placed her hand on his arm. "Naturally I must call on you tomorrow to return your fan. In gratitude, you will grant me a drive in the park."

She laughed buoyantly, loving the feeling of being swept along by the force of his interest. Why was it that behavior that might irritate her in another man simply made him more attractive? She set the thought aside for another day. What mattered now was this moment, and the excitement that bubbled through her veins like champagne.

Leah did not have a chance to speak with her godmother until they were in the carriage on the way home. Lady Wheaton started the conversation by saying, "You're bouncing like a kitten, child. I gather this is about Duncan Townley, since you shamelessly partnered him for two dances in a row."

"Am I that transparent?" Leah said with a laugh.

"It's one of your charms," her godmother said gently. "I'm continually amazed that a girl with your beauty is as direct and unaffected as you."

Leah's mouth twisted ruefully in the darkness. She was not sure that she deserved such a compliment, just as she felt that tributes to her beauty should go not to her but to the faery whose spell had created her appearance. But she could not say that to her godmother. "Captain Townley is a most attractive man," she said truthfully. "Tell me about him. I found that he has no wish to discuss his heroic deeds."

"Duncan is the nephew and heir of an old beau of mine, Viscount Townley," Lady Wheaton replied. "Though he was plain Will Townley then. We were quite infatuated for a time, but I wished to marry and he felt unready for such a commitment. So I accepted Wheaton, and Will went off to India. He was a great success there, I hear."

Wondering at the note she heard in her godmother's voice, Leah asked, "Are you still in love with Lord Townley, Aunt Andrea?"

"Nonsense," Lady Wheaton said briskly. "Wheaton was the most doting of husbands. I'm very attached to my stepchildren, and I have a comfortable income and the use of Wheaton House for the rest of my life. Altogether it was a most satisfactory marriage." Her voice softened. "Still, I do have fond memories of Will. I hear that he's recently returned from India, so I expect that eventually we'll see each other at some ball and laugh at just how young we once were."

To Leah, it seemed that perhaps her godmother protested a bit too much, but she did not pursue the point. "Have you known Duncan long?"

"Since his christening. His parents lived not far from us in the country."

Leah leaned forward in her seat eagerly. "What was he like?"

Lady Wheaton hesitated. "For all that he's so handsome and dashing, the word that comes to mind is—sweet. He was the most agreeable boy. Intelligent—he always had a book. Kind. Reliable. A little shy. But I haven't seen him since he came down from Cambridge. His parents died, and he went into the army and became that splendid masculine specimen that is coveted by every woman who sees him. He may be very different now from the boy I knew."

"Why is he considered a hero?"

"At Waterloo, the French tried to break through the line where his regiment was stationed. All of the senior officers were killed or wounded in the first assault, leaving young Duncan in command. Though he was wounded himself, his courage and leadership prevented the enemy from breaking the line."

Leah nodded, understanding better why he disliked the label *hero*. It had been bought at a very high price. Proceeding to the critical question, she asked, "His affections are unattached?"

"I believe so. As I said earlier, he has not been going about much in society. Dislikes being lionized, I believe. But I understand that he's been more visible in the last fortnight." Lady Wheaton laughed wickedly. "Good hunting, child. If you can't capture him, I don't know what woman could."

Leah leaned back, expression determined. This was why she had accepted a faery bargain for beauty—so she could win the heart of a man like Duncan Townley.

Even though mortals could not see him, from habit Ranulph stayed in the shadow of a massive rhododendron as he waited in the park opposite Wheaton House. As always, his Leah attracted an endless stream of male callers.

Then a smart sporting carriage drawn by matched bays swept into the square and halted in front of Wheaton House. The driver, a strikingly handsome young man of military bearing, gave his reins to his groom and jumped lightly to the ground, then entered the house. In a remarkably short time, he emerged with Leah on his arm. She was looking up into the man's eyes, her face bright with laughter.

She was exquisite, his little harpist. Ranulph greedily absorbed the sight of her slim, graceful figure and delicate features. He felt a surprising urge to reveal himself and wrench her away from her young man. Goddess, but he'd spent too much time observing mortals! He was developing some of their vices, such as jealousy.

He watched as the young man helped her into the carriage with tender care. Then the man left his groom to wait at Wheaton House, and drove off with Leah.

Ranulph scowled. He should be pleased. If he was any judge, his little harpist was finally well on her way to falling in love, which meant that the day when he could claim her was not far off. That knowledge only increased his impatience.

"Surely in London you can find other amusements while you wait to net your mortal miss," a familiar purring voice said.

Ranulph was becoming accustomed to Kamana's silent appearances. This time when he turned, his hand was not on the hilt of his sword. "There is enough greenery here to sustain faery life, but it is locked into strange, unnatural shapes. I shall be glad when the time comes to return to my wood." He suppressed a sigh. His longing for the familiar green peace was almost as powerful as his desire to have Leah there as his consort.

"It won't be much longer now," Kamana said. "The

silver threads are crossing now, creating shared destinies. You'll be home again soon.''

"I hope so." He studied her appreciatively. Today she wore an Indian costume that swathed her magnificent figure with provocative snugness. Necklaces of golden coins jingled around her neck and drew attention to her dark silky skin. "What are your London amusements, Lady Kamana?"

She shrugged, the gesture creating a tantalizing possibility that her wrapped garment would come unmoored. "Observing the passing scene. Visiting the green margins of the city. Did you know that by the river in Chelsea there is a wonderful apothecary's garden that contains plants from my own land?" She gave a dazzling smile. "But mostly I watch these strange, intriguing mortal creatures."

"Surely you cannot wish to stay in London forever."

"Oh, no," she said positively. "Soon I shall return to the country. I've visited the great faery courts in Somerset and Derbyshire, and some smaller ones as well. I know what home I would prefer, but I will not speak of it until I'm sure I will be accepted."

He smiled down at her. For all her regal bearing, she was really quite a small creature. "I'm sure that whatever court you choose will welcome you gladly."

"We shall see." She pressed her hands together in front of her chest and bowed gracefully. "As we say in Hind, *namaste.* Until next time, Lord Ranulph."

She vanished in a shimmer of light. A good trick. He must learn how to do it. Then he turned and glided unseen through the street to Hyde Park so he could continue observing Leah and her mortal.

Leah enjoyed watching Duncan as he drove expertly through the crowded London streets. Heavens, she would enjoy watching him groom a horse or weed a garden. By the light of day he was every bit as handsome as he had seemed last night. More so.

Yet she was even more struck by the quality that Lady Wheaton had mentioned the night before. Beneath the facade of a bold and dangerous-looking hero was a disposition of surprising sweetness. The expression in his golden eyes when he'd called for her had been almost shy.

Duncan had come at an unfashionably early hour so they would not be constantly interrupted by acquaintances. When they reached the park and the traffic no longer required his complete attention, he glanced at her and said, mirroring her own earlier thoughts, "You are even lovelier than I thought last night. Helen of Troy could not have surpassed you."

"That is a very pretty compliment," Leah said seriously. "But I would not want to launch a thousand ships. So much suffering! Not that I think it was Helen's fault. Surely Menelaus and Paris could have resolved their differences in a more civilized fashion."

Duncan grinned. "I've often thought the same. A duel would have been far more efficient. But the truth is that the Greeks simply liked to fight. I expect that any excuse would have done as well."

"Then they shouldn't have blamed the Trojan War on Helen," she said firmly. "It's the same as Adam blaming Eve for his own weakness. Most reprehensible."

He gave her a smile that made her knees weak. "I see that you are a radical."

"Not really, but I've read Mary Wollstonecraft Godwin and agree with much of what she said." Leah smiled ruefully. "I promised Lady Wheaton that I would not reveal my bluestocking tendencies, but with you, I forgot my promise."

"I'm glad. Women with ideas are far more interesting than those who haven't two thoughts to rub together."

Leah glowed at his words. The compliment seemed to belong to her more than his praise for her beauty.

He continued, "Tell me about your family. Parents? Brothers and sisters?"

"No brothers and sisters," she said with regret. "I came late, when my parents had long since given up all thoughts of having a family."

"And . . . ?" he said, perhaps hearing something in her voice.

She hesitated, then said aloud what she seldom admitted even to herself. "My parents had little patience or interest in a child. They did their duty, of course, but . . ." Her voice trailed off before she continued, "Though my childhood was a quiet one, I always had my books and music. I was . . . content."

"I see," he said quietly, and she suspected that he did see.

"What of your family, Captain Townley?" she asked.

"Call me Duncan," he said with a warm look that reached deep inside her.

She seemed to be having trouble with her breathing. "Very well, Duncan. But . . . but you must call me Leah."

His answering smile was like a touch. How could the simple exchange of names feel so intimate?

"I was fortunate, for my parents were unfashionably interested in their offspring. I have two older sisters who alternately spoiled and tormented me." He grinned. "That's normal for families, from what I've seen. Jane and Caroline are both married now. At last count I had five delightful nieces and nephews."

Trying not to sound too envious of his family, she asked, "Did you always wish to grow up and join the army?"

"Actually, my inclinations were scholarly rather than military." He concentrated rather more than necessary on steering around two stopped carriages. "But shortly after I finished at Cambridge, my parents died within a month of each other. I felt the need for a change." He smiled with wry self-mockery. "I also had romantic notions about

serving my country, so I went into the army and was sent
to the Peninsula just before the big push into France.''

He'd had a baptism of fire. She did a swift calculation,
and decided that he was only about twenty-five now. War
had matured him early. ''You may deny being a hero, but
at the least, you served your country well,'' she said quietly.
''Don't apologize for that.''

He pulled his horses to a halt, then turned to her, the
reins tight in his hands. ''We both seem to have the ability
to hear more than what the other person is saying.''

So the deeper levels of this conversation were not in her
imagination. She asked, ''Is that bad?''

''No.'' He snapped the reins and set the horses into
motion again. ''Not bad at all.''

For the rest of the drive, they talked about anything and
everything. Leah had never found anyone, male or female,
with whom she could converse so easily. And Duncan was
obviously enjoying himself as much as she was. Could falling in love be this simple? She prayed that it was so.

As Duncan drove back to Wheaton House, he said with
a touch of diffidence, ''Tomorrow is the last night that
Vauxhall will be open before closing for the winter. My
uncle, with whom I'm staying, has suggested inviting you
and your godmother to join us. Apparently she and my
uncle are old friends. Might you be able to come?''

''Let me ask Lady Wheaton when we reach home. I
believe we're free tomorrow night,'' she said, ruthlessly
jettisoning invitations to three loud, crowded rout parties.

With a private smile, she guessed that her aunt would
be almost as interested in the excursion as Leah.

Chapter Five

After spattering rain all day, the skies began to clear as dusk approached. Leah gave thanks—she did not want the evening at Vauxhall canceled. She was ready and bouncing with eagerness an hour before Lord Townley and Duncan were due to arrive.

Monique, who styled Leah's hair, shook her head sadly. "You must not wear your heart on your sleeve, m'zelle. Men like Captain Townley enjoy the hunt. Where is the challenge in a woman who falls into the hand like a ripe plum?"

Shadow, who was sitting on the vanity table with her paws tucked primly under her, gave a soft, scornful yowl. Feeling supported, Leah said, "Captain Townley is not like that. He would despise such games." She was not sure how she knew that, but she was quite positive that she was right.

After Monique left, still shaking her head, Leah stroked Shadow's luxuriant black fur. Now that she thought about it, she realized that the cat's eyes were the same transparent gold as Duncan's. An interesting coincidence.

She spent the next hour playing her harp, and wondering if Duncan would like the traditional instrument as much as he had enjoyed her piano playing. Wryly she recognized that every thought in her head involved Duncan one way or another.

When a maid summoned her, she raced down the stairs like a hoyden. Outside the drawing room, she made herself pause to take a deep breath. Then she went in.

Duncan greeted her warmly and made the introductions. Lord Townley was a lean, handsome gentleman with silver-touched hair and an unfashionably brown complexion. He bowed over her hand. "I had thought my nephew exaggerated your beauty, but I see instead that he understated the case."

Leah liked the twinkle in the viscount's eye, and the obvious affection between him and his nephew. One of the bits of female advice that Lady Wheaton had offered was that a man who could get along with his relations was a good prospect for getting along with a wife. Leah had learned more such useful things in a few weeks with her godmother than in twenty-one years with her real mother.

Lady Wheaton swept grandly into the parlor, looking particularly fine in a navy blue costume trimmed in military-style gold braid. Lord Townley swung around, and there was a suspended moment while they looked at each other. Both of them were very still until the viscount said softly, "You haven't changed at all, Andrea."

To Leah's amazement, her worldly godmother blushed. "Nor have you, Will. You're still an outrageous flirt."

"A flirt?" he protested. "I'm a simple man, dedicated to the pursuit of truth."

"Hmph. The truth isn't in you," she said, but she took his arm eagerly when he offered it.

Leah and Duncan exchanged a glance of mutual surprise and amusement. As they followed the older couple out to the carriage, Duncan said under his breath, "I had thought my uncle a dedicated bachelor. But perhaps I was wrong."

Leah laughed and tightened her clasp on his arm. Magic

was in the air. Why shouldn't Lord Townley and Lady
Wheaton also feel the enchantment?

Ranulph had visited Vauxhall Gardens several times.
During the day, the acres of trees were a welcome respite
from the stone and stink of the city. He'd come several
times at night as well. The concerts weren't bad, though
nothing as good as faery music, or Leah's lilting airs. But
in the tree-shadowed paths, it was simple to find women
who would lie with a handsome stranger. The physical
satisfaction he'd found in such encounters was fleeting,
but easily come by.

Tonight was different because Leah was here, along with
her damned suitor. The young man was definitely a
suitor—a blind man could see that.

Leah and her party had promenaded along the Grand
Walk, watched the Cascade, and dined in a supper box.
There was something afoot between the older man and
Leah's godmother as well—Ranulph could see the energy
glow between them. Not as intense as the radiant bond
between Leah and young Townley, but definitely there,
and growing stronger. The lot of them were having such
a good time that they were like feasting court faeries, he
thought acidly.

After the fireworks display, the couples separated and
went off to promenade through the gardens, wanting pri-
vacy to talk—or for other reasons. Ranulph drifted through
the shrubbery, watching Leah. The provocative sway of her
hips as she walked intoxicated him. And her breasts, ah,
those perfect little breasts . . .

He caught his breath as an idea struck him. What if a
patch of fog rolled in from the river while Leah and her
suitor were on the Dark Walk? No one would think anything of it. In the mist it would be easy to separate Leah
from Townley. Lost and confused, she would run to her
suitor in relief when she found him. Except that it would

be Ranulph she would find, guised in the form of the man
she desired.

He gave a great shout of laughter as the plan took form
in his mind. He'd have her tonight, and pleasure her so
well that she would be mad for the young man whose face
he wore. Then, when her wits were scrambled with love,
it would be time for Ranulph to collect his price, and she
would be his.

In his bed—and in flower-filled glens and mossy bow-
ers—he would bind her to him with the erotic arts learned
over centuries, skills no mortal could hope to match.
Through passion he would swiftly overcome any resentment she had at being compelled to leave the world of
mortals. Not that he expected much resistance. Once she
adjusted, how could she not prefer eons of pleasurable life
in the glittering realms of Faerie?

He waited until Leah and her escort left the lighted
Grand Cross Walk for the Dark Walk. Then, his gaze following her graceful figure, he raised one arm and summoned
the fog.

Thick and soft as cotton wool, the dense mist rolled
over the trees and walkways of this corner of the gardens,
muffling sounds and reducing vision to a matter of two or
three feet. Even Ranulph could see little.

All about him were gasps and feminine squeals of surprise. Ranulph smiled and snapped his fingers as he murmured a few words in the ancient tongue of magic. A spell
of confusion formed in his palm, a dim sphere with dark
swirling streaks inside. He tossed it toward Leah and Townley. The spell was a small one, and would affect only them
and an area of fifty feet or so around.

Then, silent as the fog, he headed toward where he had
last seen her. He'd done his work too well, for even he
became confused. She was not where he had expected,
and neither was her escort. Ranulph stopped and searched
the dense fog with scent and sound and intuition. Trees

to the left, beyond that two people coupling, and not with the partners they'd come with. But where was Leah?

He heard light steps on the gravel path. A soft voice said uncertainly, "Duncan?"

Vibrant with excitement, he made himself visible to mortal eyes in the guise of Duncan Townley. He took a moment to familiarize himself with the new form. He had to admit that it was not a bad body, for a mortal. Then he called, "Here, Leah!"

He stepped forward, and almost ran into her. She gasped, "Oh!" as he caught her shoulders to steady her.

"Are you all right?" he asked, the words coming in a deep voice that was not his own. Slowly he ran his hands down her arms as he studied her delicate features.

She smiled, shamefaced. "I am now. I don't know quite how I lost you. One moment I had your arm. Then the fog came, and I got confused."

"I know. I was worried." He drew her into his arms and held her close. After making a small sound of surprise, she nestled close.

Reminding himself that he must go slowly, he kissed the top of her head, then gently moved his lips to her temple. She tilted her head back questioningly. The damp fog caused tendrils of hair to cling fetchingly to her throat. No longer able to restrain himself, he claimed her lips.

She gave a shiver of surprise. "I . . . I shouldn't," she whispered into his mouth.

"I was so worried," he said again, and kissed her bare throat, stroking her rapid pulse with his tongue.

Her mind might have doubts, but her body didn't. She pressed against him even as she murmured another vague protest. With a few steps he moved them to a mossy bed that he had created earlier, safely away from the graveled walk.

"This . . . this is most improper," she said weakly as he dropped to his knees, then tugged her down beside him.

"You're wrong," he said intensely. "For us, it's the most

proper thing in the world." He started to say that he loved her, a phrase that worked like a magical spell on any mortal female who was already as aroused as Leah was. Yet he could not utter the words. In some indefinable way, it seemed wrong to lie to her about that.

He kissed her throat again, at the same time slipping her shawl from her shoulders and deftly unfastening the tapes securing the back of her gown. The bodice fell away, revealing her lacy underthings and the tops of her perfect breasts.

"Oh, Duncan." Eyes wide and startled, she made an ineffectual attempt to cover herself properly. "You really shouldn't do such things."

"I must have you, Leah," he said tightly. Though he wore the form of a mortal, it was Ranulph's own need that burned through his words. He captured her mouth, swallowing her protests while his hands delved beneath her gauzy garments.

He should have let his passion show sooner, for suddenly she was responding with a desire that matched his own, her small hands biting into his back. She was like a flame, her lithe body twisting beneath his, her hands and mouth eager.

Madness swept through him, a scorching need to make her his own. Yet even as he possessed her, their bodies joining with a wildness that seared his senses, he realized that something was wrong. *Something was wrong.*

He cried out at the same time as she, drowning in passion's inferno. In that same instant, as he felt the fierce heat of her response, his partner suddenly transformed. Her slight body became more voluptuous, her tawny hair turned into a tangle of silken tresses as black as night.

With shock and incredulous rage, he realized that it was not Leah but Kamana who lay beneath him, her shapely limbs twined around him and her golden eyes filled with wicked amusement. Violently he wrenched himself from her embrace. "Damn you!" he panted. "How dare you interfere with me!"

She laughed, unabashed, and rolled onto her side, propping her head up on one hand. Her clothing had vanished, leaving her naked except for the gossamer spill of her raven hair. "Why are you so angry? You seemed to be enjoying yourself." Her free hand drifted to her breast, where the mark of his teeth still showed. "I thought I played the innocent very well, until the end."

He flushed. "That is not the point. You had no right to deceive me."

Her brows arched. "Yet you had a right to deceive that child, to take the virginity that mortals prize so much? That would have been unkind." Her voice became husky. "I thought that you were in need of a diversion, so I sacrificed myself to that cause."

He snorted. "Sacrificed! You mated like a she-panther. The marks on my back will not disappear quickly. Is that why you came to England, to find bolder lovers than the Folk of India?"

Her laughter pealed through the fog that enclosed their private glen. "Sexual congress is one of the great arts among my people. There are none in Angland that could match the sensual skill of one of my kind."

Seeing that he was on the verge of explosion, she added kindly, "Oh, I admit that you are not without a certain talent in this area. With practice, and the teaching of a skilled partner, you might someday equal a lord of Hind." She stretched a hand lazily toward him, her fingers trailing sparkles of light.

Cursing, he leaped to his feet before she could touch him. "You witch! You were probably driven out by your own kind, and that is why you've come here to plague me."

She dropped her teasing manner. "Not at all. But I will not let you hurt that child wantonly. The fact that she is bound by the faery bargain she made does not mean she must be your prey now. Have patience, and you will soon have all that you desire."

"What I desire is to be free of you," he said viciously. Then he whirled into the fog as her laughter followed him.

One moment Leah was smiling at one of Duncan's remarks, and the next the thickest fog she had ever seen had fallen with amazing swiftness. She gasped and turned around, then realized that somehow she had let go of Duncan's arm. At first she was not alarmed, thinking that he must be within touching distance.

But he wasn't. He had vanished. She moved toward where he had been, or where she thought he had been, without success. Fear began to rise in her. The fog was uncanny, menacing. Struggling to contain her panic, she called, "Duncan?"

There was no answer. Hands clenched, she called again. Why could she hear nothing? It was as if she had fallen from the face of the earth into a nightmare.

Then she heard a faint, "I'm here, Leah."

She exhaled with relief, but in the fog it was impossible to tell from where his voice had come. Uncertainly she turned in a circle. "Where?" she called back.

"Stay where you are," he ordered, his voice a little closer. "If we both move, we'll never find each other."

Obediently she stood still, drawing her shawl tight against the biting chill. After what seemed like forever but was probably only a couple of minutes, Duncan emerged from the fog in front of her.

"Thank heaven!" She reached out with both hands.

He caught them, his grip warm and secure. "Are you all right?"

She nodded, ashamed of her fear. "Just a little disoriented."

His hands tightened on hers. "I had a strange feeling

that there was some great danger in the fog. Danger for you. I was terrified that I wouldn't find you in time."

She swallowed. "I was afraid too, until you came."

He cupped her face in his hands, his gaze intense. "I don't know what I would do if something happened to you, Leah. I feel as if I've known you forever instead of just a few days."

"I . . . I feel the same way." Tears stung in her eyes, and she didn't know why.

"You are so lovely, Leah," he whispered. "The loveliest creature I've ever seen."

Then he bent his head and touched his lips to hers. The kiss was exquisitely gentle, totally different from the Duke of Hardcastle's rough embrace. But sweet, so sweet. She yearned toward him, feeling the effect of the kiss in every fiber of her body.

When he lifted his mouth away, she said shakily, "Is it wicked of me to enjoy that so much?"

"If so, we are wicked together." He wrapped her in a warm, protective hug. With a sigh she relaxed against him, feeling the beat of his heart. She was in love. Though she'd never experienced the state before, it was as unmistakable as a sunrise.

Duncan held her for long minutes, stroking her head and back. Finally he said reluctantly, "I must return you to your godmother before I do something I shouldn't."

She nodded, but didn't have the will to move away.

Slowly he disengaged himself from their embrace, his hands skimming over her back and hips as lightly as butterfly wings. "The fog should thin as we move away from the river," he said in a determined voice. "If we follow the gravel path, we'll be all right."

They set off, her hand locked in his. She counted her steps. Twenty. Fifty. A hundred. They walked out of the fog as abruptly as if they'd entered a lighted room. "How odd," Leah exclaimed, looking around at other revelers who were discussing the strange mist.

"Indeed," Duncan said thoughtfully. "Almost unnatural."

As they watched, the fog began to disperse as quickly as it had formed. Within a few minutes it was no more than a strange, dreamlike memory.

Lord Townley and Lady Wheaton appeared from where the mist had lain, both of them looking pleased and suspiciously mussed. As the older couple came toward them, Duncan said swiftly, "May I call on you tomorrow? There is . . . something very important I want to discuss with you."

"Of course you may call," Leah said as her heart jumped. Might he be intending to offer for her? Though they hadn't know each other long, there seemed to be a rare harmony, a matching of minds and tastes, between them.

She hugged the possibility, knowing that she was grinning like a fool. She didn't care. She was in love, and she thought he loved her.

She had never been happier in her life.

Chapter Six

Too nervous to eat, Leah was glad that Lady Wheaton was abstracted at breakfast the next morning. Downright dreamy, in fact, with a smile hovering around her lips. She looked ten years younger and far less jaded than when Leah had first come to London.

Leah regarded her godmother fondly. If not for Lord Ranulph's magic, it was unlikely that the two women would have ever become acquainted. Now there was a bond between them that was warmer than what existed between Leah and her mother. She owed the faery lord a great deal.

For the first time in days, she wondered what he would want in return, but she felt too happy to worry about that. In olden times, favored servants were sometimes leased houses in return for a peppercorn a year, or something equally trifling. Lord Ranulph had said that he loved her music, and it was only the laws of his people that required him to exact a payment in return. No doubt his price would be like those peppercorn rents.

Unable to eat, Leah mangled a piece of toast and hoped

that Duncan would call early. But he did not come until afternoon. She spent the morning playing the harp and thinking about the evening before. The memory of his kiss, and his embrace, caused tingling energy to flow through her body. In a very real sense, she felt truly alive for the first time. Perhaps that was what it meant to be in love.

It was a relief when a maid arrived to tell her that Captain Townley was waiting in the drawing room. Leah took a swift glance in her mirror. She looked beautiful. It had become hard to remember exactly the differences in appearance from before Ranulph had worked his spell, though she remembered with icy clarity how it felt to be so plain that she was almost invisible in her own life.

Leah felt a little sadness that Duncan would never have noticed her as she was before. Winning his regard this way seemed almost like cheating. But her beauty gave him pleasure, so she was more grateful than guilty.

After composing herself, she went downstairs to the drawing room, carefully leaving the door ajar for propriety's sake. Duncan was leaning casually against the mantelpiece. As she watched the sunlight define the chiseled planes of his face, Leah said involuntarily, "You're the most beautiful man I've ever seen."

Instead of being pleased or embarrassed, he became still as a statue. Then, releasing his breath in a sigh, he said, "I can't think of myself as beautiful."

"Would you prefer handsome? Dashing? Heroic? You are all of those things," she said, amazed by her own boldness. "I love looking at you."

"I'm not the man you think, Leah," he said with sudden vehemence. "I'm not a hero, not dashing, not at all out of the common way. I'm a plain man who likes books and country living and music, who merely did his duty as the situation demanded."

His golden eyes darkened. "The only thing special about me is how much I love you. Meeting you was like . . . like

coming home. I know it's too soon, and that I should not
speak to you before talking to your father. I know also that
you are a jewel who should be gracing the finest society
in Britain, and I can't give you that. But is it possible''—
his voice wavered for an instant—"do you think that you
could be happy sharing a quiet life with me?''

He really was shy, she realized with amazement, perhaps
as shy as she herself. Overcome with tenderness, she said,
''I would like nothing better, Duncan.'' She went to him
and took his hands before saying haltingly, ''I love you. A
rational person might laugh at us both, but I feel that . . .
that in you I've found the other side of myself.''

He scanned her face with riveting intensity. ''Would you
love me if I were ugly, or if this scar was far worse, or if I
had never been called hero?''

Recognizing how much he cared about her answer, she
took time to think before saying slowly, ''I love your kindness, your humor, the way you make me feel safe and
cherished.'' She gave him a shy smile. ''I love the person
I am when I am with you. I think that would be true no
matter what you looked like, and even if you had never
been lionized by London society.''

His smile was radiant and relieved. ''Then I'll go into
the country and speak to your father. Is there any chance
that he might refuse to allow me to pay my addresses?''

''None at all. You are not only wonderful, but wonder-
fully eligible.'' She smiled teasingly. ''I'll be getting the
best of this bargain, you know.''

His expression turned wry. ''Never think that, Leah. If
only you knew.''

Leah bit her lower lip. ''My parents dislike surprises. I
think it would be wise for me to go home first and prepare
them for your visit.''

''Good. That means that as soon as I have his permission,
I can come to you and make a formal offer.'' His arms slid
around her. ''Oh, Leah, Leah . . .''

She went into his embrace gladly. "This is very forward of me, but I'd like the engagement to be short."

His laughter was rich and deep. "As short as we can decently make it."

She sighed with delight. It was hard to believe that such happiness could be real. As she rested against him, loving his warmth and strength, a dreadful thought struck her. Surely Ranulph couldn't ask for her firstborn child! But there were ancient tales of faeries asking such a price.

The thought had not occurred to her when they had made their original bargain, probably because the idea of having a child was so far from her mind then. But it wasn't now. When she imagined marriage to Duncan, children were as much a part of the picture as Duncan himself. She would never give a child of theirs to a being who was as incomprehensible to her as the far side of the moon.

Surely her fears were pure, overwrought nonsense. Nonetheless, it was good that she was returning home now. She would find Ranulph and settle her debt. Then she could go into her new life freely.

Leah found it strange to be back in the bedroom she'd occupied since leaving the nursery. She'd changed so much, yet the room looked exactly the same. Well, the same except for Shadow, who had returned from London with her usual aloof dignity.

Her father had been bemused by Leah's announcement that a Captain Townley would be coming to speak with Sir Edwin on a matter of great import. However, he'd decided that he approved of the prospect after reading Lady Wheaton's letter that described Duncan's character and financial situation.

Rather sadly, Leah recognized that her parents would be glad to have her off their hands. Yet the knowledge didn't hurt the way it once had. As long as Duncan loved her, she could accept the fact that to her parents she was no more than a regrettable obligation.

On the morning after she arrived home, Leah slung her harp on her back and asked her dozing cat, "Would you like to come for a walk in the woods with me? There should be mice to chase and similar delights."

Shadow gave her mistress a look of contempt, then closed her eyes and swished her black tail over her nose. Leah chuckled. The cat was a good companion, but not overinterested in exertion.

It was a lovely autumn day, with a clear sky and pleasantly warm sunshine. Leah hiked into the woods to the glade where she had first met Ranulph. There she sat on the trunk of the fallen tree and played her harp. She sang of love and joy, and silently asked for the faery to come.

She'd almost given up hope when Lord Ranulph abruptly appeared in front of her, his golden hair drifting in the wind like thistle down. Leah caught her breath at the suddenness. This time he didn't wear the garb of a fashionable Englishman, but elegant garments of medieval cut, with a sword swinging at his side and dark hose that displayed the powerful muscles of his thighs. He was dangerously masculine, with an untamed light in his green eyes that made him seem far more alien than on their first meeting. But his tone was courteous when he bowed. "You wished to see me, my lady."

Setting aside her harp, Leah stood and curtsied. "Your magic is strong, my lord. I went to London, as you arranged, and became very successful, as you predicted."

"I know," he said coolly. "I observed you in London myself."

She found the knowledge that he had spied on her disturbing. Had he eavesdropped on her private, tender moments with Duncan? She hated the idea.

Remembering his ability to read her mind, she tried to suppress the thought, but guessed from his cynical expression that he knew how she felt. She made herself smile.

"I won the love of a hero, as you said I could. Soon I will be married. If it is agreeable to you, I would like to settle my debt now."

"Your timing is impeccable, Leah." He stalked across the clearing like a restless golden lion. "If you had not come here today, I would have summoned you."

Suppressing her uneasiness, she said, "You told me I would have three choices, my lord. What are they to be?"

"Can't you guess what I really want?" He stopped and turned to regard her with drugging eyes. "I want you to become my consort. I want you to live with me in Faerie, surrounded by music and beauty always. I will show you wonders such as you have never imagined. Come to me, Leah." He extended one long beautiful hand.

She felt the fierce power of his desire, the dark strength of his magic tugging at her. "No!" she said violently.

She retreated until the backs of her legs were pressed against the fallen tree. "I don't belong in your world, Lord Ranulph. I would never agree to such a thing."

His uptilted brows arched, and she saw that he was laughing at her. "But you will, my dear girl. It is the best of the choices I offer you."

She ran her tongue over her dry lips. "Tell me the other two."

He began to pace around the glade again, his sword swinging by his side. "You say that you are to be married. Captain Townley, I assume." Ranulph gave her a glance that demanded a reply.

"Duncan and I have an understanding," she said reluctantly. "After he has spoken to my father, our betrothal will be official."

"A handsome youth," Ranulph said musingly. "A warrior hero."

Leah nodded warily, not sure where this was leading.

The faery lord halted at the far side of the clearing and turned to face her. In a voice that chilled her to the bone, he said, "Your second choice, my dearest girl, is to bring me his heart."

Leah stared at Ranulph. "What do you mean? The fact that he has pledged me his heart does not mean that I can give it to another. Love isn't like that."

The faery's eyes narrowed. "I was not speaking in metaphor, Leah. Never fear, I shall make the task easy." A silver dagger materialized in his hand, the blade glittering wickedly. "This is an enchanted blade. Even a small creature like you will find it easy to slide the dagger between his ribs and cut out his heart when he is dead."

"You're mad!" Shocked beyond words, she gagged, on the verge of vomiting at the horrific image conjured by Ranulph's words. To look into Duncan's smiling eyes, then murder him . . . She pressed her hand to her mouth as her stomach heaved.

Bland as butter, Ranulph continued, "I suggest that you do the deed when on a walk in my wood, so you will not have to go far to deliver your payment. You need not fear retribution from your own kind. Simply weep prettily and claim that you were set upon by a madman who slew your lover. No one will believe that a woman so beautiful, so fragile, so in love, could perform such a bloody deed."

He smiled satirically. "After a suitable mourning period, you will be free to seek another husband. That duke who mauled you in his garden, for instance. He was angry then, but I'm sure you could win him back with a single enchanting smile." Ranulph pressed the silver dagger into her numb hand. The hilt was cool against her palm.

She stared at the shining weapon, her horror intensifying. "I can't. I *won't*."

He tilted his head, wicked, inhuman amusement in his eyes. "I didn't think you would. That's why I waited until now. It would take a fierce woman to kill her lover."

"You needn't have waited so long," she said in a shaking voice. "I could never do such a thing even to a stranger."

"You are that sentimental about all mortals?" he said,

surprised. "If I had realized the extent of your squea-mishness, I would have come to claim you sooner."

More than anything else he had done, that statement made Leah realize how utterly alien he was. He simply had no understanding of humans. "What is your last choice—my firstborn child?" she said bitterly. "If you ask that, I swear I shall use your dagger right now." She raised the weapon in shaking hands and held it to her breast, wonder-ing if she would have the strength to kill herself. He'd said the blade was enchanted. Perhaps it would slide home easily . . .

Ranulph leaped across the clearing in one bound and wrenched the dagger away from her. "Goddess, and you think *I'm* insane?" he said furiously. "I don't want your life, nor another man's squalling brat."

He tossed the dagger aside. It vanished in midair. More calmly, he said, "A babe fathered by me—now that would be more interesting. The Folk are not prolific, but in an eternity of mating, we are bound to produce a child now and then."

He truly intended to own her body and soul. Shaking her head in revulsion, Leah said, "You owe me another choice, Lord Ranulph. Whatever it is, it cannot be as evil as what you have already suggested."

He smiled at her, as splendid and amoral as a wild beast. "Your last choice is not evil at all. Such a simple thing."

She laced her trembling hands together. "Don't play with me, my lord," she said tightly. "Just tell me what you want."

"A simple thing," he repeated. "But, I think, the highest price of all. If you decline the other choices, it will cost you your beauty."

Chapter Seven

Leah stared at Ranulph, her eyes wide and shaken. "My beauty?"

He winced inwardly at her distress, but it was necessary. He'd set the order of the choices deliberately, knowing that her first reaction to leaving her own kind would be refusal. Only after hearing all the choices would she take his proposal seriously.

Careful to keep all sympathy from his voice, he said coolly, "Don't play the fool, Leah. Refuse me, and you'll become again the plain creature you were before. Dull and colorless, almost invisible. Most people will not really understand the change, though anyone who saw you during your London triumphs will be unable to remember why he thought you such a great beauty then."

His voice dropped. "But your suitor will remember. He'll look at you with shock and revulsion. How many times did Captain Townley praise your beauty? How often did he murmur in your ear about your loveliness? When your beauty vanishes, so will his love. You will live the rest of your life alone and despised."

He gave a bored shrug. "I suppose that since masculine honor is involved, you may be able to hold him to the betrothal. In that case, you will have the pleasure of living with a man who despises you for deceiving him."

Her eyes, an emerald mirror of his own, filled with tears until she closed them. Her exquisitely expressive face revealed that she was imagining exactly what Ranulph had described: rejection by her lover, a return to her empty existence.

Judging it time to change his tactics, he said softly, "Now do you understand why I said that becoming my consort was the best choice? Come with me and I shall give you passion and beauty beyond your wildest imaginings. Great caves shimmering with secret jewels. Forests with a majesty that would humble the greatest human cathedral. We'll ride the wind and sing the seas, and you shall never regret your decision."

Confident that the web of words he'd spun would change Leah's mind, he stepped forward and took her hand between both of his. Goddess, but she was lovely. He felt himself hardening with desire. Passion would sweep away the last of her doubts.

He drew her into a kiss. Her mouth was soft, her scent as fresh as spring flowers. He used all his erotic skills, he focused all his desire, weaving an enchantment that would leave her begging for more.

But it didn't work. She tore herself away, wiping her mouth with the back of her hand in revulsion. "Do you think I could ever prefer your touch to that of Duncan?" She lifted her harp and clutched it like a talisman against harm. "Perhaps you can cloud my mind with magic, but I will never be your whore voluntarily."

He stared at her, shocked that she could resist his sensual spell. Who would have thought that she had such strength? He produced his magic mirror with a snap of his fingers and held it up as a reminder of what she had looked like. Ruthlessly he used an image of her at her worst, with her eyes swollen and her nose pink from crying. "Is this what you choose?" he said cruelly. "Or will it be your lover's heart?"

She paled at the image in the mirror, but said resolutely, "Return me to what I was, Lord Ranulph. I was plain all of my life. I . . . I can learn to be plain again."

"You don't know what you're saying!" he exclaimed, incredulous. "It was bad enough to have no looks before, but now you have known the delights of beauty. The adoration, the power, the fame. To lose those things after briefly tasting them will be infinitely more painful than never to have known them."

"Do you think I don't know that?" she cried out, clutching the harp even tighter. "But I can bear it. I shall have to, since both your other choices are unthinkable. I could never harm Duncan, nor any other innocent. Nor can I give up my whole world to become the slave of a creature who is as beautiful and alien as a tiger."

"I want you for my consort, not my slave!" he snapped in a voice like a whip.

"Isn't it slavery if I go against my will?" Her mouth twisted. "You and I are made of different stuff, Lord Ranulph. You think beauty more valuable than freedom, more precious than another person's life. I can no more understand that than you can understand me. Goodbye, my lord. I presume that by the time I reach my home, I will be plain again, and our bargain will be fulfilled."

She slipped away from him and headed across the glade. Before entering the woods, she paused to say quietly, "I . . . I'm sorry that I cannot be what you wish."

Stunned that she was really leaving, for an instant he stood frozen. Then he gave a wild shout of anger. *"No!"*

He flung both arms to the heavens, and thunder boomed from the clear autumn sky, rolling across the wood with a force that shook the trees. Leah flinched, and he saw alarm in her eyes.

Realizing that if she feared him all hope was gone, he

said tightly, "I shall not harm you, Leah. Not now, not ever. If ever you become disenchanted with being plain and lonely and despised, you know how to summon me."

She gave a faint nod of her head, but he knew with despair that she would never change her mind. Except for her music, she was as much a mystery to him as he was to her. Was that because she was a mortal, or simply because she was female?

Saturated with pain, he watched her disappear among the trees. She was gone, and he was alone.

Then rage returned. With a gesture of his hand, he removed the faery glamour that had dazzled all of London. Viciously he contemplated how her lover would react to the discovery that his ravishing betrothed was now as plain as a barn mouse.

The restless churn of his anger turned toward Kamana. *Damn* the treacherous female! Her predictions that Leah would come to him were empty, more of her mocking games. She would answer to him for her lies. She had power, but he was her equal. She would be unable to refuse if he summoned her.

He closed his eyes and visualized Kamana until her exotic, teasing image was burned in his brain. Then he uttered the words of Power that would bring her to him, against her will if necessary.

She'd pay for her interference and lies, the traitorous witch. Aye, she'd pay.

Leah was still shaking when she reached home. Not wanting anyone to see the tears on her face, she crept up the back stairs and into her bedroom.

Shadow still lay on the bed. At Leah's entrance, the cat opened her eyes and gazed at her fixedly. Leah tried to smile. "Don't tell me that you'll abandon me, too. I would have thought that at least my cat would accept me as I am now."

Shadow leaped from the bed and came to rub Leah's ankles, purring warmly. A little comforted, Leah scratched the cat's neck.

Then she turned to her mirror. Any faint hope she'd harbored that Ranulph might not exact his price died. Drab hair, thin figure, ordinary gray-green eyes reddened from tears. She glanced at her left palm. In the center, she could still see the faint iridescent glimmer of the cut Ranulph had made when they'd sealed their bargain. Apparently it would be the only lasting sign of what she had been.

She inhaled painfully and forced herself to stare at her reflection. Had he made her plainer than before, or did her appearance seem worse because of the contrast to what she had been? No matter. This was the face she was born with, and would die with. She reminded herself that she'd had no real choice. Murder was unthinkable, and so was going into whatever strange, inhuman netherworld Ranulph called home.

She winced as she remembered Duncan's worshipful gaze, the number of times he'd told her that she was the most beautiful creature he had ever seen. He was too much a gentleman to break his pledged word when he saw what she had become, but Ranulph was right. It would be even worse to live with Duncan and know that he despised her than to live without him. She must release him from the betrothal.

The thought of losing him shattered her last shreds of composure. She threw herself onto the bed, sobbing uncontrollably. Shadow followed and touched her cool nose to Leah's cheek, but that did nothing to allay the pain. Merciful heaven, Leah would have been better off if she'd never met Ranulph of the Wood, or if she had been wise enough to refuse his damnable bargain.

Or would she? She rolled onto her side and cradled the cat's warm, fluffy body. The cost of Ranulph's bargain had been bitterly high, but she had learned what it was to be beautiful, and that beauty was not an unalloyed blessing. She wouldn't miss the hungry stares of strangers, or the resentment of other woman.

Nor would she miss the endless balls and parties. After the first excitement of being admired had worn off, she'd realized that she was simply not a very sociable creature. She preferred a country life with her music and a small circle of friends, and would no longer yearn for the delights of London.

And Ranulph's bargain had allowed her to learn the joy of loving. Someday, when the anguish lessened, she would be glad of that.

But now the wound was still too raw. She buried her face in Shadow's silken fur and wept.

Exhausted by tears, Leah dozed. She was jerked awake when one of the housemaids tapped at her door. "Miss Leah, there's a fine young gentleman called Captain Townley here to see you," the girl called through the door. She giggled. "He's just spoken to your father. Is there going to be an announcement?"

Leah pushed herself upright with a gasp of shock. Dear Lord, Duncan had already arrived and asked her father for her hand! She had thought he wouldn't come until tomorrow at the earliest. But he was impatient, as she had been.

She raked her fingers through her hair. She couldn't possibly see him like this. In fact, perhaps it would be best to write him a note. She'd apologize profusely and say that after serious consideration she had decided that they would not suit.

An image appeared in her mind of what his expression would be when he read such a letter. She realized that Shadow was staring at her, disapproval in the great golden eyes. The cat was right. It would be unforgivable to take the coward's way out and leave Duncan to a lifetime of wondering what had gone wrong. When he saw her, his love would evaporate painlessly, leaving him free of the misery that tormented her. She could find some small solace in that.

"Miss Leah?" the maid called again. "Aren't you in there?"

"Ask Captain Townley to wait in the morning room," Leah replied in a strained voice. "I'll be down in a few minutes."

She went to her washstand and splashed her face with cold water to reduce the redness. For pride's sake, she would look no worse than absolutely necessary. Luckily, her apple green gown was very pretty, one of her London acquisitions, and it made the best of her slight figure and fair complexion. Her hair was a disaster, so she combed it out and tied it back simply with a green ribbon, leaving it soft around her face.

Shadow was watching again. In her mind, Leah heard the words *Beauty is as much confidence as it is physical perfection.*

Leah blinked, realizing that was true. Lady Wheaton was not a classic beauty, but her graceful posture and confidence always made heads turn when she entered a room. Leah had carried herself differently after she'd become accustomed to her faery beauty.

Remembering how she had felt when she made an entrance and known that all eyes were on her, she raised her head proudly. She would not hold Duncan against his will, and she would not weep in front of him.

Farewell. Shadow was suddenly next to Leah, the golden eyes somber.

Leah swallowed hard at this unexpected loss. "I'm going to lose you, too, aren't I? You came with Ranulph's magic, and now you must leave since it is gone."

Sorrowfully she lifted the cat for a last hug. As she did, the image of a kitten appeared in her mind. A playful black kitten who would dance into Leah's heart, and soon.

The knowledge was some comfort, though Leah knew there would never be another cat like Shadow.

After setting Shadow on the bed, Leah opened the casement, though if the cat was of Faerie, she probably didn't need an open window to leave. Then Leah headed toward the door. With black humor, she told herself that Duncan would be lucky to escape her, since clearly a woman who held imaginary conversations with her cat was half mad.

As she left the room, she felt a comforting warmth in her mind, almost like a purr.

Since the morning room faced east, it was dim this late in the day. Leah entered to find Duncan standing in front of the window, his broad-shouldered form a dark silhouette. Even when he turned, his features were too shadowed for her to read. That was a small mercy, she decided. "Good day, Duncan."

"Leah." He bowed, but didn't come to her.

Her heart died a little when she saw the ominous rigidity in his figure. He must be shocked by her drab appearance. She halted in the middle of the room, reminding herself to keep her head high. She could not change her looks, but she could at least behave with dignity. "You've spoken with my father?"

"Yes, and he gave his blessing willingly. But"—Duncan hesitated, then said in a rush of words—"before I make a formal offer, there is something I must say."

Suddenly desperate to speak first so that she needn't hear his confused, embarrassed questions, she said lightly, as if it was a matter of no importance, "No need to say anything. It's perfectly obvious that it was a mistake for us to consider marriage." Her gaze slid away and she blinked back tears. "Farewell, Captain Townley. I enjoyed our . . . flirtation."

She glided toward the door and was on the verge of escape when Duncan darted across the room and caught her arm. This close, she could see his shocked expression as he said, "Please don't go. At least, not yet." He swallowed hard. "I . . . I understand that you do not wish to marry me. I'm sorry, Leah. I warned you that I was not the man you thought. A woman as beautiful as you deserves so much more. But I, too, shall treasure our . . . flirtation."

She stared at him. " 'A woman as beautiful as me'? Duncan, look at me! I'm as plain as a fence post. People would laugh at you for taking such an ill-favored wife when you can have any woman in England."

His gaze ran over her. "You do look a little less spectacular than usual today, probably from worrying how to tell me that you prefer to end our understanding. I'm sorry this has been so difficult for you." His voice roughened. "But even upset, you're still the loveliest sight I've ever seen, Leah. I . . . I shall never forget you."

The sincerity in his voice shocked her. If he still thought she was beautiful, it was because the room was too blasted dim. Grimly accepting that she must reveal herself in all her plainness, she took a candle from the table and thrust it into the small coal fire, then ignited a whole branch of candles so that light blazed over her. She turned to Duncan. "You're wondering what happened to the girl you wanted to marry," she said flatly. "It's quite an interesting tale, though hard to believe. At the end of the summer, I met a faery who offered to make me beautiful, for a price to be paid later."

She smiled without humor. "Not only was I made beautiful, but the thought was planted in Lady Wheaton's head that she'd like to present me, and presto! I was in London. Excellent magic, wasn't it?" She shrugged with elaborate unconcern. "But the faery and I couldn't reach an agreement on the payment, so my beauty was revoked. It would be impossible to believe such a tale, except that the truth is written on my face."

He frowned. "Kamana came to you also?"

"Kamana?" Leah said, perplexed.

"The faery." Wearily he raked a hand through his brown hair. "She told me at the beginning that the change in my appearance could only be temporary. I knew you and I could not become betrothed until you had seen me as I really am, so yesterday I asked Kamana to remove her spell. She did so with a snap of her fingers, then told me not to worry, that all would be well. I didn't believe her, and rightly so. A woman with your beauty and charm deserves the very best, not an ordinary man like me."

Leah studied him, looking for changes in his appearance. Now that she looked, she could see that his eyes were no longer golden, but a pleasant hazel with flecks of green, and his hair had gone from near-black to medium brown. Though he was still broad-shouldered and fit, the dashing and dangerous aura that had drawn women like honeybees was gone. Yet he was still unmistakably Duncan.

Perplexed, she said, "The faery who came to me was male, Ranulph of the Wood. He dwells right here, on my father's land, I think. Could he have transformed himself into a female to speak to you?" Even as she said the words, she rejected them. Ranulph was too wholly masculine ever to take the form of a woman.

Equally perplexed, Duncan said, "Kamana is from India. She came to England on the ship that carried my uncle and a hold full of plant specimens. After Waterloo, when I was recovering from my wounds, she appeared and said that my uncle had saved her life. In return, he'd asked that I be protected in battle." Duncan gave a lopsided smile. "She apologized for not being able to turn aside all harm, but her spell surely preserved my life and caused me to heal quickly. You see why I should not be called a hero? Because of my uncle's good deed, I was protected from the guns that killed my comrades. I deserve no credit for that."

So that was the source of his self-deprecation. "Nonsense," Leah said vehemently. "Did you know during the battle that you were protected?"

When he shook his head, she continued, "Then how does a faery spell diminish your deed? As far as you knew at the time, you could die at any instant, as your friends had. It wasn't magic that rallied your regiment and stopped the French advance. It was your courage and skill. Your heroism, Duncan."

As she scanned his beloved face, trying to infuse him with her belief, she recognized that he had been wounded more gravely than she had known. She went to him and tenderly touched the rough scar that ran from his temple to the middle of his cheek. This was not the thin line that had seemed like an elegant accessory to the dramatic good looks of a drawing room hero, but the mark of a savage injury that might have taken his life. "To me, you will always be a hero," she said quietly.

He flinched away from her fingers. "Ugly, isn't it? In hospital, I couldn't even face myself in the shaving mirror. And there are a dozen more scars in less obvious places." He swallowed hard. "When Kamana came to me, she insisted on granting me a season of faery glamour so that I would not hide from society. Perhaps it would have been better if I had not agreed to that, for her magic merely delayed the time when I must come to terms with my disfigurement."

His voice softened. "Yet if not for Kamana's spell, I would never have met you, much less had the courage to speak, or . . . or to kiss. I cannot regret that."

"You're not ugly," Leah said vehemently. "Even without faery glamour, you're the most attractive man I've ever known, Duncan. I love the way you look, just as I love your strength and kindness and conversation and a thousand other things about you."

A startling thought struck her. If she loved Duncan even though he was not the dashing, Byronic hero who had made half of London swoon, there was a chance that he might love her even though she was not beautiful.

She took a deep breath, then asked the hardest question

of her life. "Do ... do you think you could care for me even though I am plain?"

Amazed, he said, "How can you think yourself plain? Though you don't glitter as you did, you are still enchantingly slim and graceful, with a smile that lights up the room and eyes as warm as winter fire. Beautiful—at least, you are beautiful to me."

He cupped her cheek tenderly. "As I told you once before, when we met I felt I had come home," he said in a husky voice. "Now that we see each other truly, I love you even more than before."

Laughing with joy, she went into his arms. How foolish she had been to think that love was only about surfaces, and that no man could love her unless she matched some impossible ideal of perfection. "Duncan, Duncan, I love you so."

They came together in a fierce embrace. As Leah raised her face for his kiss, she gave passionate thanks for the miracle of having found the other half of herself.

Chapter Eight

Raging, Ranulph stalked about the glade until Kamana appeared before him in a blaze of light. Magnificent and terrible, she wore an Indian garment of scarlet silk that brilliantly emphasized her dark, sultry skin and the raven hair that swirled around her.

"You summoned me, Lord Ranulph?" she said with cool composure.

He scowled at her. "Time and again you interfered with my pursuit of Leah. Today she rejected me, despite your assurances that she would be mine." His voice turned to ice. "You influenced her, didn't you? Perhaps even bespelled her so that she could resist my magic. Why, damn you? What have I done that you take such pleasure in thwarting me?"

"I never said that Leah would accept you, Ranulph. Only that your destined consort would soon be yours, and that is the truth." Kamana glided toward him, her figure swaying provocatively and her bare feet scarcely bending the autumn grass. "Why do you think I came halfway around the world? Destiny, my lord."

She was taunting him again. Furiously he wrapped his hands around the warm flesh of her throat, wanting to see her fear, wanting her to plead for mercy.

Kamana laughed at him, her slanting eyes glowing like new-minted coins. "Is the thought of me as your consort that dreadful, Ranulph? I thought our encounter in the park was rather pleasing."

"You mocked me then, and you mock me now," he growled. His fingers tightened until he could feel the hammer beat of her pulse beneath his thumbs. "If we were really destined mates, why not simply say so?"

"You're a stubborn creature," she replied calmly. "All your thoughts and dreams were centered on that mortal child. How would you have reacted if I'd announced that you and I were fated to be together?"

She was right again, damn her. His hands dropped and he stepped back. "I'd have said I'd sooner mate with a hedgehog than share my life with you," he growled.

"You shall find me a much better companion than a hedgehog." She tossed her head, her silken hair shimmering like an ebony veil. "You cannot fight fate, Ranulph. Come, I have something to show you."

Kamana crossed the clearing to where a rivulet of water formed a small pool before trickling away. She waved her hand, and an image of Leah and her young man appeared in the water. They were sitting side by side on a sofa. Townley said something and Leah laughed, turning to rest her forehead against his shoulder as she laid her hand lightly on his chest. His arm came around her, and he kissed her soft temple.

Ranulph saw the tenderness, and ached inside. "Are you saying that mortals, with their short lives and eternal souls, are more fortunate than the long-lived, soulless Folk?"

Kamana gave him a glance of mild exasperation. "All things that live are formed of spirit, Ranulph. The trees around us, the grass beneath us, all creatures great and small. That includes the Fair Folk, so I'll hear no more talk of our lacking souls.''

His gaze went back to the image of the two young mortals. They were kissing now, and Leah was beautiful. Beautiful in a quiet, far more profound way than the dazzling faery glamour that Ranulph had granted her.

"Those two are soul twins, which is why their love could not be affected by faery spells," Kamana said softly. "When Duncan's uncle asked me to protect the boy, I traced the thread of his destiny, and found that without magical aid, he would die at Waterloo."

She shook her head with regret. "Despite my efforts, he was injured in body, and even more in spirit, on that terrible day. The physical wounds were not hard to heal, but an injured spirit is much harder. When I looked again at his destiny line, I realized that the best remedy would be to bring him to Leah. Ordinarily it would have taken them longer to come together, longer still to realize that they were true mates. But because you and I had touched them with faery magic, they both sensed their fate almost instantly."

"It sounds to me as if you interfered with their so-called destiny," Ranulph said with heavy sarcasm.

"I was merely an instrument of fate, a way of bringing them together. The same is true of these two." She gestured and a new image showed in the pool. Lord Townley and Lady Wheaton were also on a sofa, but the activity they were involved in was nowhere near as innocent as mere kissing. Ranulph's gaze sharpened with interest at the sight of the tumbled skirts and passionate movements, but before he could get a clear look, Kamana waved away the image.

"Lord Townley asked nothing for himself, but I thought I would speed him toward the secret wish of his heart," Kamana explained. "My aid was not essential. I merely helped him recognize his destiny sooner."

Exotic and beautiful, Kamana gazed at Ranulph with

slanting eyes that had seen mysteries half a world away. She was so alluring that he almost reached out to draw her to him. Instead, he retreated, scowling. "So you went to London as a spy."

She grinned. "Indeed I did." There was a shimmer of light, and the faery was replaced by a large black cat with long silky hair and golden eyes the same shade as Kamana's. Purring, the beast rubbed against his ankles in sensual invitation.

He had to smile. Scooping the cat up in his arms, he said, "You're an excellent shapeshifter." Still purring, the creature settled into the crook of his arm. Ranulph stroked the soft-furred belly, thinking that a cat might be a good companion in the lonely nights of winter.

Suddenly Kamana returned to her own form and he was holding a glorious, half-naked female in his arms. She was warmly alive and scented with the rare perfumes of Araby, and his hand was on her full, silk-clad breast.

Throatily she said, "Shapeshifting isn't all that I'm good at." Her hand slid down his body, arousing him with indecent ease.

Furious at how cleverly she manipulated him, he dropped her like an armful of burning timber. As she gave an acrobatic twist that landed her on her feet, he snapped, "You said that I was carnally unskilled compared to the Folk of your land. Why would you want to mate such a clumsy creature as I?"

"There is more to mating than mere technique." Her eyes gleamed wickedly. "You're quite arrogant enough already. I didn't want to feed your vanity by saying that never had I known such passion, or such satisfaction."

"But *why*?" He caught her shoulders, trapping her so that she must look at him. "Why me? Why risk a journey halfway around the world to become the consort of a stranger?"

She became utterly still, her gaze locking with his. "Because of who and what you are, Ranulph," she said quietly. "Our people mate often, but seldom love. Few of the Folk desire the kind of bond you wanted to have with Leah."

She raised her hand to his face, her fingers light. "You were mistaken in your choice of mate, but not in the truth of your heart. You have a rare capacity to love, Ranulph, though it is a word the Folk never use."

Kamana closed her eyes for a moment. When she opened them again, she let him see into her soul, to the vulnerability and desperate yearning that she hid behind her teasing. "I wanted love, but could not find it in my own land. Like you, I was a solitary who yearned for my true mate. Finally I went through the door of dream-time to find if such a being even existed. The Great Mother gave me a vision of a wild and golden faery lord who lived in a far distant place. I knew then that my true mate existed, though to find you I would have to risk my very existence. But if I succeeded, the silver threads of our destinies would knot and become one forever."

Her eyes searched his, uncertainty and hope in the golden depths. "I thought I recognized you the moment we first met. Was I wrong? Did . . . did I allow my yearning to distort my vision?"

In the drowning pools of her eyes, he saw an end to loneliness, a craving for union that matched his own. He'd never found such longing among the Folk of his land, had not believed that it existed anywhere except among humankind. That was why he had become obsessed with Leah—because he'd known that the mortal girl had an immense capacity to love.

With wonder and deep humility, he recognized the rare and precious gifts Kamana was offering. Companionship. Passion. A love for all eternity. This was what he had longed for, this shining creature from a far place who knew the shape of his spirit, and would complete it with her own.

Huskily he said, "No, Kamana. You were not wrong." Then, with a blossoming of joy, Ranulph drew her into his arms, and surrendered to his destiny.

And they all lived happily ever after.

ABOUT THE AUTHORS

Jo Beverley is the author of seventeen romance novels, all set in her native England. Her fiction has garnered many awards, including four Ritas, romance's top accolade, and a place on the *New York Times* bestseller list as part of the collection *Married at Midnight.* Jo lives in British Columbia, Canada, with her husband and sons, and once more has a garden to play with. Perhaps, if she plants the right flowers, the faeries will come

Karen Harbaugh has always loved fairy tales and myths and could never quite let go of them when she grew up. As a result, she became a writer and started making up her own, except she called them romance novels. In 1995, *Romantic Times* gave her their Reviewer's Choice Award for Best Fantasy Regency. Her most recent book is *Cupid's Mistake,* yet another myth disguised as a Regency romance. She lives in Washington State with her husband and son, and has, of course, a garden.

Barbara Samuel is a triple Rita Finalist and Janet Dailey award winner who has written five historical romances and several fantasy novellas under her own name. She has also written more than a dozen contemporary romances under the pseudonym Ruth Wind.

A *New York Times* list bestselling author, Mary Jo Putney has written nineteen novels and ten novellas. Her books have won numerous awards, including two Ritas, a *Romantic Times* Career Achievement Award, and the first Aphra Award for Book of the Year from the published authors chapter of the Romance Writers of America. Her most recent novel was *One Perfect Rose.* She lives in Maryland with her nearest and dearest, both two and four footed, and surrounds herself with as many flowers as she can persuade to grow.